FORBIDDEN DREAMS—
THEY WOULD DARE
TO MAKE THEM
COME TRUE. . . .

REBEKAH—A ravishing Jewish beauty, her fiery passions drove her to make any sacrifice to lay a foundation for freedom and power in a turbulent new world . . .

SIMON—Rebekah was his by right of marriage. Once he had promised her freedom. Now she would claim it for her own . . .

JARRETT—Marked by family disgrace, he would defy his aristocratic Southern heritage to possess Rebekah and make her mistress of Wild Oaks . . .

LUCY—A fragile beauty, her slave blood condemned her to serve men's lusts . . .

BENJAMIN—The child that should have been born to Rebekah . . . the son she would defend with her life. . . .

THEY SCANDALIZED THE SOUTH.
THEIR PASSIONS RAGED LIKE A . . .
FEVER ON THE WIND

FEVER
ON THE
WIND

Adrien Lloyd

A DELL BOOK

Published by
Dell Publishing Co., Inc.
1 Dag Hammarskjold Plaza
New York, New York 10017

Dell ® TM 681510, Dell Publishing Co., Inc.

ISBN: 0-440-12613-4

Printed in the United States of America

First Printing—June 1980

Part One

CHAPTER ONE

*KORNEUBERG, AUSTRIA. THE JEWISH
QUARTER. 1868.*

Her sister Sarah adjusted the veil over Rebekah's face.
Miriam, the dearest of the cousins, held the glass for
her to see. Look how beautiful you are, they all said,
and when she wept, they made a ring around her and
held her close.

She *was* a beautiful bride. Young, less than eighteen, she was already renowned for the grace of her
bearing and for her exquisite amber-colored eyes. The
fact that the amber eyes could often become opaque
and inscrutable seemed not at all to detract from her
charm. She was a quiet, serious girl, the middle of
three sisters, and, because of her beauty and her father's venerable position as the foremost Jewish merchant of Korneuberg, her hand in marriage was much
sought after. Already her father had turned down proposals made by the widowed baker, the miller's son,
and the lame but moneyed cousin from Tulin. For
her elder sister Sarah her father had not been so
choosy. Sarah, who was heavy and whose puckered eyelids gave her a strange, out-of-focus look, was quickly
dispatched to the tailor's apprentice Mischa. As for
Rebekah's younger sister Hannah, she had died in the
same wave of fever that had claimed Rebekah's moth-

er. A marriage made with joy seemed out of the question, and so her father held on fiercely to Rebekah until a prosperous match might present itself.

As far as Rebekah was concerned, the right match had presented itself. For the last six months she had secretly been seeing Jacob Leiber, a student at the Yeshiva. She adored Jacob: he was a small, wiry man with finely cut features and slender hands that were constantly, nervously involved with pieces of string or leather. He was a young man of intimidating intensity, and Rebekah found a satisfying role in protecting him with her softness. Sometimes they would go to the woods that lay beyond the pastures and fields of Korneuberg, and they would lie together under the shadowed sky, a hidden place made for them by the thick circle of linden trees, and Jacob would whisper to her the magical names of the stars. Orion. Hydra. Sagittarius. Jacob knew so much and read so widely; she felt that there were no other men for miles around who knew what names to call the stars. Just then, when they lay together in the luminous night, she would gladly have given herself to him.

He was a modern man, her Jacob, and that was why she loved him. He questioned all things, all principles, and when he was with her, Rebekah felt as though she were part of a new world that allowed for wisdom and love and innovation. She dreamed of lying with Jacob, holding his taut body next to hers, but he would not have it. He was a man of new ideas in all things except one, and he had resolved that he would not have her unless she could become his bride. The fact remained, however, that she could not become his bride. Her father disliked Jacob for his dangerous ideas and regarded him as a radical and a hothead. There was no way that her father would ever let Rebekah throw her life away in this manner, and both she and Jacob knew that their love was not destined to blossom in marriage.

Jacob ran off to Vienna, and Rebekah stayed at home with her devastated dreams. Some nights, after her sister and her father had gone to sleep, she would lie awake and, in the dim light that the eye manages to seize out of the darkness, she would look at her body. How mysterious it was to her that her body had become beautiful. She touched herself and there was softness and she felt a faint, aching weakness. Oh, Jacob, she murmured to herself. It was true that she didn't quite know what giving herself to a man was all about, but she was willing to take the risk. Even though her cousin Fannie, who was married to the butcher Kalman Meyer, told her that the marriage bed was a woman's curse, Rebekah did not believe it could be so. At least not with Jacob. Jacob was so kind and gentle that nothing he did could possibly hurt her.

But there would be no more Jacob for her. After he left Korneuberg, Rebekah's cousin Josepha wrote to tell her that Jacob had been conscripted into the army. Rebekah wept bitterly over the letter, and when her father sought to comfort her, she said terrible, disrespectful things to him. She called him a tyrant and a torturer. Sadly, soberly, he beat her with a length of leather cord and then he withdrew into a grave and melancholy silence. Both the father and the daughter remained in their own regretful, righteous camps, and Sarah, the sister, was unsuccessful at negotiating a truce. Finally her father, a stubborn but ultimately pragmatic man, unearthed a solution: he would accept the very next request that was made for his daughter's hand. Because she was a beauty, a wealthy merchant's daughter, and a virgin, neither Rebekah nor her father would have to wait long.

The lucky benefactor of this situation was a young man named Simon Weiss. Rebekah had a very old and vague memory of him. Ten years older than she,

Simon Weiss and his family had left Korneuberg to go to Vienna when Rebekah was just a child. Then, just in this past month, Simon Weiss had returned to Korneuberg to visit a consumptive cousin and had made Rebekah's acquaintance. It was an auspicious meeting, for it seemed that as soon as Simon had encountered Rebekah, he decided that she would become his wife. He was a determined and forceful young man who told everyone that he worked "in trade." Rebekah did not know what that meant, and she was too shy to ask. Most everything about Simon Weiss, in fact, made her shy and she didn't like to feel shy and, in fact, she didn't much care for Simon Weiss. She had to admit, however, that he was an impressive figure of a man. He was rather tall, and he made himself even taller by carrying himself with an erect military bearing. He had large blunt hands and a bristly sand-colored moustache. His eyes, gray and blue and small and hard like two polished pebbles, were piercing and seemed incapable of gentleness. When she looked at Simon Weiss, Rebekah saw a handsome, dauntless man who made her long for the likes of her sweet lost Jacob.

What Simon Weiss saw in Rebekah was an excellent catch. He was in need of a wife, for he was planning a great journey. His life was about to turn around altogether—he was going to go to America—but he needed the money to get there. Rebekah Kraus could supply that money, for she was promised a substantial dowry. And so, no more than two weeks after he arrived in Korneuberg, Simon Weiss found himself meeting with Chaim Kraus to ask for his daughter's hand in marriage. Their meeting was ceremonial and brief and more than a little surprising to the enterprising young man from Vienna. Simon Weiss did not know, of course, about the disaffection between the merchant and his daughter, and so he was unprepared for the ease with which the terms of the marriage were arranged.

When Rebekah found out about the impending marriage that the two men had arranged, she fell into despair. It meant that she would never have Jacob at her side again. The notion, so astonishing in its awfulness, had never really been seriously considered by her before. Suddenly there seemed nothing worse to her in the world than being married to a man she didn't love. One day, as Sarah helped her polish the silver candelabra that would serve as part of her dowry, Rebekah burst into tears and ran far out into the hayfields. She lay there beside a great bale of hay, her wracking tears making her feel weak and sickened. She heard Sarah's heavy breathing as she ran into the fields after her. She wanted to hide, to dig a hole and never come out of it, but Sarah kept calling her name, and she knew that there was no escape.

Her fat, good sister held her in her arms, and she wept some more. Then Sarah took Rebekah's face into her hands and made her look into her sympathetic eyes.

"Rebekah," she said, "there is no use in crying."

"But I don't love him," Rebekah protested.

Sarah laughed gently and sadly. "Don't you know anything, my little Becky?" she said, hugging her sister close.

Rebekah looked up into Sarah's eyes. "Don't you love Mischa?" she asked.

Sarah's round, pale face fought against the frown that sought to fix itself to her lips. "He's my husband," she replied.

Rebekah withdrew a bit from her sister; there seemed nothing to say. How indeed could Sarah love Mischa? Mischa was sallow and hollow chested and laughed like a fool and had warts on his chin. How could she possibly love him? But that was Sarah's lot,

Rebekah thought. Rebekah had not yet given up on love. Love was her only escape out of servitude. If she had married Jacob, then to be his wife would have been all she would ever have asked for. She looked at Sarah: was there nothing they shared in common? Were their dreams really so very different? The truth might be blunt, but it could not be denied: Sarah was fat and unattractive and she, Rebekah, was a beauty. She felt she deserved more and, for a moment, she hated her sister for conspiring with her father in carrying out the inequities of the world.

"Rebekah?" Sarah murmured, reaching out for her sister's hand.

"I *won't* marry him," Rebekah cried fiercely. "You can't make me and Father can't make me. No one can make me."

"Rebekah, don't be a child . . ."

"Just because you've decided to settle for less doesn't mean that I . . ."

"Rebekah!" Sarah said harshly. "Don't say any more. You *will* marry Simon Weiss. When you accept that fact, you will have an easier time of it."

Silently they walked back through the hayfield. Silently they resumed the polishing of candelabra and the little silver pitcher and the litle silver goblet that had been her mother's. She wished that her mother was here with her now. Her mother had loved her. Her mother had held her on her lap and had stroked her long dark hair. Rebekah began to cry again, quietly now, and Sarah ignored her, resolutely fixing her attention on the silver polishing.

Shortly thereafter Simon Weiss came by to take Rebekah for a carriage ride. It had been arranged that Rebekah's cousin Miriam would accompany them as chaperone, and the three of them set out in the small worn landau that Simon borrowed from his family in Korneuberg.

It was a brilliant day. The sky was cloudless and all objects on the horizon—trees and hills and the gently winding road—were limned by a pure and exquisite light. Korneuberg, an ancient city with a great spired church looming over it, was set at the hub of a valley, and the road led off in all directions to pastures and meadows and woods. As they rode along, heading toward the dark cool woods, doves and swallows made rings around them, and the air was spiced by the sweet fragrance of the Russian olive that grew along the side of the road. The three of them drove in silence. After awhile Miriam began to hum a plaintive little lullaby, and Rebekah found her eyes slowly starting to close.

"Am I so very dull?" Simon asked her.

Quickly Rebekah opened her eyes. "I'm sorry," she murmured.

He looked at her and smiled. "I don't think I'm quite so dull, you know. I have ambitions and drive and everyone expects me to be quite successful. Everyone thinks we make quite a good match, you know."

"No," she said softly. "I don't know. And what's more, I don't care."

Simon flushed a deep red and urged the horses on with his crop. Rebekah saw Miriam's startled look, but she didn't care a bit. Simon Weiss was insufferably smug, and she wouldn't stand for it. She wanted her Jacob, and if she couldn't have Jacob, then at least she wanted a man she could love.

Simon stopped the carriage and directed the party toward a small lily pond that one approached through a grove of copper beech trees. Finally he took the arms of the two women and helped them step over the brambles that littered the crude path. When they arrived at the pond, Rebekah was captivated by its beauty. It was small and it shimmered in the sun; water hyacinth grew up above its surface, and she could see, on a lily pad, a bright green frog.

"Oh, look!" she cried to Miriam, pointing to the frog, which gazed at her with its ancient, unblinking eye.

"Would you like me to catch it for you, Rebekah?" Simon asked.

"Oh no," she protested. "Leave it be. It doesn't matter and you might . . ."

"It's nothing," he said, scooping down and seizing the creature in his hand.

He brought it up to show her, and when he opened his hand, the little green frog lay crushed in his palm. In his enthusiasm he had been too rough, and his little present had inadvertently turned macabre. Rebekah stared at the dead thing, and her lower lip began to tremble.

"We'll catch another," he said, casting the tiny corpse aside.

"You beast!" she cried. "I hate you!"

He reached out for her, but she raced into the woods. She wanted to run and run and run, and when a thorned branch grazed her cheek, it was a minute or two before she stopped to register the pain or the blood. She leaned against the trunk of a tree, and her body heaved with the effort of her sobs. She heard him coming through the woods, and she wanted to race some more. But where would she go? The idea that there was a world beyond Korneuberg seemed dreamlike and unsubstantial to her. She saw him come toward her, and he was like a sleek, fit, feral animal, a wolf perhaps or a panther. He stood before her, breathing heavily, his color high, beads of sweat lingering above his eyebrows.

"Are you hurt?" he panted.

She shook her head.

"You're bleeding," he said, reaching out to touch the wounded cheek.

She flinched away, turning her face into the tree.

"Stop this nonsense," he said harshly.

"I hate you. I loathe . . ."

"I said stop this!" he ordered, pressing close against her. "I'll get you another frog. There are millions of frogs in the world, don't worry."

His callous words made her sob. "Leave me alone," she wept. "Go away and leave me alone."

He turned her face to his and stared into her eyes. "You're going to be my wife, Rebekah," he said. "Whatever you do, you're going to be my wife."

"Why?" she demanded to know. "Why do you want me? I don't love you. I'll never love you. Can't you find someone who loves you?"

He shook his head, amused by her naïveté. "What does love have to do with anything?" he asked. "Do you think your father loved your mother? Do you think your sister loves her husband?"

"I don't care . . ."

"You're either very ignorant or very presumptuous," Simon said. And then in darker tones, "You must come to terms, my girl. You're going to be my wife, you know that, don't you? You come with enough property, enough position, enough health, enough strength, and enough beauty. You meet my needs, and that is what I am concerned about in this life: meeting my needs. Your father has consented to give me your hand, and that's the way it's going to be."

"I think you're horrid," she spat out. "I think you're ruthless and awful."

"Many women would be glad to have me. Your cousin Miriam for one."

"Then take my cousin Miriam," she cried. "Just leave me alone."

"But I want *you*," he said calmly. "I like your spirit. I will be making an adventurous new life, and I need a woman with spirit."

She stared at him. He was handsome and strong

and bold and she felt nothing for him. Would she one day feel something? Love or, at least, affection? Would something in her heart respond to him? She couldn't believe it would ever be so.

"Now I will kiss you," he announced in the same calm, measured voice.

He bent toward her, and she averted her face. Roughly, decisively, he took her into his arms. She beat at him with her small fists, but he seemed not to feel anything, and he forced his lips onto hers and made her join him in this first painful intimacy.

"Now there," he said, pulling back. "That wasn't so bad, was it?"

They rode back to the village in silence. Miriam chattered on about the weather and her new dress and her mother's impetigo, but Simon and Rebekah were both in their private worlds, reviewing the significance of what had passed between them. When Simon left her off, Rebekah bid him a grave good-bye. Suddenly, during the course of this afternoon, she seemed to realize that her youth and her dreams were gone. She was now a woman, and a man was taking her for his wife. Like all the other women she knew, she was leaving behind something—a fantasy, a vision, a romance. She would either have to get new dreams to replace the old ones or do without altogether.

Sarah was the first to notice the change in Rebekah. One day, as the two of them were doing the laundry, she turned to Rebekah and stared at her.

"What is it?" Rebekah asked when she noticed her sister's scrutiny of her.

"You've changed, haven't you?" Sarah whispered.

Rebekah looked down at the ground. "What do you mean?" she said.

Sarah shook her head. "It's just that you're different, that's all."

"Well, I'm going to be married, you see," Rebekah said with a savage irony.

"It will be all right, Rebekah," Sarah said. "I promise you. You'll have a man who'll take care of you and, besides, Simon is such an attractive man and so ambitious and has such a future . . ."

"Yes, Sarah," Rebekah said coldly, closing the conversation.

She would not hear any more from Sarah. Sarah had betrayed her. She had let her own dreams fly out the window when she married Mischa, and now she wanted the same thing to happen to Rebekah. Very well then, Rebekah thought. If she were to be traded off like chattel to a man she didn't love, then so be it.

She, too, would reap some reward from this arrangement. That night, in the darkness, she touched herself in the same way that she had touched herself when she was in love with Jacob, but this time she felt nothing. The nothingness that she felt frightened her and, despite the resolution she made, she found herself crying. Was her softness going to vanish so quickly? Was she going to become hard and exacting so soon? She wept, and then she could weep no more.

Jacob had always said that they were in a new age, and she had always thought that this new age was so very strongly linked to love. But then Jacob was gone, and Simon was in his place, and Simon seemed a modern man too. Hungry, intent on acquisition, a man "in trade." Perhaps he could bring her along into this new world as Jacob would have done. There seemed no other way: if she were to survive, then she must fight for what she could get. If she could not get joy, then at least she might acquire property.

With that resolution in mind she received Simon in her father's parlor, and she put out tea and cakes for him. It was all very businesslike as they discussed aspects of their future life together.

"Would you like a biscuit with some jam?" she asked her husband-to-be.

He nodded, an amused smile on his lips, and watched as she prepared this treat for him. "You've changed your attitude, I see," he said. "That's good. That's very good."

She answered him with a tight smile. "You're absolutely right," she said. "I have learned the error of my ways, and I now see how fortunate I am in having been chosen by such a man as you."

His smile hung on his lips a few moments after his amusement evaporated. "Yes," he said quietly. "How very fortunate we both are."

His tone struck her with its loneliness, and she searched his face. "I hardly know you," she said, her voice full of a very real wonder. "I don't know who you are or what you are or what you want or how you plan to go about living your life—our life. All I know about you is your name, your face, and the fact that you were strong enough to crush a little frog."

He set the delicate teacup and saucer down on the table. "My name is Simon Weiss," he said. "But then you know that much, don't you? I have no father, I have an invalid mother, I have a blind brother who weaves, and I have a lovely, golden-haired sister named Clara whose ambition it is to sing on a stage. My father sold poultry. In the ten years since he died, I have supported my woeful family. I tell people that I am 'in trade' but, in fact, I peddle shoes on the street. Somehow I manage to make a living. Fortunately my mother's brother, a wealthy merchant, left us a tidy sum of money, and that, and that alone, has kept us from being destitute."

She stared at him, her face shocked and appalled, her mind not quite able to absorb the stilted, seemingly rehearsed narrative that he had just unleashed.

"Don't look so alarmed, Rebekah," he advised. "I wouldn't bring you into all of that, now would I?"

"But my father . . . does he know of this?"

Simon gave out a harsh bark of a laugh. "Of course he doesn't. Do you think he would have handed you over so quickly, even knowing how urgently he wished to be free of you?"

She blushed, her face contorted by outrage. "How dare you! You must be a fool to think such a thing, you must be . . ."

He held up a silencing hand. "The lady doth protest too strongly," he said, the wretched smile coming back to his lips. "Your cousin Miriam told me the whole story. All about this great lost love of yours, this Jacob fellow, and the terrible disrespect you showed your father."

She was trembling with rage. "Don't you ever mention Jacob's name," she warned. "You're not worthy of mentioning his name, you're not . . ."

He laughed uproariously this time. "I think you've read too many French novels, my dear Rebekah," he said. Then, trying to catch himself, he added, "I really shouldn't laugh. It's unkind, I know, but you have so many foolish ideas, you see."

She could have wept from shame, but she didn't want him to see her crying. She never wanted him to see her crying again. "I'm glad you find me so amusing," she said, composing herself with a mighty effort. "But I'm afraid you have presented certain problems. I have no intention of going to live in the near squalor you have described, and I will certainly tell my father what you have told me."

He nodded, pleased to see that she had as much of a mind of her own as he suspected she had. "Of course you won't live in squalor," he said. "If you'd been listening more carefully, Rebekah, you would have heard me say that I have no intention of exposing you to all of that. You would have remembered our previous conversation when I told you that I wanted you to join me in an adventurous new life."

Now that he said the phrase, she had a vague memory of his having used it before. This time she felt much more interested in what he had to say.

He saw her quizzical look and leaned toward her, his large, hammish hands on his knees. "Listen carefully to what I have to tell you," he said. "I don't like to have to repeat myself as much as you require me to do."

She thought to protest, but then she sighed and settled back into her chair.

He cleared his throat. "Now listen to me, Rebekah," he said. "We are going to America."

"America!" she cried. "What do you mean? What do you . . ."

Again he held up his infuriating, silencing hand. When she was quiet, he continued. "I have already booked passage on the *Germanic*, leaving from Bremen on the twentieth of October."

"But that is less than two months from now! That is only six weeks after our wedding!" she cried, rising slightly in her chair.

"Yes," he said softly, "so it is."

She tried to think a moment. Her face threatened to crumble into tears, but suddenly there didn't seem to be time for such a thing. There didn't seem to be time for anything. America. America. The word ran through her mind. How could she leave? Her home, her family, Korneuberg—everything she had ever known—and in its place everything that was strange and foreign and remote.

"I won't do it," she said. "You must be mad. Truly you must be mad. Who do you think you are? Do you think you can just come into my life and tell me that you're going to take me to America and tell me that I'll never see anyone that I care about again and think that I'll just trot along by your side like some kind of faithful old dog? Is that what you think? You stupid, conceited fool, you!"

"Rebekah," he warned, staring at her, her fury causing his smile to form once again on his lips.

"Stop your wretched smile!" she hissed, which only made him smile more. She hurled her teacup at his head, missing him by inches and shattering the fine china against the wall.

Sarah came running in, wiping her hands on her apron, her fat, pale face dimpled with concern. "Rebekah!" she cried. "What is it?"

"Get out!" Rebekah cried to Simon Weiss. "Get out, do you hear?"

Simon rose with great dignity, the smile just faint now, his hat in his hands. He bowed to Sarah and then to Rebekah. "Good day, ladies," he murmured, and then he was off.

Rebekah thought she would go insane with anger. She crawled over to where the broken remains of her mother's teacup lay on the floor, and she cradled the artifact in her hand. She loved the fragile teacups, translucent and pearly yellow with violets painted around the rims, and here Simon Weiss had made her go and destroy it. He was a spoiler, she thought, and going against the rule she had made for herself, she gave in to her weeping and let Sarah comfort her in her arms.

That evening she went to speak with her father. Conversation between the two had been minimal for some months now, but she had to know what he felt about her and whether, indeed, he was truly willing to abandon her to this strange, dangerous man who had come into their lives from nowhere.

He was reading—an activity from which they were trained never to interrupt him—but she knocked softly on the door and waited for him to admit her.

He looked up and stared at his youngest surviving daughter. "Yes?" he said. "What is it you want?"

Her mouth felt dry, and she licked her lips. "I want to talk with you, Father," she whispered.

"You want to talk with me," he repeated after her, stroking his long gray beard. "Have you learned how a daughter talks to a father?"

"Please, Father," she said. "Will you never forgive me for what has happened?"

"It is not in my domain to grant you forgiveness, Rebekah," her father said sternly.

She thought of continuing her defense, but there didn't seem time. "Father," she said, "I don't want to marry Simon Weiss."

"Who do you want to marry?" he said in a whisper.

"A man I love," she pleaded.

"Jacob Leiber?" he cried. "That firebrand? Is that what you want?"

"No, Father. . . ."

"The man who counseled you on how to betray and humiliate your father?" he railed in a mighty roar. She stared at him: he was like a wild-eyed Jeremiah, and she didn't see how she could reason with him, but she would do everything to try.

"Father, will you let me speak?" she said, the anger rising in her again despite all her efforts to suppress it.

He saw this new defiance in his daughter, and he stared at her as though he could pound her into a paste. "You fail me, my daughter," he said in a whisper. "All the joy I once had from you has ended in bitterness. I can find no more love for you."

So, she thought. So her father had said the unthinkable. With dignity she rose and walked wordlessly from the room. She stood in the vestibule, her head pressed against the wall, her breathing shallow but steady. Her father had made it impossible for her to retreat, to go back into the protective shell of this family, and what was there left for her except to take up Simon Weiss's offer? She might, if she worked very hard at it, convince her father to let her marry some-

one else, but who would it be? Another sallow
Mischa, another gross butcher like Kalman Meyer?
Although her mind was racing, she tried to think
very, very carefully. If she went with Simon Weiss to
America, at least something good might happen. She
would be entering a new world, a new age. America
was the land of opportunity, was it not? Once she
would have lived like a poor little mouse to be at the
side of her beloved Jacob, but Jacob was gone and
love was gone and Simon Weiss was left. Perhaps she
could form a partnership with him, and together, in
America, they would seize whatever wealth they could.
If she couldn't have love, then she would try for
wealth, for perhaps wealth might buy her freedom.

She sat down and wrote her fiancé a brief note:

> Dear Simon,
>   Accept my apology. Forgive me the hurled tea-
> cup. I wish to see you as soon as possible. Make
> arrangements with Miriam.
>
> > R.

She had her cousin deliver the letter, and a meeting
was arranged for the next day. Simon waited for
Rebekah in a small cul-de-sac off the Lindenstrasse,
behind the bakery. He watched as his bride-to-be
walked toward the appointed destination and, in a
private moment of scrutiny, he took in all the details
of her beauty: the fine olive skin, the lush black hair,
the rounded figure, the exquisite amber eyes. He
helped her up the stairs of the gazebo, and he saw that
her expression was serious, almost grave.

"Hello," she said with a small, tense smile.

He kissed her hand.

"I can smell the bread baking," she said in a faraway voice. She stared at him. She knew she must
speak frankly.

"Simon," she whispered, "my father has no feeling for me. I won't try to keep it a secret anymore. He mistrusts me; he doesn't love me."

"You don't need his love anymore," Simon said softly.

She stared at him. "Do you love me?" she asked, hopeful in spite of herself.

His lips parted as if he were about to say something, but then he remained silent and merely blinked at her with a sort of confusion.

She gave a wry, desperate laugh. "Of course you don't love me," she said. "How stupid of me. I don't love you. How could you love me?" She covered her eyes with her gloved hands; suddenly she was very, very tired. Wearily her hands dropped to her side, and she looked up at him. "But mustn't someone love me, Simon?" she demanded to know. "Mustn't there be some love in my life?"

He shook his head. "We can live without love. I've lived without love all my life, and it hasn't hurt me a bit as you can see. I'll offer you adventure," he said. "It's the best I can do." He reached out and took her limp hand. "Let's just throw our fates together, Rebekah, and hope for the best."

"But how can you just run away?" she cried. "Your mother, your brother, your sister—how can you just leave them?"

Simon's eyes turned hard and cold. "I've thought about it, and I've made my decision. I've spent so many of my years peddling shoes on the street to keep their stomachs full," he said bitterly and then, seeing the shock on her face, he softened his tone. "There is my uncle's money, and there will be the money we'll send from America. Beyond that, I don't know. They'll have to beg like all the others who are lame and blind."

His words almost made her physically ill. She felt

her stomach tighten with nausea, and she turned away from him, breathing deeply to keep herself from spilling her sickness over the railing of the gazebo.

"Are you all right?" he asked with disinterest.

She thought a moment. "Yes," she finally murmured.

"Yes," he repeated after her. "Yes," he said harshly. She turned back to him, and she saw his face red and angry. "Yes," he said, "so you've found out that I'm not a saint. You've found out the terrible news that I have dreams of my own that I will pursue at any cost."

"Can I live with such a man as you?" she wondered aloud. Her tone was not vindictive, but, rather, truly perplexed. "Can I live with a person who has left a needy family behind with no care for their welfare or survival?"

He stared at her. "You have very little choice, I'm afraid," he remarked dispassionately after a moment's time.

She felt the wind whipping at her face. "Yes," she said with a grave nod. "I have very little choice."

She returned home and began seriously to work on the preparation of her dowry and her trousseau. The talk with Simon had disturbed her deeply, but after awhile her unease dissipated. She knew he was marrying her so that he could use her dowry to pay for their booking abroad, but, somehow, the reality of the situation had become acceptable to her. She would be Simon Weiss's wife; she would travel with him to America; she would conspire in the desertion of his family and her own; she would help him to achieve his dream and, if possible, she would find a new dream of her own.

As she stood for Sarah who fitted the dress for the wedding, she felt guilty keeping the momentous secret of her future from her sister, but that was the way it had to be. Sarah chattered happily about how their two families would visit, how their children would play together, and what joy there would be for all of them, and Rebekah nodded mutely. Indeed all of the excitement about the wedding that was generated by Sarah and Miriam and the other cousins was at odds with Rebekah's sober acceptance of the fact and the occasion. She would, of course, be a beautiful bride, but there would be no gaiety or delight when the day finally arrived.

And it was not long before the day did arrive. As was the custom, Rebekah had not seen Simon for a week. It had been a nervous week, filled with preparation, and now she found herself ensconced in the special bride's room, attended by Sarah and Miriam. She felt famished, for, as befitting Jewish custom, she had fasted this day of her wedding. She was to purify herself—but to what end? This marriage was not consecrated to love; this marriage had nothing to do with love.

Sarah adjusted the veil over Rebekah's face. Miriam held the glass for her to see. Look how beautiful you are, they all said, and when she wept, they made a ring around her and held her close.

Soon they brought Simon to her, and she looked at him as though he were a stranger. But of course he *was* a stranger, she thought. She didn't know him, but here he was, in his best suit, his face washed and gleaming, his eyes calculating and just vaguely familiar, his small smile perched on his lips, his possessive posture making it known that he was here to claim her.

Her father produced the wedding contract, known as the *kettubah*, which had been signed in the presence of witnesses. Thus it was in writing that she was to be a good wife and he a good husband. The rabbi gave the groom a handkerchief, which he lifted above his head and then returned: this was the ceremony of the *kinyan*, signifying the undertaking of the obligations of the marriage contract.

The groom and the others left the bride alone with her father. Her father sat stiffly on a chair, the expression on his face impassive and without regret.

"Will you be as good a wife as your mother was?" her father said finally in a weary, perfunctory voice.

"I will be as good a wife as you are a father," she whispered in a mockery of humility and respect.

Her father rose to his feet. He was a tall, broad man, physically impressive, even more so when angered. He took his willful daughter by the shoulders, and he shook her until her teeth chattered; then he held her arm so tightly that it hurt.

"You're hurting me," she cried.

"There is so much pain in the life of a man with a daughter such as you," he moaned, his voice wild and hollow as a wind organ.

She pulled away from him, pressing herself against the wall, her breath coming heavily through the veil. "Then be rid of me," she cried. "Take me to my husband and let me be rid of you."

Her father's gray-bearded face twitched slightly, and then he walked to the door. He waited for her to join him, and she did, her fear dissolved by anger. She watched as her father went off to lead the groom to the ceremonial wedding canopy known as the *chuppah*. She waited for Sarah and Miriam to lead her to the *chuppah* with their lighted candles. As she walked toward her groom, Rebekah felt strange, unearthly. She felt as though she were in the middle of something that had nothing to do with what she wanted. She was to be Simon Weiss's wife—a condition that had more to do with history and event than it had to do with her. Somberly, in some shadowed chamber of her heart, she surrendered herself to the inevitable.

Soon she heard words that were mysterious and punishing. For an instant she felt faint, and the glowing candlelit room seemed to spin, but Simon held onto her and she passed through this feeling.

He who is supremely mighty,

she heard.

He who is supremely praised; He who is supremely great; May He bless this bridegroom and bride.

The rabbi led Rebekah seven times around the groom to ward off evil spirits, and then there was drinking from the goblet and then there was the smashing of the goblet beneath the groom's foot to recall the destruction of the temple of Jerusalem.

Suddenly they were man and wife. But no, not quite yet. It was hardly over. While the sounds of the banquet that was being set up filtered through the rooms, the time had come for Rebekah and Simon to consummate their marriage, the traditional moment known as *yihud*. They were led into a little room reserved for just such a purpose, and they closed the door behind them, shutting out the crowd that waited eagerly for this resolution.

It was a small, barren room, fitted out only with the barest essentials, and slowly, for there was no other place to go, Rebekah sank down close to the edge of the bed. Through the veil, which she hid behind, she watched Simon Weiss. She could see his smile, broader now, cunning.

"So you have got what you wanted, is it not so, Simon?" she sighed.

"Yes," he admitted. "Yes, I have."

She stared at him for a moment. "Then you can

have me," she said dully. "You have won me, so take
me now."

He walked over to her as if there were all the time
in the world. With a quick, easy motion he reached
down and pulled her veil back. Her lips parted as
though to protest, but what was there to say? Roughly
he pulled her up by the elbows and pressed his mouth
against hers, pushing his thick hot tongue between
her lips. She tried to push him away, but everything
she did only seemed to fuel his lust. She let him
remove her clothes. He alternated between a slow,
numbing pace as he undid her buttons and clasps
and then sudden jerky graspings when he reached her
underclothing. Suddenly she was nude before him,
and she could feel his dry, cracked hands probing at
her.

"Stop it," she murmured like a fool, but of course
he wouldn't stop it. She watched as he began to dis-
robe. She watched as the articles of clothing fell in a
heap on the ground, and then he was standing before
her, his body white and gleaming and looking cold to
the touch, like a statue, like a platinum statue.

"Have you ever seen a man?" he demanded to
know, holding himself in his hand and waving his
fullness at her.

For a moment she felt giddy, as though she might
laugh and never stop, but there wasn't time. He stole
away all the time in the world. Before she could
laugh, he was atop her, covering her with his hard
white body, all bone and muscle and sinew, all
voided of blood and warmth and tenderness. Then
she felt his hands below, spreading her roughly, and
then, before she had a moment to prepare herself, he
plunged into her and the pain made the room seem
afire, and she afire, her body afire, her dreams curling
up in smoke, her capacity for love burning down to a
cinder. Jacob, she moaned to herself, thinking of her
lost love's gentle, nervous hands, and then, when she

thought she could bear it no more, it was over, and he slipped out of her, falling at her side like some great sated beast.

She reached down, and there was blood. In spite of her vow she began to cry and, with the blood on her hands and the tears on her cheeks, she felt like she was just substance, substance that was oozing out and leaving behind an emptied shell.

"Get up now," he instructed, pushing her to the edge of the bed.

She watched as he gathered the heavily stained sheet and swaggered across the room. She watched as he opened the door a crack and threw out the evidence of his achievement. As she stood shivering behind the screen, pulling on her wedding gown, she listened to the wounding cheers that went up outside the door, and she swore to herself that she would never succumb.

CHAPTER TWO

"You can put your things there," Simon's mother said, indicating a small, dank wardrobe that seemed to hold generations of mustiness.

Rebekah felt herself being watched intently as she brought out her trousseau. "Such pretty things," Frau Weiss said, a whine in her voice.

"Thank you," Rebekah barely whispered.

"I never had such pretty things," Frau Weiss continued, obsequious and bitter at once. "I've only had trouble in my life."

"I'm sorry," Rebekah said, placing her shawls neatly on the shelves.

"Sickness, poverty," the small disheveled woman sighed, launched on a litany that was well rehearsed. "I've not had everything handed to me as you have."

Rebekah did not respond. She concentrated on folding her lace kerchiefs and placing them in the wardrobe. But just then a large red bug darted from one of the crevices, disturbed by the sudden imposition of neatness, and Rebekah cried out in fright.

"Silly girl!" Frau Weiss said, her expression having suddenly, miraculously lost its melancholy aspect as she laughed heartily at her new daughter-in-law. "It's just an old beetle."

Rebekah felt her face on fire. "I was startled," she explained. "We didn't have such things."

Frau Weiss stared at the beautiful young girl and fingered a lock of gray greasy hair that was clinging to her cheek. "I didn't come from such a fine home as yours," she continued in her cringing tone. "A rich man's daughter!" she said with a faint sneer. "Such honor Simon has brought us."

"Thank you," Rebekah said pointedly.

Suddenly she felt her mother-in-law's hand on her arm. "Listen to me," she said urgently. "You must listen."

"What is it?"

"Promise me you'll listen," she cried desperately.

"Yes. Yes, I'll listen."

"It's Simon," Frau Weiss said confidentially, but then her voice turned fierce. "Don't you take him from me," she warned. "I need him. Joseph and Clara need him. Don't you take him from us, or I promise you, you'll be sorry."

She stared at her new disagreeable mother-in-law and found herself speechless. She was being accused of stealing Simon away when in fact it was much more the other way around. "I have no intention of 'steal-

ing' Simon," she said finally in a quavering voice.
"Nor do I think you have provided me with a very
hospitable welcome."

"Did you think we would honor you like royal
blood?" she said nastily. "Princess Rebekah of Korneuberg?"

"I thought perhaps you might have cleaned the
room," Rebekah replied disdainfully.

The woman's small yellowed eyes seemed to pop
from her head. "Joseph!" she cried furiously. "Joseph,
come here!"

Rebekah heard the clicking of a cane as Simon's
brother advanced. He was a small, undernourished
youth with a large, misshapen head and two sightless
eyes the color and opacity of boiled egg white.

"Your broom, Joseph!" his mother cried. "Where
is your broom?"

The blind boy's constant inexpressive smile was
wrenched from his lips.

"Yes, quickly!" Frau Weiss shouted. "Your new
sister likes her room to be clean!"

There began a series of confused, wasted motions
as the boy shuffled back and forth until Rebekah went
over to him, putting her arm around his shoulder.
"It's all right, Joseph," she said. "It's all right."

The smile, which had nothing to do with sweetness
but which evoked instead the scared subservience of
an abused domestic animal, reappeared, and he clung
to her. "Oh, thank you, Sister," he murmured piteously.

"But I thought you wanted your room cleaned,"
Frau Weiss persisted.

"I do."

"Then who shall do it? Me? With my rheumatism
and the consumption knocking at the door?"

"I'll do it, Mother," Joseph said timidly.

"Shut up!" the woman cried viciously.

"What about Clara?" Rebekah asked. "Why couldn't she have cleaned the room before . . ."

"No," Frau Weiss said angrily. "My Clara will scrub no floors. My Clara is made for better things than scrubbing floors."

Rebekah stared at the miserable woman. So, she thought, she was being told just where she stood in the hierarchy of the Weiss family. At the very bottom, amid the dust and the cobwebs.

"Very well," she said, removing her hat. "Then I shall have to be the one to scrub the floors."

She collected the mop and the bucket and went about getting years of filth off the pitted wooden floors. Simon, who had been stabling the horses, came back and found her on her knees. "What are you doing?" he demanded to know.

"I am cleaning the floors," she replied, gazing down into the bucket of black water. "I can't live in such a place as this."

"Mother, is this what you have my bride doing?" Simon said to the pallid creature lurking near the hearth.

"No, Simon," the woman replied anxiously. "We begged her to let us do it, but she's a fussy, take-over kind of a girl."

They all knew that Simon's mother was lying. Simon stared at Rebekah, his new bride, with her elbows soiled by the grimy bilge. "You mustn't be that way, Rebekah," he cautioned.

She turned to look at him. She felt beset by a great fury, and she had an impulse to heave the filthy water at him. But she controlled the impulse as she had learned to control much of her anger toward him. She returned to her labor, silent and remote.

She spent all of that first week cleaning the tiny hovel as it had never been cleaned before. She waxed the floors. She bleached the grimy curtains. She polished the brass knocker. She scrubbed the stoop and beat the rugs. One day, as she worked, Clara laughed at her.

"I never saw anyone work so much for so little," Simon's sister said.

Rebekah stared at the girl. Clara was four years younger than she, making her fourteen, but still there was already something womanly about her, despite her doll-like golden curly hair. Her lips were full and sensual, her figure already quite developed, and she pinched her cheeks to keep them rosy.

"Don't you like your house to be clean?" Rebekah asked.

"What do I care?" she said with an impudent little grin.

"Well, I should think you would. After all, it is your home."

"It's not my home!" she said emphatically. "Just because I was born here doesn't make it my home."

"Then where is your home?" Rebekah asked, not wanting to close off this communication.

Clara gave Rebekah a penetrating look. "The stage!" she whispered confidentially.

"The stage?" Rebekah asked, unable to keep the amusement out of her voice.

"Yes," the girl said, annoyed by her new sister-in-law's amusement. "I have a God-given voice."

"Do you indeed?"

"Yes, I do." To demonstrate, she launched into a bit of improvisational *Lieder* that evoked the shrillness of a rabbit being tortured. "There," she said, satisfied. She gave Rebekah still another penetrating look. "Can you keep a secret?"

"Yes. I think I can," Rebekah said, pleased to be taken into the girl's confidence.

"What if I told you I was already an established comedienne?"

"I would be very much impressed."

Clara giggled excitedly. "Well, I am, you know. I perform with a troupe in the Heldenplatz."

"On the street, you mean?"

"*Bien sûr*," Clara said, dismissing the question. "I play all the Columbine roles."

"And do you get paid for this?"

"Of course," the girl cried, laughing gaily. "I've taken in quite *un peu* so far."

Rebekah was annoyed by the girl's affected sprinkling of French, but that wasn't the important issue. "You mean you make money and you give none of it to your family?"

Clara's small, cheeky face fell a bit. "You won't tell, will you?" she cried.

"But Simon works hard to support you . . ."

"You wouldn't tell, would you?" Clara pleaded, clutching Rebekah's arm. She stared into her new sister-in-law's eyes. "Because if you should tell, I would hate you eternally."

The melodrama of the girl's words made it hard for Rebekah to take her seriously. "Oh really, Clara . . ."

"I mean it," Clara warned, her cool gray eyes suddenly fierce and resolute.

All through the remainder of that day Rebekah could not keep from wondering what kind of family she had joined. There seemed so much fear, anger, suspicion, and selfishness. She could not help but think of dear Sarah, who would never have wanted to hurt her. When she had left Korneuberg, scarcely a week ago, she would not have anticipated missing Sarah, feeling her a part of the conspiracy against her. But here she was, in some wretched corner of the great city of Vienna, among people who mistrusted her and sought to abuse her, married to a man whose principal aim seemed to be her utter degradation.

At night he took her wordlessly, with no pretense of concern or tenderness. He used her to the accompaniment of his mother's wheezing and the scratching of vermin in the walls. She tried to be stoic about it, but it grew harder and harder until finally she broke down sobbing at the conclusion of one evening's coupling.

"Stop your crying!" Simon hissed.

She couldn't. She was so lonely and so full of pain and sorrow.

"What is it?" he demanded to know.

"I'm your slave!" she cried, devastated by the reality of what she said. "I'm your slave, and I wish I were dead."

"Stop this!" Simon ordered. "You're my wife. Stop saying such things."

"Then why do you have me scrubbing your mother's floors? Why am I beating the rugs and polishing the brass like some common serving girl?"

He touched her face with his hand. She had the urge to fling his rough hand aside, but she decided to let it rest. "Rebekah," he said gently, "you are my wife. The promises that I made to you I shall keep. We will be leaving here soon. I have our passage on the *Germanic* for less than a month from now. We will be sailing from Bremen to Baltimore, America." His voice was a rising whisper of excitement to which she felt herself responding. "Soon we will be gone from here forever. So let my mother win her battles now, Rebekah. Will you do that?"

"But why must I suffer?"

He took her hand and held it to his face. "I want to leave them with something," he said haltingly. "If the only thing I can leave them is a clean house, then that's what it will have to be."

She reached out to touch his fine sand-colored hair that fell over his forehead. "Oh, Simon," she said, "I'm glad. I'm glad that at least you want to leave them something."

Her words irked him, and he arched away from the touch of her hand. "Don't tell me what makes you 'glad,'" he said viciously. "I don't care what makes you 'glad.' I'll do what *I* want to do. If I want to leave them the filthy beggars that they are, then I'll do so, and if I want you to get on your hands and knees and scrub the floor until your flesh is raw, then I'll do that. It's what *I* want to do that matters, do you hear me?"

She remained in a shocked silence, and so he shook her. "Do you hear me, I say?"

"Yes. Yes, I hear you."

"Then I have some further news for you," he said, releasing his tight grip on her. "You're to go out tomorrow and get some washing from the Gentiles. My mother will tell you where to go."

She could hear her heart pounding; she wondered if he could as well. "What do you mean?" she tried to ask as calmly as she could.

"We need money!" he cried.

"Simon, is there anything wrong?" his mother called from another room.

"No!" he shouted furiously. She saw him wipe a hand across his brow and then his mouth. "Look how she torments me," he said with a grim laugh. "You all torment me. Why? Why do you all torment me?"

She was silent. She stared at the low ceiling, the ceiling that she had washed this morning with a filthy black rain falling all around her. My God, she thought, was he mad? How could he speak of his torment when it was she who was being abused without hope of rescue? She turned away from him and waited in vain for sleep to give her release.

After two more weeks of washing laundry and sharing a house with Simon's family, she would have taken a steamer to Madagascar if it had been offered.

"Soon we'll be going," Simon reassured her. "Another two days."

She felt giddy with expectation. She was going to

the New World; she was leaving behind all that was old and fussy and worn and predictable. Just then she thought of Sarah, from whom she had received a letter only yesterday, and she realized that they might never see each other again. This grim reality erased all her fantasies about gold-paved streets, and she took the letter from her pocket and read it again, hearing Sarah's voice as she read.

> Dear Rebekah,
> I miss you so terribly. I never expected to be so lonely, but Father and Mischa do not know me as you do . . .

Tears came to Rebekah's eyes. She wished that they could have said kind, loving things to each other before they parted, for this letter was not enough to fill the void.

Still there was no way to go but forward. Perhaps when they were settled in their new country, they could send for Sarah and her family. Now she had to decide what they would be able to take with them tonight. Stealthily she packed two valises and slid them under the bed. There was such a sense of intrigue in the air: she felt weak with tension. They were to leave after midnight, when the rest of the family was soundly asleep. Then they would take the carriage and drive it to the outskirts of the city where they would deposit it with a friend of Simon's who would bring it back to Frau Weiss the next day with an account of Simon's intentions.

She no longer felt sorry for Frau Weiss and Joseph. They were cruel, manipulative, and concerned only with their own well-being. Moreover she guessed that they would survive. Frau Weiss would take in washing, and Joseph would beg. Regrettably begging did not seem to be alien to the boy's nature. He begged for everything until it got to the point that one felt one might do anything to get some peace and quiet. No, she didn't feel as bad as she thought she would at the prospect of leaving them. She did feel, however, that Simon would never lose his guilt and that he would carry it with him wherever they went.

About Clara, however, she felt differently. Clara was so alive; in the weeks she had been here, she had developed a fondness for the girl, who could be unspeakably silly and frivolous but who was so open and vulnerable and budlike that it touched her deeply. To leave Clara behind would be to abandon her to a life without hope, and this she could not abide.

The night before they were to leave, she had confronted Simon on the matter. "I won't go with you, Simon, if we don't take Clara with us," she said bluntly.

"What are you talking about?" he cried in a whisper. "I won't have it."

"We can't just leave her to take care of the family you're abandoning. It's not human. It's not just."

"She'll drag us down. She'll be a weight."

"We're taking her with us," Rebekah said firmly. "We'll be three working people. We'll be able to send money back to support your mother and Joseph. That's the only way I'll consent to go."

He stared at her, his face red and furious. "Very well," he muttered. "But tell her she'll have to carry her weight."

The next day she sat Clara down and told her she had something very important to say.

"What is it, Rebekah?" she cried. "I can't imagine."

"Simon and I are going on a journey," Rebekah said, "and you are to come with us."

"But where to, Rebekah?"

"America."

Clara's mouth opened, but no sound emerged. "America," she said finally. "Is it true?"

"Yes, it's true, and if you are to come, you must be a hard worker. That's the condition."

"I will, Rebekah. I promise." She hugged her brother's wife, but then she pulled away. "What about Mama? What about Joseph?"

"They are to stay," Rebekah said. "And we will send for them when there is money," she added, even though she was hardly convinced of it.

Again Clara was silent as she tried to think. "Very well," she whispered, and Rebekah couldn't help but be amazed by the willingness with which these children were ready to leave their mother and brother.

Rebekah flew about the room all morning like a ladybird, too wrought up to stay in one place for more than a few minutes at a time.

"What's the matter with you?" Frau Weiss cried. "You're as jumpy as a hen."

"I don't know," Rebekah said, wanting her face to stop blushing. "It must be the heat."

"It's not hot in here. Is it, Joseph?"

"Oh no, Mother," the boy said with the perpetually wasted smile.

"You're not already with child, are you?" Simon's mother said with exasperation.

"No. No, I don't think so."

"Another mouth to feed," the woman said bitterly. "Don't you know anything?"

"Oh, be quiet!" Rebekah said, and her mother-in-law did as she was told. Rebekah never would have dreamed of saying such a thing to one of her elders, but this seemed to be what someone like Frau Weiss understood best.

The day passed with impossible slowness. She wanted to get out—out of this house, out of this city, out of this country, out of this world. When Simon came back at the end of the day, she felt like embracing him. She might not have loved him—she didn't love him—but he was her partner. She would be making a great voyage with him, and if they had nothing else, then at least they had that.

"Rebekah's been so nervous today," Frau Weiss said as her daughter-in-law placed dinner on the table.

"Like a hen," Joseph said, feigning innocence.

"Do you know what, Simon?" Frau Weiss said, displeased by her son's lack of reaction. "I think your bride may be carrying something."

"You're mistaken, Mother," Simon said. "Rebekah is exactly the same as when I married her."

"Well, what if she does have a baby?" Frau Weiss grumbled. "How shall we have the money or the food for another one?"

In disgust Simon pushed away his plate of soup. "That's enough talk for now. Come, Rebekah, we shall retire to our room."

"Thank you," Rebekah whispered, once inside.

He laughed unhappily and shook his head. "I don't know why they dislike you the way they do. There's no reason for it."

"They would have disliked anyone you brought home," she said with somewhat more sympathy than she actually felt.

He took her hand and kissed it passionately. "You understand me, Rebekah. That's why I'll always cherish you."

I don't want you to cherish me! she felt like screaming. I just want you to be decent to me and to treat me in the way that it is proper for a man to treat his wife. Don't tell me you'll "cherish" me. Don't use any of your falsely pious words on me.

"What's wrong?" he whispered, sensing her discontent.

She shook her head. "Nothing, it's nothing. I'm just nervous about the trip, that's all."

"Yes," he said, patting her hand. "It will be a difficult voyage."

"And when we get there, we'll know nothing of the language or the customs."

"But it will be all right, I promise you, Rebekah. America is the land of opportunity. Fortunes can be made there, even by such as we."

She shook her head. "I'm scared, Simon. We're leaving our world, and who knows if we shall ever see it again."

"Rebekah, there's nothing here for people like us. The only hope we have lies in some other frontier. You believe that, don't you?"

She remained silent for quite a long moment. "I suppose I do, Simon," she said at last. "I suppose I do."

"Good girl," he said intensely. "And it shouldn't be too hard. We have money beyond our passage and, from what I hear, it should go a lot further in America than it would here."

For hours they lay on the bed together, waiting for the appointed hour. The house was still; everyone had fallen asleep. She closed her eyes and moved into the crook of Simon's arm, a gesture more involved with need than with affection or intimacy.

In the very early hours of morning Simon nudged Rebekah awake.

"It's time," he murmured. "Time to go."

She felt a swift, sinking sensation, prelude to an enormous, palpable fear, and quickly she fixed her appearance and checked to make sure they had everything.

"The valises are under the bed," she whispered, and she marveled at the quietude with which he collected them.

They moved as quickly as possible through the small black house. She wondered if this didn't presage something—this surreptitious, stolen exit—but there wasn't time to think. Clara was waiting for them at the door, as arranged; her little heart-shaped face was pink with excitement. Then they were in the landau, and Simon was hitching the horses. Were they going to make it? It seemed unlikely that anything they did would proceed without complications.

Simon stared at Clara. Already he felt that things were not going as planned; already he felt himself tied down by responsibilities he had not anticipated. And perhaps worst of all he could see the alliance that the two women were forming against him.

"Say good-bye to it," Simon instructed.

"I have, Simon," Clara said impassively.

He looked at the squalid little house, perhaps for the last time ever, and with his crop he struck the horses' flanks and they raced away from this part of their lives.

It was a long and arduous journey to Bremen. They figured it would take a full two weeks by combination of railroad and carriage. Most of the journey was executed by horse cart, for it was not difficult for them to obtain rides from obliging farmers and peddlers. The most difficult aspect of their traveling was the unceasing complaints of Clara, who proved every bit as troublesome as she had promised not to be.

"I'm so tired and hungry," the girl whined at every junction.

"But we had some bread just a few hours ago," Simon sighed with huge exasperation.

"She's used to sweets," Rebekah explained.

"Nonsense! Where would she have gotten the money for sweets?"

Rebekah shot a significant glance in the girl's direction. "Clara, is it sweets you want?"

"No," Clara murmured, suddenly timid, afraid that Rebekah would tell the secret of her street performing and the money she had withheld from her family.

"Then are you satisfied?" Rebekah said sternly.

"Yes, Rebekah."

Simon marveled at his bride's powers. She was able to keep Clara enough in check to enable them to keep moving toward their destination. She seemed to wind up making many of their decisions: when to stop to eat, when to stop for sleep, whose directions to trust, which bend in the road to take. He marveled at her powers, and quickly, very quickly, he began to find himself envying them.

"What shall we do in America?" Clara asked one night after dinner.

"We shall become very rich, and we shall have the finest house made with the finest woods and the finest marble. And we shall have servants to bring us tea and we shall have servants to put the sugar in our tea and we shall have servants to butter our bread."

"In other words," Rebekah said, "we shall have our servants do everything but eat for us?"

"That's right," Simon laughed.

"Well, you know very well it's not going to be that way," Rebekah said coolly.

"Oh, it is!" Clara said petulantly. "Simon says so."

"The fact of the matter is that Simon knows no more about America than we do. The fact of the matter is that everyone cannot be rich in America."

"What do you know?" Simon said angrily. "America is a land of opportunity, is it not?"

"Yes, it is, but . . ."

"Then why do you argue with me?"

There was a very tense silence. "I have one question," Rebekah said at last. "If you're going to have a servant to bring you tea, to sugar it, and to butter your bread, and if America is a land of rich men, then why are there so many servants to each man?"

Simon stared at her, perplexed and annoyed.

"And who cuts the sugarcane?" she demanded to know. "And who churns the butter?"

Simon shook his head and turned to Clara. "My, so

many questions your sister-in-law has, isn't that so, Clara?"

But Clara didn't want to tease Rebekah. Perhaps there was something in Rebekah's tone that signified greater seriousness and that demanded greater attention. "Will we be all right, Rebekah?" Clara wanted to know.

Rebekah thought a moment. "If we work hard and if we're honest and if we watch out for each other, then perhaps we shall succeed."

The impact of this statement weighed heavily on Simon, and he ran it through his mind obsessively in the next few days. So his wife already had a prescription for their success. How kind of her to let him know. He brooded continually until Rebekah finally spoke to him.

"We won't be able to get ourselves a ride if you make yourself look so very grim," she chided gently.

"So!" he cried, his finger jabbing the air. "So then it is all my fault!" he shouted wildly.

"I don't know what you mean," she murmured. He was a child, and she must think how to calm him. "You're tired," she said.

"And I suppose you're not?"

"Why do you suppose such a thing? Of course I am. I'm very tired. You must know that."

"I know nothing of the sort. You're trying to present yourself as being fresh as can be while the rest of us are wilting away. But it won't work, do you hear me?"

She thought to retaliate with something harsh, but she controlled herself. "Yes, Simon. I understand."

After another few days of dusty travel, during which their tempers frayed and their personalities ate away at each other, they arrived by rail in the city of Bremen. The station was a great mob of people pushing and shoving toward destinations that were unclear. Many of them were clothed in unfamiliar national costumes and spoke a language that was incomprehensible and vaguely rude and frightening, perhaps because much of it was screamed as parents searched for children, siblings for siblings, friends for friends.

"Don't lose me!" Clara cried out to Simon, fearing his darkest impulse.

"Stay close," Rebekah said, pulling the girl next to her.

"Do you know where to go?" Clara asked accusingly of Simon.

He looked around. There were so many people—more than he could ever have imagined seeing in any one place. He wondered where they came from, where they were going, why they were going, what they hoped to achieve. They couldn't all be rich men, could they? he heard Rebekah asking, and maybe she was right. Some of them looked too old or too dull or too dirty to become rich men. There were too many people, he thought, feeling hollow in his stomach.

"Where should we go, Simon?" Rebekah asked, feeling exhausted and in need of rest.

"Just a moment!" Simon cried angrily. "Why must you badger me so?"

It was evident that he didn't know what he was doing and that he intended to punish her on that account. She knew by now, however, that it was best to avoid whatever could be avoided and to take matters into her own hands.

"Come," she said, pointing to a spot nearby. "There are Jews there."

Simon and Clara followed her as she introduced herself to the family whose name was Stern and who came from Trier, Germany.

"Do you know where to go from here?" she asked the father.

"Have you passage?" the dignified old man said.

"Yes. For two of us."

"Well, you must go to one of the agents to buy passage for the other in your party and then I hear that there are lodging houses at the piers."

Rebekah turned to Simon. "Then that is where we must go," she whispered, and he nodded stiffly.

"And don't forget," the old man said, "you need provisions. And water as well."

Rebekah shot a frightened glance at Simon who would not look back at her. "Yes," Simon said. "We know that."

"Well then, go in health, my friends," the old man said.

"Thank you, sir," Rebekah murmured. "You've been most kind."

They headed out of the station, each of them holding onto the next. They, too, had to push and shove to make their way through this sea. Once they got outside, there was some fresh air—sea air—and there was time for questions.

"Did you know about the provisions?" Rebekah asked.

"Of course I did," Simon said. "What do you take me for?"

"Oh, Simon!" Clara cried. "We're going to see the ocean!"

Yes, Rebekah thought. Yes, that was something thrilling, and she wished she could have anticipated it with more joy. But when she saw the scared faces of all the people, she could think of nothing but the vast unknown that they were moving into.

They walked a long way before they got to the pier. What they found when they got there was utterly remarkable: a harbor full of ships, a pier crowded with people, and, beyond all of this, the ocean stretching blue and boundless.

"The ocean!" Clara sighed, throwing out her arms theatrically.

"Stop making a spectacle of yourself," Simon said. "Come. Let's find our lodgings."

They went to the nearest place, a grim warehouse crammed with men, women, and children.

"It's vile-smelling in here," Clara complained. "Can't we go elsewhere?"

"Where? For a penny a night? Just where do you suggest?"

"Well, couldn't we afford just a bit more, Simon?" Rebekah asked.

"Stop questioning me, both of you!" he ordered. "This is where we'll stay."

She decided it was best not to make this into a battle; there were too many other battles she would be forced to fight; these lodgings she could endure if she had to.

They found two beds where they would pass the night. "Stay here," Simon said. "I will go arrange booking for Clara."

He made his way back into the sea of people collected at the pier. Men who were well dressed, who smoked cigars, and who stuck out from the crowd were plainly identifiable as agents, and long lines of shabby, frightened men waited in turn for an audience. Simon looked down at his clothes. Yes, he, too, was shabby. And frightened? Yes, that too. What would they do if he couldn't arrange booking for Clara? He wished they could leave her here, just run off, but no—no, that was too without honor. If he could marry her off perhaps . . . but she was only fourteen. Damn her! he thought. Damn her to hell.

He stood in line for hours—he didn't know how many hours, but it was too many hours—until finally he was at the head of the line.

"Please, sir," he said, hat in hand, "a booking for the *Germanic*?"

"None left," the agent said with a shake of his head.

He felt the sweat break out on his brow and his

back and above his lips. "Please, sir," he repeated. "Passage for one on the *Germanic*."

"Next," the agent said.

"How much?" he cried.

"You don't have it."

"How much?" he demanded.

The agent quoted a price that shook Simon to his limits. "But it's everything I have!" he cried.

The agent shrugged. "Next," he barked.

"All right!" Simon cried, seeing that there were no second chances. "Here!"

He pulled out a billfold and handed over the prescribed amount, which represented nearly the entirety of their savings. He watched the money disappear into the agent's cashbox, and he had a sudden startling impulse to cry.

Now he had Clara's ticket but hardly anything left. He felt a terrible nausea overtake him, and his throat burned with his unexpelled sickness. What was he to do? Did he have money left for provisions? No, not a voyage that might take thirty days or more. What was he to do? He felt his pulse beating wildly. What would Rebekah say? Dear God, what was he to do?

He walked around the piers for quite a long time. He saw many men as dejected as he, but he felt no kinship with any of them. If he thought of himself as one of those failed men, then indeed it would be over for them all. He simply had to keep his mind clear in order to think.

As he sat, his head in his hands, he witnessed a group of men going into a shed. They all had the same intent, hungry, expectant looks on their faces— a look which told Simon that something of value was being exchanged in that shed. He got up and went closer; looking inside, he saw that a game of cards was in progress. He couldn't possibly know it, but already his face had taken on the same hungry, expectant look that the other men possessed. This was

his last chance, his final hope, and he had no other
option but to seize it.

He sat down at the gambling table. Already there
were some men who were finished, destroyed. The expectant look was gone and, in its place, was something stunned and desperate. Simon took out his
billfold; he was going to put all of his money into the
pot. He had no other choice.

The tension of the next few minutes made everything around him a blur. It was a moment outside of
history. He forgot Rebekah, Clara, and America. All
he thought of was his cards and the essentiality of his
winning. He saw the hand that had promise and then
he asked for two cards. For a second—that's all he
had, a second—he didn't want to pick up the cards,
for if he lost, his punishment would be poverty, a life
of poverty, the kind of poverty that would cause him
to be old and wasted before his time.

He had to pick up his cards and so he did. What
he found almost made him explode with excitement.
Could it be? Yes, yes, it appeared so. A straight, queen
high. He waited for his turn to show his hand; when
it was clear that he had won, he had to keep himself
from sobbing with relief.

But it was not over yet. He couldn't leave the game
yet—he knew they wouldn't let him leave—and it
would be easy for him to lose everything he had won.
But in hand after hand he won more than he lost.
When the game finally broke up, there were lives
ruined, but his was not one of them. There would be
enough money to buy provisions for the voyage and
there would be enough to buy them a few weeks in
the new country before he was faced with the same
nightmare of their annihilation.

"Simon!" Rebekah cried. "Where have you been?
We were worried out of our minds!"

He stared at the two women. He felt removed from

them. He felt he didn't like them very much. The whiskey he had bought to celebrate his victory made him want to run wild and find himself a woman who would cater exclusively to his needs and who wouldn't ask him to give accounts of his comings and goings.

"Simon, where have you been?" Clara demanded to know.

"Enough of your questions!" Simon warned, showing them the back of his hand.

"He's drunk," Rebekah said disgustedly.

"What of it?" Simon shouted. A few people in the lodging house looked around, but everyone was used to family quarrels turned into public spectacles.

"I didn't know he drank," Rebekah said, feeling her lips pursing angrily.

"He doesn't," Clara cried defensively. "Simon, what are you doing?"

"Shut up!" he said brutishly, and they did as he said. That night the two women shared a bed, made uncomfortable at first by this forced intimacy but then surrendering themselves to it.

"Rebekah?" Clara murmured.

"Yes?"

"Rebekah, I'm scared."

"I know, Clara."

"What shall we find when we get there, Rebekah?"

"I don't know," Rebekah said, scared herself but holding on to the promise of a new life.

"No one knows me there," Clara whispered. "No one but you and Simon."

"They will," Rebekah assured her.

"Rebekah, I'm scared," she said in a teary voice.

Reluctantly, but inevitably, Rebekah put her arm around Clara, and thus it was that they fell asleep.

They had to wait more than a week, lodged in the wretched boardinghouse, before they were able to set sail on the *Germanic*. When the call came that the ship was boarding, there was a huge, wild crush of people. It was said that a ticket did not ensure the actual right to board the vessel; so the crush became a mob as people pushed their way toward the edge of the pier. Rebekah watched Simon shoving and trampling people to make his way, and when she stopped to help a woman who had stumbled, he pulled her roughly along with him.

"Simon!" Clara screamed when it was her turn to stumble, and he ran back to retrieve the girl whose face had lost all its color and whose lower lip trembled uncontrollably. Rebekah could not believe his fierceness. He had the strength of an animal when it came to a situation that required force, but when the situation required decision, he was at a loss.

"Move, damn you!" he shouted at her.

She felt herself flirt with faintness, but no, she mustn't. Did she have what she was supposed to have? The potatoes and the salt? Yes, yes, she did, thank God she did. She felt her entire being throb with an awful, thrilling fear and, in the final push, she felt herself almost weightless as she reached the deck of the boat, carried by a force far greater than her own energy.

"All right," Simon panted. "All right, we made it."

"Clara!" Rebekah cried. "Where's Clara?"

"Clara!" Simon shouted. "Clara!"

"Simon!"

They looked down. They could see her on the dock, her small white face, the rose gone from her cheeks, her hair improbably gold and curly. They could see her fighting to make her way, but she was losing inches at a time.

Simon stared at her, frozen to his spot. He didn't want her, he didn't want her, and this was the way he could lose her.

"Simon, help her!" Rebekah screamed.

He could not move. He did not want to move.

"Simon!" Rebekah screamed, beating at him, pushing him, and then he woke up and looked around him, filled with shame.

"Help her!" Rebekah ordered, and he forced himself down the gangway, through the crush of people, until he got hold of her hand and dragged her along with him.

"Clara," Rebekah cried, holding out her arms, and the girl rushed to her. Rebekah stroked the girl's golden hair and stared at Simon who looked away. Then they began to move, so suddenly, so without warning.

"Look," Rebekah murmured to Clara, and the girl saw the shore moving away from them. "We're going," Rebekah said. She saw the knots of despairing people on the dock, their hopes dashed, their lives robbed of its promise. "We're going," she said again as if to convince herself.

"And when we come back," Clara said, "we'll be rich."

But Rebekah doubted that she would ever see this shore again. She looked at Simon, lost in his own thoughts, and she wondered what their life would be.

CHAPTER THREE

They had expected the voyage to be difficult. They had expected discomfort, privation, and their fair share of illness. But their expectations, which were designed to prepare them for hardship, proved totally inadequate to the task. The voyage was more hellish than difficult, and they knew no good way to prepare themselves for hell.

There was no room to breathe; there was no air to breathe. It was as if air were a precious commodity rather than something that they were guaranteed as an inalienable right. They suffocated in steerage, crammed in with an incalculable mass of fellow travelers whose combined states of agitation created a din that dwarfed the Tower of Babel. There were Finns and Letts and Ukrainians and Litvaks and Glissanos and Croats, all pitched in separate camps, waiting to do battle over the alleged theft of a piece of bread.

The voyage was supposed to last a month, but it had been known to go beyond that. Rebekah didn't know if she could endure. The stench of unclean people, the absence of air, the constant noise, the impossibility of uninterrupted sleep, the impossibility of a bath, the impossibility of achieving any measure of privacy—how could she endure it for this length of time? Here they were, gone just a few days, and she felt she might go mad if she didn't get some air, but the only air that was available to her was provided early in the morning, for perhaps half an hour, when they were allowed on deck to view and smell the sea.

That was the sweet moment of the day, designed to soothe the spirit, although by the time they were sent up top, they were already too desperate to really enjoy it, being so afraid of having it taken away from them. People fought to be first to reach the deck, and so animosities were fostered with one voyager intent on avenging himself against another who had elbowed his way ahead.

But the deck was the deck, and they needed its renewal. There they stood as one, gasping for air, planting their feet firmly, allowing themselves to get a sense of the sea, an option which they did not even consider in the fetid steerage compartment below. The first efforts at real communication were made:

landesmen found each other and spoke tentatively, comparing their plans against those of the others. It became a time for whatever merriment could be seized. Clara delighted everyone by borrowing a concertina from one of the crewmen and performing a song and dance concerning a little yellow bird who thinks she's an albatross and flies across the sea. The audience cherished her and cried for more, and to Rebekah it was a revelation. Even though Clara's voice might not have been a polished instrument, the girl possessed a charm and vivacity that easily compensated.

"She shouldn't be doing this," Simon said sternly.

"Why not?" Rebekah replied. "She is a talent. Look at how she is enjoyed."

"Yes, look," Simon pointed. Rebekah saw a trio of men handcuffed to each other. They were the most brutish, dangerous-looking men she had ever seen, and they were staring at Clara with a lust that was terrifying.

"Who are they?" Rebekah whispered.

"Prisoners. I don't know from where or where they are going."

Now Clara was doing a little dance which required that her skirt be hitched up just a bit to show her dainty feet and ankles.

"Stop her," Rebekah cried, horrified by the brutes' enjoyment of her.

Simon pushed his way through the crowd. "Come, Clara. It's enough."

His little golden-haired sister flashed a furious look at him. "Not yet, Simon."

"Clara, come with me."

"Not *yet*."

"Let her sing!" the crowd roared, and she launched into another divertissement, saucier than the last.

Finally the call came for them to go below. Simon

roughly seized his sister's arm and smacked her
soundly across the face.

"Simon!" Clara cried. "Simon, stop it!"

"You wouldn't listen to me, you little fool! You
tramped around like a little strumpet."

"You're hurting me!" she cried, trying to pull away
from his grasp.

"You'll be lucky if I'm the only one who hurts
you."

"Rebekah! Rebekah, he's gone mad!"

"Let her go, Simon," Rebekah said, and disdainfully he pushed the girl away. She ran to Rebekah
and began to sob. "What did I do?" she cried. "Tell
me what I did."

"You didn't listen to Simon," she said. "Don't you
know that you must always listen to him?"

"No," she said. "I know nothing of the sort."

Simon's hands clenched into fists. "I should beat
some sense into you. You're good for nothing but
trouble."

She began to cry like a small girl. "What did I do?"
she moaned.

Rebekah patted the girl's head. "Enough, Simon,"
she said, and again he listened to her.

As their voyage progressed, it seemed that things
might grow easier, but they did not. It was worse as
they continued: little problems loomed larger; smells
that started off as mere insinuations soon became full-
blown nuisances; people grew sick and people died. In
a short space of time a catalog of disease managed to
introduce itself and establish a foothold. There was
measles and dysentery; in time they could expect
ravaging waves of smallpox or cholera or yellow fever
or typhoid. The first horror came with the lice. She
would never forget the moment when she discovered
them on her person—the searing itch and then the
frantic searching of her skin and her garments.

"What is it?" Clara asked.

But she could not answer. She could not speak. She would surely go mad. She had to get above decks. She ran to the stairway, and there she encountered a crew member who would not let her pass.

"But I must!" she cried. "Let me up!"

"Go on back," he barked. "You're let up once a day."

She tried to fight her way past him, but he pushed her roughly, knocking her against a wall, and soon there was a crowd surrounding them. She saw Simon making his way toward her, and she could hear herself sobbing, but it was as though she was lost in another life and she didn't know what action to take.

"Rebekah!" Simon cried. "Take your hands off her!" he demanded of the crewman.

"She was trying to go up top."

"If you ever touch her again, I'll kill you."

Oh Simon, Simon, she heard herself say, and she fell into his arms and he took her back to their station deep in the hole.

She sat on the filthy mattress, and her sobbing became more anguished still.

"What happened?" Clara said.

She just wanted to hold on to Simon. She wanted to thank him for letting her hold on, for being with her, for protecting her.

"Tell me what happened," he said sternly.

She wondered at his tone—the sudden rudeness of it, the sharp withdrawal.

"Tell me why you made a scene. Tell me why you've turned the crew against us."

She didn't know what he meant. "I had to go up top. Can't you understand?"

"No," he replied stonily. "Explain yourself."

"I've got . . ." She didn't want to say it, for to say it meant that she could never take it back.

"Say what you have to say."

She stared down at the rotted floorboards. "Lice," she whispered.

They recoiled, but within a few days their story was no different than hers. There was not a traveler on board left uninfested by the loathsome creatures. At first it seemed like utter madness might result. She would have liked to fly off the ship and drown the creatures even if it meant drowning herself. But, in time, she made her adjustment. She would have to live with the lice; she would have to give them their space.

Indeed the trial of the lice was only the beginning in a series of curses. The next assault came from the rats. She had always feared rats, even on the farm where they were comparatively mild and inhibited in their growth and manner. Here they were obscene, monstrous creatures, a foot long, gray and black and ravenous. One could hear them everywhere; oftentimes one could catch a battalion of them scratching at a larder. Some nights, when their offensiveness had been greater than usual, a hunt would be organized, and groups of men with clubs would overturn barrels and trunks where they might be hiding. The men would catch their share—one could hear the harsh, bitter squeal and then the thud—but there was more than this. There was the panic of the women as the rats dispersed and raced in all directions intent on preserving themselves. Rebekah often felt that she would rather have them alive than displaced in such a manner and made more intrusive on account of their desperation.

But the intrusiveness of the rats was not the most serious problem the vermin presented. The combination of rats and lice made for disease. The measles and dysentery—ghastly at the time but now almost innocuous in light of more recent developments—gave way to an undiagnosed illness known generically as "ship fever." Rebekah watched people fall all around her. The illness started with a rosy flush that developed into a rash, and the rash soon covered the body. Then there was the loss of fluid in the constant wracking diarrhea that caused the chamber pots to overflow and that made the steerage compartment reek like some particularly loathsome corner of hell.

She waited, they all waited, for the fever to make its way. It seemed impossible that there were individuals who might escape, for, in these close quarters, nothing was private. Their universe was marked by sickness; there were no avenues for renewal. And so she waited, and then, one day, she felt the grim beginning of what she had expected. It hit her very suddenly as she was preparing dinner. She had imagined—what? a mule kick?—but it was different than that. An inexorable tide was pulling her toward an abyss. She held on to the nearest person, fearing she might fall, but suddenly she was no longer a person. She was a contagion, and, as such, the person she was holding on to shook her off and laid her down on the foul straw bedding.

She was entering a new world. Yes, surely she was; surely this was the new world. Here she could float, here she could disappear from her body, her spirit sailing faster than the ship. It was a hot equatorial place she had entered; then, sometimes, the world would turn arctic, and she would cry out for warmth, speaking a language that no one understood.

"It's all right, Rebekah. Stay quiet, my girl."

To whom were they talking? She couldn't understand. She was thrashing on the straw bedding. She wanted to rip off all of her clothing. Sarah! she cried. Mama! Sarah!

"Quiet. You'll wake the others."

Sometimes she would seem to fly for days, exhausted, unmoored. Then she would feel something cool on her brow, and she would cry with relief. But then she would be burning again, the world would be burning, and she would scratch at herself, wanting to rip off a layer of skin.

For a while she came back to life. She opened her eyes; she saw Simon sitting next to her; she felt his hand graze her scalp.

"You're cooler now," he said.

She stared at him, not yet understanding.

"You've had the fever. A very bad case. You've been sick six days."

"Am I well now?"

"We'll see," he whispered.

She'd been away for six days. She felt fear now, fear that the illness would come back and find her.

"I dreamt I was a bird. Like the one Clara sang about."

She was very feeble. "Mustn't talk," Simon said.

No, she mustn't. But she had to. How could she not? She had to tell him where she'd been while there was still time. "I've been so far away," she cried. "I didn't know how I'd ever get back."

"Be still," she heard him say. "Be still."

And then as night approached, she found the fever returning. Oh, Simon, she thought to call, but it was too late. She was going already, being pulled away too fast to protest. She didn't want to go back there—everything was too fast there or too slow. It was true she could fly like a bird, but she wasn't free. She had to struggle; she had to sweat in order to hold on.

She felt the cool water again. Simon, Simon, Simon. There was something she remembered from the other world: she remembered Simon. Mustn't talk, he told her. But she had to call him because she was lost, and it was up to him to bring her back.

Simon! Simon!

Could he not hear her? If she opened her eyes—which took all of her strength because her eyes were so heavy, so encrusted—she could see dim black forms edged in white. One of these must be Simon. If she reached out to touch him, he would take her hand. But still she was lost, still he was unable to retrieve her. Finally the fever broke once more, and she found herself staring at him, like a sailor washed up on the shores of a strange island.

"Yes, it's me. Simon."

She looked at him wonderingly and so very fearfully.

"It's back for good now, I believe."

"You said it last time."

"No. Never."

"Hold me," she moaned.

He took her into his arms, and she wept there, reclaimed at last.

"Was it you who saved me?" she asked at last.

He thought a moment. "You saved yourself," he whispered.

But she knew it wasn't true, and she knew she would be bound to him always.

When the illness had subsided, she was left without energy or strength. Clara and Simon, both of them miraculously passed over by the savage fever, divided her chores between them. Rebekah remained all day on the straw bedding, barely able to remove herself to the deck each morning for the fresh air she needed so badly. Simon would tie a kerchief around her head, place a shawl over her shoulders, and carry her up top to join the others. She took the sun and began feeling much better, until her recuperation was savagely interrupted.

It was midway in their voyage; the sea had been calm. She knew that the sea was a dangerous place; she knew that there were vessels which set sail and which never reached their destinations. At the bottom of the sea were relics of other ships which held the remains of the lives and histories of those people who had aspired to make this same crossing. She knew the

sea was a dangerous place, but she was fully unprepared for the limitless fury of it.

They first sensed something coming in the hour before dinner. The quiet before the storm and, yes, the
calm.

"What is it?" Clara whispered, but there was no
answer. It was one of those moments when there is no
time for answers; there is only time for the careful
attention paid to details and signals and impending
needs for action.

From this stillness, which seemed so far-reaching
and vast, came a sudden wolfish wind, mournful, in-
dicative of savagery, scratching at the portals.

"It's just a wind," a voice cried, but the voice belonged to a fool, because anyone could tell that the
wind was a prelude to something terrible. She found
herself sickening at the pit of her stomach. The boat
was beginning to rock; dishes crashed to the floor.

"Oh, *Gott in Himmel*!" someone shouted.

Mustn't shout. For to shout meant to fear and to
fear meant to lose and she wouldn't lose. She would
fight and she would win.

In moments the wind grew louder and more urgent,
and the stillness dissipated altogether. The wind
grew enormous, gargantuan; it sounded like some
huge pyramidal mass crashing down upon them.

"What should we do!" someone screamed.

Hold on. Yes, hold on. She held on to Simon and
Clara held on to her, and it was as intimate as they
had ever been or might ever hope to be. They held
each other's lives—pulsing in their hands—and if they
let go, who knew what might happen?

And then the sea broke into their universe. It
ripped away a large chunk of the craft and sent the
storm around them. There were shrieks. The sea
pushed its way in like a hand, reaching around,
tickling at them, tearing at them, seizing a few and

shaking them and then pulling them out through the hole in the hull.

"Mein kind!" a mother cried. But there was nothing to be done about the lost child. What had to be done was the stopping of the hole, and men with quick, active minds sought the means to stop the sea wall from invading further.

"Mein kind! Mein kind!" But the child was gone, taken to sea.

The immigrants hung on for hours, watching the configurations of their fates announce themselves. Would they survive? And if they survived and the boat did not, what would happen to them next?

"Mein kind!"

She thought of what it might be to have her own child and to see him lost, pulled away as this child had been pulled away. Dear God, what greater cruelty could there be than to travel to a new land with such a tragedy as this?

"Oh, Rebekah!" Clara cried. "I'm so afraid!"

And she held the girl tighter. Don't let anything happen to Clara, she prayed fervently, not knowing why she prayed, but knowing that Clara was their innocence, something young and in need of nurturing that they were bringing with them to this new world.

"Don't let go of her," Simon warned, and Rebekah held her tightly, bent on riding out the storm together or not at all.

When the storm had passed, and when it was clear that the boat would not be lost, and when all those who survived had the opportunity to tell themselves that they had stayed alive, then they began to count their losses. Seventeen in all had been taken by the sea. One hundred and eight had been taken by the various fevers. Death was an entity of increasing prevalence.

The next day their spokesman requested that the

passengers be allowed on deck for a greater amount of time. What were they after all? Prisoners? Slaves? Captives on a pirate ship? They wanted more time up top and they got it. The sea that day was a strange sight: all churned up, gray, brown, brackish in spots; seaweed and beds of kelp stretching out like nets and weird creatures stirred up from the depths—jellyfish, almost bloody—looking as large as sundials, schools of cuttlefish, squid swimming in ink. They wondered at the sea; they wondered if they would ever really cross it entirely or if they would just keep going, like a phantom ship, doomed to a perpetual journey.

Rebekah looked down into the hideous dark waters and felt the familiar sickness again, the nausea that threatened to overtake her and that frequently did. She was not made for the sea. She came from a world of wheat and linden trees and wild roses.

"You look unwell," Clara said.

"It is not a serious thing," Rebekah replied, and it wasn't. It was merely the disaffection between herself and the sea and to counter it, she let her face feel the cool wind.

"Look!" Clara whispered.

She turned; she saw something she did not want to see. She saw a tiny corpse, swaddled in black; she saw and heard the anguished mother alongside it, imploring the crew not to do what it had to do. This, Rebekah realized, was one of the children killed in last night's storm, thrown against the floor, the skull fractured, the life torn instantly from it. She heard the captain make a prayer. Why were they doing this now? she wondered. Why, in front of everyone, were they giving evidence of such grievous loss and such mortality?

"Josef!"

So that was the child's name. She turned her head; she did not want to see the child committed to the sea; she did not want to hear the hysterical mother being led away.

There was a silence. The sadness of the event covered them tightly. With much delicacy Clara rose and began to sing a song that served as a lament for the occasion. Although the girl's voice was untrained, she sang with such feeling that the experience moved the crowd collectively. She would have sat down afterward, but the crowd would not let her, and so she sang a graceful melody about riding in a carriage through the park.

"She mustn't," Simon whispered, but Rebekah held up her hand. Of course she must: the crowd needed the kind of relief she was offering.

Simon saw the trio of convicts eyeing his sister. It was clear that they were not viewing her as everyone else did. She was not offering them comfort or catharsis. They were viewing her as something they wished to possess and probably to destroy. Well, damn it all, he would not rescue her again. He would let them lust after her as they wished, and so be it.

Rebekah also saw the men. They wouldn't harm her. Why would they harm her? She was a child. There would exist no one so bestial as to hurt her. But it was best, on any account, to be careful.

Later that day she tried to talk to Clara.

"You must not be willful, Clara. You must listen, and you must do as you are told."

"I haven't set out for America so that I could be told what to do!"

"Clara, you will make trouble for yourself and for us."

"*C'est très fou!*" the girl cried. "I won't be told what to do."

"If you don't listen to us," Rebekah said sternly, "then you'll have no one. Can you understand that? We will leave you to your own devices, and you shall have to fend for yourself."

"What do I care? I can sing and I can dance. You see how they like me. Don't you think I could make my living on the stage?"

"You don't understand," Rebekah said furiously. "You can get hurt. Don't you understand that?"

"Yes, by you!" the girl cried. "You want to hurt me! You and Simon! You want to tie me up and lock me in, but I won't have it!"

"Clara!" she cried, but the girl ran down the length of the steerage compartment, away from her.

Clara flew down a flight of stairs, deeper into the hold of the ship. It all smelled of tobacco, for that was the cargo; the passengers were merely gravy on a more profitable commercial venture. She moved along the dark alleys of the ship. She wanted to be alone; she searched for some private place. When she found it—this smelly, damp spot, deep in the bowels of the ship—she sat there and, like a child, she sang to herself, warding off her fear.

They were just three days from Baltimore harbor. Soon they would be landing at Locust Point, ready to become Americans. The ship was filled with happy, excited people ready to put behind the weeks of sickness, filth, and, in many cases, loss.

"Will we meet again?" people asked of their enemies, willing to consider reconciliation.

In the evenings there was much singing and dancing. Even the quality of the air seemed lighter, although one presumed it wasn't. One morning, as they stood on deck, they saw whales and porpoises following their ship.

"So many new things to see!" Rebekah cried, but Clara, still feuding with them, would not even deign to look.

"Have you heard that the prisoners are escaped?" an elderly man said to Simon.

"Since when?"

"Just yesterday."

"And they're not yet found?"

"Not yet. There be lots of good places to hide aboard this here vessel."

Later, down below, Simon cautioned Clara once again.

"You will not be out of sight while there is danger about," he warned her.

"Stop giving me orders!"

He took her shoulders and shook them. "You will listen to me!"

"Why should I? You're nothing to listen to. You're less than nothing . . ."

"Clara!" Rebekah cried. "He's your brother."

"Who cares? He's nothing but a filthy swine to leave his family like a thief in the night."

He struck her harder than he had intended. He could see his finger marks, red and livid on her white skin, and he waited for her to cry because there were, in fact, tears in her eyes. But she, more and more willful, would not resolve this exchange in such a way. She went to bed early, silently, filled with anger and hatred.

She knew that they would be unable to maintain a constant vigilance over her throughout the night, and so she waited to hear their sounds of sleep. It didn't take long because the enormity of their fatigue was never much below the surface. She crept through the steerage compartment, waiting until she was some distance from them before she lighted her candle.

The candle led her down the flight of stairs in search of the private place she had carved out for herself. She had never been here at night. She hummed the tune about the little yellow bird. She smelled old, stale tobacco. Should she go back? No. They must learn a lesson. They must not give her orders as though she were a child. She would hide all

morning in her private place and let them be worried
sick; then perhaps they would value her more.

As she searched for her private place, there were
those who saw the glowing light and who heard the
sweet low hum. They were the Polish prisoners, being
transported to America to work on the railroads. They
had been, respectively, a murderer, a thief, and a
bandit. Together they had conspired to kill their
jailer. Now they roamed the ship, staying one step
ahead of their pursuers; their minds, crippled by long
years of imprisonment, frantically trying to figure
out what they would do when the ship came to port.

She found her special place of refuge, and it was
a stone's throw from where the men were hiding. She
fixed the candle to the floor, and in a very quiet voice,
barely more than a murmur, she continued her song.
The men, as one might expect, could hardly believe
their eyes at first and then their good fortune. They
watched her intently and the murderer, really large
enough for two men, began to rub his penis. Yes, this
was a very good idea, the thief thought, and so he did
the same, and the bandit, perhaps rougher even than
the other two, moved toward her.

Clara, lost in the sweet calm of the music, did not
hear them until they were right there, beside her. At
first she just stared, quite full of surprise and wonder,
and then she just opened her mouth, as though to ask
a simple question, and then, when she was ready to
scream, it was too late, for they had pounced upon
her and covered her mouth with their rough and
filthy hands.

They wanted to have her, but, beyond that, they
wanted to hurt her. At the sight of her unblemished
skin and at the apparency of her virginity, they conspired in a cruel, thrilling venture to tarnish her and
wound her and to destroy her. They never took the
time to ask themselves why—it didn't matter why—
there are so many people in the world who would do

the same, who would rip the petals from a flower, who would scratch their names into something fine and flawless, intent on ruining what they couldn't have or understand or deserve. They had found their kind, and they worked well together, beating her down to the floor when she struggled, holding her limbs, tearing her clothes from her, reaching down into her private places.

They had her there all night. They used every part of her, many times. The floor, the insides of her thighs, and the wounding sex of each man was smeared with blood. When she fainted, which she did more than once, they slapped her into consciousness, and then they started in again. They were three men, collectively without a woman for twenty-two years. They used her brutally, without worry that they would use her up, and reluctantly they left her as morning approached.

When finally she was alone, it was as though she were lost forever. She could not get hold of herself; she could not find her place in time. She kept moving from a pain too total to be imagined into a nightmare-ridden, breathless sleep. Now and again she would hear herself moan; she was disinclined to scream; it was too late, and it would hurt too much. She felt down below; there was new blood, there, on her fingertips. She was going to die. Oh, dear God, why had she come down here? If she had only stayed behind, then they wouldn't have . . . hurt her, they had hurt her, they had hurt her.

"Clara!"

They were calling her. They were coming back to her. What were they going to do to her next? They had hurt her breasts. They had squeezed the nipples black.

"Clara! Clara, can you hear?"

She wouldn't make a sound. She would hide, and they would never find her.

* * *

The ship's doctor, a dissolute, drunken man, crudely stitched the tears in Clara's body. Rebekah held the girl's hand, also bruised—there seemed no part of the girl that had not been mauled. "I hurt," Clara murmured, sounding every bit a child.

Rebekah looked to Simon. His face was twisted with anguish and outrage. Surely he would kill: that was what his face meant. She felt her sickness again, growing still more intense.

"They haven't found the men yet, have they?" asked an inquisitive woman, poking her way into the scene.

"No," Simon muttered.

"The devils," the woman, a Finn, said. "They should burn in hell. They should burn in hell for a thousand years."

Clara moaned and clutched Rebekah's hand.

"A young girl like that," the Finnish woman clucked. "Ay, they made a woman out of her all right."

"Oh, Rebekah," Clara moaned again.

"You're upsetting her," Rebekah said to the woman.

"What do you mean? I'm trying to help and here you . . ."

"Thank you," Rebekah said firmly and finally.

"The Jews," the woman exclaimed bitterly to an unseen audience, and she turned to leave.

Simon hadn't heard a word of this exchange. All he could think of were the men who had ravaged his sister. They would be caught; they would be punished; they would die; they would be food for fish.

He found himself standing at the central point of the steerage compartment. "Who among you are men?" he cried hoarsely.

The crowd stiffened its collective back, waiting for his next words.

"They've ruined my sister," Simon shouted.

Rebekah held a wet compress against Clara's brow.

Don't listen, she wanted to say. He's taking away your honor and your life, she thought. Your brother's writing you off, so don't listen, Clara, don't listen.

"Are there men among you?" he cried.

"Aye!" a roar went up.

"Then we will find them!" he roared back.

Rebekah watched them go off, some of them armed with clubs, others willing to use their bare hands. They stalked the decks, and the convicts fled as desperately as the rats had fled. They caught up with the three men in one of the cargo rooms. Don't hurt us! the little thief cried, but of course they would hurt them. They began to hurt them right away, beating them with their hands and with their clubs. One of the vigilantes, a coarse and giant Lett, took out a knife and sliced off the bandit's nose. The little thief quivered like a bird and the murderer, a giant himself, began to moan as Clara had moaned. The vigilantes dragged them up top; the crew watched, smiles on their faces. The little thief and the murderer watched as the bandit was thrown overboard.

"Please God. Please Jesus. Please Mary," the little thief cried.

It took six men to seize the huge murderer and hoist him overboard where he sank like a stone.

"It was them!" the little thief cried. "Pray have mercy! Mercy!"

They all laughed at the little thief. They dangled him overboard, teasing him, enjoying his piteous screams. Rebekah covered her ears. The nausea overwhelmed her. She found herself being sick on the floor.

"Pray God, have mercy!" the little thief shrieked, and yes, there was mercy for him as they ended his torture and flung him to the sea.

Simon, white as the sea foam, went below to his wife and sister. "It's done," he said, wiping the sweat from his temples.

The coarse, giant Lett appeared by Clara's bedside. He opened his palm, showing the bloodied, severed nose. "It's yours," he said, and the girl began to scream in horror.

"Simon!" Rebekah cried. "Take it away!"

Simon led the hurt Lett from the girl's bedside.

"Oh, Rebekah," Clara moaned. "I shall never be the same again."

"Poor baby," Rebekah murmured, stroking the girl's hair.

"Oh, Rebekah. I want to die. I want to die."

"Poor baby," she gasped, not knowing what else there was to say.

CHAPTER FOUR

The place called Locust Point appeared in the distance. America. They had reached America. In view was the harbor of the city called Baltimore in the state called Maryland in the country of America. She felt Simon take her hand, and she allowed it even though she felt nothing for him. No, that was wrong: she did feel something, if nothing else some aspect of alliance, for theirs was a partnership tightly bound by circumstance and need. She didn't like his hand—it was rough and cruel and grasping—but she let him take her in his grip, and she didn't say a word.

"Things will be better," he whispered, perhaps sensing her discontent.

Still she remained silent. She glanced at Clara, who

held tightly to the railing, her eyes quite blank, even now, confronted by this vista of a new world.

"Look, Clara," Rebekah said with strained enthusiasm. "There's America."

Clara stared at Rebekah, her blackened eyes dull and lifeless. Bruises, bruises everywhere. The girl hobbled; she could not dance. Yes, surely, one day she would be able to dance again, but would she want to? The bandits and the thieves had stolen so much from her.

"Things will be better," Simon said once more.

Clara managed a derisive little laugh, which silenced them all quite thoroughly. She hardly spoke at all anymore, except to communicate her physical needs or her general contempt. Simon and Rebekah were tyrannized by her sullen fury, by her pain, and by the wasted dream she had come to represent. Rebekah did not know how she could comfort the girl, and it would be her responsibility to do so. Simon would not stay with them long. He had already discussed the idea of purchasing a stock of hardware and peddling his way down south. Simon's absence was something that Rebekah knew she would have to reckon with, but she had not been counting on caring for Clara in her present state.

"We're going to be rich," Simon murmured lamely.

Rebekah shook her head. What did it matter to Clara, she thought, if they were rich or not? Clara would never be able to buy back the things that were taken from her: her youth, her innocence, her high spirits, her capacity for happiness. She wanted to reach out and touch the girl except the girl would not be touched; so they stood stiffly next to each other.

The boat would be landing within two hours. All of their property had been neatly and securely tied. There was nothing to do now but wait for the slim strip of land on the horizon to become bigger and broader and more worthy of the portal to a conti-

nent. There was no one they need say good-bye to.
They had become, since the assault on Clara, something of pariahs. No one wanted to know their pain,
for pain was infectious.

Simon put his arms around Clara and Rebekah.
"You remember what was said, don't you? If we're
good to each other and honest, then we shall thrive
here."

Both women remained silent until the awkward-
ness hit them in the face. "Yes, Simon," Rebekah felt
obliged to say.

Simon frowned down at Clara. It was his inclination to pummel her out of what he considered her
obstinacy, but he controlled himself. "Clara," he said
with grating gentleness, "I don't hear you."

Clara stared at the strip of land that she found unspeakably ugly.

"Clara," he said sternly, taking her by the elbow.

She let out a small soft shriek. He released her, and
she backed away from him, white-faced, her hands
held defensively.

"Clara," he sighed, stretching out his arms to her.

"Don't touch me. Don't *touch* me!" she cried as
though he were someone she had never before seen.

Rebekah watched Simon's face sag. There were
times like this when she felt a compassion for him
that was both enormous and confusing. He was a
difficult man; she could see him becoming a dangerous man. His anger was very great, and yet his will
was shaky. She watched him stare at Clara, his expression a conflicting outrage and sorrow.

"Did they turn you against me, Clara?" he whispered.

Rebekah could see the girl's pain. The small
bruised mouth twitched downward.

"Did they make you hate your brother?"

"Stop it. You must stop it," the girl cried. "You
must!"

Rebekah felt the familiar nausea climb up inside her. She left them to each other; she could not abide what they had to say. She moved along the deck to a quieter place. Here she waited for the strip of land to become larger and more definable. Here she waited for her nausea to pass. She was beginning, after weeks of foolish obliviousness, to realize what the nausea meant. It did not mean the sickness of the sea. The sickness of the sea had nothing to do with the soreness of her breasts. What the nausea meant and what the soreness of her breasts meant was that she was with child. *So soon?* she could hear Frau Weiss cry. *Another mouth to feed?* Yes, she thought, so soon.

She wasn't sure how she was supposed to feel. She was eighteen years old; she was an acknowledged beauty; she was married to a man she didn't love; she was to give birth to his child. And so she would be trapped further. No, no, she mustn't think such things. It was wrong to think such things, she told herself. She was Simon's wife; she would be the mother of his child. She would love the child; the child would make them happy. The child would bring them together and she would bear the child in this new land and they would prosper and make themselves into a family. The child would erase the pain of Clara's violation. The child would absorb the thread of innocence that had been broken in Clara. For the first time since the terrible night of Clara's rape, she found herself crying. Why was she crying? For Clara, for Clara, she wept, and yet surely for herself as well. As they neared the green strip of land, she wept for the life that she was leaving behind.

When they disembarked, they entered a new world that was marked more by bedlam than by anything else. Thousands of people converged all at once as ships unloaded their inferior cargo. Within moments this swarm was channeled into a number of lines, each one designed for purposes of hygienic investigation. Rebekah waited her turn, her anxiety producing an intensification of the nausea that had consistently enveloped her these past few weeks. When a harsh gray-faced man sent Simon in an opposite direction, the nausea threatened to overwhelm her.

"Simon!" she called, and he turned back to look at her, his face furrowed with fear, but then he was ushered onward.

"Oh, Clara," she said suddenly. "I'm frightened."

Clara had nothing to be afraid of and so she maintained her stony silence. It was heartless of the girl, she thought angrily, and she moved several steps away.

Among the women and children there was a wild, insistent babble of voices as frenzied questions were asked in foreign languages. What will they do to us? And will it hurt? And don't let them, Mama, don't let them. She never felt more alone. She was passing before some tribunal that was mysterious and powerful, and she had no one to give her comfort.

She entered a large white room. There were doctors and nurses everywhere. She glanced at Clara, but still Clara would not look at her or do anything to reassure her.

"Next," called a tall white-haired nurse.

She entered into a cubicle where a doctor and another nurse awaited her. The doctor began to examine her and then turned in exasperation and disgust to the nurse. "She hasn't been deloused yet!" the doctor remarked querulously.

"I'm sorry, Doctor. I don't know how it . . ."

"Just get her out of here," the doctor said between clenched teeth.

She was dispatched to still another room. No one noticed that she was quivering with outrage and mortification. She had not understood the doctor's words, but she did understand well enough that she had been treated like filth, a creature without feelings.

Was this the way of her new country? She had expected to be welcomed, or at least to be greeted civilly, but instead she had been considered as something less than human.

She stepped beneath the hose and allowed herself to be deloused. It quite shocked her, as she stood there, to realize that lice had been feeding on her for many weeks. Just a short while ago if anyone had told her that she would be living with lice, she would have thought them mad. It was clear to her now that one allowed oneself to be degraded with very little resistance; that deprivation and filth and poverty came naturally to the human animal.

"Filthy things!" a flinty redheaded nurse said to no one in particular, shaking her head.

Rebekah looked at her as if to say she did not understand.

"*Schwein!*" the nurse cried impatiently. "Do you understand that?"

She felt her eyes sting with sudden tears. She had an impulse to spit at the woman, but surely action would be taken against her, and so she said nothing.

After a few moments they directed her back to the stark white cubicle.

"Come in, come in," the doctor said. He was a short fox-faced man of indeterminate age. "You're cleaner now?"

Again she was forced to stare blankly, maddened by her incomprehension, not knowing whether to smile blandly or to flash a furious look at him.

"You're a pretty one," he said jovially. "Especially when you're clean."

There was something in his voice that suggested intimacy, and she didn't want to hear it.

"If you saw some of the sows I have to examine . . . Isn't that right, Nurse?"

The nurse remained absorbed in her prim, disapproving silence.

"But this one," he groaned lasciviously, and she knew, quite clearly, what it was that he meant. She turned deeply, furiously red, and she made motions to leave this confinement.

"Achtung!" the doctor laughed merrily, pleased to have successfully tormented her. "There's no place for you to run to."

She had never felt more confused. She didn't know what to do, where to go, what to say. She understood nothing, except that the doctor was foul and hateful.

"Just simmer down," he said with what was intended to be a soothing sibilance.

She had no choice, and so she decided not to resist. She let him examine her thoroughly, ignoring the fact that his hand lingered in her private places.

They checked her out for all things infectious. They didn't want her to taint their fine country. They suspected her of strange, horrible diseases bred in filth and captivity. Tuberculosis, diphtheria, measles, cholera, typhoid, yellow fever. They wanted to see if she carried them on her person, ready to dispense them at will amidst the general population. Quickly, startlingly, they flicked back her eyelids with a buttonhook to check for trachoma. The doctor pored over her assiduously, his hands alternately sensual and disinterested. She felt sore at her nipples when he touched them, and the soreness and the nausea and the relentless search through her body for infection was taking its toll. She began to feel a general weakness, laced throughout with sharp, clutching pains. What was happening? What had they done to her? She began to moan and hold herself, the pain at her pelvis becoming excruciating.

"What is it?" the doctor demanded.

The moan grew into a quick, feverish panting. She began to feel all wet down below, and suddenly there was blood on the floor. She collapsed into the nurse's arms, her head spinning, her eyes open just enough to see color and form but no detail.

"Good grief!" cried the fox-faced doctor. "What in God's name is it?"

The tone of uncaring and nervousness that the doctor conveyed only made matters worse, and so Rebekah began to cry, edging toward a state of complete hysteria.

"I think she's miscarrying, Doctor," the nurse ventured.

The doctor, caught in a blatant show of ignorance, quickly sought to cover up. "Of course she is!" he declared as if annoyed by the nurse's retarded rate of recognition.

She kept her eyes closed. Simon, she moaned, Simon, Simon, Simon.

"Oh, good grief," she heard the doctor saying.

It was the baby. She was losing the baby. And she'd just come to realize that the baby was within her and she'd just come to realize that she wanted the baby . . . the baby would make her happy . . . happy, she wanted to be happy, and the baby was to make her happy and she was losing the baby. She felt the blood on her fingertips, and she began to thrash wildly on the table.

"Stop it!" the nurse hissed.

She was dreaming. What were they doing to her! They were cruel, cruel, and she was defenseless. Simon! she screamed.

"She's bleeding like a pig!" the doctor cried.

Simon! Simon!

"Achtung!" the doctor shouted.

Simon! She was howling. All of the anguish of these past months finally found expression, and she could not stop herself from screaming. It was not that the pain was so great as much as it was that her fear and her sorrow were so great. Simon! she screamed. What did she want him for? Look what he had done to her, look! And what would he say to her? She had failed again, and what would he say to her?

"Sit still," the nurse said sternly.

No. *Nein. Nein! Simon!* she shrieked. They were torturing her. *Simon!*

Just then another doctor came into the room.

"What's going on here?" he asked.

"It's the Jew," the fox-faced doctor complained. "She's miscarrying, and she's behaving like a wretch. She's just carrying on like a . . ."

"Let me handle this," the young doctor said.

"Just a minute, Dr. Russell," the fox-faced doctor said. "You can't just come in here . . ."

"Let me handle this, Dr. Wilcox," the young doctor repeated firmly.

Dr. Wilcox stared coldly at this other doctor and then turned sharply to leave.

"You may leave too, Nurse," the young doctor said.

Rebekah stared at this new doctor. What was he going to do to her? He was coming to punish her. She lay on her side and she pulled her legs up to her chest. She grimaced in pain. Was he going to touch her? He mustn't touch her, he mustn't.

"You're very frightened," he said in a gentle, easy tone.

Still she stared at him, her extraordinary amber eyes unblinking.

He smiled a bit. "It's natural for you to be frightened. You're having a miscarriage. From the look of things it shouldn't be a serious problem for your health, but I know that it's a difficult thing for you as a woman."

She understood nothing of what he said, but she felt herself responding to the gentleness of his tone. There was a kindness to his expression as well, and after a moment or so she noted the unusual fineness of his face. Each of his features had the appearance of having been made with remarkable care and precision, and his long, slender hands showed that same firmness. His hands, in fact, brought to mind Jacob, her lost love, although this young doctor, for all the delicacy of his features, seemed larger and darker than Jacob.

"But there will be other babies," he continued. "You seem like a reasonably healthy young woman to me."

She opened her lips as though to speak, but then she felt so tired and she closed her eyes.

He touched her brow, and her eyes shot open. She shook her head, and her hands went to her mouth.

"It's all right," he soothed. He stared at her. "You don't understand me, do you?"

She shook her head again.

"Parlez-vous français?"

She stared at him, feeling like a fool.

"Sprechen sie Deutsch?"

"Ja," she cried, nodding furiously.

"I see," he said, beginning to converse in German. "Isn't it fortunate that I can speak your language?" He smiled again, more broadly this time, and she began to feel a bit better.

"Let me take care of you now," he said, and he proceeded to give her expert medical attention. After awhile she felt better, and some color came back into her face.

"My name is Dr. Russell," he said as he swabbed at her.

She smiled weakly in response.

"And you? Do you have a name?"

She blushed. "Rebekah Weiss," she whispered.

"Are you married?"

"Of course!" she cried, her eyes suddenly full of anger.

"I'm sorry. I meant nothing. Does your husband know you're here?"

"I don't know," she murmured.

"Are you German?"

She shook her head. "Austrian, we are."

"Jewish?"

"*Ja.*"

"And will you live in Baltimore?"

"*Ja.*"

"You're a young woman of few words," he said wryly. "That's a very rare thing these days."

She felt her eyes well up with tears. "Herr Doktor," she said, "I will be able to have another baby yet?"

"Oh, surely," he cried, taking her hand. "This is not uncommon. This happens to women more than you can imagine."

She stared at him and then began to sob.

"Fraulein, listen," the young doctor said. "It will be all right."

"But it was my baby," she cried. "And what will he say? He'll say it was all my fault, I know he will."

"Nonsense! It's nothing of the sort. It's no one's fault. Your husband will understand." She continued to sob, and so he stopped himself. He didn't know if he could believe in what he said. So many of these women he saw were married to brutish, ignorant men who beat them or abused them in one way or another. This young woman here—her beautiful face was filled with fear. "You mustn't think it's your fault," he murmured.

"I didn't know till a day ago that I had a baby," she said, whimpering slightly. "If I knew, I would have taken care not to be sick. I would have been strong. I would have . . ."

He held up his hand and hushed her. "You've done nothing wrong," he said emphatically. "Do you understand?"

"But I shouldn't have been sick . . ."

"There was no way for you to avoid it. These ships are breeding grounds for illness. You're fortunate to have survived altogether. I've been with Immigration for three years now, and I tell you that you're lucky."

"Herr Doktor?" she said.

"Dr. Russell," he corrected her.

She managed a small, embarrassed smile. "Dr. Russell," she said, stumbling over the unfamiliar surname, "will they let me in here?"

"Who? In where?"

She made a vague, circular gesture with her hand. "Will they let me into America now?"

He stared at her. She was beautiful; her eyes were very beautiful. And she looked so foreign, with her black shawl and her black dress and the black hat that had fallen to the floor. What was her name? Rebekah. "Yes, Rebekah. They will let you in," he assured her.

"And my husband?"

"If he's healthy."

"Ya, he's strong and healthy." She thought a moment. "Herr Doktor Russell," she said tentatively, "my husband has a sister . . ."

Her voice trailed off, and she looked away.

"Yes? What about her?"

She looked back at him. His gray eyes, warm in spite of their color, were concerned and questioning and urged her on. "Her name is Clara. She's very young. She's only fourteen years old."

He smiled. "And how old are you?"

"Eighteen," she said, not willing to be condescended to.

He nodded. He was ten years older than she, a considerable amount that seemed vast when he considered what had happened to his life in that time. Ten years ago, when he was eighteen, the world seemed a joyous place, full of possibilities, and he, a gifted young man born of a fine family, was eager to test those possibilities. He was Jarrett Russell, son of Jarrett Russell, grandson of Jarrett Russell. His ancestors had been

heroes of the Revolutionary War. The Russells were
one of the first families of Mobile, Alabama, and ten
years ago there was nothing stopping young Jarrett
Russell from becoming the finest of all the Russells.
But that was ten years ago, and all the promise had
faded. The war had slashed through the life of the
Russells like a sword, and young Jarrett Russell was
still in pain from his wounds.

"Herr Doktor," Rebekah whispered to the young
man who was lost in thought.

He looked at her, and his fine face seemed pinched
and rather gaunt. She noticed now that his clear gray
eyes were pouched in dark hollows; he looked suddenly tired and almost sad. "I'm sorry," he said,
shaking his head. "I was just reminded of something."

She stared at him, awaiting permission to go on.

"What were you saying?" he asked, confused now,
touching his brow.

"I was telling you of my husband's sister."

"Yes, the young girl."

"Yes. Clara."

"Clara. What about Clara?"

"She . . . something happened to her on the voyage."

"Fever?"

"No."

"What then?"

"She was . . . they attacked her."

"Who did?"

"Convicts. Aboard ship. They attacked her. They
raped and they beat her."

His face, serious all along, took on a grim aspect.
"Was she treated?" he asked, but Rebekah looked at
him uncomprehending. "Did she see a doctor?"

She smiled bitterly. "If you call it a doctor," she
muttered. "Some old drunken thing. He sewed her
up."

"I want to see her."

She looked up at him, surprised, poised at happiness but fearful of crossing into it, even if for only so brief a moment. "Do you mean it?"

"Of course," he said shortly. "I'll have a nurse bring her to me."

In a short while one of the nurses ushered Clara Weiss into the small white room. Rebekah watched Jarrett's face when he saw the beaten girl, and it was a face that registered horror, pity, and disgust all at once. Clara stood in the corner, staring at Rebekah and then at the young doctor and then back to Rebekah again.

"Come here, Clara," the young doctor said gently.

The girl shrank into the corner, her bruised hands held up to her bruised face.

"Go to the doctor, Clara," Rebekah said.

"I won't hurt you," he promised.

He examined her wounds; he examined her where she had been sewn up. The medical attention she had received was abominable; he had never seen such crude and careless stitching. Infection had set in—infection that could lead to deadly peritonitis—and he opened her wounds again, cleaning them, stitching them neatly so that hopefully one day she would be able to use those parts of her body that had been so ill treated.

"I know it hurts," he said to the squirming Clara, "but you shall be the better for it. Trust me if you can, Clara."

Rebekah watched the young doctor do his work. As she sat there, she found herself beginning to grow calm, even after the horror she had experienced: the horror of the ship; the horror of Clara's violation; the crudeness of the examination she had been given; the panic of the miscarriage; the fear she faced regarding Simon and how he would receive this news. And yet she began to feel herself grow calm. She trusted this young doctor, this Dr. Russell, and when she watched the care he took with Clara, and the tenderness he conveyed, she felt safer than she had in months.

"I want you to come see me again, Clara," Dr. Russell said. "You've been hurt very badly. I don't want to see you suffer anymore."

Clara stared at this young doctor for a long moment. Her eyes filled with tears, and she began to move her lips with much difficulty. "I hurt," she said at last, her first words to him. "I hurt."

Dr. Russell reached out for her and put his arm around the girl's narrow shoulders. "I know, Clara," he said, his voice filled with sadness. "I know you do."

The nurse took Clara from the room, and Rebekah watched her go, the limp a painful souvenir of the assault.

"You see what they did to her," Rebekah said bitterly.

"Yes," the young doctor murmured.

"Beasts. They are beasts. They are beasts."

He took her small clenched fists, which she had been pounding against the examining table, and he held them. The gesture was intimate; they allowed it for a moment; and then it was over.

"You may go in a few more hours," he said. "First you must rest. The nurse will show you a cot."

She stared at him, still thinking of the moment past when he had taken her hands and looked at her as though he really knew who she was.

He turned away and wrote down something on a chart. "I want you to bring back Clara in a week. Will you do that?"

She nodded.

"Good day then," he said crisply, walking to the door.

"Good day then," she whispered, watching him go.

She lay on the cot. There was no pain. She had expected there to be pain, because if there was pain, then she would be able to remember what had happened. Now all she knew was that hours ago there had been a baby within her and now there wasn't and she had met a doctor who was kind to her and who made her feel safe and he had brought her to this cot here and now she waited, she didn't know what for, Simon she supposed, but what would Simon say? Simon wouldn't make her feel safe; Simon would make her feel as though she had done something wrong.

She lay on the cot and all around her were others laying on cots. There was sickness and misfortune all around her. Old people and women like herself and children coughing. She wanted to be away from here, but she didn't know where she wanted to be.

Suddenly she saw him coming toward her. Simon. His fair-skinned face was very flushed, and his walk, although rapid, was heavy-footed and clumsy.

"Simon," she called, sitting up a bit in the bed.

He strode over to her and stood there, staring down at her. "What did you do?" he asked, his question and his stern visage chilling her with their bleakness.

"I . . . I was sick, Simon," she stammered.

"Sick? Do you want to ruin everything? You were sick on the boat. Will you be sick forever now, is that it?"

"I couldn't help it, Simon. I was sick and I . . ."

"Do you think I came to America to be with an invalid? I could have stayed in Vienna if I wanted to be with invalids!" he cried, his red face furious and full of hatred.

"Stop it," she muttered. She turned away from him, pressing her face into the pillow, and he reached down to her shoulder and pulled her roughly around to him.

"Get up," he said savagely. "I won't have you lying around here like all the other wretches, waiting to be sent back where they came from."

"Stop it, I said! You have no right!" she cried.

"What do you think I'm doing here? I'm here because you gave me a baby and now it's gone!"

His face, so violently red just moments before, suddenly lost its color as the shock of her words registered on him.

"That's right," she said spitefully. "It's all gone, and it's not going to come back."

He sat down on the edge of her bed. "What did you do?" he whispered. "You did something to it. What did you do?"

She laughed out loud. "I knew you'd say that. It's funny how well I know you in so short a time."

His large, rough hand darted suddenly and seized her slender wrist. "What did you do?" he said viciously.

"Let go of me," she warned. She hated him and she feared him. "Let go of me or I'll scream and they'll take care of you, they will."

He dropped her wrist and sat there staring at her.

"You're no better than the beasts who hurt Clara," she accused. She rubbed the wrist he had chafed. "And you were so quick to murder them, weren't you?"

"You rotten, no-good . . ."

"Shut up," she cried. She was wild with anger and with the sense of exhilaration that her anger gave her. "I don't want to see you. Why don't you just go? Ay? You got my dowry; you got yourself over here. Why don't you just leave me alone, and we'll go our own ways."

"Because you're my wife," he said with a little smile. "For whatever it's worth, you're my wife."

"But I'll never love you. I swear it. I'll never love you."

"Do you think I care? You're the woman who has my name, I don't care for anything more. You want what I want. Freedom. That's what you want and you'll work hard to get it and the harder you work, the more you'll be worth to me."

"I won't go with you!" she cried, oblivious to the looks she was getting from nearby patients.

"Get your bag because we're going now," he said, standing and straightening his tie.

"But the doctor won't allow it. The doctor will . . ."

"I don't give a fig for no doctor," he said with an arrogant smile, and he took her hand and fairly dragged her from this place where she had felt safe.

CHAPTER FIVE

Their rooms were small and dark and close. They lived there, massed together like birds in a rookery, except that they never got to fly. Lloyd Street was their address, off of Lombard Street, the center of Baltimore Jewry. There was nowhere else in the city they would have gotten lodgings; this was where their people lived, for better or, mostly, for worse.

They lived on the fifth floor of a narrow, decaying building that smelled of cabbage and cinders and human offal. The three of them shared three rooms with three other people—a widow, her child, and the child's elderly uncle. The rooms were dirty, cramped, and airless, looking out on a shaft which was used as a receptacle for garbage that was flung from the windows. If the boat that took them here had been a sort of hell, then this address, theirs for God only knew how long, was a sort of purgatory.

"So here we are in America," Clara said scornfully. She had begun to talk again, growing almost voluble in her expressions of contempt and bitterness. "We're to be rich here, are we, Simon?"

And Simon sat there silently, over his plate of cabbage and cheap, coarse bread, trying not to lose patience with his sister because her mind was in a delicate state, easily unhinged, and maybe, beyond that, because what she said was true.

"Nothing to say, have you?" Clara goaded. "My, my, Rebekah. How does it feel to be married to a fool?"

"Enough, Clara," Simon warned.

"You shouldn't talk to your brother that way," said the widow, a Pole named Milner.

"Who asked you?" Clara cried. "Did you hear anyone ask you?"

"Such a mouth," the elderly uncle moaned. He was a Hasid, with a long white beard and a large fur cap atop his head.

"Shut up, you old fool!" Clara screamed in a rage, and Simon rose and took the girl and shook her shoulders.

"You stop this!" Simon shouted. "You stop it!"

"Oh no!" Clara began to shriek. Her piercing cries rang through the tenement. "Oh no! Don't hurt me! Don't hurt me!"

Simon, shocked and appalled, let her go, and she ran out onto the landing where she began to wail like some dumb, abused animal.

"Rebekah," Simon whispered, his lower lip quivering as his eyes implored her to help.

She rose wearily and went out onto the landing. She sank down to her knees, next to the kneeling Clara. "Don't do this, *mein fagele*," she murmured, calling her sister-in-law a little bird. She *was* a little bird to Rebekah, a little yellow bird who had tried to fly the ocean and who had had her wings broken in the process.

"He hurt me," Clara whimpered, letting Rebekah

take her into her arms. Rebekah was the only one she would allow to touch her, and so she became Rebekah's entirely, and so Rebekah had come to love her.

Later, after the girl went to sleep, after the other lodgers went to sleep, when they were alone and there was a moment of privacy, she waited for Simon to speak, but he only sat there, staring down at the floor.

"She will never get better," he muttered at last.

She almost began to deny it, but then she remained silent, not willing to lie for him, not willing to comfort him with falsehoods.

"Did I do wrong?" he demanded to know, his face, once handsome, now dirty and twisted with his troubles.

She stared at him for a long while. "No," she finally whispered, finding him more pitiful at the moment than hateful. "You didn't do wrong."

He was so grateful to her that he suddenly began to cry. She couldn't believe it. A man as hard and cruel as he crying like that—and she was so moved that she went to him and took him in her arms.

"Oh, Rebekah," he breathed, pressing his face close to her breast.

She stroked his head and kissed him lightly at the temple. Did she love him? *No*, she heard a voice within her shouting, *No*! They went to bed together. He was eager for her, hungry; he sucked at her breasts and she closed her eyes because then she could enjoy it just a little, if she didn't have to see him, if she didn't know that it was he. Jacob, she whispered to herself, although Jacob was fading, becoming a thing of the past, and she wasn't so much longing for him as she was longing for something other than what she had.

"I want you," he groaned. "I want you."

She took him between her legs. She had become familiar with his wants; she no longer fought him. She made a point of trying to satisfy him, because it was easier that way, but it was evident that her heart was not in it. She would perhaps have liked it better if he were slower and took more care, because he was a good-looking, strong, well-made man even though she didn't like the way he smelled, the odor of the cigar factory on him where he worked rolling cigars, the air brown and thick with tobacco dust, and him coming home all covered with it and she wondered what it did to his lungs and she thought that she would retch when she smelled him making love to her, even though she didn't smell so good herself, what with her working all hours in a sweatshop sewing pockets, and even though she tried to keep herself clean, she didn't have clothes to wear and she couldn't keep her things laundered the way she would have wanted and sometimes she could smell herself and it was to her like the lice, her feeling so unfamiliar with her body, and she felt so sad and angry and she didn't want to be touched, least of all by Simon who used her roughly, ramming at her, taking great pride in the fact that he could hurt her and when she moaned, he thought that there was pleasure but he was wrong, as he was wrong about everything . . .

"Oh, yes," she heard him crying. "Oh, yes." And then he was at her side, all sweated and breathing hard.

She stared at the ceiling. She knew that everyone had heard them; there was a residue of shame, but she tried to put it out of mind.

When he fell asleep, she felt a deep, satisfying sense of relief. It was another day done. She knew that she was too young and too pretty to want her days finished fast, but that was the way it was. She was getting nothing she wanted. She could just as well be back home as in America.

The shop she worked at was run by an old German Jew named Rosenzweig. He called her Weiss, and he had little patience when she was slow and fell behind in the rate of pockets sewn. She was the slowest of the girls; much slower than Goldie, who wasn't nearly as shining as her name would imply, and Fannie, who had thick glasses and swollen hands and yet who still managed to outstrip her.

"Mr. Rosenzweig, he won't give a damn if you smile pretty at him," Goldie said vindictively. She was a homely, embittered spinster who bridled at the very appearance of Rebekah. "Mr. Rosenzweig, he likes a job well done, that's all."

"Leave her, Goldie," said Fannie, fat and kindly. "She's a 'greener.' She'll learn."

In time she did learn, as Fannie had predicted, and she spent twelve hours a day at the shop, which was cold and damp and poorly lit. But not all of it was bad; she became friendly with Fannie and each day they took lunch together. Fannie would say, "Come, Rebekah. We're gonna talk English now." Rebekah was amazed at how quickly she picked up the language. Simon, impatient as always, had learned very little, but Rebekah seized every opportunity to practice.

"You're becoming a regular American lady, aren't you?" Simon said sarcastically.

"Why not? We're here, aren't we?" she replied.

"You're a Jew," cried the elderly Hasid who lived with them, and his sister, the widow, glared at her.

"What does she care?" Simon said.

She stared at Simon. Now he wanted to be cruel to her again, and she wouldn't let him. "I wanted to keep the Sabbath," she cried, "but you said we don't do it. You said we're Americans now, not Jews. You're lying for them," she accused, indicating the observers, "just as you lie about everything."

"What I do is one thing," he said. "What you do is another. Don't you go doing things without asking me, you hear?"

"Doing what? Learning English? Is that what you mean?"

"*Ya*, that's what I mean."

Each day they spent together in this new country, they grew more embittered with each other. Simon thought he would go mad from his work. The cigar factory was a bad dream, umber colored and choking. He worked with a layer of tobacco dust on his clothes, in his hair, on his scalp, on his eyelashes. He had not yet begun the wracking, constant cough, but others around him were unceasing and through each silence he waited for the next cough; and when it came, he gnashed his teeth. He hated what he did: there was more money than he had had in the old country, but he hated the cigar factory more than he had hated peddling shoes on the streets of Vienna, and when he had done that, he couldn't imagine anything worse.

One day he sat over the bread and the old cheese that Rebekah had packed for him and he spoke with Horowitz, the man who worked at the table next to him, a Jew ten years his senior, small, sallow, and usually silent.

"Tell me, Horowitz" he said in Yiddish. "This is how America is?"

Horowitz, eating some gray indistinguishable slice of meat, said nothing.

Simon laughed wearily to no one in particular. "I was a dreamer," he whispered. "I was going to be a rich man, and all I am is a 'greener.'"

Horowitz chewed, looking down at his filthy brown fingernails.

"You don't talk?" Simon challenged.

Horowitz turned and stared at the brash fellow beside him. "What you want me to say?"

"It's got to get better, doesn't it, Horowitz? I mean, this is America. Doesn't it get better?"

"Are you a fool?" Horowitz whispered. "Ay, man? Are you a fool?"

The conversation so unnerved Simon that before he went home that night, he bought himself some gin and drank himself drunk. He came into the lodgings much later than usual, finding the dinner boiled out and Rebekah and Clara seated in silence at the table.

"Don't ask me where I been!" Simon shouted, raising a fist to them.

"No one asked," Rebekah replied.

"Smart girl," he sneered. He leaned down and wrapped a hank of hair around his fist, and Rebekah blanched with fright.

"Don't hurt her!" Clara cried, rising halfway in her seat.

"If I didn't have either of you, I'd be on my way!" Simon bellowed. "I'm a young man. I could go to California. I could go to Panama. But no, I've got you two wretches to take care of."

"Let me go," Rebekah demanded, and he did so. "Coward," she muttered. "It's only a coward who would hurt a woman."

Clara, touching her bruised face, looked so faraway that Simon, in his guilt, turned on her. "If it wasn't for you . . ."

"Simon!" Rebekah warned.

"It's true! She'll drag us down. Look at her. What good is she?" He couldn't believe what he heard himself saying, but he couldn't stop. "Why don't you get out of here and leave us alone? Why don't you get away, you goddamned leech!"

"Simon, stop it!" Rebekah cried, unable to bear it.

"Get out!" Simon shouted at Clara, again raising a fist to her, and the girl, terrified, bolted to the door. "And don't come back, you tramp!"

They heard her running down the stairs. Rebekah, paralyzed for a moment, pulled herself to the landing. "Clara!" she screamed hoarsely. "Clara! Come back! Clara!"

There was no answer. She stood, hanging over the banister, for several long moments, and then she went back into the room. "You see what you did," she said in a low, ominous voice.

He felt his head pounding from a combination of liquor and shame. "She . . . she'll come back," he croaked.

"Drunken cur!" she whispered. "You no-good rotten swine."

His watery blue eyes grew even more liquid with sudden, stinging tears. "What did I do? What did I do?" She watched him wringing his hands. "What did I do?"

She continued to stare at him with contempt for a few moments, and then she seized a pan from the stove and rushed at him, flailing at him, joyous when she heard his ooophs of pain. She felt like a mother whose child had been harmed. Clara—he had hurt Clara—and she would hurt him, yes, she would hurt him.

"Enough," he moaned, holding up his hands.

She locked him out of their room that night, and in the morning she found him hunched over the kitchen table, his head pressed against it, his mouth open, his tongue lolling. He was a repulsive sight, she thought. "Wake up!" she ordered, poking at him, and he awoke with sloppy, startled movements. He was pathetic, she thought, loathing him now, wanting him away.

"Rebekah," he groaned, "where is Clara? Did she come back?"

"No."

He sort of whimpered. She couldn't believe how weak he was and how strong she would have to be.

"What will we do, Rebekah? What will we do?"

"You drunken thing." She liked to insult him, to call him names. "You drunken thing, you. Look what you've done."

"Don't, Rebekah. Please don't."

"You'll have to leave," she said dispassionately. "As long as you're here, Clara will never come back."

"What shall I do? Where shall I go?"

"Can't you think of anything yourself?" she said viciously. "South. Go South. Get yourself something

to peddle and peddle it and make some money and
send it up here. Do you understand? Or can't you do
anything right?"

She liked him wounded and wounded he was. He sat
there, holding one large blunt hand in the other.

"Or aren't you a man?" she asked finally. "For all
your noises, maybe you aren't a man at all."

A few days later, with Clara still not returned, he
was ready to go on his journey. Rebekah went with
him to the train station, and they stood mostly in
silence, waiting for the train to come and take him
away.

"Savannah," she said. "That's what we heard is good
for men who peddle. Savannah. Can you understand?"

"I'm not a fool, Rebekah," he said, trying to regain
his poise but being weakened irreversibly by the behavior he had shown.

"And I'll look for Clara," Rebekah said, ignoring
him. "I'll go to the theaters. That's where she's likely
to be. She'll be trying to sing and dance, but I don't
know. I don't know if they'll have her, her all beat-up
looking and all."

"Will you tell her I'm sorry? Will you tell her I beg
her forgiveness?"

She maintained her silence, staring at the platform
with its contingent of fine-looking people waiting to
board the train.

"Rebekah, please. Will you tell her?"

"Yes," she muttered. "I'll tell her."

And the train arrived. They looked at each other;
they didn't know when they would see each other
again. If he ran away, she would find him and kill
him. "Richmond, Norfolk, Charleston," the conductor
cried. The world was filled with smoke from the mighty
locomotive.

"Then I'm going," he whispered, his face white with
apprehension.

She nodded.

He put his hands on her shoulders. She knew he would try to kiss her, and she didn't want it. But then he bent down, and she let him touch her lips with his.

"Go on then," she said to his surprise, and in moments he was lost in the crowd.

She waited for Clara to return, but Clara did not return. No one had heard of her; she had been lost and, as a result, Rebekah found herself unable to sleep or to eat.

The weeks passed. There was finally a letter from Simon.

Rebekah,

it read,

I am out of Charleston now and headed toward Savannah. There is money to be made. Here's fifty dollars. Come down with my sister as soon as you can. Tell her I beg forgiveness. Tell her we'll start anew. All of us.

Your husband,
Simon Weiss

She sat in the park and read and reread the letter. Should she go? What choice did she have? She was still his wife, and according to Jewish law she would have to remain his wife. If there had been another woman, that would be reason for her to ask to have them separated. As it stood now, she owed Simon another chance. According to her Jewish contract of marriage, she was still bound.

But what would she do about Clara? She was still gone, and Rebekah had been unable to find traces of her.

One day at work the spinster Goldie approached her with a triumphant smile.

"So," Goldie began, "you're looking for your husband's sister, ay?"

Rebekah stared at her. "Yes," she said. "What of it?"

The tall raw-boned woman found her hips and placed her hands there. "Her name's Clara?"

"Yes."

"I thought so. I heard you talking with Fannie. I heard you talking about 'Clara this' and 'Clara that.'"

"What about her?" Rebekah cried impatiently.

Goldie smiled a little. "I got a cousin who lives on Lombard. Her name's Sophie. She's from my town. She was telling me about another woman from my town—a woman named Rosie Schweitz. She was telling me that Rosie Schweitz went and got herself a house and that there was a Jewish whore who worked there— a girl named Clara who maybe didn't even have the curse yet. And I thought to myself: Clara? *Ya*, that whore could be the one."

"What are you saying?" Rebekah whispered.

"I'm saying that there's a whore named Clara. Is it your Clara, *mammele*?" Goldie mocked, using the Yiddish endearment for mother.

"What's she saying, Fannie?" Rebekah demanded to know. "She's saying Clara's a whore? I'll kill her, Fannie. I tell you, I'll kill her," she cried wildly, grabbing a scissors in her hand.

"Mr. Rosenzweig!" Goldie cried. "Look! She's gonna kill me! She's gonna kill me!"

"Weiss, what's this?" Mr. Rosenzweig roared. Rebekah dropped the scissors; she felt herself begin to tremble. "Get back to work, girls," Mr. Rosenzweig croaked like an ancient rooster overseeing his brood.

For the remainder of the day she sat, lost in her thoughts, allegedly involved in the sewing of pockets. Goldie, frightened by Rebekah's reaction, remained silent and cautious. When the day came to an end,

Fannie approached Rebekah and put her hand on her shoulder. "What can I do for you, *mein kind?*" she asked.

"Do you think it's really Clara?" Rebekah whispered. "Clara, *my* Clara . . . do you think it could be? A whore? My Clara a whore?"

"Shush," Fannie scolded. "That Goldie is no good. Don't you go listening to what she got to say."

But the next day Rebekah went over to Goldie. "Tell me," she said tremulously, "where do I find this Rosie Schweitz?"

Goldie concentrated on her sewing and did not look up. "It's down on the piers," Goldie said finally, after keeping Rebekah waiting for a reply. "Where else there's gonna be a whorehouse?"

That night, after work, she put on her coat and headed down the stairs.

"Rebekah," Fannie cried, "where are you going?"

She didn't look back. She headed down to the piers. The wind was cold and salty, and the streets were empty. At one point she turned a corner and came face to face with a tall, debauched old man in rags who begged her to give him something, and she had to run, almost slipping on the wet cobblestones. But then she was safe again, and in another moment she saw some lights that turned out to be a tavern. Because, as a woman, she felt she could not go into the tavern, she waited for some men to come out and then, gathering her courage, she asked them if they knew where Rosie Schweitz was.

One of the group, a sleek, bearded man, looked her up and down quite carefully and admiringly. "You one of Rosie's girls?" he asked.

"Where is she?" Rebekah persisted.

"You're a pretty one," he said, reaching out to stroke her chin.

She jumped away from him. "Don't touch me," she warned.

"I guess she's not one of Rosie's girls then," the man said jokingly to his companions.

"Maybe she's after her husband," a crony suggested.

"Should we tell her?" asked another.

"Down two blocks, first left up the stairs," said the bearded man at last.

She ran the distance. There was, in the vestibule, a red light, and she felt her heart begin to pound. She walked up the stairs and knocked on the door. "Rosie's?" she whispered. They let her in. She faced a room full of men and women.

"Look, Rosie," a thin pale-skinned whore called. "A new recruit."

Rosie came in from another room. She was a great, fat woman, close to six feet tall with arms the size of hams. Her face, multichinned, was painted thickly, and she wore a rhinestone-studded cap to cover her balding head.

"What, dearie? You want something?" she said in a voice that was tough and honeyed at once.

Rebekah looked around her. The house was not well appointed; the furniture was cheap and worn. The crowd gathered around her and stared with smiles on their faces. She was their diversion, and she hated them for it.

"Where's Clara?" she demanded to know.

"Clara?" Rosie Schweitz echoed, her tone amused and curious. "The *shane kind*?" she asked, identifying the beautiful child.

"Where is she?"

"What do you want with Clara?"

"Clara!" she screamed suddenly. "Clara!"

"Shut up!" Rosie Schweitz said.

"Clara!"

"Throw her out, boys!" Rosie Schweitz ordered.

"Clara!" she screamed again. "Clara!" She felt two men take her by the arms and lead her down the stairs.

She kicked at them and struggled, but they didn't even seem to notice.

She found herself on the street, and she paced back and forth. Should she call the police? She wanted to speak to Clara. *Oy, mein fagele,* she murmured to herself, not knowing what to do, and then she heard a tapping from an upstairs window. She looked up and saw Clara's golden curly hair; the girl was holding up a hand that pointed to a warehouse down at the piers. Rebekah understood and went there and waited for her.

In a short while Clara appeared. Rebekah watched her approach, a shawl around her head, the limp still present.

"You shouldn't have come," Clara said breathlessly.

"Not come? I searched for you and here you are and I've come to take you home."

Clara shook her curly gold head. The bruises had cleared from her face, but the prettiness had not returned, perhaps because the injuries had turned her features hard. "I can't go," she said.

"Simon's gone," Rebekah explained. "He's gone South. He's gone peddling."

"I hope he dies," she muttered bitterly, turning her face into the darkness of the warehouse.

"No, Clara. You don't mean it."

"Don't tell me what I mean!" she whispered fiercely. "I wish he was dead! He called me a tramp! He called me a tramp and he turned me out of his house and that's what I've become!"

"No, you're not, Clara. You're not what he said, you're not . . ."

"I'm a whore!" she cried hoarsely. "I'm the best goddamned whore Rosie Schweitz has to offer!"

There was a ringing silence. A rat, big and brown and bold, ran past them. Rebekah felt herself grown faint, but she had to hold on.

"So go back, Rebekah," Clara murmured. "Just go back and forget about me."

"I won't. You're my sister. I care about you."

She saw Clara's back hunched over in pain. "I tried," the girl said. "When I left you, I tried to get something decent. I went to the theaters and I said I can sing, I can dance. But they said, 'Look at you!' And I did look at myself, Rebekah, and you know what? I'm not pretty anymore."

"You've been hurt, Clara. Give it time. Soon you'll be . . ."

"No," she said firmly. "My face has changed, and it's not going to change back. So there I was. My singing . . . well, I guess it never was good enough to carry me along on its own. What could I do? I met another girl at the theater who took me here. They're good enough to me, Rebekah. The men . . . they know I'm young and they don't treat me too rough, not too rough, and I don't have to . . ."

"No," Rebekah whispered, holding her hands to her ears. "Don't tell me any more. I won't hear it!"

Clara stared at her. "Then what do you want, ay?" she said bitterly. "Then what are you coming down here for, ay?"

Clara's hardness astonished and frightened her. "Simon begs your forgiveness, Clara," she said quickly. "I don't know what he'll do if you don't come back. Come back, Clara, and it will be our secret."

"Ours and everyone else's," she laughed out of the side of her mouth. "It's no use, Rebekah. Can't you understand? Once a whore, always a whore."

She grabbed Clara by the shoulders. "Listen to me, Clara. It doesn't have to be. We can go to another city. We can go to Richmond or Charleston," she cried, grabbing at vague names she had heard. "Don't surrender, Clara. Come back with me, please come back."

Clara looked at Rebekah, her eyes suddenly hazy

and indistinct. "I can't," she said suddenly. "You're good. You're good to want me. But I can't."

"Why, Clara? I don't understand."

"Because I . . . I hurt, Rebekah. I hurt, and they give me something to make it stop hurting."

Rebekah waited for more, but there was no more forthcoming. "I don't understand," she murmured. "I just don't understand."

Clara laughed suddenly, but the laugh turned into a sob. "They give me something," she said. "They give me something."

"What? What is it?"

And now the girl laughed again. "Are you an idiot?" she asked angrily.

What did they give her? Oh, dear God, they gave her some kind of potion, and they kept her tied to them that way. "Clara," she whispered, and she reached out for her.

"Don't!" Clara screamed, slapping at her. "Don't touch me!" She ran from the warehouse, back toward the arc of light.

"Clara!" Rebekah screamed as if to a drowning girl. "Clara, come back! Come back, Clara!" But the girl had already slipped away.

She waited at the door to his office. She had been waiting a long time, and still she had not caught a glimpse of him. She didn't know why she had come here—she wasn't sure that he would even talk to her—but he had told her to come back with Clara and he had looked to be a kind person and she needed a kind person to talk to.

It was the end of the day. The waiting rooms had cleared out; all the sick people had dispersed, full of broken dreams and false hopes. She saw him emerge. He wore a hat and a long black coat; he seemed very tall and dark and thin, wraithlike almost, and for a moment she wondered why she had come.

"Herr Doktor," she whispered, recovering herself, feeling again that she had nowhere else to turn.

He stopped and turned; he stared at her.

"Herr Doktor," she said, her hands at the knot of the shawl around her head. "Can you help me?"

He peered at her. "Who is it?" he asked, his pale gray eyes tired, his face quite drawn and gaunt.

"Rebekah," she murmured, feeling like a fool. "Rebekah Weiss."

He continued to stare at her, shaking his head just slightly.

"Never mind," she muttered, turning to leave, her face on fire.

"No, wait," he called after her.

She stopped; she didn't want to face him.

"I remember now," he said. "You're the girl . . . yes, I'm sorry, I remember now."

She didn't know why she felt like crying, but she did. "Should I have come?" she said, her voice strained and full of pain. "Is it all right?"

"What's happened to you?" he asked, putting down his black bag, waiting for her to speak.

She tried to think of how to tell him, but then she began to sob, and he took her in his arms. "There, there," he said, patting her back. "There, there."

"I'm sorry," she said awkwardly.

He smiled. "You've learned a bit of English, haven't you?"

She nodded and wiped her eyes and cheeks.

"You were supposed to come back to see me with your sister, weren't you?" he asked, remembering more now, remembering her quite vividly as he looked at her lovely face.

"I know," she murmured. She wanted to leave now. She didn't know why she came. She didn't want to tell him about Clara. What could he say to her? What could he do for her?

"Tell me what's the matter," he urged.

She stared at him. He had been kind to her; his face was kind; he held her kindly, but she didn't trust him. She mustn't trust him. How could she tell him about Clara? What if they punished Clara? She didn't know what to do. She felt more confused and afraid than she could possibly have imagined. She felt so . . .

"What is it?" he demanded, growing gray with fatigue and suddenly stern with her.

"Nothing," she whispered. "A mistake. A mistake."

"But you've come down here in a state and you're telling me it was nothing? I don't believe it. I don't . . ."

"Nothing!" she cried, and she ran from him.

"Hey! You! Come back! Come back here!"

She ran. She ran down the stairs and out onto the street. There was sleet; she felt the cold hard rain hit her in the face. She ran, the hem of her dress becoming soaked as she stepped in puddles in the street. When she got on the trolley, she was breathless, but, more than that, she wasn't sure why she had run; she was fearful that she had gone mad.

Several weeks passed, weeks that she would only be able to remember in the future as being characterized by a deadness within her. She went to work and she went home and she slept as much as she could, losing herself in that deep, narcotic sleep that represented her only escape. There were more letters from Simon, filled with encouraging reports and promises of continued success, and she wrote him lying letters back, telling him that Clara had returned, safe and sound, and that they would soon join him.

She was writing just such a letter the night that Clara returned. She was sitting in the kitchen of the squalid rooms, and she wrote her husband:

Simon,

she wrote,

* * *

All is well with us . . .

But all was not well. There was a knocking on the door. So late? Who? Who could it be?

She went to the door, and cautiously she opened it a crack.

"Help me, Rebekah, help me!"

It was Clara, crying for help. She was holding herself. There was blood all over her dress and on her hands.

My God, my God. She just kept hearing herself saying, my God. Clara fell into her arms, and Rebekah helped her to the bed. The girl's face was chalk; there was a map of blue veins at her temples, and she shook as though from a deep chill.

"I did it wrong. They showed me how, but I did it wrong, Ay, ay, ay. It hurts me. Look. Blood. Look! Look! I'm dying, I tell you, I'm dying."

She put the girl in bed. There was a steady unchecked flow of blood coming from between her legs, and Rebekah placed a towel there.

"They showed me how, but it hurt me. Here, a feather, they said. They said, 'Here, take this feather and in turpentine you dip it.'"

"Ssssh," she whispered to the girl who was delirious.

"Turpentine. But it burned!" she shrieked. Rebekah realized that Clara was describing an abortion, some crude kind of abortion, a whore's trick that had backfired and that looked to have ripped her womb away. "Ay, it hurts!" she cried.

"Clara," she called. "Clara, I'm going for the doctor."

"Don't leave me," Clara sobbed. "I don't want to die!"

"Mrs. Milner!" Rebekah called. "Mrs. Milner!"

The widow who shared rooms with them padded out in her nightgown. "What?" she cried when she saw Clara. *Gott in Himmel!* what is it?"

"Stay with her," Rebekah said. "Don't leave her alone."

"Go!" the widow squawked. "Run!"

Run she did. She ran through the streets. She tried to find a doctor, but there were none who could understand her or who would come with her the distance or who would walk up the five flights of the tenement building. She found herself screaming aloud in the streets. A man in a carriage stopped and offered to help her. She had him drive her to Locust Point where she searched for the young doctor, and there she found him, late at night, his head on the table, a cup of coffee and a smoking cigarette beside him.

"Doctor!" she cried, waking him, pulling at him.

"What? What is it?" he asked, disoriented.

"Help me!" she cried. "Help me!"

"It's you," he said. "What is it?"

"Clara! She's dying! She's got blood all over. She's dying!"

He grabbed his coat and his bag and they raced out to the carriage. The ride was black and frigid. She shook life a leaf, and her voice quavered as she tried to explain.

"She came to me, and she was bleeding," Rebekah moaned. "And I tried to get a doctor but no one would come and so I came to you."

"You came the other day. Why did you run? What did you want to tell me?"

She hesitated, and then she blurted it out. "That Clara's become a whore," she cried. "And now she's gone and tried to kill what some bum has given her. She said something about a feather and turpentine—I don't know—she wasn't talking sense."

They raced up the five flights of stairs.

"She's going," the widow cried, wringing her hands.

"Clara!" Rebekah screamed.

"Mama, it's all right," the girl muttered, lost in her delirium. "It's only to sing in the streets, Mama, and they give me coins, Mama. All the Columbine roles, Mama. And they say I sing like a bird, *Mammele.* I sing like a bird."

Jarrett's hopes fell when he saw the butchery that she had committed on herself. She was hemorrhaging, and blood poisoning had set in. "Quiet now," he said, placing his hand on her feverish brow.

"Mama, they're hurting me!" she suddenly shrieked, writhing on the bed. "Don't let them touch me! No! You mustn't! Ay, it hurts! Mama! Simon! It hurts!" She began to beat her fists against the mattress. "Not there! Don't you touch me! I'll tell! I'll tell and they'll punish you! No! *Mammele!* Simon!"

It was the rape she was reliving, and Rebekah found herself turning away, unable to bear the piteous cries. Don't let her die, don't let her die, she prayed.

"With a feather," Clara groaned. "Here, just a touch. Ay, I hurt. No, Rosie, not with him, no, he'll hurt me. Don't beat me, Rosie, pray God, no, look, he's laughing at me and I hurt. Rosie!"

"Ay, *mein fagele!*" Rebekah sobbed.

"She's got to get to a hospital," Jarrett said. "There isn't much time."

"No! Rosie, he's hurting me! No!" Clara screamed and then, sitting up in bed a bit, she looked around her, her eyes suddenly lucid. "Rebekah," she moaned, reaching out her hand, and as Rebekah went to take it, she collapsed back onto the bed.

"Clara!"

But it was over. Over. Over. She was gone; she would not be coming back.

"Doctor?" Rebekah whispered.

He took her pulse, even though it seemed academic, for he had watched the life go out of her as clearly as he had seen the sun set that day. "I'm sorry," he said. "There simply wasn't time."

"No," Rebekah whispered, backing away from him.

"Ay, *mein kind*," the widow Milner cried, reaching out for her.

"No!" Rebekah shrieked, moving into a corner of the room. "Clara!" she screamed. "Clara!"

"She's gone," Jarrett said, moving toward her.

"They murdered her!" Rebekah screamed. "They murdered her!"

He tried to place his hands on her shoulders, and she struck out at him. "You let her die!" she accused, having succumbed wholly to her hysteria. He took her hands and held them as she thrashed wildly, spitting at him, trying to kick at him. When she had no energy left, when her anger had disintegrated into wracking, aching sobs, she collapsed into his arms, and he held her there, whispering soothing words to her.

"She was too young," she moaned. "She was only a child."

"I know," he said. "I know."

"They murdered her."

"Yes," he said grimly.

"Did you hear her? Rosie, she called, don't let them hurt me. They drugged her, did you know that?"

"Ssssh," he soothed, patting her back.

"I want to die," she cried. "I want to die."

"No, you don't, Rebekah. You know you don't."

She hid her face against his chest and continued to sob. "Hold me," she begged the doctor, hardly more than a stranger. And he did as she asked, holding at bay the terror and the anguish that threatened to consume her.

The day of the funeral was icy; the sky was salted with gray. She had scraped together some money that Simon had sent her; she had sold a string of pearls; she had bought a coffin and a burial place. She sat now, in a small, darkly lit synagogue, along with the widow Milner and her elderly brother, her friend Fannie, and

Jarrett Russell. She listened to the rabbi make the *Kaddish*.

Yiskah dahl v'yis kah dash sh'may rahba

Magnified and sanctified be the name of the Lord. She held her hands on her lap and stared straight ahead, considering the plain pine coffin that Jewish law decreed, considering the image of Clara, laid wasted, brought to her final place.

Ayl malay rachamin . . .

God in his compassion look over the soul of Clara Weiss. With Clara dead, Rebekah was free now, she thought. The thought made her look around to see that no one was reading her mind. Was it a shameful thought? She supposed it was but she couldn't keep herself from having it. She was free now, even though that gave her no pleasure. For her freedom meant that there was no one she cared about. Her father and her sister Sarah were memories: she could keep their lives in a locket in a drawer. Clara . . . gone. And even with Simon at her side, she would be alone. Simon was weak; Simon was full of cowardice and betrayal. She had the sense that she would be linked inextricably with Simon but that was all. She couldn't ever love him or respect him or even feel friendship toward him. In a very real way, it was Simon who was responsible for Clara's death. The only thing Simon could give her was a child and now, at the funeral of this lost *kind*, she knew how much she wanted to be heavy with child, to give birth, and to hold something pure and innocent and alive in her arms.

The procession to the cemetery was silent and grim. It had rained for weeks on end and the ground underfoot was marshy and their boots got wet. There were no tears: none of the mourners had really known the girl, and Rebekah herself was drained of tears and longing for conclusion.

She faltered at the grave site. It was too cold; it was happening too quickly. Simon, she heard herself murmuring. Simon, your sister, your sister. She trembled as the rabbi read the *Kaddish* once more.

Yiskah dahl, v'yis kah dash sh'may rahba

Sad words. Such sad words. The chant of it snaked through her mind. She remembered her mother's passing, and she began to shake violently. As they lowered the coffin into the ground, she began to moan and then she felt an arm around her, supporting her, holding her up. It was Jarrett Russell, and she felt so reliant on him at that moment that she allowed herself to sag further.

"She's gone," she heard herself cry. "She's gone."

Then it came time for them to bury the dead. As the only family of the deceased present, it was incumbent upon her to throw the first clod of earth over the coffin. She took the shovel and she heard the soil hit the thin pine wood. Then the others joined, all the others, except for Jarrett who was a Gentile.

Soon the coffin was covered altogether. It was over, all over, and the mourners were anxious to find some warm place.

"Come now," Fannie said, taking Rebekah's arm.

"No. You go on. I want to stay here a moment."

"Ay, *mein kind*," Fannie cried. "Why? Why do this to yourself?"

Then she heard Jarrett murmur something. He would stay with her. She looked at him in surprise, and he nodded shyly. She turned around and saw the fresh, rude mound of earth. She felt something wrench in her throat. She had thought she had no more tears, but she was wrong. They came in a flood, and she kneeled at the wet, cold crest of the grave.

"Good-bye, *mein fagele*," she whispered. Would there be a headstone? No, no money, no money, but she would work for it, yes, she would, she promised. "Ay, Clara, Clara." She felt her hair come undone in the cold wet wind and then she felt Jarrett take her by the arm and lift her and pull her away from here.

"But she'll be so scared," Rebekah whimpered.

"No," Jarrett said. "It's all over now. It's all over."

She sold the possessions that she would be unable to take with her. To the widow Milner she gave her pots and pans, and to Fannie she gave books and linens.

"Will you come back?" dear Fannie cried at their parting.

She did not answer. She did not know. She kissed Fannie on both plump cheeks; she doubted she would ever see her again. She was leaving still another part of her life, the part that had to do with Clara and the shop where she sewed pockets and the young doctor. Before she left, she stopped by his office to thank him for everything he had done.

"So you're going South?" he asked, his thin mouth a bit crooked and discontent.

"Yes. To my husband. To Savannah," she said, making the last sound very exotic indeed.

"They'll not know what to make of you nor you of them."

She smiled wanly. "It doesn't matter now."

"You're just searching for a place, is that it?"

"Yes," she nodded. "And we'll find it," she added with sudden fierce determination.

"I hope you do," he said sincerely, his voice tinged with sadness.

"And you?" she asked.

He seemed surprised by her question. "I don't know," he said frankly. "Maybe here, maybe not."

She knew by now that he was a lonely and troubled person. She sensed that his life was a secret, its mysteries not even decipherable to him. "This isn't your place?" she asked.

He laughed, but it wasn't a good laugh. "No," he sighed. "This isn't my place." He waved a hand about. "Is this anyone's place? It's just a moment, between coming and going, and I'm just a keeper of the gate."

"Then where will you go?" she asked urgently, concerned for him.

He shook his head. "It doesn't matter," he said, recalling her words.

There was a long, difficult silence as they studied each other.

"Good-bye then," she said at last, offering her hand. "And thank you."

"Good-bye," he whispered, and with a swift, light motion, he kissed the hand she had offered.

When she left him, she felt a deep, gnawing sadness that she had not anticipated. The doctor was a kind man, and now she would never see him again. How strange life is, she thought, with all its entrances and exits, all the people who touch you and then disappear.

She walked to the railroad station, her suitcase in hand. She was journeying again, this time alone. The station was crowded with people. She heard the conductor calling names for different trains: Boston, Philadelphia, Hartford, New York, Buffalo, Richmond, Trenton, Charleston, Savannah. Savannah: her destination. She looked around her. There was every sort of person here. Women in fine dresses and fur muffs; black servants in starched whites; soldiers; children in sailor suits; immigrants bound to distant points; and people like herself, a suitcase in hand, alone, lonely, unsure, anonymous.

The platform was adrift in smoke. She was losing still another part of her history. She boarded the train, ticket in hand, and placed her cheap cardboard suitcase on the rack above. She sat down in a worn, once

plush velvet seat and looked out the window. The
station, the city, the world . . . all in smoke. A hot
white fire was licking at her feet, and she was escaping
into an unknown place that promised no special haven.
Almost imperceptibly she raised her hand. Good-bye,
Clara, she whispered to herself. And then the train
began to roll.

CHAPTER SIX

The country was marshy at first, with low scrubby yews
and pines and the sun remote and cold like a small
white grape in the sky. All she knew was that she
wanted to sleep. She closed her eyes and tried not to
think.

Just then someone entered the compartment. It was
a woman—small, middle-aged, heavily made up,
elaborately bonneted. She held a lace hankie to her
nose and made small, querulous noises as she had a
porter arrange her hatboxes and valises around her.

"Is everything here?" she drawled.

"Yes'm," the porter replied.

"I don't believe you," she pouted. "I'm forever
losing luggage on these trains. I tell you, a woman
should not have to travel alone."

The porter left them, and they sat in silence, the
two of them eyeing each other carefully.

"I just hate to travel alone," the woman said finally.
"Don't you?"

"*Ya,*" Rebekah said with a nod.

"I tell you, we haven't gone much further since the days of highwaymen, have we?" she persisted.

Rebekah shook her head. She did not want to appear uncommunicative, but there was much in the woman's conversation she could not understand.

"My daughter just got married," said the woman, launched on a new and possibly unrelated topic. "She's a lovely girl, just your age, I'd say. How old are you?"

"Nineteen," Rebekah replied.

"Well, she's just eighteen, you see! She married a lieutenant in the navy, Lieutenant Stephen Larsen. He's got a fine career ahead of him, and they're very much in love. But he's being sent to Vera Cruz, and I don't know how I'll make do without my little Mary Lee. She's such a comfort to me. Ever since the death of my beloved husband, Colonel Winslow, Mary has been my life. And now she's gone away, and I'm a woman traveling alone, just like you."

Rebekah remained silent. The woman gave her a flinty-eyed stare, and Rebekah could see that there were beads of perspiration at the high, sparse hairline.

"Where are you bound?" the woman asked impatiently.

"Savannah," Rebekah said, pronouncing the name peculiarly.

"Why, you're foreign, aren't you?" the woman exclaimed.

Rebekah nodded.

"Oh, my, there are times when I could be declared deaf, dumb, and blind! Where are you from, child?"

"Austria," she said, placing her hands on her black wool skirt, feeling foreign again, strange, uncomfortable, and acutely observed.

"Austria? Oh, my, what a divine land. The Alps, the waltz, Strauss and Schubert. How simply divine. Whatever are you doing on a train bound to Savannah?"

"To meet my husband," she explained. "He has found employment there."

"Is that so? What kind of employment?"

Rebekah thought a moment. "He sells."

Mrs. Winslow looked surprised. "What does he sell?"

"Many things."

The woman scrutinized Rebekah even more carefully. So her husband was a peddler. The people one
ran into on trains these days. "I see," she said, dis-
tancing herself with a moment of coldness.

Rebekah stared out the window. As they went south,
the land became greener and warmer, and there was
more that was pleasant to look at.

"The green is here again," Hattie Winslow said,
placing her need for conversation over her innate sense
of snobbism.

"Ya," Rebekah murmured, herself a bit cold at this
particular juncture.

"You should learn to say yes," Hattie Winslow said
firmly. "It won't do you a bit of good where you're
going not to speak the language."

Rebekah's face flamed. She thought to change cars,
to do something in response to this insult. But then she
considered the woman's words, and she checked her
anger. There was something to what the woman said,
she thought, and perhaps there were things she could
learn from this woman.

"Savannah is a very special place, you know," Hattie
Winslow continued. "It's got its way of doing things,
and don't you go thinking that certain things aren't
noticed. Everything is noticed, child, believe me."

The woman's words made Rebekah feel nervous.
She would do everything wrong, and there would be
still more trouble with Simon.

"But once you get down there, you'll be very happy,"
Mrs. Winslow continued. "Of course they may not
know what to make of you nor you of them, but . . ."

Rebekah stared at her.

"Did I say something?"

She shook her head, startled and confused. "It's just that someone else said that to me right before I left."

"Really? How odd."

"Yes. And he was from the South too."

"Was he? Did you get his name?"

She thought of him. "Yes," she said. "He is a doctor. His name is Jarrett Russell."

"Oh, my Lord, how extraordinary life is!" the woman cried. "Jarrett Russell! I won't believe it. I simply won't!"

Rebekah just stared in surprise, waiting for an explanation.

"Why, he's from my town!" Mrs. Winslow declared. "Mobile! Mobile, Alabama. I knew his father and his grandfather. I knew the whole rotten pack of them. Traitors, that's what they are! Traitors down to the very last man!"

Rebekah's surprise was now in contention with her anger. However brief their association had been, she had valued Jarrett Russell, and she did not enjoy hearing him slandered in such a way.

"Where did you meet 'Doctor' Russell?" Mrs. Winslow inquired, making the word "doctor" seem like a profane parody.

She didn't know whether she should tell, but then she had no good reason not to. "At Locust Point. He treated me there."

"Locust Point? The immigrant station?"

Yes, Rebekah nodded.

"Well, my, my, my. Haven't we come down just a little in the world." There was a smug look of satisfaction of the woman's florid face that Rebekah could not understand but that she knew he didn't like. "Jarrett Russell, the fine young prince, swabbing disinfectant for a living."

"He treated me kindly," she said in his defense, knowing full well that to defend him would be to alienate this woman across from her.

"Well, of course he did," Mrs. Winslow laughed. "A traitor can still be a gentleman. And besides, what have *you* got to do with anything?"

She didn't know how to respond to that and so she didn't, remaining silent, just sitting there, feeling like a fool.

"Let me tell you a thing or two about Jarrett Russell," Hattie Winslow said. "Jarrett Russell's family was the finest the South had to offer. A family of lawyers, doctors, senators, judges. The Russells were to Mobile as . . . Romulus and Remus were to Rome. Do you understand what I'm saying?"

"Yes," Rebekah said distinctly, fascinated by and eager for these revelations into the young doctor's life.

"Why, I can't tell you how many evenings we spent at Wild Oaks. It was the finest house in Mobile. My little Mary Lee went to all the cotillions there, and they were the most wonderful, starlit nights." There was a silence as the woman gazed out the window. "I can't tell you what the South was, child. The South was music and sunlight and gardens and people being so kind and gentle with each other. The South was honor, my dear, and we fought to defend our honor."

Rebekah watched the woman fold and unfold a fan as she evidently ran thoughts through her mind too bitter and painful to relate.

"We lost but we fought valiantly, and so our honor lives on. It isn't easy though to live in a land that's been taken over by filthy carpetbaggers. Why, all sorts of trash is pouring into the South every day, like sand pouring into an hourglass. And the niggers—why, you'd think it was Mardi Gras every day of the year. Oh, all of that is bad enough, but we can abide it if we must. One day, don't you worry, we'll have our place in the sun again. What we can't abide is cowardice and betrayal. We can never forget that, and we can never forgive it."

Rebekah waited for more, but Hattie Winslow had shaded her eyes, seemingly overcome by this recitation.

"Tell me what happened," Rebekah whispered.

The woman sighed and folded her fan once again. "Where shall I begin? The father of the young man you met was named Jarrett Russell, Junior. We practically grew up together, you know. He was a dear and beloved friend of my brother, Winfred, and, in fact, it was taken for granted that we would one day marry. But things taken for granted rarely occur, do they? And when Jarrett went off to college, he soon met and became engaged to Miss Sarah Fenn of Charlottesville, Virginia. Oh yes, my heart was broken for a time, but young hearts mend quickly and, besides, it turned out that we had never been in love anyway. I found out what love was when I met and married my husband, Colonel Winslow. Well, child, the world is a different place when love is about, don't you think?"

Rebekah nodded dutifully.

"Don't you find that with your husband?"

"Yes," Rebekah murmured after a rather lengthy pause.

"Well, my goodness, I surely hope you do, for life isn't worth living if you never have love."

The woman's words caused Rebekah a deep, internal sadness. She gazed out the window, and she found green hills in the distance.

"Anyway," Mrs. Winslow sighed, interpreting Rebekah's silence as a sign of boredom, "let me get back to my tale. Jarrett Russell married Sarah Fenn and brought her back to Wild Oaks. He became a military man, which was an unusual thing in his family. His was a family of intellectuals and politicians and judges. Brilliant men and, in a very different way, General Russell was a brilliant man as well. But he was a fiery man, and that was his flaw. Nothing was ever good enough for General Jarrett Russell. I tell you, his slaves lived in terror of him. Not that he abused them physically, but he would treat them as though they were creatures without feelings and I, for one, always have said that niggers are people too. But it wasn't just his niggers that the general spat upon. It was everyone. It was the men in his outfit. It was his neighbors. It was his wife. Why, his wife was like a flower when she first came to Wild Oaks, but it took little time to turn her into a poor wilted thing. No one was spared his temper and his contempt except for one person."

Rebekah waited for the woman who had paused for dramatic effect.

"And do you know who that one person was?" she asked at last.

Rebekah shook her head.

"His son. Jarrett Russell the Third. Prince Jarrett, we called him. That child had everything, let me tell you. Tutors, trips abroad each year—I think it was a profligate childhood."

Rebekah looked at her quizzically, not understanding the word.

"Waste, my dear. Sheer waste. Jarrett turned out to have as fiery a temperament as his father. Many was the time we were at Wild Oaks when it seemed sure that father and son would come to blows. Well, what did you expect? The boy was spoiled rotten on the one hand and pushed to his limits on the other. General Russell wanted his son to be President. Can you imagine? Not that young Jarrett was lacking the intellect or the personal charm to attain that office. But how can a young man achieve when his home is such a terrible place? And that's what Wild Oaks was—a terrible place. General Russell sucked the life from poor Sarah Fenn, and she died when she was still a young woman. Oh Lord, I loved that girl even though she started out as my rival. I saw her through miscarriage after miscarriage . . ."

The word made Rebekah start in her seat.

"Oh, child, are you faint?"

"No. No, it's all right."

"Well here, have a sip of brandy," she said, pulling a flask from her bag. "I know," she said, resuming her narrative, "that I never could have married the general because I was too strong and he wanted someone weak. Well, he found that someone in Sarah, and when she died, young Jarrett left home. He went to medical school, a choice that the general deplored because it was the end of the dream that one day his son would become President. They remained estranged up to the time the war broke out."

"Did they ever get back together?" Rebekah asked, thinking of her own father and the way in which she left him.

"The war brought everyone into each other's lives, child, be it in a good way or bad. Young Jarrett joined the medical corps and the general . . . well, the general's story is well known."

"Tell me, please."

"The general," she sighed, "may have been a strategist, but he was not a warrior. In his very first battle he retreated. Oh my yes, he showed his yellow streak. Wouldn't you know it? Bullies are always cowards. The great general, the man who sought to embody all the virtues of his heritage, the man for whom nothing was ever good enough—he ran like a cur with his tail between his legs."

"And what happened?" she demanded to know.

"It was my brother, Colonel Schuyler, who brought charges against him. It was my brother who had fought beneath his command and who saw the men in his battalion fall like flies. It was my brother, the one man who had remained General Russell's ally through it all, who made it his goal to see the coward punished. But the coward didn't even have enough courage to take his punishment. On the eve of his court-martial he sat in his tent and blew his brains out."

There was a thundering silence as the first part of

this tale came to a close. It was a terrible story, and she could only think of the young doctor's drawn, gaunt face.

"And what happened to the son?" Rebekah asked.

"Well, I suppose there you know nearly as much as I do. What I do know is that it left the young prince badly damaged. He seemed to have a need to avenge his father's death. I couldn't begin to tell you why that is. There was no question that the general was a contemptuous coward; there could be no hope of honor redeemed. Perhaps young Jarrett simply could not bear the truth. Perhaps he longed for forgiveness from his father and the only way he could get it was by vainly trying to protect his father's name. Whatever it was, the poor young man engaged in one fight after another. His attempts to duel were endless and terribly disruptive. On top of it all he took to drink. Eventually it was said that he was asked to leave the medical corps. And that was the last I'd heard of him until you told me that he treated you at Locust Point."

The sadness of the story was utterly piercing. She kept thinking of Jarrett saying that he was looking for his "place," and now she understood.

"What did he treat you for?" Hattie Winslow asked, unabashedly prying into something that was none of her concern.

Rebekah hesitated a moment, but then answered. "I lost my baby," she whispered.

"Oh, poor child," Mrs. Winslow cried. "We women have the hardest job, don't you know. But you're such a fine-looking, healthy young thing. Don't you worry about it."

Rebekah smiled a bit and nodded her head a bit.

They both slept for what seemed many hours. When they awoke, they were in a foreign place that was warm and sunny and that thrilled her to the bone. Through the window she could see cedars and palms and palmettos and the ocean glittering and studded with lush green islands."

"Where are we?" she cried.

An awakening Mrs. Winslow rubbed her eyes and yawned. "We're between Charleston and Savannah, child."

Savannah. She whispered it to herself. It seemed a magical, musical word. "We will soon be in Savannah?"

"Yes, very soon."

She felt her whole body come alive. She felt her heart pound; she felt the blood coursing through her veins. Savannah. And Simon. Simon would be there, waiting for her. She wanted to see him. She was lonely for him or, at the very least, she was lonely for someone who was not a stranger to her. She heard the train pull into the station, the harsh joyous whistle lifting her spirits even higher, and she rose from her seat and collected her things.

"Savannah," Mrs. Winslow sighed. "Lovely Savannah. Enjoy it, child."

"Thank you," she replied. "It has been most good talking with you."

"What's your name?" Mrs. Winslow asked. "Isn't it funny I didn't get it?"

"Rebekah Weiss."

"Well, I wish you luck, Rebekah Weiss." She offered her hand. "And if you're ever in Mobile, you'll have to come to White Meadows."

"Thank you. I will."

"Just ask for Hattie Winslow. Everyone knows me," she said in a strange, emphatic, and somehow distant voice. "My husband was a hero."

She stepped down onto the platform. Simon. Where was he? She felt an instantaneous sinking sensation as she thought that he had deserted her. Was he capable of such a trick? Yes, yes he was, yes.

She stood on the platform and watched it empty of people. She felt herself begin to cry like a lost child. What would she do? And where in God's name could she go? She sat down on her suitcase, and her body was trembling. Just then she saw him running down the platform.

"Simon!" she shrieked.

He took her in his arms. "I'm sorry," he cried. "I didn't mean to be late."

"I was so frightened," she said, her voice a mixture of anger and relief.

"But now you're here. Let me look at you," he said. "You look fine, just fine. Where's Clara?" he asked, turning around, looking toward the depot.

She stared at him. He looked better than he ever had, his face fairly glowing, his clothes clean and well tailored.

"Is she inside?"

She shook her head.

"Where is she?"

"She isn't here, Simon."

His face fell a bit. "She stayed behind in Baltimore?"

Her silence was construed as verification.

He darkened noticeably. "She's a willful girl," he muttered. "You would have thought she had learned her lesson by now, but evidently she has not."

"Don't, Simon," she said, finding his words too painful to bear.

"Why not? Look how she defies me!" he cried, launching into his wrath.

"You don't understand, Simon!"

Now he peered into her eyes quite seriously. "What is it?"

She knew she had to tell him, but she found herself shaking her head ever so slightly.

He seized her roughly, almost wildly, and began to shake her. "What is it? Tell me what it is!"

"Let me go!" she cried, and he released her. She saw his stricken face.

"Tell me," he whispered.

"She's dead," Rebekah said, feeling her throat swell up as she spoke the words.

"No," he said. "No, it isn't true. You're lying. I know you're lying."

"She's dead, Simon. I buried her. She's dead."

Reflexively he lashed out and struck her across the face. Then, when he saw what he had done, when he remembered what he had done to Clara, he let out a wail that was too horrible to hear, and Rebekah covered her ears.

"Clara," he moaned, sinking to his knees. "Clara!"

She held his head and he wrapped his arms around her waist and he wept, pressing his face against her stomach.

"Sssssh," she soothed, stroking him.

"How did it happen?" he managed to ask between great, gulping sobs.

"Fever," she said after a moment's pause. "We did everything we could."

"Did she suffer?"

"No. I was with her throughout."

"You didn't take care of her," he began to accuse. "You didn't feed her. You didn't keep her warm enough."

"Stop it, Simon," she warned.

"When it was you who had the fever, no effort was spared. Clara and I kept a vigil at your bedside to see you through it. And how were we repaid? By letting her die like a dog!"

He stamped away from her, leaving her alone again on the platform. Go then! she cried bitterly, taking her bag and moving in an opposite direction. She would make do without him. All she got from him was abuse and accusation. She would become a seamstress and she would work her fingers to the bone and she would succeed and she would be free because that's why she had come to America, to be free.

She counted her money. She had perhaps enough for one week's lodgings. Where to? A trolley? Once more she felt lost and abandoned, but she would not succumb to fear. She walked a few more blocks. She suddenly realized that this was a beautiful city, warm and sunny and renewing, and she picked up her pace, even though she had no idea where she was going.

"Rebekah!" she heard.

No, she would not turn around. Damn him, she would not turn around.

"Rebekah, wait!"

She dashed across a crowded street, eager to get away from him.

"Rebekah! Please! Listen to me!"

She heard his footsteps nearing hers. Then she felt his hands take her by the arms.

"Don't touch me!" she cried.

"Stop it! You're my wife! Don't say that."

She struggled with him; she lashed out at him with her fists. People stopped and stared at them like they were freaks, jabbering in some arcane Eastern tongue, and yes, she supposed they were, but she hadn't the time nor the inclination to worry about it.

"I don't want to see you!" she spat. "Never again. Do you hear me?"

"Don't say that, Rebekah . . ."

"You think I didn't take care of Clara? You think I let her die like a dog? Well, let me tell you, when she came to me, it was too late to do a thing. Fever! She had no fever. She slaughtered herself like a butcher slaughters a calf. Fever! I just told you that to protect you from the truth."

"What truth?" he demanded. "Tell me!"

"She was a whore," Rebekah whispered. "You made her into a whore. You turned her away in a drunken rage, and what do you think becomes of a girl on the streets? She fell into the hands of thugs, and they did her up good. And when she made a mistake and got herself with child, they showed her how to butcher herself. She did as they said and she came to my house in the middle of the night, her womb ripped apart, and I had to run to find a doctor and when I returned, she was dead."

Simon's silence shut out all the noises of the street. His broad, blunt hand was held to his forehead as if to shade himself from a sun that was not, in fact, hot.

"I gave her a proper burial," she said, feeling herself suddenly choked with emotion.

"What have I done?" he gasped. "What have I done?"

"Don't, Simon," she said, dryly, pulling back on the grief she could feel on a moment's notice.

"I killed her, didn't I?"

"Don't, Simon. It will do no one any good."

"Oh, Rebekah. I'm a monster . . ."

"Simon . . ."

"Kill me, Rebekah. Kill me."

She picked up her bag and began to move away from him.

"Don't go, Rebekah!"

"I must, Simon," she said, shaking her head. "It hurts me to be with you. Can't you understand? And anyway, you don't love me."

"I need you!" he cried like a child, holding out his hands to her.

"Let me go, Simon," she pleaded.

"I need you, Rebekah. I need you."

"Let me go," she murmured. But then he had her bag in his hand, and he was leading her down the street.

The rooms he had found for them were makeshift by any standards, but after the tenements of Baltimore, they seemed fresh and airy. The smell of the oyster heaps and rotting fish that lay beyond their balcony were, to her way of thinking, immensely preferable to the odor of human filth. All around the row of houses were dense vines of violet flowers known as bougainvillea. From the window they could see boats in the harbor, and they could see the horizon where the sea met the sky and gave the illusion of boundlessness.

"It's comfortable," he said timidly, "and there are breezes off the water."

"Yes," she said. "It's fine."

There was an awkward silence. He kept putting a hand to his forehead, a confused gesture that had suddenly seemed to become very characteristic of him.

"Some tea?" he asked eagerly.

"Yes. That would be nice."

For a long time thereafter silence reigned. Now it was her turn to speak.

"You've done well," she remarked, "haven't you?"

"Yes. I have. There's opportunity here, I know that."

"In peddling?"

"Yes."

"You peddled in Vienna and you loathed it."

"I wasn't making money in Vienna," he said fiercely.

"Will we travel?"

"No. You'll stay here. I'll have to travel, but it's no life for a woman."

"You're wrong. I won't stay here. Do you think all I want to do is be your wife? *Your* wife? We have no marriage, Simon, understand that. You said you needed me. All right then, I'll work side by side with you, and I'll share whatever is good and whatever is bad. We'll work together and maybe that way we'll survive. At least we have our health, and if we work hard enough, maybe something good will happen to us. If that's agreeable to you, then I'll stay here. Otherwise you will force me to go."

She thought his eyes would pop from his head. "Are you telling me what to do?"

"I'm offering you a proposition," she replied.

He stared at her, very hard, intent on melting her position. But he saw that he could not succeed, and so he nodded wearily.

"All right, then," he said. "You've won."

From there on the rest of the evening was easier. She made eggs and coffee, and they sat, sating their hunger, feeling closer than they had in such a long time.

"Life goes on," he said softly, puffing on his cigarette, "and there are so many changes."

"It will become easier," she assured him.

"I will never be free of Clara," he said, full of fear. "She'll come back to haunt me, you'll see."

"Hush," she said sternly. "Stop with your talk of ghosts."

"You'll see," he said. "You'll see."

Sooner than she had expected, it became time for them to go to bed. She dreaded it utterly. Now she felt about their intimate encounters something quite different from what she had ever felt before. Before she had sensed his cruelty, his selfishness, and his ruthlessness. Now it was his need that she felt. As he lay upon her, whispering her name, asking her to hold him, she felt she might suffocate. She couldn't bear to have him so close to her, and she began to push at him.

"What?" he demanded to know.

She couldn't explain to him. "Let me breathe," she said. "Just let me breathe."

"Are you ill?"

"Yes. Yes, I'm ill," she cried, clutching at his suggestion.

He eyed her suspiciously. "Well now, this came on suddenly, didn't it?" he asked, a trace of bitterness in his voice.

"Just let me be, Simon," she repeated.

He turned over, presenting his tense and rigid back,

and she found herself so grateful that she sought to find some kind words.

"It will be better, Simon," she promised, although in her heart she could not believe it.

"Everything's wrong," she heard him utter. "Everything's wrong, and it's all bound to get worse."

She closed her eyes and tried not to think.

CHAPTER SEVEN

Again she was journeying. It seemed she would never stop; it seemed she would never find rest. She was young and there had never been a question of stamina, but she was weary nonetheless. There was so much to learn, so much to cope with, and she had such meager resources to give her comfort and support. When she set out in the wagon alongside Simon, she felt a sense of union in purpose but not in spirit. They were poles apart; the more time they spent together, the greater the distance grew.

He had bought pots and pans, a stock with which he had enjoyed some success in the past. He had sold boots, ladies' shoes, flatirons, brooms and brushes, and table linens. He had peddled in Maryland's Cumberland County, in the vicinity of Richmond, in the Piedmont country of North Carolina. He had enjoyed his share of success in most of these locales, but he was just one of many peddlers working the same territory, and there he had some difficulty. Being a saturnine sort of man, his visits were not regarded with the same sort of expectations that awaited his competitors. A peddler was not only expected to sell, but he was expected to bring diversion as well. It helped to be able to tell a joke or to know the news of the capital or to pass on the newest treatment for a dry cough or to be the sort of man who could remember the names of children and grandchildren. Simon was deficient on all these counts, and he knew it.

He dreaded going to peoples' homes. It was, in its way, worse than it had been in Vienna even though he made more money here. In Vienna, on the street, the patch of turf he had claimed was his, and all the other peddlers knew not to intrude. Here he traveled the same circuit as everyone else, and it had happened more than once that some harsh, raw-boned country wife, tired of visitors, had taken a broom to him and chased him from the porch steps as though he were a skunk or that ubiquitous local creature known as a "possum."

He knew he was without charm and that he had more difficulty gaining an audience than others did, but he compensated by working furiously, even obsessively. He drove himself as though he were a dray horse rather than a man and this took its toll on his nerves. He rarely slept anymore; when farmers offered him lodging, he tossed and turned all night in the hay. He would be on the road for solid weeks at a time until he sold out as much of his stock as the territory would support and then he would go back into town— Raleigh, Richmond, Greensboro, Charleston, Savannah —to replenish, to wash up, to send money north. His only release had to do with drinking, whoring, and cards. In the latter he had thus far been lucky, winning more than he lost. Now with Rebekah at his side everything would be different. He would no longer have his releases, or, at least if he did, they would have to be clandestine. This realization, which hit him fully as they began their journey, served to make him even edgier and more irritable than usual.

"Then are we ready to begin?" Rebekah asked impatiently when Simon appeared to have finished loading the wagon.

"We're ready when I say we're ready," Simon barked.

She thought to retaliate in anger, but then she held herself back. If they were to quarrel over every injurious remark that Simon made, there would never be any progress. It was best to hold her tongue and to try in subtle ways to get what she wanted.

After a silent hour or more of working their way toward inland plains, she decided it was time to speak again.

"What a strange countryside this is," she remarked, looking out at dry, dusty fields.

"Peanuts," he muttered.

She had never heard of it before. "What is it?" she asked.

"A crop," he replied, exasperated.

"Is it eaten?"

He ignored her thoroughly. They rode on and then the road became cooler, shaded by towering pecans. It was not a road he had ever traveled before, but it looked not much different than many other roads he had been on. For five months now he had lived on the road. At first he carried his load on his back and then, when he had made some money, he was able to get this wagon.

"It's so terribly hot this time of day, isn't it?" Rebekah remarked.

"Complaining already?" he said nastily.

They passed another peddler who was walking along the road, burdened down by a pack that weighed a good hundred and twenty pounds. The pack had sewing things and aprons and pots and pans, but the young man carrying it had a jaunty walk nonetheless.

"Good day to you," the young man said in Yiddish. It was a reasonable assumption on his part that his fellow peddlers were Jewish.

"Good day," Rebekah said. The young man must have been her age or so, and he had a smile that made her feel good, particularly in counterpoint to Simon's glowering presence.

"I'm Jacob Reich," he said.

Jacob. The name and the youthful charm of the peddler made her think of her own lost Jacob. "Rebekah Weiss," she said, "and this is my husband Simon."

Simon nodded almost imperceptibly. He didn't like strangers, and he didn't like competition.

"Business is good for you?" Jacob asked.

"Oh, we're just starting out," Rebekah said.

"Hold your tongue," Simon ordered.

The young man looked surprised. Among the peddlers there was a tradition of camaraderie that was not in evidence here. "I'm just another egg-eater," he said. "Egg-eater" was a term for Jewish peddlers who would only eat eggs while out on the road in order to observe the kosher dietary laws.

"Well, I don't happen to be no egg-eater," Simon said scornfully. He had given up being kosher as soon as he set foot in the United States, and he was proud of it, as though it were a move that signaled his progressiveness.

"You're a Jew, ain't you?" the young man asked, and Simon shrugged, much to Rebekah's mortification.

"Of course we are," she said.

"Well, don't hide it," the young man said. "Around these parts they like to meet a Jew. Most of them never met a Jew before. In fact one of them asked me if I was a Baptist Jew or a Methodist Jew—and they think we're all good friends of Moses and Isaiah and such."

Rebekah gave the young man a quizzical look, and he laughed. "They're all great Bible readers down here. Don't you see the names of the towns? Mount Olive and Pisgah and Cedars of Lebanon. They love their

Bible and you'd best be up on it 'cause they think we're all authorities."

"Well, I ain't no gospel preacher," Simon said.

"What are you selling anyway?" Jacob asked.

"Pots and pans," Simon said. "Can't you see?"

"Why, with this nice rig, you should be selling banjo clocks and mattresses. That's what they're hungry for down here. It ain't often they get to see an egg-eater what don't have his wares on his back."

"Can we give you a ride?" Rebekah asked. "It's so hot."

"Why, thanks," the young man said. But before he could get on, Simon urged the horses away.

"What are you doing?" Rebekah cried.

"No free rides," Simon barked. "That's a rule."

"But he's a Jew."

"Shut up, I say. It's me who makes the rules here."

They rode on in silence for what seemed a long time before they saw a house with people. There, down in a sort of glen, was a small rough-hewn farmhouse.

"We'll try there," Simon said, the unnatural calm of his voice belying the tension underneath.

He pulled the wagon to the side of the road and disembarked. "Stay here," he instructed her. She watched him walk toward the little house. He should have let her go with him, she thought as she stayed behind in the hot wagon.

He knocked several times, and then, finally, the door opened. A tall, skinny young girl, perhaps thirteen, no more, stared at him with a blankness that he had never before encountered.

"Your mama," he said. "She is home?"

She continued to stare as before.

"Your mama?" he persisted.

"Mama," she cried like a tired loon, "it's the peddler man."

The mother, older but otherwise identical, came to

the door. He could see that she had a brood behind
her, all with the same stringy, blank appearance.

"What you want, peddler?" she demanded to know.

He could feel himself arch his back. He hated when
people called him "peddler." It was as though he were
no longer a man but a thing, and a thing rather low
down on the scale of things.

"What you want?" she cried again.

"Pots and pans," he said quickly.

She stared at him—blankly. Her eyes had a blind,
shiny glaze, and the skin on her face was worn leather.
"Don't need no pots and pans," she said.

"You'll be sorry. This is an opportunity you
mustn't . . ."

"Don't need none. Git now!"

He turned around in a huff, and there, standing in
the doorway, was Rebekah. The suddenness of her
appearance brought to mind how rare and moving her
beauty was.

"Please, may I have some water?" she asked.

The woman looked at her as though she were an
angel or some other celestial being.

"Vila!" the woman cried out to her eldest daughter.
"Git her some water!"

Rebekah held the ladle to her lips. "Thank you,"
she said after a long draught. "You've been most kind."

"Well," the toothless woman said, "I ain't never denied a sip of water to a thirsty traveler."

Rebekah smiled in warm appreciation. "My name is
Rebekah Weiss," she said, offering her hand.

The woman wiped her hands on an already filthy
apron. "Talma Jean Burns," the woman announced as
they shook.

"My husband didn't take the time to explain the
pots and pans to you, I'm afraid," Rebekah said with
a small, tinkling laugh. "But then I suppose men don't
know quite so much about such things, do they?"

The blankness of the woman's expression dissipated a bit, making way for a bovine, good-natured smile.

"I can tell you, Mrs. Burns, that I have used these pots and pans since our wedding and look at my husband—he looks to have an appetite, no? They are fine pots and pans, heavy, lasting, and most well priced."

Simon watched his wife with a mixture of outrage and fascination. She was usurping his role completely, but there was something so cunning in her approach that he could not take his eyes from her.

"But I can't," the woman whined. "I ain't got enough money for them kinds of pots."

Rebekah nodded compassionately. "How much would you spend on a new pot?"

The woman went wearily to her cupboard and pulled out a jar. "Jes' what I got in here. No more."

"Well, Mrs. Burns, that's enough to buy this round casserole."

"No! Well, my, my. I'd think it'd be a far sight more 'n that."

They concluded the deal. The casserole was sold for less than suggested, but they still made a profit. Simon watched Rebekah take the money and put it in her purse.

"Thank you, Mrs. Burns," she said as they left.

"Thank you," the woman cried, proudly holding her new acquisition.

They got into the wagon and rode a long while in silence.

"Did I do wrong?" she asked at last, her voice indicating that she would fight him on this if he said yes.

"I told you to stay in the wagon," he said darkly.

"I was hot in the wagon. I wanted to . . ."

"Stay in the wagon!' he shouted. "I told you to stay in the wagon!"

"I don't care!" she said spitefully. "I made the sale, and you were going to lose it."

In the middle of an arid and hazy stretch of land he

brought the wagon to a halt. "I'm telling you never to do that again, do you hear?"

"You forget what our agreement is," Rebekah said. "I won't sit in wagons while you make sales. We share everything or we share nothing."

There was a long silence as he thought to shift tactics. "You're very proud of your sale, aren't you?"

"Yes. Yes, I am."

"And you're proud that you took that poor woman's last dollar, aren't you?"

"What are you talking about?"

"Just what I said. You took from her no different than a thief. You took her last bit of money, but, instead of using a gun, you used your cleverness."

She felt momentarily confused by Simon's assault. "That's rubbish!" she cried.

"Is it?" he asked, feeling for a moment cleverer than she. "Did you see her face? Did you see how without defenses she was against your persuasion?"

Now she was beginning to consider this; now she was beginning to let Simon hurt her. "Stop it!" she said. "You know you would have done the same given half a chance. But you couldn't make the sale and now you want me to feel bad and I won't, do you hear? I won't."

"Do as you wish," he said with infuriating calm.

"She will enjoy what she bought," Rebekah said half to herself. "She will feel that she got something good and she got it at the best price."

"Think what you will."

She would have liked to slap him. It was so total, this struggle between them; it bound them together and pulled them apart. "Don't you want me ever to be happy, Simon?" she asked with genuine curiosity. "Don't you want me ever to feel good?"

"Of course I do, Rebekah," he replied, hurrying the horses along. "It is you who seems to make that impossible."

Their life on the road was without comfort or pleasure or any promise of joy. They worked with equal diligence and responsibility; Simon, having no choice, had come to accept this. Indeed, on many occasions, they had used the original gambit, with Simon beginning the sale and with Rebekah suddenly appearing, on the pretext of a need for water, and then going on to cinch the sale by exercising her considerable charm and talent for persuasion. They began to take in real money.

They compared themselves with other peddlers that they met on the road. Almost all of them were Jews, mostly Russian. Some of them were so young—only boys, not more than seventeen or eighteen—and they sold shoes and woolens and kitchen things and their faces were still bright and alive with expectation. Others were old men with packs on their backs, jingling with their pots and pans as they made their way down the country roads, and they looked for all the world as though there was no hope in their lives.

There were other married couples. In Macon they had met Rose and Philip Weissman, who sold elixirs and hair tonics, and near Charlotte they met Shaina and Louis Lipkind who sold books and toys—but it was a rare thing. It was a rare woman who would agree to a life on the road. Rebekah supposed that most of them did it out of love.

By the time they had made their sweaty, dusty way through Georgia and had reached Florida, they had sold out their stock of pots and pans.

"Shall we rest now for a few days?" Simon asked.

"Why?" she demanded to know. "Are you so tired already?"

"Yes," he said wearily, angrily. "I am not quite so strong as you."

She laughed, enjoying his admission. What he said was evidently true for in any given situation, it was

always he who was ready to retire for the evening or
for lunch or for a midday nap.

"Very well then," she said, "but remember that I
did this for you."

They checked into the Hotel Navarro on Monroe
Street in Tallahassee. Late summer now the climate
was hot and humid, and the large overhead fans did
little to tame the heat. Each of them took hot baths,
however, and Rebekah had never felt anything quite
so satisfying. There was fresh fish to eat and melons
and oranges and sugared pecans, and she realized how
hungry she was.

"You don't know how to enjoy yourself," Simon said
to her after their fine dinner.

"I think I do. I think I just ate a very good dinner."

"No, listen to me. We have money now. You must
learn that money can be spent and should be spent."

"Simon, we haven't made quite so much money that
we can afford to be free with it."

He shook his head. "Ah, Rebekah. What a difficult
woman I married."

She did not choose to respond. She sat with him in
the hotel bar, watching him drink a whiskey that they
called bourbon.

"How much are you going to drink?" she asked him
after his third.

"Don't go keeping count, you hear!"

Eyes turned, and she found herself wanting to leave.

"I do what I want to do, do you understand?"

"You're very loud. Everyone's looking at you."

He gripped the edge of the table until his knuckles
turned white. "If you weren't so cold with me," he
whispered fiercely. "If you weren't so damnably
cold . . ."

"Be still, Simon," she said primly.

"You enjoy it, don't you? You enjoy driving me
mad."

"I can't imagine what you mean," she said coolly. "I've never heard such foolishness."

He stared at her. "Very well, Rebekah. Have it your way."

Later on, when they returned to their room, the liquor made him pick up where he had left off.

"You must not be so cold, Rebekah," he said urgently. "Because if you're cold, then you shall dry up, and it will be so sad because you're beautiful. And if you're beautiful, you mustn't . . ."

"Please, Simon. I'm tired."

She had used these words so much of the time they had been together, and they both knew that she was rarely tired and that she had enough energy for two. But mostly he had accepted it, and they had not slept together as man and wife for many weeks now.

"Rebekah, you're not listening . . ."

"I said I'm tired."

He sat down on the bed and ran his fingers through his hair. He took out a flask and sipped from it. Then he spoke again. "I tell you I can't stand it. You have duties to perform. I have needs that must be . . ."

"What do you want, Simon? You have needs? Then go find a whore, but don't come to me. I can't bear to have you next to me."

He was staring at her again, and she looked away from him. "I can't believe you mean that, Rebekah."

"But I do. I mean every word of it."

There was a silence and then, without any sort of warning, he threw the flask against the wall and there was the sound of glass breaking and she jumped up, stunned by the sudden violence.

"I won't go to no whore!" he cried furiously. "You're my wife and you'll be my wife!"

"Don't," she warned, backing away.

He lunged at her and grabbed her around the waist. She pushed at him, but he pulled her down to the bed and covered her with his body.

"Don't," she demanded, but he wasn't listening. He knew what it was that he wanted, and he had the force to acquire it. He tore at her clothing—her good clothing—and when she was nude, he lowered his trousers and pushed himself between her legs.

"Stop!" she cried, but of course he wouldn't stop. He began to ram at her and the pain was immense and so she told him to wait, please wait, and she began to rock with him and when he saw that she would cooperate, it excited him and he lifted her legs up to his shoulders and he moved in firm measured strokes.

"Do you feel it?"

"Yes."

"Do you feel it?"

"Yes," she cried.

"Do you feel it?"

"Yes!" she screamed.

Then it was over. He fell exhausted at her side, the sweat in pools on his belly. She went to the bathroom and washed herself and wept. She was his wife, she thought, and just when she was beginning to feel free, he had captured her again and claimed her for his own.

The respite that Simon had demanded was beginning to turn into a binge. They had been at the Hotel Navarro for two days, and their money was rapidly diminishing.

That night, at dinner, she gave him an ultimatum. "We're leaving tomorrow, Simon," she said. "We've stayed long enough."

"Don't tell me what to do," he muttered, lost in an alcoholic haze and high on his recent abuse of her.

"We cannot afford to be . . ."

"I'll win it all back tonight," he said with a strange, conspiratorial wink.

"What are you saying?" she demanded to know.

He shook his head. "Nothing," he mumbled, momentarily chastened.

"Cards? Is that it, Simon? You're planning on taking our hard-earned money and losing it in a drunken game of cards?"

"You don't understand . . ."

"Oh, I think I do," she said, rising to leave.

She waited for him in the room, and before long he returned. Again—still—he was very drunk, and it didn't take him long to fall into a sound postprandial sleep. He was far enough gone for her to be able to unbuckle his money belt and collect what was rightfully hers. She left him a third of what was left, figuring that he had already drunk a good portion of his share.

She left the hotel, took the wagon, and found a rooming house some distance away where she would be able to stay the night. She had left Simon, this was clear, and her heart was pounding. That night she made up her mind to purchase a stock with the remaining money and to go back on the road. She knew that some would call it madness—a woman alone, on the road—but what choice did she have? The worst that would happen to her is that she would be robbed and molested, which was exactly what Simon sought to do to her.

She went, that next morning, to a wholesaler. She was limited in her choice of stock to a commodity that she understood and that she could easily manage on her own. She selected needles, pins, thimbles, threads, and bolts of fabric. This way she could sell to women, if, indeed, they would approve of another woman selling.

She set out on the road to Pensacola. This was red-clay country she was passing through, studded with innumerable small lakes. It was not unpleasant—everywhere there were water lilies—and she did not feel as frightened as she might have. She was determined, and she knew she had a talent. Time and again she had seen evidence that people liked her and trusted her and were willing to buy from her. She knew, somewhere in her spirit, that she would survive, even if it meant that she would have to pass through great fear in order to do so.

She traveled many miles, many hours. At one point she paused to sip from the water and to soak a bandanna and wrap it around her neck. The midday sun was brutal, and the incessant buzz of mosquitoes seemed like a prelude to some experience in madness. Just then, with the wagon stopped and the sun beating down and her skirts dank with sweat, she heard something quite strange and ominous on the roadside. It was a dry, rattling sound she heard, something skeletal and fearsome. She looked below, and saw a snake as long as two people laid one behind the other and with an obscene, enormous girth that undulated even as it seemed to stay in place. The horses, scenting snake, froze on their hooves for a moment and then, snorting wildly, began to panic. She lashed at them, not knowing what else to do, feeling herself move into panic, feeling the power of the monstrous snake, and just then, seemingly quite oblivious of them all, the snake sidled across the road and removed itself to the bushes.

The horses, now stamping their hooves, refused to be budged, and even as she lashed at them, they remained steadfast. Finally she had to turn them around, and, through a series of maneuvers, convince them that they were not, in fact, passing that treacherous spot. Once beyond it she felt her tension explode into sickness, and she relieved herself over the side of the wagon.

It was then that she had her strongest impulse to surrender. This was a country she did not know and that was clearly full of pitfalls. She had been an utter fool to try it on her own. She would ride out to Pensacola and there she would try to find work in a store or, failing that, she could hire herself out as a laundress, she thought bitterly. She loathed Simon for bringing her here and then for failing her. She watched the road for snakes. She hadn't ever planned on anything quite so terrifying as snakes.

After another few miles she saw a dwelling in the distance. It was a rather ramshackle cabin in the midst of tobacco country, but it was surrounded by signs of care. All around the house itself were sunflowers and primroses and hollyhocks. There were clean white sheets on the line and a finely painted sign that said: TURNER. It all added up, in Rebekah's mind, to evidence of a woman. She brought her wagon to a halt and walked toward the front door. She suddenly realized that this was her first stop alone, and she felt her mouth go dry. She knocked on the door and waited for someone to open it.

"Hello?" said a pretty young woman, roughly her own age.

"Good day," Rebekah replied, feeling her upper lip drenched in perspiration. "My name is Rebekah Weiss. Might I show you my line of dry goods?"

The young woman smiled. "Why sure. Why don't you come on in?"

The interior of the cabin was absolutely immaculate. The planked wood floors were polished to a high sheen, and there were braided and rag rugs underfoot. The windows were hung with starched white curtains, and all the brass implements of the hearth shone. In a hand-hewn cradle slept a tiny baby who was covered with a light summer quilt.

"My name is Leona Turner," the young woman said. "Would you like some coffee?"

"No, please, you must not bother on my . . ."

"It ain't no bother," Mrs. Turner said cheerfully.

Rebekah looked around the room. "This is most lovely."

"Thank you," the young woman replied, returning with the cup of coffee. "I been noticing how you talk. You a foreigner, ain't you?"

"Yes."

"Whereabouts?"

"Austria."

"Where that be?"

"In Europe. Near Germany."

The woman lifted her delicate little hands to her cheeks. "You mean from across the ocean? Oh, my!"

Rebekah smiled and sipped from the coffee. "How old is your baby?" she asked.

"Five months."

"Your first?"

Mrs. Turner thought a moment. "My first one born."

"Oh," Rebekah said. "Oh, he's lovely. What's his name?"

"Andrew Seth."

Rebekah rocked the cradle gently. "He's as fine-looking as he can be," she said.

"You got chillun?"

"No. Not yet."

They both watched the sleeping baby, then Rebekah spoke. "Are you in need of sewing notions and fabrics, Mrs. Turner?"

"Oh, my yes. I always am."

"Well, let me show you what I have," Rebekah said excitedly. The woman admired all of the calicoes and the chintz and the gingham and selected more yards than Rebekah had expected as well as needles, pins, thread, a buttonhook, a crochet hook, and knitting wool. It was an excellent first sale; Rebekah brightened noticeably.

"You traveling alone?" the young woman asked incredulously as Rebekah prepared to leave.

"Yes. Yes, I am."

"Well, I declare. Imagine that."

"But are you here alone?"

"No. My husband's a trapper. I wouldn't think of living alone out here. Don't you got a husband?"

Rebekah nodded.

"Then where he be?"

She thought a moment. "He will meet me soon," she said.

The woman shrugged. "Well, come again next time you be in these parts."

"Thank you. I will."

With her first sale completed, she felt somehow heartier than she had before, and she set out on the road to Quincy. She stopped at every house along the way and, twelve miles later, she had made sales at more than half of the houses. Of course the sales were modest because the commodity she dealt in was modest, but the point was that she was selling and that was what mattered.

She pulled into Quincy, a small tobacco exchange, in late afternoon and found a seedy lodging in a seedy rooming house. She would leave at dawn, and all she wanted was a place to sleep for the night. When she found it, and when she reached her bed, she succumbed to the exhaustion that the day had produced.

In the morning she rose, washed, and dressed and made her way to the wagon. She set out on the road to Marianna. After a mile or so of traveling the winding, dense, wooded road, she heard a movement in the back of the wagon. Turning, she saw something coming out from beneath the trunk. She began to shriek, but there was no one around to hear her. She jumped from the wagon and began to run through the woods, and then her pursuer called her name.

"Rebekah!"

Breathless she turned around and saw it was Simon.

"Oh, my God," she cried. "What are you doing? Are you mad? What do you think you're doing?"

He tried not to smile. "I had to talk to you," he explained.

The shock he had given her was beginning to take its toll. She felt her knees threaten to buckle, and she had to steady herself against a tree. "How did you find me?" she asked in a shaky voice.

He laughed a little now. "I figure you'd go to Pensacola," he said. "I know you so well. I feel what you feel."

"How did you get here?" she demanded to know.

"I stole a horse, Rebekah." He ran a hand through his hair. "You left me no other choice. I stole a strong, black horse, and I rode through the night like the wind."

She stared at him. In a single awful moment she realized that he was truly unwell and that he was capable of almost anything. "You shouldn't have done that, Simon," she said, struggling to keep her voice calm. "You shouldn't have stolen the horse, and you shouldn't have followed me."

"But what choice did I have, Rebekah?" he cried angrily. "You ran from me, and I had to follow you, didn't I?"

She didn't know what to do and so she began to walk toward the wagon. "Go back to town, Simon. Go back to Quincy. I don't want you with me, do you hear?"

"Oh yes," he said bitterly. "I hear you."

She got up on the wagon.

"Wait, Rebekah!"

She looked and she saw that there was a gun in his hand.

"Simon," she whispered, "no."

"Why not? You desert me. All alone you want to leave me."

"No, Simon," she pleaded, not wanting him to hurt her, praying he wouldn't hurt her.

"I told you Clara would haunt us," he laughed. He held his hand out straight, pointed the gun at her, and then, very deliberately, he bent his arm and inserted the barrel of the gun into his mouth.

"Simon!" she shrieked. "Don't! Don't do it!"

She saw him cock the gun, and she thought she would die. "Simon, come with me," she cried. "Do you hear? It will be all right. Everything will be all right."

Tentatively he removed the gun and let his arm drop to his side. He began to sob piteously, and she ran to him and held him in her arms.

"It will be all right, Simon," she repeated over and over and over again until she began to feel him stop shaking.

Things did get better. They worked their way all along the Apalachicola River, and their customers noted the quality of their service. At Rebekah's insistence they continued to sell sewing notions and fabrics, and Rebekah remained the primary salesperson. They found that women were delighted by Rebekah's visits and that they bought from her eagerly in return for the advice on style that she could give them.

"I don't suppose you need me at all," Simon would grumble.

"Don't be so foolish. You're always looking for ways to aggravate yourself."

"What do you need me for? It's you who does the selling, it's you who picks the fabrics, it's you who does the books. What do I do? Drive the wagon—that's what I do."

He would go on like this until she would begin to cry. She didn't have to cry—she didn't feel like crying —but this was one way she got him to stop, when he knew that she was in pain as he was. At night they slept together and she tried to comfort him with her body. She felt better about him than she had, perhaps because she had finally come to recognize the full breadth of his need. She would never love him, for he was incapable of love, but she was his wife and it was her duty to take care of him. Sometimes at night he would thrash in his sleep and cry out wildly from some dream that he had suffered. When she awakened him, he would clutch at her and he would whisper: "Ghosts!"

Oftentimes she would let him drink, with something approaching moderation, for that seemed to take the edge off his unease. She would actually ration out his liquor, as though it were a medication, and for this he was grateful even though there were times when he screamed at her that he needed more and she would have to watch him sob like a child when she refused him.

From the Apalachicola region they headed southward back to the Gulf coast. They had made a good deal of money, and now they would be working the rich Gulf areas. They went through Chattahoochee, Marianna, Cottondale, Bonifay, and Ponce de Leon. Their customers numbered among them many freedmen, anxious to utilize their new economic freedom.

"We're making money," she said one evening, satisfied after a good day's work.

"I could have told you that," he responded, rolling himself a cigarette. "Now maybe we can take it a little easier, ay?"

"That's always your first thought, isn't it, Simon? Just as we're doing so well, you want to pull back. Well, that's not the way I work."

"That's not the way *you* work? So it's *you* who's calling the rules, is it? Well, what if I just left you flat?"

"Do it. Do it and see what happens."

There was a furious silence as he continued to roll his cigarette and as she wrung out the laundry she had been soaking. She felt her stomach tighten; she felt her mouth pursed so tight. He was making her hard, and she hated him for it. He was turning her into a bitch, and she didn't know what she could do about it. All she could do was keep on struggling to try and make some money, for with money came freedom; and the vision of freedom, abstract as it was, kept her going.

A night later, as they camped on the outskirts of Pensacola, as Simon snored loudly and monotonously beside her, she felt herself filled by a sense of dread. Everything seemed so quiet, so silent, and all she kept thinking was that they must go, they must. She didn't quite understand what it was that made her feel this way, for the nights with Simon were always hard and restless, but this was different.

She got out of the wagon and walked onto the road. There was something wrong with the sky. She couldn't say what it was except that it was dark and foreboding. She ran back to the wagon and roused Simon.

"What?" he grunted.

"We have to go!" she cried. "Something's wrong. We must go!"

"What are you talking about? Go back to sleep."

"You don't understand. There's something wrong."

"I understand you're carrying on like a fool."

"Go look for yourself. You'll see . . ."

"Just let me sleep, will you?"

He rolled over and pulled the blanket up above his head. She lay down beside him, letting her body touch his, looking to him for warmth. But he would have none of it, and he moved away from her.

After a while it began to rain. The rain was surprisingly gentle at first, but she could hear it grow in intensity.

"Simon," she whispered.

He chose to pretend he was sleeping.

"Simon!"

"What is it now?"

"It's raining."

"Well, what of it?"

"We have to go."

"Stop acting like a damned fool!"

"Listen, Simon. Listen to the wind."

He listened, and he heard the low frightening

whine. "What kind of a wind is that?" he wondered, suddenly feeling the wind everywhere.

"Let's go, Simon," she cried. "Hurry!"

He rose quickly. He hitched the horses. The rain was growing stronger each moment, pelting him fiercely as he went about his work. Hurry, Simon! he heard her call. What did she want of him? Wasn't he doing the best he could?

They set out on a road that was already muddied from the rain.

"How far is it to Pensacola?" she cried, feeling that there they might find adequate shelter.

"Ten miles," he shouted. "Maybe more."

They would never make it. Already the palm trees were flapping wildly in the wind. The rain was beginning to blow in great, drenching sheets. He lashed at the horses, trying to make them race ahead, but the wind had frightened them into their own wildness and obstinacy.

"Giddyap, you swine!"

"What are we to do, Simon?" The sky had turned ashen, and the whine of the wind had escalated into something between a squeal and a howl.

He couldn't answer her. There was no answer. The wheels of their wagon became mired in the mud, and the horses strained at their harnesses. Now the palm trees swept the ground, and the canvas that covered their wagon and their stock ripped at its lacing.

The wind was screaming at them, whipping at their faces and their clothes. They began to feel themselves tossed about, weightless as corn husks.

"We have to find cover!" he cried, trying to make himself heard above the wail of the wind.

He unleashed the horses and tried to save some of their stock. He grabbed bolts of fabric only to have them blown from his hands. "Help me!" he screamed. As she went to help him, another gust of wind ripped off the canvas and carried it above the bowed trees. They watched their stock lifted and scattered.

"Run!" Simon screamed. "Run!"

Rebekah felt herself lifted and carried for yards. "Simon! Simon!" There was the sound of tree trunks breaking like giant bones, and she could see timber flying through the sky. They would die, she thought; they would die.

"There!" he said, sighting something that might save them. It was a boat, moored in the water that was lapping onto the road. They fought their way there and he lifted her into it and they held on to each other. After a length of time that would remain in her mind forever incalculable—it could have been hours, it could have been minutes—the wind passed over them. There was a sudden shocked silence left in its wake.

"Is it over?" she dared to whisper.

He lay rigid, and she had an instant, hysterical phantom of a thought that he was dead.

"Simon! Simon!" she shrieked, grasping at him.

"Ssssh," he hissed. "Listen."

She heard what sounded like a huge volume of water sluicing toward them. "Oh, Simon. Simon, what is it?"

It was the water level rising. When it reached them, with its terrible force, it ripped their craft from its mooring and sent them on an interior journey through a weird, broken landscape that had never before been navigated. There was almost no light, and the drowned earth was swamped with the carcasses of dead animals.

"Where are we going?" she cried.

"It's hell, you see. We're in it."

"What are you saying?" She couldn't bear to hear him go on. She wanted to live and she wanted him to help and she didn't want to hear him go on.

"She's come back to haunt us, you see . . ."

"Shut up!" she screamed. She began to weep. She

didn't know where they were going; all she knew was that they were lost in a maze of channels.

The sun baked them. Their lips and their throats were painfully swollen, and all they could do was dream of slaking their thirst. In the water around them writhed water moccasins by the dozens. They could see, stranded on tiny newly formed islands, rabbits and rats and coons and possum, all united in an uneasy truce.

They had been on the boat—their salvation and their prison—for at least a full day now. The air smelled of rot and carried the suggestion of fever. Is this how it would end for them? she wondered. No, she couldn't believe it. She couldn't believe that it would end now, just when there was so much that she wanted. She found herself weeping again, as she had done so often these past twenty-four hours, weeping childishly, purposelessly, and achingly.

"Don't," he shouted.

She couldn't stop.

"Don't or I'll throw myself over. I'll throw myself in with the snakes."

She made herself stop then. "What are we going to do?" she moaned.

"We're going to die. Can't you see? We're going to die."

"That's what you want, isn't it? You want us to be punished. You want us to be punished for Clara's death. Well, I won't! It wasn't my fault, and I won't be punished! I hate you for wanting it, do you hear? I hate you!"

He grabbed her, and they struggled.

"What are you doing?" she managed to say.

"I'm taking you with me!" He got her about the waist and began pulling her toward the side of the boat. She shrieked and flailed at him, gouging his cheeks with her nails.

"We're going to die!" he screamed. "We're going to die!"

She didn't know whether he was mad from sun and thirst or whether he was just plain mad. She didn't care. She beat at him and she hurt him and when he cowered beneath her blows, she felt like hurting him even more.

"There!" she said, slapping at him. "There!"

The battle had sapped her of all strength. She lay back against the oarlock, panting heavily.

"Are we going to die?" he asked in a small voice.

She laughed even though there was nothing funny.

"Are we going to die?" he begged to know.

"No. We're not going to die."

Hours later they heard voices calling out.

"Help us!" she screamed. "Help!"

They set up a continuous din that didn't stop until they saw the ripple of water and the boat moving toward them.

"D'ere be two," one of the rescuers cried. There were two men in the launch, dark, swarthy, they could be Indians.

"Help us!" she cried hoarsely.

They pulled up beside them and helped them into their boat.

"Water," she groaned.

They held up a jug, first for her and then for Simon.

"Where are we?" she asked when her throat had been moistened enough for her to speak.

"Yeller Creek," one of the men said.

"Near Pensacola?"

"Pensacola be dere," he said, pointing. "Real close."

"Then we're saved?" she whispered, more to herself than anyone else.

"Saved, lady," the man nodded. "You saved."

She dipped her finger into the jug and wet her lips again. They were back to the beginning, she thought. Their stock, their wagon, their horses—all swept away.

Simon lay on his side, holding his feverish head in his hands. She looked around her, and everything was changed. The storm had made the terrain into something new and twisted and more full of danger than ever. As they glided through the brackish water, she realized that a new journey had begun, and she could only think that she was glad to be alive.

Part Two

Part Two

CHAPTER EIGHT

The road was their home, and she had come to hate it. It seemed like a lifetime ago that she had a real home, with a real bed and candles on the table and china in the cabinets. There was so little left of that life: letters to and from her sister Sarah had become few and far between. The last one brought the grim news that her father had been killed, run over by a wagon driven by wild, drunken thugs. She just sat with the letter in her lap for hours and hours. She had never reconciled with her father. He had died without forgiving her and the sense of loss that she experienced was both unexpected and enormous. She promised herself that when they went to the next big city, she would find a synagogue. She would have *Kaddish* said for him, and each year on the *Yahrzeit*, the anniversary of his death, she would light a candle for him.

"What are you carrying on for?" Simon asked with a scornful laugh. "You couldn't wait to be free of him."

"You don't understand," she said. "You don't know what it is to have a family you care about."

"You hated your father."

"I didn't hate him. I never hated him. He didn't understand me and he made many mistakes, but I never hated him."

"You're a liar. Look, you even lie to yourself."

"What can I say to you? You couldn't possibly understand. You left your mother and your brother in the middle of the night. Like a thief you left . . ."

He covered his ears with his hands, and his face went white.

"I'm sorry," she whispered, knowing that she had gone too far, knowing that to hurt him when he hurt her gave her no victory.

It was true that he knew nothing of family nor home nor love. Perhaps it was her fault that she couldn't teach him, but the fact remained that he wouldn't learn. Each time they rode into town—whether it be Biloxi or Gulfport or Natchez or Port St. Joe—he got himself drunker than the time before and he found himself a whore to keep him company. She knew all about it—he conscientiously flung it in her face—but after the first few times she had managed to come to terms with it. She let him whore; she let him do anything he wanted to keep him out of her bed. She appreciated his not making demands on her, and she gave him his freedom. She minded not a bit sleeping alone. All she ever wanted from him was a child. And she would have a child even if it meant waiting until they had made enough to settle down somewhere and open a proper store.

To her way of thinking they already had enough to launch such a venture. In the wake of the hurricane that had stolen their stock and that had left them without even a wagon with which to peddle their wares, it seemed that they were without prospects. They had to stay for weeks in Pensacola, living in the most squalid of circumstances on Zaragoza Street. It had seemed like still another foreign country they were passing through, that was how strange it was, with its Spanish streets—Intendencia, Moreno, Gonzales, Tarragona—and its gabled, pilastered, and colonnaded houses cast in stucco. They worked there like field slaves—he digging ditches, she taking in laundry—and it was hard, monstrously hard. It was so hard that they feared they might never get out of this hole and that was when they edged toward despair. But when they saw that indeed they could manage to save a portion of what they earned, their hopes lifted considerably, and they resolved to stay as long as they must. It did not turn out to be as long as they had expected; within three months they were able to purchase a stock of sewing notions and fabric. Without further delay they were back on the road, and, by now, principally through Rebekah's acumen, they had not only recouped their loss but had shown a profit.

They worked for solid weeks, seven full days, sleeping only a few hours each night, eating out of hand. They traveled at night and sold by day. It came to the point that she didn't want to stop because she knew that then her body would be in revolt against her, her back aching, her muscles fairly vibrating. She would have liked to keep on going, but Simon would not have it. Simon accused her of trying to destroy him, and perhaps, she thought, he was right. In the end, though, she would bow to his wishes, and they would spend two days in the best hotel in whatever city they happened to be near.

Just now they were staying in the Montross Hotel at Beach and Lameuse streets in Biloxi, Mississippi. She liked the hotel, and she liked Biloxi. They had been here before, and the management made a point of knowing them and treating them graciously.

"What shall we do today, Simon?" she asked as they sat over their breakfast of toast and marmalade and *café au lait*.

"Why don't you just do what you want to do?" he said, altogether too eagerly.

"My dear companion," she said with a wry little laugh. "You don't wish to holiday together?"

"Don't be idiotic. We're with each other all the time. Isn't that enough?"

He still had the power to hurt her. She felt her face

flame and, shaking badly, she lowered the coffee cup and saucer, hearing them clatter as they met the table. She didn't want to see Simon's cruel, mad grin, but she couldn't help it. "I suppose you're right, Simon," she said at last.

"Of course I'm right. Don't be a fool. Just go your way, and I'll go mine."

She stared at him. "Don't get yourself in trouble, Simon."

"Rebekah . . ."

"Just don't. I don't want you getting shot for cheating in any card games and I don't want you locked up for drunkenness and vagrancy and I don't want you picking up any filth you see and bringing it . . ."

"Rebekah!"

". . . home to me. If you want a woman, then find one who knows how to keep herself clean. Here," she said, pulling several bills from her purse, "add this to your allowance and go to the best house in town."

He looked at the money that she had folded and stuck in his hand. For a moment it seemed as though he might either cry or scream in rage at her. But then, silently, he put the money into his pocket and folded his hands on his lap.

She felt disgusted with him. To look at him made her feel almost physically ill. She began to gather her things.

"What shall you do?" he asked blandly.

"That's my affair."

"When shall you return?"

She stared at him very hard, displaying more anger than she wished. "We're leaving here tomorrow morning, Simon. Make sure you're around."

Then she rose and left him without another word.

She had the day to herself. She wasn't quite sure what to do. She thought to write letters—there was still Sarah and cousin Miriam back in the old country, and

dear Fannie up in Baltimore—but she couldn't bring
herself to do it. Perhaps she could purchase a novel,
Hugo, perhaps, and she could read it in the garden.
What could be more pleasant? she wondered hollowly.

She found herself wandering rather aimlessly about
the hotel lobby. The concierge, a haughty but not unkind émigrée from Paris, spotted her and inquired if
she might be of help.

"I really don't know," Rebekah confessed shyly. "I
suppose I am rather at loose ends."

The concierge gave her a confused and displeased
look, and Rebekah felt that the remark sounded somehow too personal.

"Can you recommend a day's activity?" Rebekah
asked, adjusting her tone. "Something pleasant to
while away the time?"

"A pleasant activity," the concierge replied, rolling
the words thoughtfully on her tongue. "Well, the
pleasure boats are always popular."

"The pleasure boats?"

"Yes, madame. A day's cruise on the Gulf?"

Rebekah thought a moment. "Yes," she said. "That
sounds ideal."

She went back to her room. She had started the day
in her usual black dress, somber but always appropriate, and now she looked in the mirror and she felt
herself horribly staid and totally inappropriate. She
did own a white dress, of eyelet lace, a bit behind in
fashion but cooler and pretty and just right for today.
She put it on and carried the parasol that went with it.
Again she looked in the mirror. Once upon a time she
knew she was beautiful, everyone in town knew it too.
She was indeed the beauty of Korneuberg. Now the
idea made her laugh; the world seemed so much a
larger place. Yet once she had been young and untouched; the beauty of Korneuberg she had been, and
the world seemed a fine place, innocent as she. Was she
still beautiful? She didn't know. She was afraid that to

look at her was to see the toil and sweat and hardship
of life on the road. She had callouses on her hands; her
feet were surely rougher than rose petals. But her eyes
—where everyone had always said her beauty rested—
her eyes were still as they were. Was she still beautiful?
She didn't know, and there was no one to tell her she
was.

She headed down to the pier. It was a balmy day;
people were out for strolls. The crowd on the streets
at first buffeted her against loneliness, but then, moments later, it seemed to lead her directly into it. She
found herself staring at strangers in the street, looking
for something or someone, she didn't know which it
was. Then, when they looked back at her, she smiled
like a fool and hurried along.

The pier was crowded, and she had to wait on line
to get a ticket. Then they admitted her to the boat, a
great big riverboat called the *Annabella*, and all
around her were families beaming with a holiday
spirit. The atmosphere was so full of festivity that she
knew it must be a special day. She saw a woman who
had four or five or six or seven children in tow—
Rebekah could not discern—and she tapped the
woman on the shoulder.

"Excuse me, madame," she said. "What day is this?"

The woman looked at her as though she were either
quite mad or just stupid. "Why, it's Easter, of course."

Easter. Of course. "Thank you," Rebekah murmured, but already the woman was off.

She held on to the railing of the top deck, and she
began to laugh. It was only a little laugh at first, but it
developed rapidly; soon she was really quite beside
herself. Here it was Easter and she hadn't known it
and she was all by herself on this boat and everywhere
around her were families on holiday. She wondered if
Simon would have trouble getting himself a whore on
Easter, and she couldn't stop laughing until she ached

deep inside of her, again feeling hollow except for the ache.

She dried her eyes and saw a little blond girl, no more than six or seven, angelic-looking and staring at her with big green eyes.

"Why are you crying?" the child asked.

"Because I was laughing."

"Why were you laughing?"

"Because I didn't know it was Easter. Can you imagine?"

The little girl gravely shook her head.

"What's your name?" Rebekah asked.

"Melinda."

"That's a pretty name."

"What's yours?"

"Rebekah."

The little girl stared at her intensely. "You talk funny."

"I know I do."

"Why?"

"Because I come from a foreign place." She pointed out across the water. "All the way over there. You can't even see it because it's so far away."

"What's it called?"

"Europe."

"I been to Baton Rouge. That's where my auntie lives. Is it further than Baton Rouge?"

"Oh yes. Even further."

The little girl continued to stare at her and then smiled shyly. "I can do the Virginia reel. Wanna see?"

"Of course I do."

The little girl spun around with surprising grace, humming a melody as she did so.

"Oh my!" Rebekah cried, clapping her hands. "What a gift you have!"

"Thank you. I hope to be on the stage one day," she said with great seriousness.

Rebekah looked at the golden hair and, when she

remembered, she felt weak again and had to hold on to the railing.

"What's the matter?" the little girl asked.

"Nothing," Rebekah whispered. "You just recalled someone to me."

The little girl looked confused, and Rebekah kneeled down beside her. "Have you a kiss for me?" Rebekah murmured.

"I hardly know you."

Rebekah laughed. "But we're friends already, aren't we?"

"Yes. I suppose," the little girl said, and quickly she kissed Rebekah's cheek. "You're very pretty," the little girl said.

"Oh, am I?" She stroked the little girl's hair. "Whose little girl are you?"

"My mother's."

She let her hand fall. "Oh. Your mother's." She laughed a little. "Of course you are."

"Melinda!" they heard.

"That's my mother," Melinda said.

A stout, fussy woman hurried over. "There you are! I declare, Melinda, you'll be the end of me." She turned to Rebekah and looked her up and down. "Excuse me, miss. She slips through my fingers like quicksilver, this one."

And so Melinda was whisked off without even a farewell. Rebekah opened her parasol and strolled about the promenade deck. She wished she had a child. If she had a child, she thought, she wouldn't be so lonely. She would have someone other than Simon to take care of, someone who would grow to be fine and healthy. If it was a boy, she would name him Jacob. She knew she should name him Chaim for her father, but no . . . she would name him Jacob. And if it was a girl? Helen, for her mother, of course.

The boat was loaded down with children. They ran past her in wild, joyful packs. She had to restrain her-

self from swooping down and picking one up and holding him in her arms, clutching him to her and refusing
to let him go. My God, she thought, how lonely I am.
The realization shook her. She held on to the railing
and leaned over, watching the great paddle wheel turn
and turn. There was music on the boat, banjos and
dulcimers, and she could hear people singing. It wasn't
right for her to be here, she thought. She wasn't like
these other people. She was not of this world. She was
not happy and innocent; she was tired and lonely and
cynical. She was a woman married to an adulterer, and
the pity of it all was that she couldn't bring herself to
care.

She turned her back to the railing and closed her
eyes. There were breezes washing over the boat; they
cooled her and made her thoughts seem less pressing.
When she opened her eyes, she saw something that almost convinced her that she had been dreaming. She
saw a face she knew. There, all the way at the other
end of the deck, she saw a tall, lean figure. She saw the
familiar gaunt face, and she knew it was he. She knew
it was Jarrett Russell. She had dreamed of him over
the years—awake and asleep—she had dreamed of
meeting him again, and she had dreamed, in her
dreams, that he took care of her and that he washed
her breasts and the back of her neck. She felt herself
suddenly wet with sweat. She didn't know what to do.
He hadn't yet seen her. It would be easy enough to
retreat to another deck. What was she afraid of? She
didn't know; all she knew was that the sight of him
thrust her into chaos. She shouldn't let him see her; it
would be more than she could withstand. And yet she
couldn't move, she couldn't take her eyes from him.
He looked just as he had the last time she had seen
him, and how long ago was that? Going on two years,
to be sure, two full years of the most arduous labor.

She kept the parasol close to her, hiding within its
shade, and she watched him. He looked older and

worn; even though he could not be much beyond thirty. He, too, was dressed in white—an immaculately white suit with a white Panama hat—but there was nothing fresh about his appearance. He stood next to the railing and smoked a long, thin cigar. He appeared to be alone. Why didn't she just go over and talk to him? She was carrying on like a fool, and she hated herself for it. Why didn't she just go up to him and say, "Good day, Doctor." But then what next? And would he be able to hear her heart pounding like a schoolgirl's?

She turned around and began to stroll in an opposite direction, circling the boat. She stared out at the Gulf, which was blue and glorious. She knew she would pass him if she kept going this way. She tried to collect her breath. What was wrong with her? He was just a doctor; he was just someone who had once been kind to her. She made up in her mind a course of action, and she walked along the deck. She saw him still standing at the railing; she saw the blue circle of smoke that emanated from his cigar.

"Excuse me," she whispered, coming up from behind.

He turned, and boldly she studied his face. It was quizzical, not having placed her, and now there was a thin black moustache, well groomed. Otherwise the face was as she remembered it and as it had played in her dreams. She had the curious impulse to touch him in greeting, but then she hardly knew him. And he didn't seem to know her at all.

"You don't remember me," she said softly.

"Yes. Yes, I do."

She stared intensely into his quizzical eyes. "No," she murmured. "I am mistaken. I beg pardon." She turned to leave.

"No. Wait." He reached out and touched her arm. She looked down at his hand, and he withdrew it. "I do know you. Surely I do."

She waited for him to say her name, but then she knew he didn't remember. She lowered her eyes to the highly polished deck. "Rebekah," she said. When she looked up again, she saw that there was recognition, and she began to smile with genuine pleasure and enthusiasm.

"Yes. Rebekah. Yes, I remember." He touched his high pale forehead and shook his head. "What a fool you must think me. Yes, of course I remember. Your sister . . ."

He caught himself. She turned to face the Gulf. She could see the faintest suggestion of Biloxi in the distance.

"Look at all the fishing boats," she whispered.

He stared at her. She was beautiful.

She turned back to him. "It's been a long time, but I have never forgotten your kindness, Doctor. I never will."

"Surely you should," he said, his voice turning a bit dry. "I did so little."

"You mustn't say that. It isn't true, and you mustn't lie."

He was to say something, but he kept still. He wanted just to look at her, both because she was so fine to look at and because she was someone who had touched him. He had forgotten her as he tried to forget most things that touched him. But here she was again, and he had the tender impulse to touch her thick black hair.

"I couldn't believe at first it was you," she said. "I never thought I should see you again."

"No. No, it's quite unexpected."

There was an awkward silence. "Are you traveling?" he asked.

"Always," she replied. "We sell. Ever since the last time you saw me. I was on my way to Savannah then. We live on the road, and we sell."

"What do you sell?"

"Sewing needs, fabrics. We do very well," she said, perhaps a bit too quickly.

"I'm so glad. You deserve to do well."

"And you? Where are you now?"

He stared at her and then laughed quite loudly and strangely. "Oh, I haven't done well at all," he said with a bitter laugh. "Not well at all."

"What is it?" she asked, concerned for him.

He puffed on his cigar and looked out over the water. "Shrimp, yes, that's what they're fishing for."

She knew he didn't want to answer her; she knew it would be inappropriate to press him. "I . . . I hope you are well."

He smiled. "Let's just say that I'm traveling too."

"Looking for your place," she murmured.

"What did you say?"

She shook her head. "I said nothing."

He straightened up and pulled the brim of the Panama down over his brow. "May I escort you back to your party?" he said, offering his arm.

"I have no 'party,' " she replied, free of pretension.

"Your husband . . . ?"

She shook her head. "I am alone," she said. "My husband . . . my husband is resting."

He stared at her as though what she said was fantastic.

"And you?" she cried, a tremor of anger in her voice. "Have you a 'party' somewhere on this boat?"

He laughed a little, pleased by her spirit. "No," he confessed. "I too am quite alone."

"Then shall we pass this time together?" she asked.

He made a vague, circular gesture with his hand. "Everyone shall talk," he whispered.

"I don't know anyone," she said with disdain. "Let them talk if they wish. It shouldn't hurt business at any rate."

He laughed. "That is your primary concern, Rebekah?"

"Yes," she said in all seriousness. "It most certainly is."

He gave her his arm, and they strolled on the promenade deck.

"I've never known a lovelier day," she said.

"Or a finer way to spend it." He lighted another cigar. "Tell me," he said, "what plans have you now?"

"We'll continue on the road until we have enough to buy ourselves something."

"A store?"

"Yes. That would be nice."

"Where?"

"I don't know yet. Where we're needed. Where we can do well."

"Of course, yes. Well, the South is open to people like you these days."

She wondered if there was something condescending in his voice, but she decided there wasn't. "We're known along the Gulf," she said.

"You've done well there?"

"Yes."

They bought fruit ice and sat down on deck chairs in a spot of shade.

"You've asked questions," she said, "and yet you haven't given any answers."

"That is correct," he said stiffly. "You see, I haven't got any answers."

"Doctor . . ."

He smiled. "I remember that you called me 'Herr Doktor.' You couldn't have known just how inadequate that made me feel. To be given such a title and to have been as much of a failure as I was . . ."

She stared at him. "It isn't so," she said at last. "You're talking foolishness."

He laughed; it seemed he laughed at her. "What a curious thing to say. You don't know what my life is—how can you presume to say such a thing?"

"A man such as you," she whispered. "You couldn't be a failure."

"Well, I was," he said sternly. "And now I am even more of one."

"What do you mean?"

He sighed. He didn't know why he should be telling her, but he was going to. Perhaps because she cared; but she didn't matter, and it was doubtful that he would ever run into her again. "I am en route to Mobile," he said at last. "My birthplace. My fine ancestral home."

His tone was so infected by bitterness that she wasn't sure she wanted him to go on, but she found herself nodding sympathetically.

"I'm coming from Galveston, you see. I've been in that area for almost two years. Just after I saw you that last time, I left Baltimore. There was nothing there for me—only sickness and despair. I didn't want it anymore. You can understand that, can't you?"

"Yes," she said. "Yes, I can understand."

"A cousin of mine asked if I would join him on a mining expedition down in Mexico." He shook his head. Again he touched his pale high forehead, and she could see the thin, quivering vein there. "It seemed like quite a fine adventure. We prospected for copper and zinc and we found some, but it was stolen from us as soon as we found it. James, my cousin, was killed by bandits, and I just managed to escape with my life. But I'm destitute now, do you hear? I haven't anything left."

"Oh, I am sorry. I am so sorry." It was a terrible story, and she would have liked to hold him as he had once held her.

"I have only one choice. I am returning to Mobile. I have a home there. Wild Oaks, it's called."

Yes, she wanted to say. Yes, I know.

"I can live there and, if possible, I will open a practice there."

In light of what Rebekah had learned from Hattie Winslow, this seemed an ill-fated prospect, but she was cautious not to say anything.

They rose after their ices and strolled again.

"Are you happy, Rebekah?" he asked.

She took a long time answering. "We're doing well," she said.

"Are you happy?" he persisted.

His question made her very tired and very unhappy. "What does it mean?" she asked. "What does it matter? I'm alive, and more than once I could have been dead. Why must I be happy too?"

He looked at her. So, he thought. So she was as sad as he was, but she was still fighting and he had worn himself out. Just then, a band, which they had not hitherto noticed, took their attention with a waltz. Soon the deck was filled with dancing couples whose children watched with a certain sense of fascination.

"Could we dance, do you think? Or would it be improper?"

She presented herself to him in response, and so they danced. Back and forth and back and forth; they floated through the air. His eyes were shining; she held her bonnet; and the music was everywhere. Sweetly they danced so close to each other, and there was no time to think of despair. Just back and forth and back and forth with the music in the air.

"I haven't danced in years," she admitted.

"Nor have I," he laughed.

It was so very gay that she wanted never to stop, but then, just so abruptly, the music halted, and the dance was very much over.

"Look," he said. He pointed to the shore. "We're back to Biloxi."

She felt something clutch within her. It was too fast and now she would be back to Simon and she didn't want it. It wasn't at all fair, not at all.

They walked with each other down the gangway

and then they stood on the pier, waiting for a word from each other.

"It's been an unexpected delight," he said. "The best kind."

"Yes," she murmured. "Indeed."

They paused, staring at each other, not wanting to leave.

"Shall we see each other . . . ?" he began, but then he let his question fade. This they could not do, they mustn't.

"And so we say good-bye," she whispered.

"We'll meet again," he cried. "Look at us now. Would we ever have thought?"

"Good-bye," she said, offering her hand.

He kissed her gloved hand, holding it at his lips longer than was proper, and then she pulled away.

"Rebekah!" he called, but already she had gone a distance down the pier and was resolved not to look back.

CHAPTER NINE

They stayed on the road another year, and they continued to prosper. They met no new catastrophes—no hurricanes, no famines—and although Simon did not and could not work as hard as Rebekah, he managed to stay on his own approximation of an even keel.

"We're ready for a place of our own," Rebekah announced one early spring day after having gone over the books.

She sat through his heavy silence, telling herself not to get angry with him.

"Isn't that what we agreed upon?" she said as calmly as she could.

"Yes, of course it is."

"Then what is the problem?"

He shook his head. "There is no problem," he said grimly.

She knew what it was. She knew that settling down represented to him the end of the dream of himself as a great entrepreneur as well as the termination of the liberties that life on the road provided. It was she who had planned their strategy, and any sense of promise and great expectations that he had once embodied, or had thought he embodied, had now clearly evaporated.

"There is no problem," she repeated after him as though he had said something quite odd and revealing. "Well, I'm glad there's no problem, Simon, because I could not endure any more problems from you."

He tied and untied a knot, refusing to look her in the eyes.

"We'll do as I say," she cried, tightening her fists, feeling the muscles of her arms twanging like tautly pulled steel bands.

"You've become so very hard," he said at last in a wondering sort of voice. "Have I done that to you? If so, I'm sorry, Rebekah."

He put on his hat and jumped down from the wagon.

"Where are you going?" she demanded to know.

"Away from you just now, but don't worry. I'll be back."

She watched him walk up the road. "Don't come back if you don't want to!" she screamed, but he didn't turn around.

She hated him. For everything he had done and for everything he had not done, she hated him. She could remember back to their meeting in the gazebo at

Korneuberg when he told her that he had a dream of freedom and that he would make her a part of it. What had it all meant? Nothing.

He returned some hours later and sat on an upended vegetable crate, waiting for her to speak.

"You've come back," she said at last.

"Yes."

"You always do, you know. Like some sort of recurring fever."

He stared at her. "There's nothing you can say to offend me, Rebekah. You've said it all."

"Look, Simon, there's nothing more between us. You know that and I know that. So shall we just end it?"

"No."

"Why not?" she cried.

"Because you're my wife."

"Your prisoner!" she shouted.

There was a silence. She knew that he was afraid to be on his own; she knew that he would use her and exploit her and that he wouldn't let her go.

"Give me a *get*," she said suddenly, referring to a Jewish divorce.

"No," he said with maddening calm.

"Why? Tell me why."

"Because such a thing would serve me poorly. You're my wife, and we are meant to be together."

She had no choice. If he didn't want to give her a *get*, then he didn't have to. He was a sick man—he knew that, she knew that—and there was no escaping him. The only way a *get* could be obtained was with the mutual agreement of both parties. The only thing she could do was try to live as separate a life as she could within the confines of this marriage.

"We're going to Mobile, Simon," she said suddenly, the idea coming to her like a flash of inspiration.

"What's in Mobile?" he asked suspiciously.

"A place for us to open a store, that's what," she said

defiantly. "If you don't want to be a part of that, then stay here. But that's what I'm doing."

"I don't want a store," he protested.

"I don't care. I just don't care."

"We have to keep traveling," he said desperately. "If we stop, they'll find us. They'll find us and they'll hurt us and we have to keep moving, we have to . . ."

He stopped himself, and they stared at each other. She knew what he was talking about; he was talking about his ghosts, and she didn't want any part of it.

"We're going to Mobile, Simon. I've had enough of this life. It's time for another kind of life for me, Simon. I deserve it, Simon. Do you hear me? I deserve it."

Within another four months they were in Mobile. She had not, of course, picked the destination out of a hat. Jarrett Russell came from Mobile, and so she saw it as a city of promise. But, beyond that, Mobile was a city of such renowned charm and reputation for *joie de vivre* that she felt it would be a propitious place to start a new business.

Situated on Mobile Bay, an arm of the Gulf of Mexico, Mobile was a city of many cultures. First colonized by the Spanish in 1559, who abandoned it a year later, it waited another century and a half before settlers made their way there again. Louis XIV sent Pierre Le Moyne, a French nobleman, to establish a colony on the Gulf in 1699. A settlement was founded on Dauphin Island, twenty-five miles south of Mobile. Three years later Pierre's brother was appointed governor, and he moved the government to Fort Louis de Mobile.

The first year was beset with hardships. Weakened by illness, the settlers did little more than build a fort and cabins. Things looked up in 1704 when the *Pelican*, arriving from Canada, brought not only messengers of the king, soldiers, missionaries and nuns, but

the twenty-three *Cassette* girls, chosen by the bishop of
Quebec as future wives for the colonists. In a month
all but one had husbands, and before a year passed the
first native child was born in Mobile.

In 1710 floods caused the removal of the colony to
the present site of Mobile, where the governor established Fort Conde, known as Fort Charlotte to the
British. In the following years Mobile served as the
capital of Louisiana. Its agricultural future was assured
when the ships *Africaine* and *Le Duc de Maine* arrived
in 1721, bringing more than six hundred slaves to
Mobile. In 1733 the town was almost obliterated by
hurricanes and epidemics. Once the capital was moved
to New Orleans, only the hardiest of pioneers remained to continue the struggle against Indians, the
forces of nature, and an occasional foray from the
Spanish settlement at Pensacola. In 1763 the Treaty of
Paris gave Mobile to the British.

In 1780 Bernardo De Galvez brought the Spanish
fleet into the harbor, forced the surrender of Fort
Charlotte, and for the next thirty-three years the flag
of Spain waved above Mobile. Finally in 1813 U.S.
General Wilkinson, using the War of 1812 as a pretext,
seized the town for the United States.

Mobile flourished under American rule. Sole outlet
for the rich agricultural lands of Alabama, it now enjoyed halcyon days. In the words of one observer Mobile was a place where: "the people live in cotton
houses and ride in cotton carriages. They buy cotton,
sell cotton, think cotton, eat cotton, drink cotton, and
dream cotton. They marry cotton wives and unto them
are born cotton children." With all that, a Mobile
style of building came into being. Some were small
"Creole cottages," with brick between wood and a
simple European pattern; others, grander, showed the
influence of the Greek revival, but also touches of
France and Spain. Balconies on all sides, fine doorways,

fanlights, and ironwork railings, wrought or cast in imaginative forms—this was the look of Mobile.

Such establishments lined Government Street, which became one of the finest thoroughfares in the South. By the 1840s Mobile ranked as one of the major centers of Southern society, a place of theater, horse racing, and elegant shops. Charlotte Cushman, Lola Montez, Joseph Jefferson, Edwin Booth . . . Mobile saw them all in turn. And the extra added touch of glamor came in 1830 when, on New Year's Eve, a party of men founded the first "mystic" organization. This society, called the Cowbellion de Rakin Society after their boisterous use of cowbells, led the way to the tradition of the Mardi Gras festival that rivaled that of New Orleans.

There was, of course, a darker side to the city. Being a waterfront town, Mobile had its rough bars and gambling places, and the city became known for its raffish opportunities. Yellow fever was also a destructive factor, and in 1853 an epidemic stole over seven hundred lives.

During the War Between the States the Mobile port served as a major Gulf center for blockade running. From the bay hundreds of Confederate ships darted out on runs for badly needed medical supplies and war materials. But in 1864, in a great battle, the Union seized the bay, and Mobile had its disgrace.

In the years after the war Mobile suffered less than other sections of the state since cotton was again shipped to world ports from the city's docks. It was into this city, coming alive after the war, faced with the problems of Reconstruction, that Simon and Rebekah came to make their fortune.

Rebekah had managed their joint finances, and she had done so like a Rothschild; there was enough for them to buy a small but promising property on Caroline Street. There was an enormous amount to do. The store had latterly housed the offices of a poultry firm. Although no actual breeding had ever transpired here, Rebekah was convinced that the odor of chickens permeated. So she and Simon scrubbed every square inch of the premises. They waxed the floors until the sheen was so high that it looked like some material much more exotic and marvelous than Georgia pine. From a notions store that had gone out of business, they purchased display cases which they refinished with such care that one would be proud to exhibit jewels therein. All the brass doorknobs were polished until they shone, and curtains of starched white muslin hung. The globes of the overhead lamps were taken down and swabbed with a cleaning solution, and the cashbox was oiled and waxed. The walls were scrubbed down, and the windows washed and washed again. They went to a sign painter and ordered a sign that said: WEISS DRY GOODS & SUNDRIES.

"Look, Simon," she cried as they stood before the newly hung sign. "Look what we have."

"Yes," he said bleakly. "But who can tell if we shall ever see a profit on it?"

"Why must you be so pessimistic? We have an opportunity. We won't fail at it. I won't let us fail."

Later on that day, as she sat doing inventory on the fabrics she had ordered, she looked up and saw him glaring at her. "What is it?" she asked.

"Oh, it is nothing. Nothing that concerns you, that is. After all, why should you be concerned about anything?"

"Tell me what it is, Simon," she said patiently, "and we shall discuss it."

"Shall we" he cried. "Well, thank you, thank you, thank you."

She felt her back break out in sweat, but she sought to keep her demeanor calm. "Everything has been going so well, Simon," she said in a voice that was just slightly, and she hoped beneficially, castigating. "I simply don't understand. Won't you tell me what it is?"

"Can't you figure it out? Can't you see that I don't matter? Don't you know that I'm invisible and that I shall disappear. And that's just the way you want it, isn't it, Rebekah, isn't it?"

"Haven't we worked side by side, Simon, fixing this place up, making it into something that people will want to come to? Don't you think I recognize the efforts you've put into it?"

"Oh, surely. Indeed. And just as soon as you have a chance, you'll cast me aside like an old shoe. Do you think I'm a fool? What kind of a future do I have here? I'll be Rebekah Weiss's husband. I'll be the one running back and forth to the stock room, waiting for instructions from you. Is that what I came to America for?"

"If that's what you want to make it, Simon, then that's what it shall be. But it doesn't have to be that way. The only person who will ruin this for you is you yourself."

"Just as I ruin everything, is that it?"

"I didn't say that."

"But you thought it."

"Simon, listen to me. Don't do this. Look around you. Everything is gleaming. Everything is fresh and clean. It's a new start, Simon, don't fall back."

"I know that you have a plan against me. Do you think I'm an innocent? I know every thought that goes through that plotting little mind of yours. You'll have me do the dirty work—the mopping and the scraping and the scrubbing—and when you don't need me any longer, you'll give me the boot!"

"Simon, listen to yourself. Listen to what you're . . ."

"Shut up!" he screamed.

She saw his face turn stark white and become contorted with rage. Suddenly she felt very afraid; suddenly she sensed that he wished to harm her. "You must rest, Simon," she cautioned. "We have been working so very hard. Now it's time for you to rest."

His face, which had been so hideously rigid, now appeared in a bright bath of sweat. "Yes," he muttered. "I have been so awfully tired."

"Why, of course you have. Is there somewhere a man who wouldn't be?"

He fingered the bolts of fabric that she had assembled on the shelves. "My, my," he said with the strangest of smiles. "So much cloth. So many beautiful dresses to be made."

"Yes," she replied. "So we hope."

"So we hope," he repeated after her as though what she had said was terribly significant and yet utterly inscrutable. "You have such hopes, don't you, Rebekah?"

She remained silent. She looked at the yards of fabric arranged on the shelves: muslins, tulle, organdy, calico, chintz, organza, lace, chenille. Many beautiful dresses. *Where are you off to? Why, Weiss's of course.* She played in her mind this imaginary dialogue between two prosperous Mobile matrons at least twenty times a day. She wanted success; she wanted money; she wanted the benefits of a well-placed situation. She wanted to lay down roots and she wanted to thrive and she wanted to reap the harvest. "Yes, Simon," she said at last. "I have hopes."

He stared at her, and then he began to laugh. It was an awful, maniacal laugh.

"Don't," she pleaded. "Don't."

"You have hopes!" he screamed. He took a scissors and, with a jerky but lightning-swift motion, he began to slash at the bolts of fabric.

"Simon!" she cried. "You mustn't! You mustn't!"

He went on, ripping at the fabric, cursing wildly, and she rushed over, intent on restraining him. There was a struggle as she tried to wrest the scissors from him, and, in a flash, she found herself stabbed in the palm, the blood already soiling her skirt. She shrieked, and he froze in his place.

"What have I done?" he muttered, dropping the scissors to the floor.

"It's nothing," she gasped. "Just a scratch. Here," she said, pulling at the shreds of fabric and wrapping the makeshift bandage around her wound. "It's nothing at all, you see."

"Blood. My God, there's blood." He backed himself into a corner. "Look what I've done. There's blood everywhere."

"Simon, please don't. I said I was all right. I said . . ."

But he didn't or wouldn't hear her. He raced ahead of her and seized the scissors. Before she could say a word, he ran the blade across his own palm, loosing a flow of blood.

"Simon! Simon, what are you doing?"

He looked at her and then, wordlessly, he ran from the store.

That evening she went to the synagogue. She had been there once before. The very first day they arrived in Mobile, looking for rooms, they had been sized up very quickly at all of the boardinghouses they had ventured into, and they were directed to Cherry Street. Cherry Street was the site of a Jewish colony—not large, not comparable to the Jewish section on Lloyd Street in Baltimore, but significant nonetheless. Simon and Rebekah had lived there in a boardinghouse run by Sadie Berman, a widow whose husband had owned a dry goods store. When they bought the store on Caroline Street, they moved into the upstairs apartment over the store. Although the boardinghouse had not been all that well kept, Rebekah felt some nostalgia for that brief time. It had been good to be in the company of her people again. They were all either peddlers or fledgling merchants—just like themselves —and they were all willing enough to share their knowledge and their experiences. That first week Sadie Berman asked Rebekah if she wanted to go to synagogue with her. Of course she did, Rebekah was quick to say. And your husband? No, Rebekah explained, my husband is not a religious sort of man.

It had been an overwhelming experience to enter a synagogue again after all this time. Her family had never been devout, but they were, by all means, Jewish in their consciousness and in their traditions. Sabbath was strictly observed (there would have been no other way for a Jewish family in Korneuberg) as were all the holidays: Passover, Purim, Chanukah, the High Holy Days. She missed the warmth that she used to experience at those times. And when she entered the synagogue and sat through the service, she said a prayer for her mother and for her father, and she felt close to them again as she once had.

Now she felt it imperative to return to the synagogue. She didn't know where else to turn. Simon's behavior was wild and dangerous, and she had to get help from someone. She went to see Rabbi Lipman, a man of advanced years, much admired in the city. She felt sure that if anyone could help her, he could.

"And you are Rebekah Weiss?" he said as they sat in his study.

"Yes, Rabbi."

"And where are you from, my dear?"

"Austria. Korneuberg," she whispered.

"Speak up, my dear. I am an old man who doesn't hear so very well."

"Rabbi, I need help," she blurted.

"What, my child?" he asked, all concern.

"My husband," she cried, and then, in a whisper: "It's my husband."

"What? Is he sick?"

"Yes, Rabbi. He's sick," she said, nodding.

"And you need money?"

"No, it's not like that. He's sick in the head. He's cruel to me, Rabbi. He's hardly ever human to me."

The rabbi nodded sympathetically. "Yes, my child. I've heard this from many wives. You, so young and beautiful, what would you know of the ways of men? But give it time, my dear, and open up your heart . . ."

"No, Rabbi. It's not what you think," she said, interrupting him. "The marriage has no love. It never did."

"Sometimes you must work at love," he said, a modicum of reserve entering his voice.

"Rabbi, listen to me. My husband Simon, he's sick. He thinks everything I do is aimed against him. He thinks I'm plotting against him . . ."

"You must help him to be happier, my dear," he said in a voice that was very smooth but that was increasingly without warmth.

"I want a *get*, Rabbi," she said bluntly.

His rheumy blue eyes widened. "What are you saying? You don't know what you're saying."

"Yes, I do! I want a *get*! I want to be free of him!"

"You're talking about a death," the rabbi said angrily. "The death of a marriage, and marriage is a holy thing. I won't hear such things."

She held up her palm that had been slashed by the scissors. "Look what he did to me," she challenged.

The rabbi stared, his thick, pale lips quivering slightly, and then he shook his head. "An accident," he murmured.

"It was no accident. It was his madness."

"Bring your husband to see me," the rabbi instructed.

"He won't come," she said bitterly. She stared down at the floor. "Then you won't set me free?"

"I can't. It isn't called for." He paused, his face

filled with doubt. "If perhaps your husband agreed . . ."

"He won't agree," she cried. "He wants to use me. Can't you see?"

"All I can tell you is to be patient, my child," he said, retreating into his platitudes. "Things have a way of working themselves out."

She left the synagogue in tears. She was so disappointed. She had thought the rabbi would help her, but instead he made it all seem her fault. And now she had to go back to Simon, and who could tell what tomorrow would bring? More madness, more grief—and no chance of happiness as far as she could see. The only thing that would keep her going would be the store. She would devote all of her energies to the store; she would make it into the best thing in her life.

The next morning they opened the store. She put on a spotless white smock, and Simon wore his best suit. The shelves, immaculate as they were, had been newly dusted and the sidewalk awning was unfurled. They awaited the customers, scheduled to begin arriving within the next hour.

They hadn't discussed further yesterday's incident. Simon arrived home very late at night, his hand bloodied but the blood congealed. She brewed a pot of tea, and they sat together at the table.

"Let me see your hand," she had said.

"No. It's nothing."

She had taken his hand and had held it in her own. "Why, Simon? You shouldn't have punished yourself."

That was all that they had said. Now here they stood before the plate-glass window of their new store, each with a private wound, trying not to think about scars, trying only to look for customers, thinking only of the success they deserved.

An hour passed, the ticking of the clock sounding

like an ax chopping into wood. She arranged and re-arranged bolts of fabric while he pursued a solitary fly much too quick and cunning for him. Another silent, stricken hour passed by before they spoke.

"It is not as you planned, is it?" he challenged.

"It is only our first day, our first morning. Don't you think these things take time?"

He laughed and began to roll a cigarette. "You know more than you're saying, don't you? You know when something feels right, don't you? And this doesn't feel right, does it?"

"You've got a victorious smile on your face, Simon, even though it's no victory for you if I lose, even though I haven't lost yet and don't intend to. So why don't you just wait awhile, Simon, until I admit defeat."

"And when will that be? When we're destitute and years in debt?"

"Oh, you have all sorts of gloom to predict, don't you? One can always count on you for that, if nothing else."

There was a furious silence as each pretended to concentrate on their midday meal. Rebekah felt that if she ingested a single morsel of food, she would be ill right there and then. So she just rearranged the food on the plate as, moments before, she had re-arranged the bolts of fabric.

It was another hour after lunch that a customer finally appeared in the store. Immediately Simon approached the woman who appeared to be an unimpressive sort of matron, and he treated her to a show of obsequiousness that was both fantastic and awful.

"Good day, madame," he began. "Welcome to Weiss's of Caroline Street."

The woman, rather worn looking, nodded while her eyes darted curiously from side to side.

"Simon Weiss, proprietor," he announced. "At your service."

The woman looked both confused and intimidated. "You got something for me to make a dress?"

He laughed richly. "My dear woman, we have the finest fabrics that can be obtained. We have the finest Belgian lace, rare China silks, Eastern brocades . . ."

"No. That ain't right," the woman said, backing off toward the door.

"Simon!" Rebekah cried out harshly. And then, in a softer tone: "I am so sorry. We do have a wide range of fabrics. Won't you let me show you our . . ."

"No. It's all right," the woman said, obviously made terribly uncomfortable by this peculiar teamwork. "I don't need nothing anyway."

They watched her leave, restraining their impulse to seize her and drag her back into the store.

"Oh, you did very well on that one, didn't you, Simon?"

"What do you mean?"

"What do you think I mean? You chased her from the store. You might just as well have used your boot on her."

"Aha! Every failure is pinned on me, and every success is yours. That's the prescription, is it?"

"Why didn't you just tell her there was nothing here she could afford? Why didn't you just send her on her way as well as . . ."

"Shut up! I tried to treat her like a queen, but she was a common sort of a woman and . . ."

"Common!" she spat. "Why, you're just a peddler. Who told you to put on airs?"

He remained silent for a long moment and then sank down into the green leather chair. "You're cruel to me, Rebekah," he said at last. "I tried and I failed. Tell me, must I be punished for it?"

She stared at him. All morning he had mocked her and tormented her. *It isn't as you planned, is it?* And then, when he had done something stupid enough to drive away their first customer and when she had complained of it, then suddenly it was she who became the villain. "Very well, Simon," she said, knowing that this was a solution most favorable to her interests, "I am sorry."

The rest of the day passed without customers. By the time night fell, one could have heard a pin or any other of their sewing notions drop.

"We're done for," he said, his voice bleak, hopeless. "We might just as well pack up and leave."

"Don't be a fool. I won't give in. If you want to, then do so. Take the wagon and get out. But I'm not quitting yet."

"Half of what's in this store is mine. If I want out, then we get out."

"No," she said. "Not half. Never half. You've done nothing to compare to what I've done, and you damned well know it."

"Then what do you suggest I do? Watch everything I have slip through your fingers?"

"Why don't you just leave me alone? Why don't you just stay home? Or, if you want to, I'll give you enough to play cards with and you won't ever have to come in."

"You take me for an utter fool, don't you? As if I have nothing to say about anything and as if . . ."

"I don't give a damn about you. I care about the store! And nobody's going to take it away from me. Do you understand?"

He looked at her very hard. "Then we're back so soon to where we were," he murmured.

"Yes," she said. "So soon. So very soon," and she felt, with all of her being, that she had never been away.

Another day passed as miserably as the first. She was beginning to believe his dire predictions, even though every fiber of her body fought against the seductiveness of his discontent. She found that her stomach

experienced a sort of strange, plucking sensation when-
ever she looked through the shop window and saw
someone headed their way. And then her stomach
fell, swooped, crashed when she saw that they had
been passed by. Two days in a store without a single
transaction—it was not something she had counted
on. And to have Simon's glowering presence as well
threatened to be more than she could bear.

"Now you'll know what it feels like not to be so
fresh and new," he laughed. "Now you'll know what
it is to have disappointment in your life."

"Don't you think I've known that?" she said in a
fury. "Don't you think I've had that in my life since
the moment I met you?"

He was without an answer.

"Disappointment," she muttered. "What a gentle
word you've given it."

He sat behind the store for the next few hours. He
rolled cigarettes, one after another, and then he
smoked them. She was glad for it. Awful as things
were, they were yet a bit better without him hanging
over her. It began to rain after midday, a dark warm
torrent, and the street traffic was reduced to nil. It
was then, in that dark hour, that she remembered
someone who might help her. She sat down and wrote
a note.

> Dear Mrs. Winslow,

she wrote,

> My name is Rebekah Weiss. We met some years
> ago, on a train going South.

She paused, pen in hand, feeling most foolish. How
could the woman possibly remember her? It had been
so insignificant and so long ago. But what choice did

she have? It was either making a fool of herself or letting the store sink into ruin.

> We spoke then at some length and you mentioned that if I ever arrived in Mobile, I should so inform you. I am pleased to tell you that my husband and I have just begun a fashion emporium known as Weiss Dry Goods & Sundries. We are located at 7 Caroline Street. We would be most pleased and honored if you would visit our store and see our fine French and English fabrics.
>
> Yours most sincerely,
Mrs. Simon Weiss

She took an umbrella and rushed out of doors, the letter in hand. "I'll be back as soon as I can," she cried.

"Where are you going?"

"On a very important errand."

It was more than that. She had come to hinge her last hopes on this ploy, and, as she went out to find Mrs. Winslow's home, she felt as though her entire future lay in the outcome of this afternoon's outing.

She stopped at the post office on Government Street. "Can you tell me where a Mrs. Winslow lives?" she asked a clerk.

"Hattie Winslow?"

"Yes."

"Why, she's up at White Meadows. Up on Spring Hill Avenue. Just north of here."

She headed north. She had to walk very far. By the time she got there, everything in her but the letter was soaking. The house was very grand. She rang the bell, and a white-jacketed black man opened the door.

"I have a letter," she panted. She handed it to him. "Mrs. Winslow," she said. "For Mrs. Hattie Winslow."

She watched him look at it.

"Will there be an answer?" he asked imperiously.

She shook her head and went back out into the rain.

The next morning she felt more nervous than ever. What if Mrs. Winslow never came? What if she didn't come for a week or even two? Simon would never last, and she didn't know if she herself could last.

"Your dear friend whom you happened to once sit next to on a train," Simon said mockingly. "Where is she? One would think she would have a bit more loyalty."

At late morning they made their first sale—a modest purchase of pins and needles to a woman who just walked in from the street. It came to nothing, at any rate not enough to assure them of an impending fortune.

"Well then," Simon cried in mock exultation, dropping the two coins into the cashbox. "Our cup runneth over."

"Laugh if you want to, Simon, but there is nothing funny. A sale is a sale. At least we have begun."

At three o'clock, when she had already watched Simon smoke innumerable cigarettes and when she felt as though she would scream if she heard another hour chime by, she suddenly saw two women approaching the store. They were dressed most fashionably, and the smaller of the two looked vaguely familiar.

"It's she!" Rebekah hissed. "She's here!"

Simon rose abruptly and straightened his tie.

"Open the door for them!" she cried.

He did as he was told. "*Mesdames,*" he said with a click of his heels. "At your service."

Oh God, she thought wildly, he's going to ruin everything. "Mrs. Winslow," she said, going to greet her. "How very kind of you to come."

Hattie Winslow peered at Rebekah. "Why, yes," she said at last. "I remember you."

"Rebekah Weiss," she said idiotically.

"Yes. Rebekah Weiss. Yes."

"And this is my husband, Simon Weiss."

Again he bowed.

"How do you do? This is my sister, Mrs. Garden."

And then still another round of "How do you do?"

There followed a most awkward silence, which Rebekah felt she must break before Simon did so.

"I took the liberty of sending you the note. I hope it was not . . ."

"Oh, it was a treat, my dear!" Mrs. Winslow cried. "I adore getting letters from mysterious sources. I simply can't imagine anyone who doesn't, can you?"

She smiled. "Won't you come in and look at what we carry?"

"Why yes. Of course we will."

They sat the women down in comfortable chairs before a table and they proceeded to bring forth a wide selection of fabrics.

"My goodness, Margaret," Hattie Winslow said to her sister. "Look at that exquisite mauve silk. It would be divine with your coloring. And that lemon silk there. Wouldn't that be marvelous for Mary Lee?"

Simon and Rebekah exchanged covert, excited glances.

"Why, you've got remarkable things," Hattie Winslow said. "Just remarkable, aren't they, Margaret?"

"Oh, indeed yes, Harriet, indeed yes."

Between the two women Rebekah rang up an enormous purchase, more than they had ever done in a single day on the road.

"It's a lovely store you have, my dear," Mrs. Winslow's sister said as they prepared to leave. Just as Simon got their parcels wrapped, it began to rain.

"Oh, heavens above!" Hattie cried. "The daily deluge!"

"Please, don't go out into the rain," Rebekah said. "Can't we make you a cup of tea?"

There was an exchange of glances between the two

sisters and, for a moment Rebekah feared that she had committed some awful breach of propriety.

"That would be lovely," Hattie Winslow said. "Just lovely."

She had Simon prepare the tea things while the women talked.

"We simply must introduce you to Madame Colbert," Mrs. Garden said. "She is Mobile's finest couturière. Simply everyone goes there to have their dresses made, and I'm sure that you'll want to know each other."

"Why yes, I would certainly appreciate such a meeting."

Simon brought out the tea. She hoped he would not allow the cups and saucers to clatter as he set them down.

"How did you decide to settle down in Mobile?" Hattie Winslow asked. "You didn't just pick it out of a hat now, did you?"

"No," Rebekah said. "We picked Mobile because it seemed like a good place to start a business. We hope we were right."

"When was it that I saw you on that train, dear?"

"Three years ago. Three very long years."

"Have they been long? When you get to be my age, nothing seems quite so long."

"Your daughter was leaving for some faraway place . . ."

"Oh yes. Now I place it well enough."

"And you said a woman should never travel alone."

"Yes. Indeed I did. Yes."

There was a silence as the apparent extent of their reminiscence had been exhausted. Then Mrs. Winslow's face brightened with an additional memory. "I know," she said, "we spoke of that terrible young man."

"Yes," Rebekah said softly.

"Who?" Mrs. Garden demanded to know.

"Who do you think?" Hattie Winslow replied. "Jarrett Russell, that's who!"

"You don't say!" Mrs. Garden countered. "Well, I never! How did you come to talk of *him?*"

"You know, I don't remember. Do you, dear?"

"Yes," Rebekah said. "I told you I knew someone in Mobile . . ." She glanced at Simon who was looking at her curiously. "I told you he had treated me at Locust Point."

"Yes, now I remember," Hattie cried. "Locust Point. You remember, Margaret, when I came home and told you the news."

Margaret looked confused.

"You remember, I told you I met a little foreign girl on the train and she told me about *Doctor* Jarrett Russell? Oh, Margaret, you never remember a thing!"

There was a silence as everyone sipped their tea.

"Has there been further news of him?" Rebekah asked, trying to maintain a casual tone.

"Oh, has there been indeed! He has only had the gall to return to Wild Oaks."

"Wild Oaks?"

"Yes, the estate. It's been empty since the war. God knows, it's nothing but a ruin."

"What does he intend to do?" Rebekah said.

"He's already doing it," Hattie replied, full of spite. "He's going to take care of the niggers."

"The freedmen?"

There was a harsh little silence. "If that's what you want to call them," Mrs. Garden said pointedly.

Rebekah sensed that it had best not be what she wanted. "How long has he been here?" she asked.

"My wife often finds herself with too many questions," Simon said suddenly. Everyone turned to look. He stood there like a headwaiter, a tea towel folded over his arm. There was one last deadly awkward silence. This time it was Hattie Winslow's turn to break it.

"See there!" she cried. "The rain is over, and we have a glorious sky again."

The women collected their things and headed for the door.

"Thank you so much for coming," Rebekah said, and Simon murmured his assent.

"Why, it's been a perfect delight," Hattie said. "And we'll tell all our people about it, won't we, Margaret?"

"Oh, indeed yes, indeed."

And so they left. Rebekah sat down and exhaled. "So," she said. "It seems at last that something has gone our way."

She waited for him to say something, but he maintained a glum silence that was quite out of keeping with the events of the afternoon.

"What is the matter?" she asked.

"So many questions you had about this doctor. What a fine memory you possess."

She started folding the bolts of fabric. "Is that all you have to say?"

"He must have made a great impression on you."

"Yes. In fact he did."

"Oh yes, he must have been some fine doctor. He must have been . . ."

"I can't bear this!" she cried. She covered her face with her hands, and then she sighed deeply. "I won't have it, Simon. I won't let you make my life miserable. We did well today. We sold a lot, and we've got people on our side. I won't let you ruin everything, Simon. I just won't let you."

"What about me?" he demanded. "Are my concerns for nothing? Do you care not a bit for me?"

"I care about the store!" she replied. "That's all I care about! Nothing else! Do you understand? I care about the store."

CHAPTER TEN

In the months that followed, Simon watched the store prosper. He recognized it as an extraordinary enterprise. Rebekah never stopped working, but, beyond that, she never stopped thinking. She ordered all the latest magazines from New York, London, and Paris, and she invited groups of ladies to tea so that they might discuss the fashions of the day. He would sit in the back room and laugh. This wife of his had presumptions such as he had never before witnessed. She thought nothing of making herself into an arbiter of fashion when she was just brief years out of the *shtetl*. But she was a quick study, this wife of his. She learned all she had to learn to push her beyond the ladies of Mobile and make them pay attention to her. And then she had Hattie Winslow on her side. She courted the woman as though she were a queen, the mistress of all she surveyed, and, in a sense, he supposed she was. She certainly helped to make Weiss Dry Goods & Sundries a store to be reckoned with.

"You Jews are so smart," Hattie said one day as she sat in the store sipping tea. "I swear you could make diamonds out of sawdust."

Simon and Rebekah exchanged glances.

"Did I say something wrong?"

"No," Rebekah assured her. "Not at all."

"I mean, I just think Jews are as smart as they come. They don't make them any smarter, no way."

"Yes, Mrs. Winslow," Rebekah said dutifully.

It was the first time in Mobile that their religion had been an issue, at least for their ears. After Hattie left, Rebekah and Simon were silent for quite some time before one of them spoke.

"You're lucky, Rebekah. You found yourself someone who likes Jew shopkeepers."

"Let's not talk about it, Simon."

"No. Of course not. Why should we talk about anything you don't want to talk about?"

"Enough, Simon. Must I always tell you when it's been enough?"

He took his hat and left the store. Altogether he spent little time there. His decreasing responsibility was never discussed at length; it was merely accepted as part of the natural order of things. Often he sat in Bienville Square, under the shade of live oaks, and tried to think about his life in a way that might make sense. He never managed to do so. He didn't know what his life was about. Rebekah had the store; he had half the proceeds from the store. But he could hardly bring himself to rise each morning and make his way to the store. There was nothing for him there; it claimed nothing of his imagination; it expressed nothing of his dream.

Did he have a dream? Still? After all this time? He liked to think that maybe there was still something alive in him after all. He didn't know what it would be. Success seemed rather a minor concern at this point. The dream that he secretly cherished had to do with romance. That was what he needed in his life; that was what he had never had. He sat at the center of Bienville Square, beside an old French cannon, surrounded by beds of azalea, and he thought of romance.

There would be no happiness with Rebekah, and so he would have to find it elsewhere. While sitting in

Bienville Square, he overheard a trio of well-dressed
men discussing Madame Jewel's house. He knew
enough to listen to what well-dressed men had to say.
Madame Jewel's house, down on Canal Street, a very
fine house indeed, so they said.

He went that very night to investigate. He put on
his best dark suit and his good bowler hat. Rebekah
never saw him; she was still down at the store, working
furiously. He walked down to the waterfront; he had
no trouble finding his destination. He saw a group of
men—well-dressed men—entering Madame Jewel's
bordello. It was quite a well-concealed little place,
nothing to distinguish it except a single blue light
(there was nothing about Madame Jewel's that was
conventional). He walked the stairs and knocked on
a blank white door. The eye opened.

"Madame Jewel's?" he asked.

He was admitted into a large white room. It was
the most eccentrically appointed room he had ever
seen. Almost everything about it was white, a scheme
that ran contrary to all the other houses he had ever
frequented where plush reds and burgundies sought
to promote a sense of intimacy. This was a world of
ivory and alabaster and white silk and white onyx.

"Crocodile, show the man in," drawled the woman
he took to be Madame Jewel.

A wire-strung black man, close to seven foot tall
and dressed in a stark white suit, ushered him in.

"I am Madame Jewel," the woman said, extending
her hand.

He stared at her with naked and unmitigated fascination. She was, beyond measure, a compelling presence. Her hair was white, appropriate to her age; her
skin was powdered the purest white; and she wore a
white dress that on some younger woman in some
other milieu he might have taken for a wedding gown.

"You are new here," she said.

"Yes. Yes, Madame Jewel."

"Then, dear gentleman, we must make you very comfortable, mustn't we?"

He thought a moment. "If you please, Madame Jewel."

"We must see that you get what you like. Everyone gets what they like at Madame Jewel's. Isn't that so, Crocodile?"

"Yes'm," the fierce-looking black man replied.

"Some people don't even know what they like until they come to Madame Jewel's," she said philosophically. "Now, dear gentleman, do you like a dark girl or do you like a fair girl?"

"I . . . I don't know," he stammered. He had been in brothels before, but never one so unusual as this, and he wore his nervousness on his sleeve.

"I think you need a dark girl," she said. "Dark girls can be very naughty. I think you would like that. Iris!" she called. "Crocodile, go fetch Iris for me."

She offered him an absinthe as they waited, and he took it and he felt warmed by it and steadied by it even though he recognized it as a sure road to ruin, even as he saw Madame Jewel's powdered white hand shaking as she lifted the glass to her lips.

"Ah, my sweet Iris!" Madame Jewel sighed as one of the girls entered the room. She was a voluptuous black girl, beautiful if sullen in appearance, and she looked Simon over more carefully than he did her.

"There is no better than Iris, dear gentleman."

"How much . . ."

Madame Jewel held up her hand. "Oh, she costs, sir. All of my girls cost."

"Yes. Yes, of course. But I was thinking . . ." He let his sentence die in midstream.

She arched an eyebrow. "Then perhaps not Iris? Go, Iris," she said with a wave of her hand. She sighed. "Yes, Iris can be a bit rich for the blood, that is true. Who then?"

Crocodile smiled.

"Oh, Crocodile," the woman said in a lascivious voice. "I wouldn't dream!"

Simon felt the hairs on the back of his neck stand on end. "What is it?" he asked, looking at the grinning black man, his mouth feeling suddenly, oddly dry.

"No, Crocodile, stop it!" Madame Jewel purred. "This dear gentleman would surely want a young lady of more dignity and reserve."

"What is it?" Simon demanded to know.

Madame Jewel sighed theatrically. "Well, if you must, dear gentleman, it's Lucy. Oh, she's just a little minx, that Lucy is. I don't see it at all, not at all." She stuck a cigarette into a long ivory holder. Crocodile was there in a flash, lighting it for her. She puffed and she puffed, and her hooded eyes made her look like some kind of ancient white lizard.

"Can't I just meet her?" Simon asked. He held his hat in his hand and looked from Madame Jewel to Crocodile and back.

She puffed some more. "I suppose it couldn't hurt. And she's such a pretty little thing, worth seeing in any case. Why don't you bring her in, Crocodile?"

He waited for the appearance of this girl named Lucy. This thing, this pretty little thing.

"More absinthe?" Madame Jewel asked.

"Just a bit, please."

He downed the liquor too quickly, and the room seemed suddenly too warm and too blazing white.

"Ah, there she is," said Madame Jewel. "There is our Lucy."

He turned. What he saw made him suck in his breath. It was the most beautiful thing, really the most beautiful thing. A small-boned, chiseled creature, with skin the light cream color of an orchid's cup. Eyes very dark blue, reminiscent of deep waters, and hair black as coal and curly, falling in masses around her face. She wore a simple white lace dress that showed her extremities—her hands and her feet—so delicate as to remind him of a Dresden shepherdess.

"Lucy, my child," Madame Jewel intoned, extending her hand.

Lucy rushed to Madame Jewel and knelt beside her chair. Madame ran her hand through Lucy's black ringlets and smiled. "Isn't she precious, sir?"

He stared at her in silence, transfixed by her beauty. The girl smiled shyly but somehow emphatically, and he felt his heart racing.

"Oh yes, Crocodile," Madame Jewel chuckled. "I can see the dear gentleman is taken. But shall we let him have her? I fear he will wrap her up in his cape and steal her away from us."

The combination of the absinthe and Madame Jewel's suggestive words made his face pour with sweat.

"Talk to her, dear gentleman," Madame Jewel said. "She likes to be talked to."

He cleared his throat. "Good evening to you, Lucy," he murmured.

She smiled enchantingly, and then there was silence.

"Enough. Show him to your room, Lucy," Madame Jewel said, dismissing them with a wave of her cigarette holder.

Lucy rose and took Simon by the hand. She led him down a hallway into a small white room that smelled of lily of the valley. She closed the door and went to sit on the bed. He could watch the pulse in her neck; he felt himself become huge with excitement.

"Come," she whispered, patting the bed beside her.

He went and sat there, holding his hat in his sweaty hands.

"Don't you want to kiss me?" she breathed so close to his ear. She turned his face to hers, and she met his lips. She tasted so sweet, and her tongue darted between his teeth. "What is your name?" she asked, and she ran her fingers through his hair.

"Simon," he said. "My name is Simon."

She smiled. With a quick, deft motion she pulled her dress over her head and she sat in her corset and camisole, showing him further glimpses of her extraordinary creamy skin. "Would you like to touch me here?" she asked, placing his hand on her smooth shoulder. She began to unlace her undergarments. In a moment her breasts were revealed, not large, but beautifully round with dark, large nipples. "And here?" she said, moving his hand to her breasts. She kissed him again, more passionately this time, her hand grazing his thigh. He held her hand and made her stop; he didn't want it to be over so quickly. When he was ready again, she removed all of her underthings and sat naked beside him. She took his hand. "Touch me here," she murmured, placing his hand in the wealth of fine, soft hair that grew at her sex. She took his hand and rubbed it against herself. He found that she was wet, and he heard himself make little moaning sounds.

She removed his jacket and she unbuttoned his suspenders and his shirt. When his chest was bare, she kissed his nipples. "I like you," she whispered, "I like you." She rubbed her nipples against his nipples. He made her stop once again, and then they continued. She took off his shoes and ran her fingers along his naked soles. And then she undid his buckles, his belt, his pants. She helped him off with his things. "Ah, look," she said. "You like me too, don't you, Simon?"

"Yes. Yes, Lucy, yes."

"Shall I do everything for you?"

"Yes, please do, please."

She kneeled down and took hold of him. In a moment she had him between her lips, and she was licking at him as if she were devouring an exotic fruit, a melon or perhaps a mango. In a flash he exploded, rocking the bed and crying out wildly. She kept him between her lips until he was hard again. Then she mounted him, pushing him into the warm wet of her, her hair falling over his chest as she held on to his shoulders.

When it was over, and it was not over too quickly, she rolled a cigarette for him, lighted it, and placed it between his lips.

"Will you come see me again?" she asked.

"Oh Lucy," he sighed. "Lucy."

"You will," she said, very much pleased. "And I shall make you so very happy."

He was in more of a daze at the store than usual. Rebekah took note and acted accordingly.

"Perhaps you're not getting enough sleep, Simon," she said, but there was no answer. He sat with a newspaper on his lap, staring ahead. "Simon?" she called, feeling herself growing angry.

"What?" he replied at last.

She laughed, her laughter etched with bitterness. "I say, perhaps you aren't getting enough sleep."

"Don't start worrying about me at this point, Rebekah," he advised. "It's rather too late for you to be worrying so."

She returned to her ledger books. For a moment the page seemed a blur of numbers, and she couldn't concentrate.

"Must you go out tonight?" she asked. "Perhaps we could go out together. The dining room at the hotel, perhaps?"

"I have made other plans," he said, annoyed by her questions.

"With whom?" she asked, trying to be calm.

"With the new friends I have made."

"I'm glad you've made new friends," she said, "but what about me? What am I to do?"

"You can always work, Rebekah."

"Do you think that's all I want?"

"Isn't it?"

"No!" she cried. "We're making money now. That's all I ever wanted. To make a bit of money and to have a home and to not have to sleep in the back of a wagon. Don't you understand?"

"I understand that you've put everything ahead of me," he said dryly. "That's been clear from the start."

"I want a child, Simon. It's time, you know. For both of us. It's something we need."

After the futile visit to the synagogue in quest of a *get,* she realized that she was bound to Simon for only God knew how long and the only thing that might assuage the bitterness and loneliness of it all was a child. He could do that much for her, she thought.

"No. No, it's wrong. It's not time."

She waited for more, but no more was forthcoming. "I don't understand," she said at last.

"I'm just not ready," he cried.

"You're not *ready?*" she said incredulously. "But you're thirty-four years old. Four years ago, when I lost a baby on the ship, you treated me like a lame horse, and now you say you aren't ready."

Now it was his turn to sit. He held his head in his hands. "What do you want of me, Rebekah?" he moaned. "Tell me and let it be."

Was she as mad as he was? Was he driving her mad? "Simon, please," she said. "I want a baby."

He stayed with her that night. Lucy would have to wait, he thought grimly. She made them a simple dinner, then they went to bed. She put on a nightgown and combed out her hair. She felt as nervous as . . . well, she didn't want to think back to her wedding night.

Very shyly she kissed him on the lips. He lay there, unresponsive to this initial affection. She kissed him again, and again there was no return. She felt angry and weary at once. Why did there have to be this masquerade of passion before she could have what she wanted?

"I want it, Simon," she said, reaching down to touch him.

He let her arouse him, thinking all the while of Lucy. *Touch me here. I like you. Ah, look, you like me too.* He could think of nothing sweeter than Lucy. *Oh, Crocodile! I wouldn't dream!* He had grown very hard and then he looked down and saw Rebekah's face and was startled when he lost his potency.

"Simon?"

But how absurd, because wasn't this a beauty and when before, in spite of everything, had he ever lost his desire for her?

"Simon, what is it?"

What indeed? How could he know? He felt himself overwhelmingly confused and then, in a single light-flooded moment, he understood. It was Lucy he loved. He had no love for Rebekah, none whatsoever. His problem was that he was filled with fear. He could not break from Rebekah because if he did so then there would be things to face, unknown things. And now, in this life that he had made for himself, he would sooner do anything than face the unknown.

Suddenly Rebekah pushed him away and turned over on her side.

"Rebekah?"

"Don't worry, Simon," she said. "I won't ask again."

"Rebekah, you don't understand . . ."

"But I do, Simon. I understand perfectly. There's someone you'd rather have, which is all well and good, but you still have an obligation to me, Simon."

"What is my obligation, Rebekah? Tell me so I'll know."

"I want a child, Simon. If you can't give it to me, tell me now so I can make other arrangements."

She waited for his response, but he was silent.

In the passing weeks his life became Lucy and Lucy his life. He felt enchanted by her, possessed by her. He lived for the moment each day when he would see her and touch her and have his life renewed by her. She knew she had captured him utterly, and when she held him, it was with a special possessiveness, as though he were her private and special pet. He brought her chocolates and bouquets of moon-white hydrangeas and a feathery kitten that she named Whistle because it seemed to come to her when she did so and white kid gloves from Paris, France, and honeycombs in syrup and white ostrich plumes and money. She accepted it all with the ingratitude and sheer excitement of a child. Soon it became clear to Madame Jewel and everyone involved that there was a specialness between Lucy and Simon. Romance, in fact, had entered Madame Jewel's house, as it had done before but never with such intensity.

The two lovers lay together in the narrow white room, and she fanned him and had him sip from a cool glass of lemonade.

"Lucy, I love you. Do you love me?"

"Oh, Simon." She blew a puff of sweet smoke called marijuana. He leaned over and placed his large, hairy hand on her smooth tan stomach.

"You're everything to me, Lucy, everything."

She laughed. "You're silly," she said, kissing his nose.

He felt even that mere wisp of a kiss along the entire length of his body. "No, I mean it, Lucy. I swear I do."

She turned over on her side, away from him.

"What's the matter?" he asked.

She shook her head.

"Please tell me."

She turned to him and smiled just a bit. "How can I be everything to you, Simon? You know what I am."

"No, Lucy. The only thing you are to me is my love. That's all. Nothing else matters."

"Oh, Simon, it isn't true. How could it be? I'm a whore." She laughed a bit. "Not a cheap whore, but still a whore. Don't you see?"

"Lucy, please don't . . ."

"Don't what? You want me to tell you how many there've been before you? Or how many there are gonna be after you've gone?"

"None!" he cried. "I'll never leave you. You'll always be mine."

He tried to kiss her, but she held him off, pushing him away with the heel of her hand. "I don't much like true love, Simon," she said angrily. "It makes things hard."

"Then what's the answer, Lucy? You know I need you. You know I won't let you go."

"There are lots of answers, Simon. Find one."

She would not let him make love to her again that night. As fragile and ethereal as she could sometimes present herself, there was also a side to her that was unyielding. She told him she was part Seminole, and it was to this that he attributed her obstinacy. Well, he was not going to give her up. She was what he wanted, and he would die before he gave her up.

When he saw Lucy the next night, they sat in the garden and sipped minted tea. The garden was cool and sweet and sublime, a perfect place for joy or melancholy or whatever mood took hold of you. Flush with white lilac and bougainvillea and gentians and larkspur and towering ferns, it was a place that was paradisal and yet a week's neglect could turn it into something rank and overgrown.

"I don't want these, Simon," Lucy said, fingering the strand of apple-green peridot that he had just now presented to her.

He became instantly crestfallen. "Why?" he demanded to know. "What have I done?"

She picked a sprig of lilac and held it to her nose. "You ain't done nothing, Simon. It ain't your fault. It just ain't right."

"But I love you, Lucy . . ."

"Love ain't all there is."

They stared at each other. Simon's eyes welled up with tears.

"Come here, Simon," she whispered, motioning for him to sit beside her on the wrought-iron bench. She held him and kissed him passionately. "It ain't that I don't love you, Simon. I do. I love you as you love me. But this," she said, making a vague, circular gesture with her hand. "This here place weren't made for love."

"But we can try, Lucy . . ."

"No. No, you don't understand, Simon. This is the best I could ever hope for. You don't know much about me. You don't know where I'm from or who my people are. You don't even know my full name, do you?"

"It doesn't matter, Lucy. I don't care what . . ."

"It *does* matter!" she cried, clenching her tiny fists. "My name is Lucy Rougier. I was born up in Escambia. My mother's mother was a full-blooded Negro. And if I didn't look the way I do, I'd be hanging out laundry somewhere."

She saw him staring at her, worldless, his jaw tight but with the faintest suggestion of a jowl.

"Madame Jewel found me when I was ten. My mama had me out working the streets, and Madame Jewel saw me and decided that there could be better things in my future. She took me from my mama, but Mama didn't care, long as I sent her money. I did,

right from the beginning, even though I wasn't working 'cause Madame Jewel don't allow no girls under
twelve to be working like that. But I guess Madame
Jewel seen some good things in my future 'cause she
sent Mama money for two years before I even started
working. But I can tell you right now, Simon, Madame
Jewel ain't never lost no money on me, not one red
cent."

He waited for more, but Lucy wouldn't talk and, instead, twisted the sprig of lilac beneath her chin.

"Now then, that's my story, Simon, or part of it anyway."

"But, Lucy, do you think it means that I don't love
you?" Simon asked. "There's nothing in the world
that could mean such a thing."

She took a few more puffs of the marijuana. Suddenly she laughed very gaily, but the laughter dissipated almost as it had begun. "You ain't been listening, Simon. You been talking a lot about love. Well,
love don't go here. Madame Jewel, she don't like it,
and what Madame Jewel don't like, we don't do. So
you'd better get all them ideas of love out of your head
if you want to keep on comin' around here."

"Listen to me, Lucy. Tell me what you want and
I'll do it for you, I swear it."

"I want you to stop coming around here, Simon,
you understand?" And quickly, without warning, she
turned and fled from the garden.

In the days that followed, he plunged again into
madness. He warred between fits of rage and jags of
crying; Rebekah avoided him assiduously and tried
to convince him not to come into the store.

"Why?" he shouted. "Have you something more to
steal from me?"

Everyone was stealing from him; everyone was hurting him. He spent hours in Bienville Square, muttering oaths to himself. His diatribes were sprinkled

with the names "Rebekah" and "Hattie Winslow" and "Madame Jewel." He would like to destroy them all, as they had conspired to destroy him. Why, he cried aloud, it was a race of women seeking to destroy him!

He went several times a day to Madame Jewel's, and he pounded furiously on the door. The eye would open, he would see something faintly glittering—Crocodile's eye, Crocodile's cold, burning eye—and then the eye would shut, and he would pound some more until his fists were black and blue.

He returned to Bienville Square. He had to try and think. There had to be a solution, if only he could think of it. But he could not think of it. Finally he sent off a note to Lucy.

> Dearest Lucy, my heart,

he wrote,

> Do you know what it is to love somebody as I love you? Surely you could not because if you did then how could you torture me so? My life is turning blacker by the moment. Don't destroy me, cherished Lucy, because I love you so and I have never considered you with anything less than absolute devotion.

> Your adoring servant,
> Simon

He went that night down to Canal Street. He wrapped the note around a rock, just as he had seen described in certain romantic novels, and he sailed it through Lucy's open window. He couldn't have said how long he had to wait before there was some kind of response, but the waiting was extended and excruciating. Then he saw Lucy peek out of the window, and then the rock was returned, landing with a thud at his feet. Before he could look up to her again, the window was closed, the shades drawn.

He picked up the message in his trembling hands. If the news was poor, he did not see how he would be able to endure it. He read the note carefully, several times, before he would believe it.

If you wish,

the note read,

we can meet tomorrow at noon beside the fountain in Bienville Square.

Lucy

He was there at noon, his stiff white collar soaked with sweat. He waited the better part of an hour, pacing back and forth, hitting his palm with his fist, occasionally groaning so loudly that others turned to look. Just when he was about to give up hope, when he felt a full-bodied scream crawling up his throat, he saw her coming toward him, dressed in white, a white parasol shading her from the brutal midday sun.

"Lucy!" he cried. "Lucy!"

For a moment he felt so afraid that she would pass him by, as if he were something loathsome, or, worse than that, invisible. But then she was before him and he could look into her eyes, blue as lagoons.

"I didn't think you would come," he whispered hoarsely.

"I told you I would."

"But you're so late . . ."

"I had business."

He stared at her. "You don't know how I've missed you. Why, they wouldn't let me in to see you. Can you

imagine? I'll burn the house down if they try it again,
I swear I will, Lucy, I swear it. I'll blow the house into
a million . . ."

She put a finger up to his lips. "Don't talk so much,
Simon," she said.

He turned scarlet. "Am I a fool, Lucy? Someone
once told me I was."

She stroked his cheek. "I don't care what no one
says. You're fine, Simon, you're a fine man."

He kissed her hand passionately, and she let him do
so for a longer moment than she had planned.
"Madame Jewel says I ain't to see you no more. She
says you ain't right in the head."

"Lucy, it's not true . . ."

She laughed. "I told you I don't care. But what am
I gonna do? I got to make a living, don't I?"

"Lucy, I'll take care of you. I swear it!"

She shook her head. "You got yourself a wife, Simon.
Where you gonna get enough to set me up?"

"I will!" he cried fiercely. "Don't you worry where
it comes from."

She thought a moment. "It'll cost you to take me
away from Madame Jewel's. It'll cost you plenty."

"She doesn't own you."

"But she do, Simon. That's what I been telling
you. And it'll cost you plenty."

He grabbed her by the shoulders and kissed her
roughly. He didn't care who saw, he didn't care. "I'll
give her whatever she wants, Lucy. You're mine, and
you'll always be mine."

She kissed him lightly on the lips and on the chin.
"You know I want that to be true, Simon. Don't you
know it? Don't you just know it, honey?"

After they parted, with renewed promises of devotion, he went to the store and lifted the floorboard
on the landing of the stairs where he had hid a good
deal of money. It was money that came from two

sources: small embezzlements he had stolen in the course of making sales and the accumulation of the allowances Rebekah had given him to send home to his mother and brother. He had never sent these allowances. He figured that they must have managed, one way or another, to survive in his absence, and he figured that he owed them nothing after all his years of servitude in their behalf. Anyway he needed the money now every bit as much as they did.

He went to the Hotel Bay Terrace and asked the bartender where he could find a card game. The bartender gave him a time and an address. He walked quickly to his destination, his mind filled with anxious anticipation and vivid memories. It seemed that so much of his life was owed to chance and that all his luck, his very great luck, was followed by a wicked, crushing sort of retribution.

He won the game of cards. It was as he expected. He counted his money again and again, knowing deep within him that the money would buy nothing and that he would be lost again and again. Once more he went down to Canal Street and pounded on the door to Madame Jewel's house. The eye opened.

"Let me in," he whispered. "I've business to conduct."

The eye closed. Evidently Crocodile had gone to convey this message, and in a moment the door opened.

"Madame will see you," Crocodile announced.

He was taken to a bath. Madame Jewel sat in the midst of steam, wrapped head to toe in drenched towels.

"Dear gentleman," she said with a laugh. "So now you see one of my secrets. This here is how I purify myself."

"I've come to discuss business with you," he said stiffly.

"Begin then," she said. "There's always time for business so long as it's touched on either end by pleasure."

"I want Lucy."

"We all want Lucy," Madame Jewel said, sipping a milky substance from a goblet. "Lucy is beloved."

"I want her for myself."

"Why, that's selfishness, dear gentleman." Her egg-like eyes twinkled. "Not that there's a thing in the world wrong with selfishness. It's just that you have to pay for it."

"I'm prepared to do that, Madame Jewel."

"You'd best be well-prepared, dear gentleman. I raised Lucy, you know. Why, she was a fawn when she came here, and I turned her into a woman."

He removed a roll of bills from his pocket. "Will this do?" he asked.

She reached out a sweaty hand. He watched her count. "It could be more, sir, but I'm not one to stand in the way of romance." She laughed a little. "Why, you know what they say, dear gentleman? She who stands in the way of romance is sure to be plowed under. Take her, dear gentleman, but treat her right. She needs to be treated right, you know, 'cause she's a special thing."

"I love her, Madame Jewel."

"I don't care about that, sir. I just mean for you to treat her right."

He collected Lucy and her things. They ran from the house like elopers, and Lucy didn't even turn to wave good-bye to the girls who were hanging from the window.

"Will you miss them?" Simon asked.

"I don't care if they all die tomorrow," Lucy said, stinging like a wasp. "They're whores. That's all they is. They're whores."

*　*　*

* * *

He set her up in a house on the bay. It was a tiny house that caught the sun and the breezes both. She brought with her Whistle, the kitten, and he supplied a bed, a fine brass bed, two cane-backed chairs, an eating table, and a cherry-wood wardrobe.

"Is it as you wanted it, Lucy?" he pleaded to know.

She walked about the room, gingerly touching her new possessions. "It's real nice, Simon. Real nice."

"Then this will be our home?"

She ran to him, threw her arms around him, and kissed him passionately. "You love me," she cried. "Don't you? Don't you? Don't you?"

He pulled her down to the fine brass bed. Without another word they were wrapped up in each other, pushing and pulling each other toward something that seemed very great. When it was over, they held each other tightly, like survivors dazed and lost in the aftermath.

"Don't you never send me back to Madame Jewel's," she said suddenly, shattering the enormous silence.

"Oh, Lucy," he said, stroking her soft black hair. "Do you think I would do such a thing? Why, I'd die before that happened."

"Do you really love me, Simon?"

"Lucy, you know I do."

"I mean, am I more special to you than anyone else is?"

He kissed her hands—her palms and her knuckles and her wrists. "You've made me come alive, Lucy. You've shown me what happiness is."

She pulled the sheet around her and walked to the window. "I seen there once a ship, Simon. It was all lighted up and it looked to be goin' to some fine place, New Orleans I suppose. I wanted to be on that ship, Simon, and I didn't never want to come back."

"I know, Lucy, I know."

"Maybe we'll go somewhere, Simon. Louisville, Chi-

cago, New York even. Maybe we'll go and we won't
never come back."

He lay in silence, restless and immobilized at once.

"Ain't that what you wanna do, Simon?" she cried.

"If you say so, Lucy, if you say so."

CHAPTER ELEVEN

In the months since its inception Rebekah watched
the Weiss Store grow and become strong and take on
personality. In a way she regarded this period as an
infancy, full of expected weaknesses and resounding
strengths and a certain innate talent for survival. She
thrilled at its successes and denied its failures; she was
content to devote all of her energies to getting the
infant on its feet. For the moment she again put aside
her plans for a natural child. Things were still too
unsettled with Simon, and the further corrosion of his
sense of responsibility made it impossible for her to
be away from her duties.

She knew now that she was as smart as anyone who
had ever come to Mobile to seek his or her fortune.
She had established an alliance with Mobile's ladies
of society, and she used enough imagination and
salesmanship to convince them that what she had was,
indeed, what they wanted. She featured, in addition
to her by now renowned stock of fabrics, a line of
perfumes, colognes and bath soaps; a selection of fine
writing papers; excellent badger-bristle hairbrushes
and tortoiseshell combs; small delicate pins in the
shapes of moths and scarabs; fans from Spain and

Portugal; and any number of additional commodities that she felt might tickle the collective fancy of her ladies. In most cases she was startlingly, spectacularly correct.

"I can't think what Mobile did before you came along, Rebekah," Hattie Winslow said. "Why, everything you have is simply marvelous."

"And I have ladies of marvelous taste to cater to," Rebekah said diplomatically.

"Well, you know what you must do next," Hattie whispered confidentially.

"What?" Rebekah said, a bit wearied by the woman's eternal vigilance and self-appointed role as confidante.

"You must open a larger store in a better location."

Rebekah laughed. It seemed an utterly absurd recommendation. "But I've only just now come here. I couldn't begin to think of moving elsewhere."

"Choice location, my girl. When you have found it, then, for sure, you will be on the road to success."

Hattie Winslow's suggestion confused her. That night, when Simon finally arrived home, she made an effort to discuss it with him.

"Hattie Winslow says we should find ourselves a choice location," she began. "Caroline Street is not choice. She says we should be on Government or nearer to it."

"I don't give a fig what Hattie Winslow's got to say!" Simon cried. She could see that he had a few drinks in him, and even though she was used to this sort of thing, she had to work to control her anger.

"*I* care, Simon," she said. "*I* care what Hattie Winslow has to say. Hattie Winslow just happens to be the most important connection I have in this city."

"I'm sick of hearing about your money and your plans and your connections. You're like a machine, nothing more, nothing less."

"It's easy for a drunkard to call names, isn't it, Simon?"

"I'm not drunk!" he shouted. "Do you think because a man wants to enjoy life, it means he's a drunkard?"

She laughed at him as though he were a fool. "What a liar you are, what a shameless liar. All you want to do is drink and keep women on the side, and I'm to support your filthy habits. Well, that's all right, I suppose. I mean, I don't care what you do, but then I don't know why I bother to ask your opinion of anything. Your opinions count for nothing."

"Watch your words, Rebekah, or you'll be very sorry."

"I have no words for you, Simon. The less I see of you or talk to you, the better."

"Just don't try to do anything without first talking to me."

"Don't be ridiculous. What do I care for your opinions? Do you have money? Or do you spend it right and left on your whiskey and your whores? Every time you come to me for extra money and I give it to you, that's money I could be using to buy you out. And that's what I'm going to do, Simon. I'm going to buy you out and that will be the end of your sucking off of me."

"We'll see who it will be the end of, Rebekah. Your pride will be the end of you, that's for certain. Just listen to me, Rebekah. Whatever you do to me, you do to yourself."

He said exactly what she was defenseless against, this sense of bonding that hung over them, regardless of everything. "But where are we going, Simon? Tell me, what are we going to do?"

"It's all right, Rebekah. Just don't ask so many questions."

She laughed desperately, not knowing what else to

do. "But you won't even give me a baby, Simon. And that's all I've ever asked you for, isn't it?"

"But we have time, Rebekah. We have all the time in the world."

She had resolved to make her own plans. She was intent on moving up, on becoming richer and better placed and well heeled. There was an obvious first move, which was to get out of the stifling little apartment above the store. She needed, or she thought she needed, a place where she could entertain, a place with an entrance gallery and a parlor and a second-story balcony. She couldn't help but enjoy a secret little laugh at the thought of it. She was moving quickly, thrillingly, dizzyingly, and yet she wasn't even afraid of falling.

One day, when Hattie Winslow was in the store, Rebekah made them a cup of tea and listened to the gossip that she couldn't have cared less about and watched Hattie eat butter biscuits one after the other and waited for her turn to speak. When it came, toward the end of their meeting, Rebekah was careful about what she had to say and how she said it.

"Mrs. Winslow," she said. "Tell me something, will you?"

"Of course, my dear."

"I want a house," she said. "Where shall I get one?"

"Well, of course you do. I imagine those are rather cramped quarters you've got at the moment." She sipped from the tea and knitted her brow. "Now let me think," she said. "Where is a good place for people like you to live?"

Rebekah felt herself tighten at the woman's words. *People like you.* What did Hattie Winslow mean, and if she meant what Rebekah thought she meant, then how dare she.

"What about Spring Hill?" Rebekah asked boldly.

Hattie's eyes widened. "Well, my dear, I don't think you'd want to live in Spring Hill."

"It is lovely, isn't it?"

"Yes, of course, but . . ."

"And I've not stopped hearing about how healthful the climate is."

Hattie Winslow's wide, red mouth narrowed into a frown. "You're in a bit of a hurry, aren't you, Rebekah?"

Rebekah rested the cup and saucer on her knee. "I just want a place I can love," she said.

"There are lots of places waiting to be loved."

"Then you know of nothing?" Rebekah said.

"Nothing," Hattie replied. "Absolutely nothing."

She would not rely on Hattie Winslow's assistance. She began to take carriage rides up in the Spring Hill area. It was a place of beauty, smelling of pine and the sea, and she knew right away that it was what she wanted. The homes were all beautiful, with expansive lawns and clusters of magnolia and tulip trees, and she could see toddlers in white gowns playing on the bright green lawns. It was what she wanted. A home and a place for her child. The fact that Simon made all of that difficult was something she put in the back of her mind.

There was one house that she noticed particularly. It was a fine white colonnaded structure, with a broad expanse of lawn and six-foot hedges surrounding it. It was a wonderful house, but it was not too grand a house. She could live in a house such as this without feeling like an interloper, or so she thought.

"Whose house is this?" she asked the driver.

"That there's the Pomeroy house," said the driver. "Saffron Hill."

"Who are the Pomeroys?"

"Oh, dey's grand folks, dey say, but dey don't live dere no more. Dey live in de small house down de road."

It turned out that the Pomeroys, an old and revered Mobile family, had suffered serious financial reversals that made Saffron Hill available. The price that they were asking was within the range that Rebekah had set for herself, and in a few meetings all the issues were resolved.

"We hope you'll treat Saffron Hill well," said Mrs. Pomeroy when Rebekah came over to sign the deed.

It was obvious that they had not wanted to sell to a Jew, even though they might like and need her money. Rebekah stared at the old woman who looked back at her as though she were some strange, almost inhuman species that she had never seen before and that she didn't particularly appreciate.

"I'll do my best, Mrs. Pomeroy," Rebekah replied.

"Saffron Hill has great meaning for us," Colonel Pomeroy cautioned.

"And I'm sure that it will have great meaning for me," Rebekah said tartly. As she signed the various papers, she glanced up and saw the faces of the old people, ashen, shocked by this cruel turn of fate that the events of the day had created. "Then I suppose that's all there is?" Rebekah asked.

"Yes. It seems so," Colonel Pomeroy replied.

"Very good," Rebekah said, rising and gathering her things. "Thank you again, and I shall inform you when I plan to take occupancy."

As she rode away, she turned back and saw Saffron Hill standing proudly on its knoll. It was hers now and, with it, came a position of importance in Spring Hill and Mobile at large. With the purchase of Saffron Hill she had completed the first stage of her arrival.

Simon held the deed in his hand. His face had an ugly, bilious look, and he held the back of his neck as though there were a very severe pain there.

"So you've gone and done it, have you?" he said.

"Yes. And what of it?"

"What of it?" he shouted.

"Keep your voice down," she warned. "I won't have everyone knowing what a common thing you are."

"Lady Weiss speaking," he snapped. "The countess of the *shtetl*. My, what a long way we've come."

"Some of us anyway."

"Don't you know you're a joke?" he asked. "The little yid shopkeeper moving up to Spring Hill. You may know how to make money, but you certainly don't know what the wise thing to do with it is."

"Perhaps you're right. Perhaps I should be out spending it on whores and gambling and liquor."

"You've developed quite a sharp tongue, haven't you, Rebekah?"

"I've had to," she said.

"How could you go out and do this without consulting me?" he demanded to know.

She laughed. "You're absurd," she said. "Whatever made you think for a moment that I would consult you."

"I'm still your husband!"

"In name only."

"That's enough," he warned her. "Don't say any more."

"In name only!" she repeated tauntingly. "You haven't done anything a husband should do. You don't earn a cent of what you pull out of the business, and you don't even have what's needed to give me a baby."

He would have liked to smash her face just then, but he controlled himself. "You? Have a baby? What kind of a mother would you be? Do you think there would be a drop of milk in your breasts? My God, if they're as dry as the rest of you . . ."

"Shut up!" she screamed.

"Keep your voice down," he said, parodying her. "I don't want everyone knowing what a common thing you are."

"Listen to me, Simon. I'm moving to Saffron Hill

whether you like it or not. If you want to join me there, I'm sure I can find you your own room. If not, that's all right too."

"What are you saying, Rebekah?"

"The same thing I've been saying for years now. If you want to end things, I'm telling you that I'm ready to do so."

There was an extended silence during which they examined each other closely.

"Did you ever love anyone, Rebekah?"

"Yes, before you came along I did." She felt like her face was on fire, that was how furious she was. "I know what love is and I know what the absence of it is. Do you have any more questions for me, Simon?"

"I don't think you know what love is, Rebekah."

"What is it, Simon?" she cried. "Is it something that's hard to find? Or can you buy it from a whore?"

"You may be successful at your business, Rebekah, but you're a failure as a wife just as you were a failure as a daughter and as a sister and as a Jew and as a woman. Just as you would be a failure as a mother. That's why I won't sleep with you, Rebekah, do you understand?"

She stared at him. "Get out," she said.

"Go move to Saffron Hill. Be a fine mistress. Because that's all you'll ever be—a mistress to a house."

"Get out!" she screamed.

He took his hat and walked toward the door. "Goodbye for now, Rebekah," he murmured.

As he closed the door, she seized a small china vase and hurled it in his path, smashing it into a great many pieces. The action brought to mind something that she had done so very long ago, so far in the past that it seemed to belong to another life altogether at the very moment that it expressed the present. She thought back to that time, in her father's house at Korneuberg, when she hurled her mother's bone china teacup at Simon's head and when, afterward, she lay holding the broken pieces, weeping at how she had punished herself.

She wouldn't punish herself again. And she wouldn't let Simon punish her. She would do what she wanted to do. She had done what she wanted to do. She had bought Saffron Hill, and now she would turn it into her home.

There was not so very much to move. They had not managed to acquire such a great many possessions. And so at first Saffron Hill would be rather a bare place, compared at least to its previous incarnations.

Wearing her smock and a bandanna, Rebekah supervised the move and ensured that none of her crockery and goblets were lost. Like all good, hard labor she relished the work involved, and the servants she had retained with the estate had never seen the like before.

"She right out there now, lifting things and all," said Sophronia to Eulalie, the cook.

"Oh my, it ain't right now, is it, Sophronia?" Eulalie said, always deferential to the sleek yellow-skinned maid.

"It ain't for us to speak at it," said Hamlin, the butler, an ancient white-haired Negro whose power in the household was being steadily eclipsed by Sophronia.

"We can all speak if we wants to," said Dover, the houseboy, Eulalie's nephew and an unreformed firebrand ever since the granting of freedoms.

"Hush up!" Eulalie cried, shaking a wooden spoon at the boy. "Don't you go talkin' back to your elders, you hear?"

"Let the boy talk," Sophronia admonished. "This Dover boy, he got to speak if he wants to."

Eulalie, fat and forever earthbound, fairly quivered in response. "If you say so, Sophronia," she muttered.

At that point Rebekah burst into the servant's

quarters. "Why are you all standing around down here?" she demanded to know. "Can't you see how much work there is to be done?"

They all stared at her, shocked and resentful of her tone. She herself didn't know what to make of them. She had never before had servants, and their presence frightened her. Her initial impulse was to do without them, but of course that would have been impossible. The workings of the house were far too complicated to be undertaken independently, and she would have been unwise to try to assemble a staff of her own. Besides the Pomeroys had recommended them unstintingly, and Rebekah received the impression that the sale was conditional upon her acceptance of this retinue. The fact remained, however, that the prospect of four in help frightened her beyond measure. She was not only reluctant to give orders, but she was terrified by the fact that she did not know what orders to give. She had enough innate business acumen to know that employees will find and exploit an employer's weaknesses. Already she could feel herself being sized up and failing the test.

"I want everything cleaned," she said. "I want the floors and walls scrubbed and the windows washed and the curtains washed and everything hung out to air."

They all continued to stare until Sophronia finally spoke. "We shall begin then, missus," Sophronia announced.

"Good," Rebekah replied with a firm, businesslike nod.

She felt as though she had won the first round, and was inordinately pleased with herself. But as the day progressed, she discovered that little was being done. Everything was proceeding with incredible and inexplicable slowness. Accidents occurred far in excess of their normal rate. A freshly polished floor was suddenly inundated by a spilled bucket. A dustpan un-

leashed its contents on a newly laundered slipcover. A
fire broke out in the kitchen. All of the perpetrators
were appropriately guilty, but she wasn't fooled. What
did they take her for, after all? Did they take her for a
fool? She knew perfectly well what they were up to,
and she was furious with them, but she wasn't at all
sure what course to take. She realized that they thought
of her as an interloper, an upstart, a strange foreign
species called Jew. It wasn't that she couldn't understand where their thoughts were, it was just that she
hated them for making these difficult times more difficult. And, hating them, she found herself too confused
to act in any firm, decisive way.

"Can't you move any faster?" she screamed at Hamlin, who was very old and unused to the difficult tasks
she was setting for him.

"No, missus," the old man replied, very close to
tears. "I cannot."

She looked around and saw the shocked, vindicated
faces of Sophronia and Eulalie and Dover. "I . . . I'm
sorry, Hamlin," she said, and then, defiantly to the
rest of them, "I will be in the parlor if you need me."

She locked the parlor door behind her and began to
cry out of sheer frustration and rage. They were beating her. Soundly and surely with all of their tricks
they were beating her. It wasn't fair that she had to go
through it all on her own. If Simon was unwilling to
share this life with her, then at least she deserved to
find someone who was. The way things were going
now, her stay at Saffron Hill could very well be over
before it began. If she was forced to fire the servants,
they would see to it that she didn't get anyone to replace them or else that she had only the very bottom
of the barrel from which to choose.

After a few hours of having sequestered herself in
the upstairs parlor, she unlocked the door and heard
a rush of gay laughter issuing from downstairs. She
had two choices: she could either explode in fury or

she could seek to negotiate. By necessity, and by virtue of her overriding intelligence, she chose the latter.

"Sophronia," she called, "may I speak with you?"

"There was a break in the laughter. "Yes, missus," answered a cool, remote voice.

This was the power behind the conspiracy, and as Sophronia climbed the stairs, Rebekah felt suddenly afraid and wholly ineffectual.

"You called for me, missus?" Sophronia asked in a voice that managed to be deferential and aggressive at once.

"Yes, I did, Sophronia. Please sit down."

"I prefer to stand, missus," the maid replied.

Again Rebekah felt her anger course through her. Again the help was telling her the rules in the rudest way possible. "Yes, of course," Rebekah said, controlling her anger, putting it away for some future time.

There was a long awkward silence. "Missus?" Sophronia said, breaking the silence abruptly.

"I think you know what I want," Rebekah said softly.

There was a pause, and then "Missus?" the woman repeated maddeningly.

"I know you know what I want, Sophronia," Rebekah said firmly. "You're smart. The others look up to you."

"They do?" she said coolly. Rebekah wanted to slap her. Everything about her was cool and strictly measured and hard as flint. One got the feeling that she could walk through fire or handle snakes or test ground glass against her tongue. But she had her strengths too, Rebekah thought, and, if need be, she would pit herself against anyone.

"Yes, Sophronia," she said finally. "They do and you know they do and I want your help."

"But, missus, I been workin' all day like the others. I been helpin' you. I do what you tell me, don't I?"

"Stop it!' Rebekah cried and then, when she saw Sophronia's cold, vengeful face, she knew she had lost ground, and she quickly sought to rebuild her bridges. "I know you don't understand what I'm doing here," she said. "I know you're all convinced that this isn't my place. But let me tell you something, Sophronia. I have as much of a right to be here as anyone does. Do you understand?"

Sophronia glared at Rebekah. "And what you gonna do if we leave? We's freed, you know. We don't got to stay nowheres we don't want to."

"I know that," Rebekah said. "And if you leave, I'll be in trouble. I don't know how this house works and I'll have to find people to show me and it will be hard but I'll do it."

"It'll be real hard," Sophronia laughed.

"But I'll do it." She paused a moment. "Of course if you stay, it will be easier."

"Why should we make it easy for you?" Sophronia challenged.

"Because I'll reward you for it! Do you want to be free? Really free? Well, so do I. That's what my whole life is about. And being free means money."

"Dat's what bein' free means?" the woman replied sarcastically.

"Yes, that's what it means. It means money, lots of it, and that's what I'm going to have and if you want some of it, then you'd better well stick around."

Sophronia stared at her and Rebekah watched the expression change. The hauteur that had seemed so implacable appeared to be dissipating.

"Well?" Rebekah cried.

"We do our best," Sophronia murmured.

"Do you mean it?"

The yellow-skinned woman thought a moment. "Yes," she said.

Rebekah watched Sophronia leave the room. When once again she was alone, she felt herself begin to tremble. As difficult as it was, she had won. The victory was hers. Now they would all fall into line, and she would make the house work as she had made the store work.

She went into her room and took out a small chamois pouch that held her most precious belongings. She took out a small lozenge-shaped object and held it in her hand. It was time, she thought. She went downstairs and saw her servants now at busy and productive work.

"Hamlin," she called.

"Yes, missus?"

"Get a hammer and nails and come with me."

He did as she said, and together they went to the front door. She opened her palm, and she watched him stare at a foreign and enigmatic object.

"It's a mezuzah," she said.

He shook his head.

"It is my faith," she explained.

Now he nodded and smiled broadly. Obviously he assumed it was some kind of a talisman, and that much he could appreciate.

"Nail it up there, Hamlin," she said, pointing to a spot on the frame of the door. "Nail it up good and tight."

She watched as he followed her orders, and in a moment the mezuzah was secured. She put a kiss to her hand, and then she touched her hand to the mezuzah. "Now it's mine," she whispered to no one in particular, and she didn't care who heard.

She had her fine house and so of course she wanted to celebrate it with something special. It had been enough time to pull the house into working order, and the lack of expensive furnishings did not deter her from wanting to entertain. She would give a small special dinner, for Hattie Winslow and Hattie's sister, Mrs. Garden and her husband, and Miss Sarah Warren, another of her steady customers, and Mr. and Mrs. Benson, the former of whom was the lawyer who had arranged for the sale of Saffron Hill, and, of course, the Pomeroys, and, of course, Simon and herself.

"Simon," she said one day in the store. "I am giving a dinner a month from this Sunday. I want you to make sure and be there."

"I am sorry," he said. "I believe I have an appointment a month from Sunday."

"All right, Simon. It's a clever little joke, but listen to me. I want you at that party."

"And if I don't come?"

"You will come, Simon. I don't much care what you do with yourself, but this just happens to be business. And it's important business. In the eyes of Mobile you and I are still husband and wife, and so when I entertain, you are to act as the host."

"*In the eyes of Mobile,*" he repeated after her in a mocking, sententious voice, and then he shrugged. "Whatever you say, Rebekah, my dear wife, my companion."

She worked furiously for the month before the party. She turned yards of fabric into draperies; she had the entrance gallery papered; she painted the hallways a sky blue. She labored to turn Saffron Hill into a real and estimable home, if not quite a showplace.

"My dear," Hattie said to her one day in the store, having ostensibly made the trip in for some needles and pins, "don't you think you're overburdening yourself just a bit?"

"What do you mean, Mrs. Winslow?"

"Well, it's just that you've so recently arrived at Saffron Hill. I'm afraid that this party you've proposed will prove far too taxing."

"Not at all, Mrs. Winslow. You know what kind of energy I have. Look around you. You see what I've done here. And that's what I want to do up on Saffron Hill."

"Don't give the party, Rebekah," Hattie said with sudden gravity.

"I don't understand."

The two women stared at each other, and then Hattie, weakening her resolve, smiled apologetically. "I'm just concerned," she said. "I don't want to see you worn out."

After Hattie left, Rebekah experienced an unsettled feeling in the pit of her stomach. Something was very wrong. What Hattie was expressing was not concern, but something far more cautionary with tinges of the ominous. What could it be about? Was Hattie upset because Rebekah had acted independently and shown herself to be less reliant on the older woman's judgment and advice? If so, what would be the ramifications in a relationship that she herself did not fully understand.

The day of the party arrived. With Eulalie's guidance a fine menu was planned, with crab bisque, saddle of lamb in Madeira sauce, duchesse potatoes, glazed carrots, fruit, Lane cake, port and brandies. She gave Eulalie, a renowned cook, total freedom in the kitchen. When she was told about the crab bisque, her first reaction was a profound shame and nausea. It was wrong, what she was doing, all very wrong. She was wandering too far from where she had begun, and she had the undeniable, inbred conviction that she would pay for her wrongs. But what was she doing? She was merely trying to survive; that was why she had to transgress and go against everything she was taught. She paused a moment in her thinking. It was untrue; everything she said was untrue. She was not trying to survive; she was looking to prosper and emerge triumphant, and it was to this end that she was willing to compromise her beliefs.

She sat at her dressing table, made desolate by this

realization. She had had Sophronia lay out the emerald silk gown, and now she looked at it blankly, not quite knowing what to do with it. She wished the idea of the party had never entered her head; again she felt that unsettled feeling as though something very wrong were scheduled to occur.

She heard a knock on the door. "Who's there?" she called.

"Simon."

"Oh. Come in."

He entered, dressed in his evening clothes, and she was shocked at how attractive they made him look. He appeared robust and confident, even rakish, and by the smile on his face, she could tell that he knew it.

"You look very well," she allowed.

"Thank you."

"Life away from me must agree with you."

"Let's not begin on that note, Rebekah."

"What note? You're being terribly sensitive, aren't you, Simon?"

"And you're terribly nervous, aren't you?"

"Oh, that's ridiculous. I'm not at all . . ."

"Of course you're nervous. You've got a lot at stake here. This is your debut as a hostess, after all, and all your connections are coming."

"I see there's a drink in your hand already," she accused.

"What of it? It's a party, isn't it?"

"Yes, it's a party. It just doesn't happen to be that kind of a party."

He laughed. "I can't imagine what kind of a party is not that kind of a party."

"I'm warning you, Simon. You had just better be on your best behavior."

He bowed. "Very well, madame. I shall be a perfect host."

They went downstairs. It was seven o'clock; the party was called for eight.

"There been a message delivered, Miz Rebekah," Hamlin said. "Here 'tis."

She opened it quickly. She had to read it several times before she could accept its news.

Dear Mrs. Weiss,

it read,

> Mr. Benson has been called to the capital on an urgent matter, and we regret that we will not be able to attend your gathering this evening.
>
> With profound apology,
> Mrs. William Carl Benson

This was the lawyer and his wife; she still could not believe it. So close to the time of the party. She could not believe how rude it was.

"What's the matter?" Simon said on his fourth drink of the evening.

"It's the Bensons. There's an urgent matter in the capital."

"And they can't come?"

"No."

"I see," Simon said.

"Well, you know how unsettled the life of an attorney is," Rebekah said desperately, ludicrously.

Simon nodded.

By seven thirty two other cancellations had arrived. The Gardens begged off, claiming a sick relative, and Miss Sarah Warren sent a cryptic note alluding to the climate, which was a bit humid but otherwise uneventful.

"The bastards," Simon said, feeling the liquor, liking the feeling of the liquor.

"Stop it!" she said. "You don't understand. It's all a terrible series of coincidences."

"Oh, Rebekah. You little fool. Are you blind? Can't you see what they're doing to you?"

"Stop it!" she cried. She felt the room spin around her, and her face burned with a humiliation of the most dreadful sort. She was en route to becoming an utter mockery. The servants, darting in and out of rooms with bowls of relish and jellies and condiments, sneaked covert looks at their mistress and at each other. She wanted to scream at them to stop. Couldn't they see that there was no party? Or were they just bringing out more and more things to emphasize the fact that she had been made to look a fool.

At ten minutes to eight, the doorbell rang again. It was Jonas, Hattie Winslow's man, bearing the one last, inevitable message.

She held the envelope in her hand, not wanting to go through with the act of reading it.

"Aren't you going to open it?" Simon asked.

She wished to God he wasn't here. She wished he would disappear as he had done so many times before.

"Come on," he goaded. "You'll have to read it sooner or later."

She ripped open the letter. At first the words were all a blur, but somehow she managed to focus.

Dear Rebekah,

she read,

I am not well. What ails me is something I cannot easily explain. I know what disappointment I must be causing you and truly I am sorry for it. Truly, Rebekah, I would have given anything to avert this.

With sincere regret,
Mrs. George Winslow

* * *

She found herself shaking with rage and then she ripped the message into many ragged pieces.

"What is it?" Simon said.

"What do you think?" she cried bitterly.

"Oh no," he laughed. "Not your benefactress. Not Hattie Winslow herself."

"Stop laughing!" she screamed. He was tormenting her, and she couldn't bear it.

"What a fool you are!" he said, still weary with laughter. "My God, have you no sense of what you can and can't do? It's bad enough in the eyes of these people that you brought into Spring Hill. Do you expect them to endorse your occupancy by coming to this party?"

"But Hattie," Rebekah cried. "She's been a friend."

"Stop it!" he snapped. "You haven't any friends. You have no one."

The absolute rightness of what he said positively stunned her. "No," she said feebly, "it isn't true."

"You have no one," Simon repeated mercilessly.

She ran up the stairs, past the servants, into her room, which she bolted against intruders. She didn't know what she wanted to do—to cry or to scream or to throw something in utter rage. By the time she considered each option, the respective emotion had shifted and so, ultimately, she was left sitting on the edge of the bed, feeling tricked, feeling drained, feeling she had so much anger and need in her that she must suppress them altogether or surely she would be swept away by them.

In the wake of this debacle she thought again of what Simon had said. She was alone. It was a fact and, as such, she could begin to deal with it. She had the store and she had Saffron Hill, but the fact remained that she was alone. She had no child, no friends, no lover, and no one but herself on whom she could rely. The realization, large and dark as a storm cloud, was interrupted by a single point of light. Somewhere in this city was a man who had once been kind to her.

CHAPTER TWELVE

They knew her well at the bank; they treated her like a queen even at the same time that they whispered of her Jewishness, or so she thought. Her bank account grew and grew, and in her mind she was resolved to follow Hattie Winslow's advice. She would find a choice location, and she would turn the Weiss Store into something bigger than anyone had ever thought possible. She would, one day, make Mobile bow down to her and kiss the hem of her skirt. She had not suffered her humiliation lightly, and much of her thought was focused on revenge.

At other points, however, she tired of her thirst for revenge, and she sought to put these feelings aside. But it was an enormously difficult thing to do, and many nights she wandered the hallways of Saffron Hill, feeling utterly alone, lost, and unable to find some relief in sleep. Some nights she went to sit in the library and held in her lap the chamois pouch filled with precious mementos, and she took from it the things that made her feel close to other human beings: letters from her sister Sarah and her mother's garnet brooch and her mother's gold-leaf prayer book. She turned to the passage from Genesis that had always held special meaning for her:

* * *

And they blessed Rebekah, and said unto her,
Our sister, be thou the mother of thousands of
myriads, and let thy seed possess the gate of those
who hate them.

Sometimes the passage helped her through the night,
reminding her of a home where the Sabbath was
observed, where candles were lighted on Friday nights,
where the cupboards were dusted with a feather in
preparation for Passover. She could smell the scents
of freshly baked *challah* and the bracing harshness of
the bitter herbs that were grated for the Passover seder.
She had, in her heart, a great longing for a home, a
Jewish home. And that meant more than a house, because here, in Saffron Hill, she had a fine house in
deed. It meant having a family; it meant a mutual
exchange of respect and affection; it meant a sharing
of her life.

On one such troubled night she fell asleep waiting
for Simon to come home. She dreamed that she had
climbed the great old chestnut tree that stood beside
her father's house. She sat in the chestnut tree, and
she could see the nests of birds and, beyond, she could
see miles and miles to the mountains at the horizon.
She was all alone in the chestnut tree and it was spring
and the world was a blooming, verdant place. She
heard someone calling her name. "Rebekah!" she
heard. "Rebekah!" It was her sister Sarah. Well, she
would be naughty, and she would hide in the tree
until they found her. But then, in a moment, the calls
became hoarse, fierce cries, full of anguish, and she
could see bright, barbed flames coming from the windows of her father's house. "Father!" she shrieked.
"Sarah!" And then she saw her father run from the
house, all aflame, his clothes on fire, his beard aflame,
and she could see Sarah's burning face at the window
and then everything was in flames and she could not

come down from the tree and she was trapped there, smelling the smoke, screaming for her life.

She woke up screaming in the red plush chair in the library. Her body was soaked with sweat. The house seemed to her filled with smoke, and she rang the bell wildly. In a moment Sophronia was at the door.

"Yes, Miz Rebekah?"

"There's a fire!" she cried. "Don't you smell the smoke?"

"Dere ain't no fire, Miz Rebekah," Sophronia replied.

Rebekah studied the woman. She was not someone to be trusted. In the months that they had known each other, there had been no increase of warmth. Sophronia performed her duties and performed them well, but it was evident that she had still not accepted Rebekah and might never do so.

"But there's smoke!"

"No, Miz Rebekah, there ain't no smoke. Come and see," she said, taking her by the arm and leading her out to the hallway. "You see."

"But I smelled smoke . . ."

"It must have been a dream," Sophronia said, the slightest suggestion of a smile on her lips.

"Oh, Sophronia," she moaned. "Oh, it was so real . . ."

Sophronia went to make her a soothing drink. She didn't want to be alone. She felt at any moment that she might lose control, that she might hang from the window and scream for help. In just a few moments Sophronia had returned, however, and she set the cup and saucer on the desk.

"Is that all for now, Miz Rebekah?" Sophronia asked without any trace of compassion.

"Yes, Sophronia," she replied with undisguised bitterness. "That will be all for now."

The cup of spiked tea did manage to soothe her a

bit. When she heard Simon come in, she went to his room and stood there.

"Yes?" he said, yawning boldly.

"I don't care where you've been or what you've done," she said in a voice that she hoped conveyed the honesty she felt. "I just want a baby."

"I see," he laughed. "Is that all?"

"Please, Simon. I need you. You've got to help me."

"Why?" he asked, his voice ironic.

"Why are you hurting me? All I'm asking for is a child. I'm so tired of being alone, Simon. I'm so scared of being alone. Why won't you help me? I've never wanted harm to come to you, you know that, don't you?"

"You have the store. That's your child."

"It's not!" she screamed. "You want me to be unhappy. It's unbelievable to me, but it's true. You have an investment in my being unhappy. Everything that's disappointed you, all your crazy broken dreams—you know you're not what you thought you'd be and you want me to take the blame and you want me to be punished. Just as with Clara."

He closed his eyes and put his hands up to his ears. "Don't say her name, do you hear me?"

"Clara! Clara! Clara!" she screamed, wanting to hurt him as he had hurt her.

He rose from the bed and started toward the door.

"Where are you going?" she cried.

"Away. I'm going away."

She flung herself at him, at first in rage, and then her need overcame her. "Oh, Simon. Don't go. I beg of you. Stay here with me. I'll go mad if I'm alone again."

"But you've got Saffron Hill, haven't you? You've got the store, haven't you?"

"I'm a person," she whispered. "I'm a woman. I want you to give me my child. There is a child that is mine to have, and you have to give it to me."

His face took on an expression that was somewhere between anguish and irritation. He tried to pull away from her, but she held to him tightly.

"I beg of you, Simon," she wept.

Something in her words—the pathetic supplication perhaps—managed to please him or at least to seize his attention. He grabbed two fistfuls of hair and looked at her stricken white face.

"You beg of me?" he said.

Her lips parted slightly.

"Let me hear you beg," he ordered her, eager to see her degradation.

"Don't, Simon . . ."

He pushed her down to her knees. "Now beg, you bitch. Beg for me."

She looked up at his cruel face. "I beg of you," she said flatly.

He pressed her face against his genitals, and she cried out. "Pig!" she gasped, rising to her feet.

He grabbed her and pulled her back down to the bed. "You bitch," he cried, smacking at her, tearing at her clothing.

"Oh God," she whispered. He hated her; he wanted to hurt her. She let him take her clothes off; she didn't know why; she supposed that she would be getting what she wanted; she supposed that this degradation would be worth it.

"There," he said, when he had finished. "There's your baby."

She rose to a sitting position in the bed. She looked at Simon's naked, sweating body. This was the man she was trying to make the father of her child. She felt filthy and violated and cold.

"Get out, Simon," she said suddenly.

"What?"

"You heard me. I said get out. Get out of Saffron Hill and don't come back. Saffron Hill is mine. It isn't yours, and I don't want you here. I've let you abuse me long enough."

His stunned face registered the strength of her words and motivated her to go on.

"Go to your whores," she cried. "Just get out of my life. I don't want you as my husband, and I don't want you as the father of my child. I'd rather be alone for a thousand years than spend another moment with you."

"It's not that easy, you know," he replied. "You owe me something."

"Nothing! I owe you nothing!"

"You owe me something, and I promise you, I'll collect."

"Just get out!" she screamed. "Get out now or I'll have the servants throw you out."

"That won't be necessary, Rebekah." He rose from the bed and began to pull on some clothes and throw some others into a bag. "I'll send for the rest of my things," he said.

"Just get out," she said again, wanting him swept up and whisked away like a clot of dust.

She watched him walk toward the door, and then he turned. "No parting words?" he asked, his voice a fusion of sarcasm and sadness.

She remained silent, saying nothing, giving nothing, knowing that this was not yet the end.

Simon sat with his beloved Lucy at their favorite spot in Bienville Square. It was quite a sunny day; Lucy wore a picture hat to shade her eyes. Each of them sipped a lemonade, and Lucy sucked on a peppermint candy that Simon had provided for her. At such moments she looked like a child. The fact was that she was only seventeen years old and that Simon was easily old enough to be her father. Consequently a thread of paternalism ran through their relationship. Simon catered to Lucy more than the other way around. When Lucy wanted tea, it was Simon who made it for her; when she wanted candy, it was Simon who dug into his pockets. Lucy was his pet, and, even when she was naughty, he delighted in her more than he had ever done so with any single thing in his life.

"Oh, Simon," she cried, clutching his hand. "Look at that lovely dress right there. Have you ever seen a prettier thing?"

He smiled. "I think it's from the store."

"Really, Simon? Oh, that peach silk—it's so lovely —imagine how it'd look on me. Oh, will you get it for me, Simon?"

Now he laughed. "Lucy, what am I to do with you? You really are a child."

"But can I have the dress, Simon? You can ask Rebekah for it. She'll let you have it."

"Oh yes. Of course she will. After two weeks without a word between us." He sighed. "No, Lucy, I'm afraid you won't have that dress, at least not for a while anyway."

Her exquisitely carved lips pursed into a frown.

"Oh, Lucy."

She shook her curly-haired head.

"Now, really," Simon chastised. "This is inexcusable behavior."

"You never want to get me nothing pretty," she sulked.

"This is becoming more outrageous with each word," he said. "I couldn't begin to calculate what I've spent on you. Just what it cost me to get you away from Madame Jewel almost wiped me out altogether."

"I don't care about all that," she said.

His shaky hand went up to his brow. "Madame Jewel said you were an expensive habit," he recalled with some bitterness. "She never said, though, that you could be ruinous."

"If you don't want to buy me pretty things, then

how can I be happy?" she said maddeningly. "And if I ain't happy, then how am I gonna make you happy?"

"I don't have that kind of money just now, Lucy. Is that so impossible for you to understand?"

"Yes," she cried. "I don't understand."

"Well then, what shall we do?"

"I don't know," she said coldly. "You'd best find some way to make that money."

"I thought you loved me, Lucy," he said accusingly. "I thought I was more to you than all the others."

"You are, Simon," she said, a bit annoyed, not understanding what all the confusion was about. "I just can't figure out why you wanted me to leave Madame Jewel's when you couldn't give me the things I want."

"You're very selfish, Lucy," he reprimanded her. "Don't you think I'd do anything to give you what you wanted? It's just that I have to find a place for myself in this town. Then, when I'm on the right track, we can begin to discuss buying dresses and hats and such things."

"When will that be?" she demanded to know.

He looked into her beautiful dark face. Dark girls can be very naughty, he heard Madame Jewel say. "Are you in such a very great hurry?" he said. "Is there nothing else that I can give you?"

Her petulant expression changed into something dreamy and far away. "Madame Jewel said I was made for beautiful things. She said, 'Lucy, you are a princess born outside the realm.' You know what it means, Simon?"

"No," he said grimly.

"I didn't neither," she admitted, "so I says to her, 'What you mean, Madame Jewel?' And she looks to me and smiles real nice and she says, 'Wherever you go, Lucy, you be a princess.'"

He realized that Lucy regarded her life as a fairy tale and that an insidious process of delusion had infected her. "What shall I do, Lucy?" he said. "Tell me what to do and I'll do it."

She thought a moment, and then she spoke. "Couldn't you go back to the store?" she wondered.

He shook his head violently.

"You was making lots of money when you worked in the store."

"Is that what you want for me, Lucy?" he said disbelievingly.

"Well, what was wrong with the store?" she demanded to know. "You didn't even have to work so hard. Your wife did all the work, didn't she? Didn't Rebekah do all the work?"

"Shut up!" he cried. "Don't you go calling her Rebekah! Who are you to be calling her Rebekah?"

The beautiful heart-shaped face paled, and her lower lip quivered in anticipation of tears.

"I . . . I'm sorry, Lucy."

"You don't love me," she moaned. "You says you do, but I don't believe it. If you loved me, you'd want me to be happy."

"What about me? Don't I count for anything?"

"I never made no promises to you," she said. "I never promised you nothing, did I?"

No, she never did. And if she had, he would have been a fool to believe her for even a moment. Sometimes he felt that Lucy wasn't a real person, and that even though he could feel her flesh and the pumping of her heart, it was not inconceivable to think of her vanishing into thin air.

He reached for her smooth and slender hand. He thought of the time that they had had together in the little house on the waterfront. "It's not the end of our great adventure, is it, Lucy?" he asked, feeling thwarted again, feeling disappointed, feeling tired and beaten and broken.

"What adventure?" she asked, slapping at a fly that had landed on her skirt.

He knew then that he would have to get more money, and only one source came immediately to mind.

In the period following the debacle of the party and her subsequent ordering of Simon from Saffron Hill, she could think only of two things: her loneliness and despair on the one hand and her memories of Jarrett Russell on the other. She knew she shouldn't allow herself to be thinking of him with such frequency. It wasn't right, and nothing good was to be gotten from it.

One day, in the store, she was paid a visit from Hattie Winslow. She hadn't seen or heard from the woman for over two solid weeks.

"Good morning, Rebekah," Hattie said as if nothing wayward had transpired.

"Good morning," she replied with a coldness that she had hoped to limit to a polite reserve.

"Isn't it the loveliest day we're having? I declare, the air is full of zephyrs."

Rebekah remained silent, not trusting herself to speak.

"I'm looking for sheeting," Hattie went on. "It's to be a little gift for my Mary Lee. She's having her second child, did I tell you?"

"No," Rebekah said. "I believe you neglected to do so."

She showed Hattie Winslow what she had allegedly come to see, not allowing more than a minimum of conversation to pass between them. When the purchase had been made, and Rebekah was concentrating more intently than necessary on wrapping the parcel, Hattie decided that she must speak.

"Rebekah, listen to me," she said in the kindliest, most caring and concerned tones that she could muster. "Hate me if you want to, but I shouldn't think it a wise decision."

"I don't hate you," Rebekah said. "I have no cause to hate you."

"Well, if you did, some might say that it was your right." She paused, having difficult thoughts to express and being unsure of the best way to do it. "I wouldn't say it wasn't your right, Rebekah. What was done was cruel, I suppose."

"You suppose?" Rebekah snapped, exposing more of her feelings than she had intended.

"I tried to warn you," Hattie said. "That day in the store . . ."

"Here, Mrs. Winslow. Here is your parcel."

"There are rules, Rebekah. There are rules and codes of conduct and they cannot be ignored. Not in Mobile, at any rate. If you wanted to stay up North, things might have been different. Rules are relaxed a great deal more than they are here. Now you've been told something. Perhaps it was told in a way that was cruel or impatient. I am sorry when such things happen. But it's over and if you want to begin again, you can do so, more slowly this time, and I promise you it won't be held against you."

Rebekah stared at Hattie Winslow. In her way, Rebekah supposed, the woman was trying to give her something. "Very well," Rebekah said.

"Then it is behind us?" Hattie said anxiously.

"If you wish," Rebekah replied, willing to play the game but unwilling to ever give the woman any real friendship again.

"I'll tell you something," Hattie Winslow whispered, eager now to give Rebekah a gift, willing to pass on some privileged information.

"Yes?" Rebekah said, giving less than a damn.

Hattie, sensing this, bristled a bit. "Well, it's about your friend."

"Who?"

"Jarrett Russell, that's who."

"What about him?" Rebekah said, not enjoying hearing his name being bandied about in gossip.

"Well, let's just say that he's been trying to continue to bring honor to the great and good name of his family and that someone has finally decided to do something about it."

"I don't know what you mean," she said, feeling most uneasy.

"Well, you heard that he's been trying to build up a practice drawing from a clientele of freedmen?"

"Yes."

"And supposedly he wasn't doing too badly. They may not have much money, but there's certainly enough of them, God knows, and they get their aches and pains like everybody else."

"*Yes,*" Rebekah said pointedly, wanting her to get on with it, to move on to the unpleasantness that was waiting in the wings.

"Well, last night his office was broken into, and his equipment was smashed."

"My God," she cried. "Who did it?"

"Those who remember," Hattie Winslow said. "Those who won't ever forget."

After the woman left, Rebekah put the CLOSED sign on the door and went to sit in the back room. She thought of Jarrett, not, this time, as a pleasant memory in her life, but, rather, as a person whose life was full of pain, just as she felt hers was. She thought of him moving through the office filled with broken test tubes and smashed beakers and torn charts. She would have liked very much to help him, as he had once helped her. It had been so long since she was able to help somebody.

She sat down and wrote out a letter.

Dear Mr. Russell,

she wrote,

* * *

I have been in Mobile for some months now. Perhaps you have heard of my store . . .

She struck out the last line. It was far too foolish to think that he would have heard of her store.

I have established a store on Caroline Street.

All of this was foolish, she thought. She didn't want to give him a history of her life; she wanted to help him, right now, in any way possible.

I have heard of the very unfortunate incident that has befallen you. I find such criminal actions more than I can endure. Please come and see me tomorrow evening at home. I am enclosing the address and I hope you will respond to the friendship I am offering.

> Yours,
> Rebekah Weiss

She looked at the note and wondered if it were not too blunt, but then she realized she didn't know any other way to be. It was not in her nature to be coy.

The next day, after many hours in the store, she went home, had the servants send up a tray, and barely touched her dinner. She didn't know why she had invited Jarrett Russell to the house; there was very little she could do for him, and she had been presumptuous in the first place to extend such an invitation.

She supposed, however, that there was nothing to be done about it now. And so she dressed for the evening. She chose a dark gray silk, cut rather severely, and she wore no jewelry except for a simple cameo at the throat. She looked in the mirror. Is this how he wanted to see her? What was she looking for in this meeting? She remembered the grace that he had brought to her; she remembered his kindness; she remembered the warmth of his worsted jacket that day of Clara's burial when she had pressed her face against him and he had held her. In that moment, years ago now, she had achieved greater intimacy than she had ever found with Simon. She supposed that there was something foolish in holding on to that moment or even the moments on the riverboat in Biloxi not so very long ago. They were just moments, just brief passing encounters, and yet she valued them with an intensity that far outweighed their significance.

As she waited for him, she felt a mounting tension that threatened to become unbearable. She began to realize how much she had invested in this meeting. She realized that she regarded Jarrett Russell as her only chance at friendship and whatever lay beyond friendship. And if he failed her, she was alone, and the fact of her aloneness would be impossible to deny.

At eight o'clock she heard someone at the front door, and she could have leaped. She sat in the richly paneled library, waiting for him, and in a moment Hamlin the butler entered.

"Dr. Jarrett Russell, Miz Rebekah," Hamlin intoned.

"Yes, Hamlin," she said. "Show him in."

She watched for him to come through the door, and then there he was, standing before her, a guest in her house.

"Hello," she said.

He smiled. He looked older to her, his face even thinner and more gaunt than it had been. His clothes, although obviously of fine quality, looked shabby and too often mended. There were, beneath his eyes, dark rings that made him look injured and in need of attention.

"I wasn't sure you'd come," she said.

"Why wouldn't I have come?"

She shook her head. "I don't know."

"I wish you would have told me you were here before now," he said. "I was surprised you didn't."

She didn't know what to say. The reason she hadn't contacted him was because one didn't contact Jarrett Russell in Mobile if one wanted to get ahead. "I'm sorry," she said. "I should have, but . . ."

"But what?" he pressed.

She thought a moment. Very well, she decided. She wanted no lies between them. "I was afraid that you would hurt me in this city."

He laughed. "May I sit down?" he said.

"Yes, please."

He took off his hat and placed it on the desk. "You're absolutely right," he said. "You would have been hurt. But tell me, why did you decide to go ahead with it now?"

"I'm stronger now," she said. "I'm not as worried about getting hurt. And," she said, "I know that you've been hurt."

There was a silence. His expression, which had been trying to appear easily social and confident, now registered the distress that must be everywhere beneath his surface.

"Let me get you something," she said.

He shook his head.

"Some sherry. Please."

He nodded. "I don't suppose I would really mind some sherry," he laughed.

"And have you eaten?"

"Oh, no, please . . ."

"You look so thin. Let me get you something."

"No," he said. "I want nothing."

She stared at him, not knowing what next to say. He looked around at the fine room with its marble fireplace and fine carved ceiling. "I knew someone had bought Saffron Hill," he said, "but from the things I heard, I hadn't realized it was you."

"What did you hear?" she asked.

He looked uncomfortable at first, but then he laughed lightly. "Not very nice things, I must admit," he said. "My man, Micah, told me about it one day as I was shaving." He laughed again, and she wondered at the sad hollowness of his laughter. "That's the only way I ever get any news, you see, through my servants. And, if I may, I'll tell you that they weren't at all pleased about what was happening at Saffron Hill."

"And what did they say was happening?" she demanded to know.

"They said that Saffron Hill was being purchased by an outsider," he declared.

"And yet you came anyway," she said sarcastically.

He was surprised by her words. "Of course," he said. "What do I care? I have nothing to protect."

"Nor, I suppose, do I."

"What kind of store is it that you've established?" he asked.

"Dry goods," she said. "Fabrics, yarns, and lots of nice things for the ladies."

He laughed, more genuinely this time. "So you cater to the ladies, do you?"

"Yes," she said, not quite sure whether to be defensive or to share in his amusement. "Hattie Winslow, Mrs. Garden, Miss Sarah Warren . . ."

Now he really laughed heartily. "Ah yes," he cried. "The dragon brigade. And are they doing well by you?"

She hedged a bit in her answer, not wanting to tell him about the humiliation she had experienced. "Yes," she said. "They do well by me."

"They must. After all, you have Saffron Hill."

She nodded.

He looked around the room again. "May I ask a favor of you?" he said.

"Of course."

"May I see the ballroom?"

The request took her by surprise, but she assured him that it could be done. She found the key and opened the great walnut doors. It was a room she had only been in once, when she first bought the house.

"It's so terribly dusty. I haven't had any use for it yet, because it's a lovely room. As soon as I . . ."

He held up a hand, silencing her. She watched him enter the ballroom, walk around in it, reach up to try and touch the dusty chandelier.

"What is it?" she said.

"I'm sorry," he whispered. "I used to come here for cotillions and the like before the war. There used to be great gaiety in this room, and for a while I was a dear friend of the Pomeroys' daughter, Madeline."

"What became of her?" she asked, half expecting some tragic story.

He laughed again, but the laughter was antithetical to pleasure, being rooted in a profound bitterness. "It's more a question of what became of me," he said. "She found herself nicely settled with Hall Burnett."

"Of Burnett Mills?"

"Yes," he said, impressed. "You learn quickly."

He moved further into the ballroom. "Mary Lee Winslow, Madeline Pomeroy, Violet Garden—they're all rather nicely settled today, and I . . . well, I clearly am not."

She didn't know what to say to him, and so she said nothing.

"This is the first of the Spring Hill homes I've been admitted to since the end of the war," he said solemnly.

"You'll always be welcome here."

He nodded heavily.

"Why did you come back?" she said suddenly. "I wouldn't think you could survive here."

"There was nowhere else for me to go," he said. "I

wandered—you know that, you saw me not so long ago—but it seemed from the first that there was nowhere else for me to end up."

"So you're at Wild Oaks?"

"Yes."

"I know. You're spoken of. Much more than I am, I assure you. And I know that you've been hurt."

"Yes, I have been."

"What can I do?"

"I've been hurt," he said angrily, "badly hurt, and there's nothing for you to do. I'll begin again. I don't care what they do to me. If it means beating me into the ground, then so be it. The fact is that I'll still be in Mobile soil and that I have a right to be here, a birthright, no matter what anyone says."

"But then it sounds like your life will be a constant battle."

"It may have to be that for a while," he agreed. He looked up at her and smiled. "We danced that day on the Gulf, didn't we?" he said.

"Yes," she replied. "We waltzed."

"You said that day that your husband was 'resting.' Is he still?"

She walked to one of the windows of the ballroom and she could see that the branches of a black willow tree touched the glass. "We are unhappy together," she said.

"I'm sorry."

"We have been for so long now, since the very first. Yes, that first time you and I met, at Locust Point—it was so very bad then, and it's never gotten any better."

"I am sorry, truly I am."

"It isn't unbearable," she said, knowing as she said it that it sounded unbearable, knowing in her heart that it *was* unbearable. "We must keep our lives separate, however. That's the only way for us."

He walked across the ballroom to her. Suddenly,

gently, he put his hand against her cheek. "Something keeps throwing us together, doesn't it?"

She would have liked for him to take her into his arms, for him to make her feel safe and loved. That was why she had asked him to come, not to help him, but to have him help her. She would have liked something from him, but it was suddenly clear how wrong it was.

"Can we leave this room now?" she said, pulling away from him, walking stiffly to the door.

"Rebekah?"

"I'm sorry," she said. "This room seems to have bad memories for you. And as for me, well, I'd never been in a ballroom before I came to Saffron Hill. They don't have ballrooms in my circle of friends."

"Rebekah, I'm sorry if I've insulted you, if I've taken liberties that I wasn't permitted and that I should have known . . ."

There was a difficult silence between them, and she felt like running up the stairs. "It's true that we seem to be thrown together time after time, but we're from different worlds. I . . . I was foolish to have you here tonight. It can't do either of us any good."

"I don't believe it, Rebekah," he said. "We're not from different worlds. We're both outsiders. We both are traveling the same route, looking for something, searching for something."

What he said moved her profoundly. Again she had the impulse to reach out and touch him. But it was wrong, very wrong, and she mustn't, she clearly mustn't.

"You must go now," she said.

He stared at her. "Do you want me to?"

"Yes. Yes, please, go."

He reached for her hand, but she wouldn't allow it, and he bowed stiffly from the waist. "Good night, Rebekah," he said, turning to leave.

"Good night," she whispered, wanting to hold him and never let him go.

CHAPTER THIRTEEN

In the days that followed all she could think of were the store and Jarrett Russell. She had not seen Jarrett since that night at Saffron Hill. She had received a letter from him several days afterward and, by now, she knew its lines by heart.

Dear Rebekah,

it read,

> However difficult the other night was for you, I can give you every assurance that it was no less so for me. I have thought of nothing else since. Whatever can be said of that evening, with all its confusion, you have lifted me from my troubles, if only for the moment. And now the inevitable question: when can I see you again? Please, let me know quickly for I am waiting.

She got the note a week ago and had not yet answered it. She didn't know that she would answer it; she tended to think she wouldn't. She didn't want to be cruel to Jarrett—it was the last thing she wanted to do—but it was poorly judged of her to meet with him. She had resolved not to see him again. But even as she ran the resolution through her mind, she knew she would never adhere to it. How could she never see him again? She needed to see him. All of her energies outside of her work went into thinking of him.

She was absorbed in all of these thoughts and feelings when she realized that someone had entered the store. It was a man she had never seen before.

"May I help you?" she asked.

He smiled at her rather mysteriously. "Maybe in a couple a moments," he said in a thick, syrupy drawl.

She watched him walk around the store, picking things up, examining them, setting them down again. He was a big redheaded man, with red freckled skin, and a great shaking belly that hung out over his belt.

"Nice things you got here," he said. "Never did see such purty cotton before."

"Thank you," she said.

He smiled and then he laughed robustly, so that his massive belly shook all the more. "You don't know me, but I know you," he said.

She stood rather stiffly and silently, waiting for more.

"You'd be Miz Weiss, ain't that so?"

"Yes."

"Well, ain't you the purty one," he said. "You the purtiest little thing I ever seen runnin' a store."

"Who are you?" she said, finding his manner unpleasant.

He chuckled. "You might say I'm the competition. My name's Chester Stiles." He took his bent and soiled hat off. "Pleased to make your acquaintance."

"You have the store on Dauphin Street? Stiles Dry Goods?"

"Yes, ma'am. That's me, all right."

She was unsure as to what she should say. She was unsure as to the purpose of this visit. "Well, thank you for coming by, Mr. Stiles. Can I get you something? Some tea perhaps?"

"Tea? No, I don't think so."

He grinned at her, the grin inexplicable and vaguely lewd.

"Then what is it I can do for you, Mr. Stiles?"

He scratched the back of his neck and grinned even more broadly. "Well, you might start by telling me how you come to Mobile."

She stared at him. "I don't think I understand the question," she said.

"Oh, no? You don't understand the question." He scratched his jaw again. "That's right. You're all from foreign parts, ain't you?"

Her heart began to pound, realizing that this was a confrontation. "If you'll excuse me, Mr. Stiles, you can see I'm rather busy . . ."

"Oh sure. I can see how busy you are. It don't come as no surprise to me how busy you are, little lady." He picked up a gaily decorated canister of bath salts. "You turnin' into an apothecary to boot, are you?"

She almost wished Simon was here. The presence of this man frightened her, and she didn't know what to say to him.

"Why Mobile?" he repeated. "That's my question. You see, we already got ourselves a store like this in Mobile. It's called Stiles Dry Goods."

"Please leave, Mr. Stiles," she said.

"But I'm payin' you a social call, Miz Weiss. It ain't friendly to . . ."

"No, you're not, Mr. Stiles," she said angrily, interrupting him. "I opened the Weiss Store on Caroline Street because I had the right to do so. Nobody said I needed your permission. And if I've taken any business away from you, it hasn't been with any deceit or trickery on my part."

Chester Stiles's grin evaporated completely. "You got a sharp tongue, Miz Weiss," he said. "All you Jewish women like that?"

"Get out of here!" she cried. "I want you out!"

He placed his hat on his head. "You see, Miz Weiss,

you should've asked me before you come to Mobile. I would've told you that Mobile weren't a good place at all for you to make yourself a store."

He turned to leave. When he was gone, she realized that her back was drenched with sweat. She went into the back room, brushed herself with talc, and changed her dress. To steady her nerves, she poured herself a small glass of the brandy she kept on hand for just that purpose.

Was she blowing this encounter out of all proportion? She should have expected something like this. She was a stranger; she was foreign; there were enemies. She would have to think about what to do, but not now. Now she was too frightened to think clearly.

A group of men gathered in a woodshed that stood on the property of their leader. There were six of them—five Ghouls presided over by a Cyclops—and they comprised a den of the Ku Klux Klan. The Cyclops was Chester Stiles; his Ghouls included three men who worked for him in the store, a deputy sheriff, and his wife's brother, who ran a one-man lumber yard. They had formed less than a year ago, but they had been proved effective. They joined, at times, with other members of the Mobile arm of the Klan to threaten, flog, exile, mutilate, stab, shoot, and hang the offenders in their midst. They eliminated Negroes who were troublesome or disrespectful or who committed crimes or who joined political or military organizations such as the Union or Loyal Leagues. They helped to drive out Yankee schoolteachers and storekeepers and carpetbag judges. They intimidated juries and punished officials who tried to register Negroes or foreclose property. They punished any Negroes or outsiders who gained land or prospered or made inflammatory statements or talked about equal rights. They worked anonymously, in long white sheets that covered them completely. But most of their neighbors knew their identities and privately commended their work.

"We all got ourselves some new troublemakers in this town," Chester Stiles, the Cyclops, announced. "That's why I called you all here tonight."

"What's goin' on, Cyclops?" one of the Ghouls asked.

"Two Jew shopkeepers," the Cyclops said. "Come over here from Europe. Come over here with all their foreign ideas."

"They the ones that got the new dry goods store, Cyclops?" said another of the Ghouls, this one being Burton Bligh, a ferret of a man who had been working for Chester Stiles well over twelve years.

"Yeah, they the ones," the Cyclops muttered.

"Well, what's the plan, Cyclops?" a third Ghoul cried out.

"We gonna ride up to the house," the Cyclops said. "These here Jews already bought themselves a fine place up in Spring Hill."

"You don't say," cried a Ghoul.

"Saffron Hill, no less."

"The Pomeroy place?"

"None other."

"You don't say!"

"That's what's happening here, brothers. The Pomeroys—one of the finest families that Mobile has to offer—is pushed out and the Jews and the Yankees and the carpetbaggers push their way in." As the Cyclops spoke, he felt the white heat of his fury inflame his listeners. This was how he had come to be the Cyclops—because he had the Word and because he knew how to spread it. "And they gonna keep on comin' in so long as we let 'em, long as we don't do nothin' to stop 'em. Is that what we gonna be doin'?"

"No!" the men roared, infected by this fury, unwilling to be restrained much longer.

"Now we ain't gonna do nothin' too rough tonight,"

the Cyclops cautioned. "Them Jews is smart. They can learn a lesson real quick. We just gonna ride up to Saffron Hill and we gonna make some noise, maybe break up a few things, and then we gonna go. You'll see, them Jews'll get the message real quick."

They mounted their horses and started off toward Saffron Hill. They always rode at night—Night Riders they were called—and they had planned this evening's outing with the full knowledge that there was only a quarter-crescent moon. They arrived at Saffron Hill shortly after midnight. The Cyclops was first to throw a rock through a window. Then his Ghouls followed suit, and the night was filled with the sounds of shattering glass. Suddenly they saw a light, and Hamlin, the butler, appeared on the veranda.

"Oh, Lord Jesus," the old man cried. "Save us and protect us."

One of the Ghouls dismounted and seized the old man. With the help of his cohorts the Ghoul ripped the shirt from Hamlin's back, and they began to flog him with the large cowhide whip that they always took with them on these forays.

"Oh Jesus!" he shrieked. "Jesus, help me!"

It was then that Rebekah rushed out. Dressed in a nightgown, with a robe pulled hastily over her and her long hair braided down the back, she could not quite believe that she was awake yet. The image she saw before her—a group of white-sheeted figures brandishing horse whips and flogging an old and defenseless man—was every bit as unreal and terrifying as anything she had ever dreamed.

"What are you doing?" she screamed. "Stop it! Stop it, do you hear!"

Then one of the Ghouls lighted a torch and threw it at a shrub right next to her which burst into flames. They threw the old man in a heap at her feet; they mounted their horrid black horses; and they rode off into the night.

She stood stunned for a moment, and then she gathered herself. "Sophronia!" she screamed as loudly as she could. "Dover! Eulalie!"

They were all right inside, hiding behind the door. When they saw that they were safe, they came to her aid. Dover threw a heavy rug over the burning bush, and Sophronia and Eulalie gathered around Hamlin.

"Hamlin, are you all right?" Rebekah cried.

The old black man held his chest and tried to catch his breath. Rebekah and the women looked at each other. It seemed that he was not all right.

"Eulalie! Get some brandy!"

The fat cook ran into the house. Hamlin's eyes were glazed with a kind of mortal, climactic fear.

"It will be all right, Hamlin," she promised.

But then his face contorted with pain once more, and suddenly he couldn't seem to breathe at all.

"Dover! Get the doctor! Quickly!"

But just as Dover mounted the horse, Hamlin let out a long, rattling groan, and then he was gone.

"He died," Sophronia said, disengaging her hand from the dead man's grasp.

"They killed him," Rebekah said.

"They're the Night Riders," Sophronia said. Her eyes were immense and flickering with fear. Rebekah had never seen Sophronia register such a human emotion before. "They come in the night, like spirits."

After the doctor had come and Hamlin was taken to the mortuary, Rebekah retired to her room. She had to make her way through shards of glass; every window on the ground floor had been smashed. She bolted her door and huddled against a corner of her bed. She had undergone the awful, paralyzing experience of having had her world invaded. Little was left untouched; certainly all sense of safety was gone, as well as a feeling of promise and discovery. She had been told to get out, and a life had been taken to illustrate the intent of her adversary. She didn't want to be alone. She thought of Simon; she had not yet let him return to Saffron Hill, but it wasn't he whom she missed. If Simon had been here tonight, he would have cowered with the servants because he was that kind of a man. It wasn't Simon whom she thought of, but, again, she knew that nothing was to be gained from such thoughts.

She was alone in this world she had made for herself, this world of broken windows and stolen lives. She snuffed out her candle, praying she wouldn't be found, not yet anyway, not yet.

The next morning, she arrived at the store and found something attached to the front door. It was a crudely printed note; its message said:

THIS STORE CONDEMNED

As with the house, the windows of the store had been smashed. The beautifully painted sign that she had commissioned at the store's inception had been torn down and smashed. She could not stop herself from crying bitterly as she made her way inside. Fortunately, miraculously, they had not destroyed her stock. It seemed that they were giving her a warning, but what was the warning? Either she could stay here and be destroyed, or she could leave everything behind and let herself be ruined that way.

She sat down to write a note to Jarrett Russell. She wouldn't wait any longer; she needed to see him and she would see him and she didn't care where it led.

Dear Doctor,

she wrote (it was too difficult for her to use his name; it was still too personal).

* * *

I would like to see you. I would like to talk to you. I need to talk to you.

She crumpled up the letter. She didn't want to correspond; she wanted to see him. He would tell her what to do. He knew the ways of this city; he knew what her chances would be against the forces that had left the wicked note on the front door of the store.

After she closed the shop that night, she got into her carriage and rode over to Wild Oaks. It wasn't all that far from Saffron Hill, no more than three or four miles off. Although she had never been there, she had no difficulty finding it. It was a grand house, much grander than Saffron Hill, set in what was almost a park with live oak trees, the tops of which were so high that they became indistinct in the twilight. It was a magical house, white, colonnaded, sitting comfortably and majestically on its plot of land. Closer up one could see that the house was in a state of disrepair, badly in need of paint, the front door cracked, the roof sagging and looking full of holes.

She knocked on the front door, and a tall, thin black man opened it.

"Yes, ma'am?"

"I have come to see Dr. Russell," she said, her voice high-pitched with nervousness. "My name in Rebekah Weiss."

"Is the doctor expecting you?"

She shook her head. "No," she said, "but please tell him I'm here. I'm sure he'll want to see me."

The black man stared at her, more with curiosity than disdain. For a moment she thought back to the time in Vienna when she had gone, as a laundress, to the front door, and she had been looked at like nothing more than refuse.

"The doctor, he ain't been feeling too well," the butler went on to say.

"I hope it's nothing serious," she said.

"No, he's goin' to be all right. Maybe it'd be better, though, if you come back another night?"

"Who's there, Micah?" she heard a voice cry.

Micah, the black man, stared at Rebekah. "You best go now, ma'am."

"I said, who's there?" Jarrett cried.

Then she saw him at the front door, a glass in one hand, the other hand crudely bandaged, his hair disheveled, his fine face unshaven, and his shirt unbuttoned.

"Oh, it's you," he said with a laugh. "What are you doing here?"

She felt her face turn a furious shade of crimson. "I . . . I shouldn't have come," she said. She turned to leave, and a terrible aching feeling passed through her.

"Hey there!" Jarrett called. "Hey, don't go!"

She walked quickly to the carriage, and he stumbled out after her, laughing idiotically. "You just got here," he said. Then he threw the glass against the house, and they heard it explode like a firecracker.

"Don't go," he murmured, grabbing her by the shoulders.

"Stop it!" she cried. "You're drunk! Stop it!"

He let her go, and she got up into the carriage. She flicked the reins and began moving away from the house, the aching feeling warring with her anger and her sense of betrayal.

He began running after her, an awkward, loping sort of run, and then he stumbled and hit his shoulder against the hard, red earth. "Rebekah!" he cried, reaching out for a hand to her. "Don't go! Don't go and leave me!"

She brought the wagon to a halt. At first she didn't turn around but just sat there, wanting to know what to do. He was drunk, just as she had seen Simon drunk, and she wished she had never seen him this way. He was weak, just as Simon was weak; and she was strong, and she didn't want anyone trying to pull her down. But she didn't want to ride away, because if she did that, then it was true that she was hard and cruel and it would be foolish of her to think of herself as a woman any longer.

"Rebekah, come back!" he called again.

She turned and saw him lying there. She jumped from the carriage and ran over to him. She got him up to his feet, and Micah came to help her walk him into the house.

They sat him in a chair in the library. She dismissed Micah and closed the door behind him.

"Don't look at me," he said, full of self-loathing. "I'm pitiful, I know I am."

"No, you're not," she said. "You're sick and you're hurt and I'm going to help you."

"I don't want you to," he cried, frustrated and suddenly remorseful.

"Why?" she demanded to know. "You once helped me. Why won't you let me help you?"

He stared at her, and then he looked away, into the fire.

"Do you do this often?" she asked.

"What?"

"Do you get drunk? I just want to know."

"Yes. I get drunk," he said. "When there's nowhere else to turn, I get drunk."

"And what did you do to your hand?"

He looked at the soiled bandage and shook his head.

"You don't want to talk about it?" she asked.

"That's right."

There was a silence, filled only by the crackling of the fire in the hearth. "You wrote me a letter," she said. "You asked when you could see me."

"That was awhile ago."

The silence deepened, but she wouldn't let it run away with them. "I see," she said. "Then when I wanted to go just now, why did you call my name? Why did you ask me to come back?"

His dark, bruised face sought to remain impassive, but she watched it crumble before her very eyes. "I'm a fool to have come back here," he said. "My God, this place"—he made a circular gesture with his hand—"this place is a hell to me."

"What happened to your hand?" she cried.

He took a deep breath. "I've been drunk for two days," he admitted, sobering up as he told the tale. "Last night—well, I didn't even realize I was doing it. I took a piece of burning kindling from the fire, and there, I threw it against the drapes."

Looking around, she saw that the draperies on one of the windows were gone. "But why? What could have made you do such a thing?"

He laughed at the question. "Oh God, Rebekah. Don't you understand? This place has called me back. I tried to run from it. You know how I tried, you know how I meant to stay away. It's gotten me back and it's going to kill me, sure as I'm telling you. It's going to kill me."

Looking into his feverish gray eyes, she knew that he meant it. "So you tried to burn it down?"

"Yes."

"I wish you had succeeded," she said suddenly, wanting to see him happy, hating to see him in such pain.

"Micah put out the fire," Jarrett said. "He put me to bed. Micah knows how to take care of me. Micah has a real talent for seeing after drunken, dissolute doctors."

"Don't say that about yourself!" she cried. "That's not what you are. You're a fine man. I won't let you speak of yourself that way."

"You don't understand, Rebekah," he said, shaking his head sadly. "The other day I said we were from the same world, a world of outsiders, but I was wrong. I *am* of this world, that's why I've come back here, that's

why I could never get away. Listen to me: one day
I'll tell you all about Wild Oaks and all about the
dishonor that the name Russell has come to signify.
And then you'll know what madness it's been for me
to come back here."

"But you can fight it, Jarrett," she said, hardly
conscious that she was using his name and that she
would use it from now on. "Look," she said, pulling
from her bag the note that had been fixed to the front
door of the store. "This is what I found this morning
when I went to the store. It says, 'This store condemned.' I know they're after me, just as they're after
you. Just as they'll destroy your office and your equipment, they'll destroy everything I've built for myself.
But only if we let them! Can't we fight it, Jarrett?
Can't we fight and can't we win?"

"Win?" he asked. "Win against the Night Riders?
How, Rebekah? How do you propose we do it?"

"By staying here," she said. "By making it hard for
them. I've got a right to be here," she cried. "I came
to this country because it was one place that I was
supposed to be able to do what I'm doing. And you've
got a right to be here. Why, you just said it to me the
other day. You said you had a birthright."

"Well, I was wrong," he said bitterly. "I suppose any
birthright I ever had was wiped out years ago."

She didn't know what to say to him. She felt like
she was losing him, just as she had lost Clara that
night, in the warehouse on the piers, when Clara ran
from her and she had called out her name. "No, you're
not going to give up," Rebekah said with renewed
determination. "I'm not going to let you. There are
people here you can help. All sorts of people who need
you and who have no one else to care for them. I won't
let you go because if you go now, then it will be over
for you. You'll be so lost, Jarrett, and you'll never find
your way."

Jarrett stared at Rebekah and then reached out his

hand for hers. They just sat there, for several long moments, in utter silence. They felt very close to each other.

"Look at your bandage," she said, pulling away. "It's so badly soiled."

She went to get gauze and scissors and some antiseptic and, with his instructions, she changed the dressing. It was a bad burn; he had given himself a very cruel punishment indeed.

"What will you do, Rebekah?" he asked. "What will you do about the store?"

"I don't know," she said. "That's one of the reasons I came here tonight. I thought perhaps you would know what to do."

He laughed. "Oh yes, of course," he said. Then, staring intently at her, he spoke with increased seriousness. "Is that why you came here tonight, Rebekah?" he asked.

She smoothed a length of gauze that had become entangled. "Is that really such a poor reason?" she said at last. "So that you might help me?"

"No. No, it's not such a poor reason at all. But I wish there was another reason as well."

She looked up from the purposeless busy work that she had created for herself. She looked at him, at his face, at his very fine face that had featured in dream after dream. She wanted, more than anything, to touch him and to have him touch her.

"I don't want you to leave, Rebekah," he said.

"Oh, Jarrett." Jarrett, Jarrett"—now she heard herself using his name. When he reached out for her, she went into his arms, and they embraced each other. And when they met each other's lips, she tasted the whiskey and for a moment she thought of Simon. But then she knew she didn't want to think of Simon, she wanted only to think of Jarrett, Jarrett only, as she felt his long lean body next to hers. She wondered how she had gone all this time without being touched, without being held.

"Rebekah, I'm so glad you came tonight. I'm so very glad."

"Hold me, Jarrett," she whispered.

He held her and stroked her fine, shining black hair. She closed her eyes and pressed her face against him. She put a hand on the smooth white skin that showed through his open shirt. She felt his hand kneading the back of her neck, and when she realized that she had forgotten completely what it was like to be touched and to feel good as a result, she couldn't stop her sudden, stinging tears.

"Don't cry," he said. "There's nothing to cry about now."

"Oh no?" she asked, tense and challenging as her mood shifted gears. "What are we to do? We haven't any answers, don't you see?"

"Well, if we haven't any answers, then we don't have to worry ourselves about looking further."

"There's too much going against us, Jarrett. We would just be fugitives again, looking for a safe place."

"But I feel safe with you, Rebekah," Jarrett said.

His remark moved her. She reached out and touched his rough, unshaven cheek.

"Stay with me, Rebekah, please."

For a moment she was ready to, wanting so much to be with him, but then she shook her head. "I can't," she said. "Oh, I shouldn't have come. It was so wrong of me. It was stupid and reckless. Can you forgive me, Jarrett? Can you understand? For whatever it's worth, I'm still a married woman."

"But what are you saying, Rebekah? Can you leave me as easily as that?"

She took his hand and held it against her cheek. "I don't want to leave here, but I must."

She rose and pulled her shawl around her.

"Don't hurt yourself again, Jarrett," she said. "Promise me you won't."

He stared at her. He had never known anyone quite so beautiful or, at least, he had never known anyone who was beautiful in the same way she was. "No, I won't, Rebekah," he said in a voice of profound sadness. "I have you for that."

CHAPTER FOURTEEN

The introduction of Rebekah into his life made Jarrett Russell come alive again. He wasn't going to let her go, even if she was married. Whatever her marriage was at this point, it didn't seem worthy of acting as an obstacle. Simon Weiss was still somewhere in Mobile, according to local gossip, but he wasn't in Rebekah's bed. If anyone was going to be in Rebekah's bed, Jarrett resolved that it would be he.

It had not taken long for Jarrett to feel sure that he loved Rebekah. She was strong, ambitious, clever, and determined, but none of that made her anything less than womanly. Aside from her beauty, which was the first thing one noticed about her, she had a warmth that seemed even that much warmer when contrasted with the sugary self-absorption of the girls he had grown up with. And for all of her strength there was a vulnerability about her as well. He felt that she had known trouble and that she needed him as much as he needed her.

Yet the fact that he loved her and was convinced that she could love him did not make the prospect of their involvement seem any easier. They were both aliens in this city—she by virtue of her religion and he, ironically enough, by virtue of his family.

Still by an effort of will that even he couldn't fully understand, he was managing to carve a niche for himself against almost impossible odds. He was becoming accepted in the Negro community as a friend and as a doctor. It gave him enormous strength to know that he was a good doctor. He felt that if he helped people, then he was wiping away the transgressions of his family. Maybe one day the rest of Mobile would leave him alone. Maybe the filthy, craven Klansmen wouldn't try to sabotage him as they had already attempted. Maybe he would just be left to treat the sick and do his job.

Somehow it was still odd to him to regard the people he served. It hadn't been altogether easy to give up his dreams of becoming a surgeon. At one point he had planned to study in Philadelphia and then in Europe; he had planned on becoming a great man of medicine. But plans are often broken, particularly so when wars are born. As soon as the war was declared, he became a lieutenant in the medical corps. He saw blood and carnage wherever he went, but he was part of a great effort, the effort to maintain the Southern way of life, and so he didn't question his beliefs. It all came to an end, however, on August 7, 1864. He was stationed at Kennesaw Mountain, where his army went down to a bloody defeat. He remembered, as vividly as though it were yesterday, coming off duty and being told by one of the other doctors that his father, General Jarrett Russell, had been taken into custody and was awaiting court-martial on grounds of cowardice. You're mad! Jarrett had cried and another young doctor, who was a longtime rival from school days, said that his father had gone to his tent, taken his gun, and shot himself in the head. Jarrett remembered leaping on the young doctor and pounding his head against the ground until he had to be pulled off and held back.

They allowed him to go home and bury his dead. Jarrett had wanted to see his father's body torn apart by jackals. He wanted to see it plucked to shreds by carrion, that's how much he despised him. His father was a charlatan; his father was a monster of deception. His father was a bully, terrorizing everyone around him, Jarrett's mother included, so that the poor woman died an early death. All the years that his father had presented himself as a noble warrior, a black-bearded Hannibal able to bend iron bars with his bare hands, all the years he had tormented everyone with his notions of conduct and then, in battle, he showed his yellow streak.

He had wanted to see his father's head on a stake, but at the same time he didn't. He wept then, and he could almost weep now at the fervency with which he had wanted to believe it was all a mistake. It had to be a mistake, hadn't it? His father, this mighty man—how could it be?

He buried his dead. The only mourners his father had at his grave site were his son and the few servants who were still around. Even his brothers, Jarrett's uncles, wouldn't come. Micah found a black minister to perform the rites, and some brief words were said. Jarrett returned for the last few months of the war and when he came back again, there was a further shock. The grave had been disinterred. Someone evidently felt that his father had not been punished enough.

There was nothing to be done. He couldn't very well place an advertisement for the return of the body. The only thing he could do was get out of Mobile. And so he joined the Immigration Service. He tried to make himself invisible. If anyone questioned him about his past, he acted as if he had none, as if he had been born without a family, without a

history, without a name. Of course his story made
itself known wherever he was stationed, and this public disgrace led to two concurrent reactions on his
part: heavy drinking and frequent brawling. He was
shifted around from one station to the next, and he
was on his last assignment when he met Rebekah at
Locust Point. When finally he returned to Mobile, it
was with the feeling that he might never overcome his
guilt and his fury if he did not confront his past.

He moved back into Wild Oaks, which was, and
which remained, in a dangerous state of decay. There
wasn't enough money to rectify the matter, and so the
building creaked and, at times, seemed to fairly sway
in the wind. Still it was his home, with all its ghosts
and all its faded grandeur. The presence of Micah,
who had been there all of his life, reassured him
further.

It was clear from the beginning that the only people
he could serve as a doctor were the freedmen. There
wasn't a white man in Mobile, poor or rich, who
would have gone to see Jarrett Russell. The name
Jarrett Russell—a name many generations old—was
anathema to this city. He began seeing patients in a
small sort of shack on Montgomery Street in the Negro
section. He set bones; swabbed burns; broke fevers;
and treated all the miscellaneous ills with which he
was confronted. Often enough he wasn't paid with
money. He was given eggs or butter or yams or even
whiskey now and then. He would have liked the
money, to be sure, but at least this was a beginning
and at least he was doing something with his talents
and at least he was home.

He had intended to remain in Mobile for the rest
of his life, but now, having found Rebekah, he wondered at the wisdom of that intention. Wasn't there
enough going against him? Wasn't he already working
against enormous odds just in terms of what his family
name meant in this city? Now, if he were, one day, to

marry a Jew, it would be adding insult to injury. His office had already been smashed up once. How many times was he willing to suffer such a violation? And Rebekah too had been threatened. The idea of his contributing to any suffering on her part made him sick with worry.

They could go somewhere else. As long as they were together, it wouldn't matter. The idea of a home no longer meant Mobile to him. The idea of a home meant being with someone he loved, and the woman he loved was Rebekah.

He would go down to the store right now, and he would talk to her. He would tell her that she meant a great deal to him. He would tell her that even though she was married, it was in name only and that was no reason to keep them apart. He was sure she would listen and, if not, he was prepared to do everything in his power to get her to listen.

Rebekah was in a state of shock. Hattie Winslow had been in that morning to spread some insidious gossip. The woman, whom Rebekah was beginning to loathe, told her that she'd heard that Simon had set up housekeeping down on Water Street with a woman named Lucy. A whore. She told Hattie Winslow that she didn't want to hear about Simon from her and Hattie Winslow protested and she told Hattie Winslow that there was nothing more for them to say to each other.

When the woman had left, a hundred questions competed in Rebekah's mind. Where did Simon get the money? Had he been stealing from her? Had he been taking her hard-earned money and finding card games? And who was this Lucy? And what did that mean? Would the rabbi grant her a *get* now regardless of Simon's desires?

The store began to fill up with people toward midday. As always she was doing a brisk business. The

Weiss Store was needed in this city, and no intimidation by the likes of Chester Stiles would convince her otherwise. Each month the store grew more important and entrenched itself further in the spirit of Mobile. It had become the place to go to get something special, to get something beautiful, to get something that was well made, to get something that was new and inventive and clever. Salesmen from all over were aware of the Weiss Store and they came to her with all kinds of cosmetics and fabrics and writing tablets and items of haberdashery that they thought she might be willing to handle. She became, in the relatively short time she had been there, a figure to be reckoned with. On the train to Mobile the salesmen would talk and talk, and the conversation would inevitably make its way to Rebekah Weiss, the beautiful young woman who had a head on her shoulders. Well, what they said was right on the mark, she thought. She was a figure to be reckoned with, and no one would drive her out of Mobile.

As she was writing up a bill of sale, she looked up and saw Simon enter. She hadn't seen him for some weeks, and now he appeared, with his inimitable timing, just hours after she had heard of his new living arrangement. He walked up to her, in front of the customers, and said, in an embarrassingly forthright and laden voice: "We must talk."

"In a few moments, please," she said, trying to keep her composure as she completed the sale of ten yards of fine paisley silk. She looked up as she packed the merchandise in tissue, and she saw Simon leaning against the wall, glowering at her. Finally, when the store was emptied of customers, she put up the CLOSED sign and waved him into the back room.

"What do you want?" she said.

"I've come here to get my money out of the store," he said bluntly.

"Your money?" she said scornfully. "You're just a

leech, do you know that? How can you be the way you are? Have you no pride? Don't you disgust yourself?"

"Not nearly so much as you disgust me," he replied. "I thought we could agree on things. I thought you'd be prepared to do as I said."

"You've done nothing for this store. Why should you get a cent out of me?"

"If it wasn't for me . . ."

"Do you think I'm going to support you in your house on Water Street?" she cried.

"What?" he said, surprised by her knowledge.

"That's right. I know all about it. All about you and your whore. What's her name? Lucy. Yes, Lucy. I know all about Lucy."

"What of it?" he said.

"Just get out of here, will you?"

"Lucy's a woman. Not like you. Lucy knows how to please a man."

"Shut up!" she shrieked. "Shut up and get out of here."

"I'll get out of here when you give me what's rightfully mine," he roared.

What was she doing? She must have been mad. He was dangerous—there was no telling what he might do. She had no other choice. She'd have to strike some kind of bargain with him, that was the only way. "Very well, Simon," she said. "I'm prepared to make a deal with you. I'll give you half of what you're 'supposed' to get now and the rest within six months. And one other condition: you give me a *get*."

He stared at her. "That won't do. I want it all now."

"Don't be a fool," she replied. "If you'd contributed anything to this business, you would know how impossible that request is. Do you think I can just hand over all of my assets to you and still run the store?"

"I don't care what you do. I just want my money now."

"Why? So you can squander it all on liquor and cards and fancy hats for your whore?" she cried.

"Shut up about Lucy," he warned. "Just you shut up."

Again she felt the full force of his menace. "All right, Simon. I just ask that you be reasonable. Do you want to ruin the business?"

"Come now, Rebekah. You should have more faith in your business ability than that. I certainly do."

She looked down and saw a pinking shears and had a quick, fleeting fantasy of running it along his cheek. "It's half now and half in six months' time, Simon. That's the only way I can manage it. Believe me, if there was any other way, I'd do it. I don't particularly want to have to see you again in six months, you can trust me on that."

He stared at her. "All right," he said. "Get me a bank check for half of the amount, and I'll call on you again six months from now."

"What about the *get*?" she asked.

"When you've paid me all that you owe me," he said. "That's when you'll get your *get*," he said vengefully.

He was like a blackmailer; he made her feel soiled. "Very well, Simon," she said. "It's a deal."

Just then she heard someone knocking at the door. She looked through the shade and saw Jarrett.

"Who's that?" Simon demanded to know.

She ignored him and opened the door slightly. "Jarrett," she whispered. "What is it?"

"Rebekah," he said, his face full of concern, "is there anything wrong?"

"No, Jarrett. It's just that I can't talk right now. Come back later," she whispered. "We'll talk then and . . ."

"Who is it?" Simon repeated, walking toward the door.

Jarrett saw a broad, blond-moustached man look at

him fiercely. "Who are you?" Jarrett said, pushing his way into the store. He turned to Rebekah. "What is it, Rebekah? Is there a problem?"

"Are you her keeper?" Simon sneered.

Jarrett turned to face Simon again. "Who are you?" he said.

"Jarrett," Rebekah interrupted, "Jarrett, this is my husband. This is Simon Weiss."

He remembered back to Rebekah's fear on Locust Point at how her husband would handle the news of her miscarriage, and now he could see why she would have been afraid. There was a brutish aspect to the man that instinctively put Jarrett on his defense.

"And who is this?" Simon inquired, a smile on his lips.

"It's none of your business who this is," Rebekah said.

"And you talking to me about Lucy. Why, with you tramping around . . ."

"Shut up!" Rebekah cried.

"You ain't nothing but a whore yourself, a money-grubbing, no-good . . ."

Jarrett grabbed hold of Simon and whipped him across the face. "Hold your filthy tongue," he instructed.

Simon, who was, if nothing else, strong as a bear, wrenched free of Jarrett's grip and smashed him across the face, sending him flying against a wall. Rebekah shrieked, and Jarrett pulled himself up and lunged at the oaf, gripping his head in his arms and pounding it against the table. It was a brawl, just like the brawls he'd had after the war, when he was going around defending the Russell name. He felt the flow of adrenaline that was, for a long time, his definition of being alive and even when Simon aimed blows at his midsection, it did nothing to stop his fury.

"Stop it!" Rebekah screamed. "Stop it!"

But they wouldn't stop it. They were like two bulls

going at each other, hating each other from the first and intent on tasting each other's blood.

"Stop it, I say!"

She grabbed hold of a broom that was resting against the wall, and she used it on both of them, bringing it down with all of her might upon their heads. It was some stunned moments before they realized what was happening and before their fight was broken up.

"Animals!" she spat. "What do you think you're doing? Do you think I'm going to stand here and watch you fight like this? Get out of my store, both of you! Just get out!"

"Rebekah," Jarrett protested.

"You heard me!" she cried. She was sick of men; she was sick of their rough, violent ways.

"All right, I'm going," Simon said, holding his bruised lip, "but don't forget about my money."

"You'll get your filthy money," Rebekah promised, "and then I never want to see the likes of you again. Now get out!"

Simon left Rebekah and Jarrett alone. Rebekah stared at Jarrett for a moment and then turned her back to him.

"Rebekah, let me explain . . ."

"There's nothing to explain, Jarrett. Please leave."

"I'm sorry, Rebekah. I know I had no right to do what I did. Can you forgive me?"

She turned around to face him. "I thought you were different," she said, tears in her eyes. "I thought you were a different kind of man, but you're all the same. Now get out, will you? Just get out!"

He bent to retrieve his hat, took it in hand, gave her one last look, and did as she said.

She began getting letters from Wild Oaks. Imploring, heartfelt letters asking her to forgive him.

* * *

Dear Rebekah,

one of his letters read.

> Don't punish me any further. I know I was wrong.
> I know I treated you like you have no mind of
> your own. That's not what I look to you for.
> You're a special kind of a woman. I was a fool,
> but can't you forgive me? I love you, Rebekah.
> Aren't I entitled to some mistakes?

I love you. When she saw those words there, she was
so startled that she had to sit down to read them
again. He loved her. Why did it seem so miraculous?
Because no one had said such a thing to her in so
many years. She thought of what Simon had said to
her, how he had tried to wound her that day in the
store. *Lucy is a woman. Not like you. Lucy knows how
to please a man.* Well, she was a woman too, and here
was a man who recognized that fact. Yes, she would
forgive him. How could she not? There was violence
in men—nothing any woman could do would ever
change that. But Jarrett was a good man. From the
first time she saw him, she could see that in his core
he was a gentle man.

She sent him a note saying that if she was wanted,
she would come to Wild Oaks that next evening. Perhaps it was a brazen thing to do, she thought momentarily, but she didn't care. She was willing to make
up her own rules and suffer the consequences accordingly.

After work the next day she drove the carriage back
to Saffron Hill and dressed for her dinner with Jarrett.
For a moment she felt wary of the evening, not sure
what she was looking for or where the evening would
go. She thought that what she was looking for was
warmth and human kindness and tenderness; she

wasn't at all sure that it would ever be available to her or that, moreover, it was ever available to anyone.

She made herself look quite beautiful. She wore a silk dress the color of rose, cut low in the bodice. When she powdered her face and did up her long black hair, there were no signs of the toil that she put in every single day of her life. She was once again the town beauty, untouchable, admired, but not necessarily loved.

She had Dover drive her to Wild Oaks. The night sky was almost silver, and the air was sweet and warm.

"Doctor Russell, he one fine man, Miz Rebekah," Dover said from up front.

"Is he, Dover?" Rebekah replied, feeling the remark somehow inappropriate.

"Why, sure he is. He jes' taken care of my aunt Eulalie. She jes' got herself some bad burn on the arm and he fixed her up fine. Nobody else take such good care as Doctor Russell do."

They arrived in no time at Wild Oaks. As she disembarked from the carriage, she looked at the house and felt the sense of ruin that she had felt the last time she was here. Waiting at the door was Micah, the head man, who admitted her into the dim, unlovely entrance hall.

"Good evening, ma'am," he intoned.

"Good evening."

"The doctor expects you in the library."

He opened the door for her, and she saw Jarrett sitting by the fire, a glass of whiskey in his hand. He looked up and then he rose.

"Miz Weiss," Micah announced.

"Come in," Jarrett said. He indicated a chair across from him for her to sit in. "You look lovely," he said, not insincerely but almost as an afterthought.

"Please sit down," she said when she had settled herself.

But he couldn't sit. He was very agitated, and he

walked toward the fire, rubbing his hands as if they were cold. She looked around this room, still fine despite its deterioration. The walls were all paneled with walnut, and there was brass and silver and faded but beautiful Turkish rugs.

"You didn't think I'd come?" she said at last.

"I was surprised when I got your note," he replied.

She smiled a bit. "That's not the way it's done around here, is it?"

"What do you mean?"

"Oh, I mean when men seek to make amends, they're supposed to get around to sending flowers and buying gifts before women forgive them."

"Does that mean I'm forgiven?" Jarrett said.

"That's why I'm here," she said intensely.

He walked over to the chair where she was sitting, kneeled down beside her, and took her hand. "I'm glad you're the forgiving sort," he murmured, kissing the hand.

"Just don't defend my honor again, Jarrett," she cautioned. "It seems you're too concerned with honor anyway."

"What do you mean?" he said again. It seemed she was full of cryptic remarks tonight, and this one touched him profoundly.

"I know your story," Rebekah said. "I've known it all along. Ever since I left you in Baltimore, I've known your story."

"But how?" he asked incredulously.

"I met Hattie Winslow on a train going to Savannah, and she was, of course, eager to tell me all the details of your family's humiliation."

"Yes," he said bitterly, thinking of yet another of his family's enemies. "I'm sure she was."

She reached down and touched his gleaming dark hair. "We both have our stories, don't we, Jarrett?" she whispered. "We both have our secrets."

"Yes, Rebekah," he said. "I suppose we do. Neither one of us is really free, are we?"

"You met my devil the other day. My Simon. Don't cross him, Jarrett. Don't ever try to fight him. He's mad, Simon is, he's a killer—don't risk your life, because if anything should happen to you . . ."

"What, Rebekah?" he said, seizing upon her intimation of love for him.

"I don't know what I should do," she confessed.

She was so beautiful; she meant so much to him. "Come, sit here beside me," he said, holding out his hand.

She hesitated a moment and then she rose, her silks making a rushing sound as she went to him. He took her hand and he kissed it, holding it to his lips, his eyes squeezed shut, his longish black hair curling over his brow. She stroked his fine hair and he looked up, into her eyes, her exquisite amber eyes, and he drew her closer to him and he kissed her, tentatively at first and then with greater passion.

"We don't have to be alone," he said. "Never again."

His words brought tears to her eyes. The idea of not being alone anymore almost overwhelmed her. "Hold me," she said, and he did, and his arms felt strong and gentle at once.

"You're so beautiful," he said.

"So are you," she whispered passionately.

The idiosyncrasy of the remark spurred him on. She wasn't like any other woman he had ever known; she was vital and forthright and stunning in her impact.

"I've wanted you for so long," Jarrett said.

He was kissing her lips and then her neck and then her shoulders. Oh God, she thought. Oh, how I've wanted you, how I've dreamed of you. When he fumbled with the buttons at the back of her dress, she leaned over, holding on to his shoulders so that he could more easily perform the task. Then he had her corset unlaced, working feverishly at the trappings; then he had her breasts revealed, beautiful white breasts with rosy nipples that were straining toward him. He took each breast in his hand, lightly at first, as though it were something exotic, rare; then he took each nipple between thumb and forefinger. She grabbed him by the thick black hair that curled at the back of his neck, and she pushed his head down so that he had his lips at her nipples, taking them into his mouth, sucking on them and running his tongue around the aureolas.

She heard herself breathing deeply, irregularly, moaning ever so slightly. Don't stop, don't stop, never stop, she wanted to cry. And he didn't stop, there seemed to be all the time in the world, and he just sucked on her breasts while she held him by the ears, by the shoulders, by the thick black hair that curled at the back of his neck. And then she was hungry for him. She undid the buttons on his shirt, the loose tie at his neck, and she helped him off with his coat. She watched as he pulled his shirt off; she could see his lean body; the ridged musculature of his chest and stomach; the dark-rose nipples; the black tuft of hair between his breasts.

She had never felt like this before, never before this hunger, only in her fantasies, but it was wrong. She wasn't to do this; he wasn't to be an adulteress.

"What is it?" he cried, feeling her withdraw.

"No," she murmured, turning away.

"I love you," he whispered. "Do you hear me? I love you."

She turned to him again. She wanted him; she wanted him so much; she had never had what she had wanted; and it was time, it was time.

"The servants," she said, and he went to lock the door.

He came back, and he kissed her with even greater passion. He lowered her dress. She watched as he lifted her a bit and pulled off the remainder of her clothes. She was nude, and she saw him staring at her. Then he touched her breasts again, her stomach, her hips, her long, silky legs. He ran a finger into the dark region, and she whispered his name. Jarrett, Jarrett, she cried. He rubbed her until she thought she would scream uncontrollably or faint from the sheer pleasure of it. She clutched him to her, and she placed her hand, gingerly at first and then firmly, desiringly, on his hardness. The proof of his need for her excited her even more. He unbuttoned his trousers, kicked off his slippers, and rolled down his pants. She stared at the vivid symbol of his longing; he was only the second man she had ever seen. Without hesitation now she touched him, played with him, and he laid her down on the sofa and, guiding himself into her, they began to move together.

She closed her eyes. She felt nothing except the fire. The fire within, her whole body on fire. She felt each subtle movement pass like a charge through her body, in her feet, in her breasts, at her scalp; and she wrapped herself around him as he moved in and out of her, gasping as he withdrew and then moaning as he gave her the full force of his desire.

"Rebekah," he cried, and she found his lips, and she sucked at his lips as he had sucked at her breasts.

He placed his hands on her bottom, lifting her up to him, the two of them groaning, and her legs shot up to his sides, thrashing as she neared the climax, and then they were there, they were there, and it seemed to last forever, this conflagration, these fireworks, this joy. As they died down, as they heard their spent bodies panting, pounding like engines, they held on to each other, not wanting to let go, never wanting to let go, luxuriating in each other's contentment, recognizing the full meaning of the experience they had just shared.

"I love you, Rebekah," Jarrett whispered.

She held him closely. She had never been told that before, never. "Jarrett," she cried, "Jarrett, I love you, Jarrett, I love you." And then she closed her eyes. Saying it had frightened her. But he knew that she was frightened and so he kissed her tenderly and held her in the crook of his arm.

"We shouldn't have waited this long," Jarrett said.

"We had to. We've done everything just as we had to. There was no other choice. Tonight, too, there was no other choice."

"I'm so glad," he said, kissing her again.

"I never thought of leaving here tonight, Jarrett. Ever since that first time I met you, at Locust Point, I knew that you were special to me. When I said good-bye to you in Baltimore that first time, it was like saying good-bye to my most cherished friend even though I'd known you only so briefly."

"Rebekah, darling Rebekah, it's been so long for me. I'd forgotten all about love. I'd forgotten how much I need it, how much I needed to be with a woman like you."

She touched his cheek. "I've never had love, Jarrett. I've had only Simon. And now you know what Simon is."

"The worst kind of monster to be cruel to you," Jarrett said.

She smiled at his gallantry. "He doesn't matter now, Jarrett. All that matters is you. All that matters is us. As long as we have each other, we'll be safe. I know that. I believe that."

"I'll always be here for you, Rebekah. I swear it."

She looked away from him, into the night, into the soft furry darkness. "Simon said I wasn't a woman. Simon said I was hard and cold and loveless. I'm not like that, am I, Jarrett?"

He smiled and kissed her again. "Of course you're not. You're so much a woman, Rebekah—too much for him."

She hugged him close. "Oh, Jarrett, I don't want this ever to end."

"It doesn't have to, Rebekah."

"I want to believe you, Jarrett, my darling, my darling." The endearments on her lips almost made her weep. "I want to, my darling, my darling, my darling," she murmured, moving closer to him and capturing him in her arms.

CHAPTER FIFTEEN

She couldn't stay with Jarrett as long as she would have wished. If she had stayed any longer, everyone in Mobile would have found out. So she dressed quickly, combing her hair, pinning it, feeling herself weak-kneed and tremulous with a combination of joy and excitement that she had never before experienced.

"I wish you'd stay," he whispered.

"You know I can't," she said quickly. It felt as though the room, with its shadows on the ceiling and the embers in the fireplace, was the warmest place she had ever been; and it was a torment for her to have to leave it. "I must go. I'll speak with you tomorrow. Come by the store at noon, Jarrett." She touched his cheek. "I love you," she said again, fearlessly this time.

They kissed once more, and then she left. The night was restless but filled with remembered pleasures. She arrived back very late, hours after midnight, at Saffron Hill. Sophronia, who admitted her, cast a baleful glance, but nothing was said right then. There was sleep to be had—she needed sleep so badly, even

though the excitement of her body made it difficult—
and she dreamed of him, just as he was, just as they
were together.

When she awoke, she had a strange feeling deep
within her that something was wrong. Perhaps it was
just being away from Jarrett, she thought. She dressed
quickly and went downstairs.

"So early, Miz Rebekah?" Sophronia said as Rebekah entered the kitchen.

"Yes," Rebekah replied hastily. "Just give me some
coffee. I have to get to the store."

"You'd best be getting more rest, Miz Rebekah,"
Sophronia said with her small cat's smile. "You been
comin' in awful late."

Eulalie, the fat cook, quivered with embarrassment,
and Rebekah felt like slapping Sophronia. "Don't
worry about me so, Sophronia. You'll wear yourself
out."

"But I do worry about you, Miz Rebekah."

"Don't," she said firmly, warningly.

She got into the landau and headed toward the
store. As she rode, she felt again the strong feeling of
danger in the air. She urged the horses on. She had
them galloping; she had them snorting in the cool
dawn air. Something was very wrong. It was the store,
she thought, feeling the pain of it all lance through
her. She felt the danger to the store the way a mother
senses danger to her child, and so she sped along the
route, her heart pounding, the horses' hooves pounding.

She raced down Government Street. She turned at
Caroline Street. She saw the orange glow from blocks
away. No. No, she cried. No! THIS STORE CONDEMNED.
No! she screamed. She tasted the smoke on her tongue,
and then she saw the blaze. The horses reared at the
sight of the inferno. She leaped from her carriage and
ran toward the site of the destruction.

"You can't go near there!" a fireman called, but she

ran anyway, not knowing why she was running, not knowing what she would do, just wanting to run into the fire, just wanting to save something from the blaze. She felt the waves of heat, she saw the waves of heat shimmering in the bright pink morning, and the fireman caught her in his arms and held her there, a wild parody of last night's events, and she struggled in his arms and then she sobbed there, feeling wretched, feeling beaten and defiled.

"This your store?" the burly red-faced fireman asked.

She nodded heavily, pulling away from him now, covering her mouth and nose with her trembling hand.

"That's too bad. This here is some bad fire all right."

"Can't you stop it?" She demanded to know, even as the flames shot out through the roof.

"Well, ma'am, let me ask you something. What do you sell there?"

"Fabrics," she said. "Notions."

"Yeah? Well, you sell silk there?"

She nodded.

"Well, you see, all them silks, when they burn, they give out a poison. Makes it hard for us to get in there."

All her silks, she thought. Her exquisite, jewellike silks. She began to sob again, holding herself, bent in half as if she were going to be sick.

In less than an hour, as businesses opened for the day, a crowd gathered to watch the blaze. It was a spectacular blaze now, forty feet high, crackling, brilliantly orange and red and yellow and white. Her neighbor across the street, a greengrocer named Robbins, hurried over to her.

"Mrs. Weiss," he called. "What's to be done?"

She turned to him, took a moment deciding who he was, and then shook her head abjectly.

"Is everything gone?"

"Everything. Everything!" she cried. "All my stock, all my equipment, all the new lines I just ordered. *Oy, Gott in Himmel*," she moaned, reverting now to the Yiddish tongue she rarely used. "What am I going to do?"

"How did it happen?" he asked. "Do they know?"

"I know!" she screamed. "I know! It was the Night Riders! They burned up my store! They want me out of town! Look!" she cried. "Look at my store!"

At the mention of the Night Riders the greengrocer excused himself and disappeared. She was tainted; she knew that much about herself. So she stood in isolation, but she held herself erect, willing to be an outsider, willing to be a sufferer, intent on standing here and watching the building burn down.

After awhile she felt a tap on her shoulder. She turned. It was Jarrett. "Oh, Jarret," she cried, falling into his arms. He didn't care who saw and neither did she. He just let her sob, and she pressed her face against his chest, remembering in the midst of everything that similar moment, years ago now, at the grave site of her sister-in-law.

"I came as soon as I heard," he said.

"They've won," she cried. "They warned me and I defied them and they've won."

"No," he said. "No, they haven't. You won't quit. I know you won't."

"I will," she rasped, feeling her throat parched by the thick drifts of smoke. "I can't keep fighting. I feel like I've been fighting my whole life, and I feel bruised by it, Jarrett. I feel bruised and broken."

He took her hand and kissed it quickly, passionately. "You'd pitch a tent if you had to, wouldn't you?" he said.

The facetious remark made her cry again. "Oh, Jarrett. It was going so well. I was so proud. I was so happy with it."

"I know, darling. I know."

"It isn't fair. They're beasts. They're dirty swine." Just as she said these words, she looked up and she saw that awful man staring at them. Chester Stiles. He was behind it all—she knew he was—and he had the temerity to come and watch her dreams go up in smoke.

"What is he doing here?" she cried.

"Who?" Jarrett said.

"Chester Stiles. He's standing right there. Can you believe it?"

Stiles saw her watching him and gave her a sympathetic frown.

"Get away from here!" she screamed, clenching her hands into tight fists.

"Rebekah!" Jarrett warned, but she wouldn't hear him.

"Get away from here, you dirty dog!"

All faces turned to see the confrontation, and Stiles's choleric complexion turned even redder than it was normally.

"I think you're makin' a mistake, little lady," he said in his thick, buttery voice.

She raced over to him and punched his shoulder with her fist. *"Gey avec!"* she cried, wild with anger, telling him in her foreign tongue to get away.

His eyes almost popped from his head. "You crazy?" he cried.

She flailed at him, and he retreated, the way a big dog might retreat from a normally lesser but herein outraged adversary, like a hissing goose, for instance.

"Who does he think he is?" Rebekah demanded to know. "Coming around here, looking at this destruction as though anyone for a moment would think he had no part in it."

"Well, you managed to scare him away," Jarrett said.

"He'll be back," Rebekah replied. "His kind like to lay their eggs in other people's wounds."

The fire continued to roar. They both stared at it, awestruck, terrified, yet in some sense unconvinced of the futility of it.

"What could I have done?" Rebekah asked rhetorically. "Get out of town? Where would I have gone?"

"Maybe we should go, Rebekah," Jarrett said suddenly. "Maybe it's wrong and reckless and unfair to ourselves to stay here."

She turned away from the fire to look at him. "What are you saying, Jarrett? Go? Go where? Where would we go?"

"Anywhere. What does it matter? We'd be together."

She took his hand and held it tenderly for a moment. "We can't go," she explained patiently. "We'd only be running again. We can't run, Jarrett. *I* can't run. I'm too tired, and there's no place to run to."

"But we'd have each other. We could go together, and we could find . . ."

"No!" she cried, suddenly angry. "You sound just like Simon! I won't run like a cur with my tail between my legs!"

He looked shocked by her response. "Is that what you think I'm proposing to do?"

She felt shamed by his question. "I'm sorry, Jarrett," she murmured.

He stared at her. "You seem so driven, Rebekah. Are you sure you're making the right decisions?"

"Yes, Jarrett," she said. "I think I know what I'm doing. I know that if I leave here now, with this defeat hanging over me, I'll never be successful again."

"There are lots of different ways to be successful, Rebekah."

"Don't lecture me so, Jarrett!" she cried. She felt desperate, and she reached out for him again. "Try to understand me, will you? I can't leave here. I'm bound here. I know what I want, and just because it's taken from me doesn't mean I'll stop wanting it. Can you understand that, Jarrett? You must be able to."

He looked down at the hand that was on his shoulder. He touched her hand with his own. "I don't understand, Rebekah, but whatever you choose to do, it's all right with me. I'll be with you, Rebekah, that much I can promise you."

She wanted to kiss him, but she couldn't, not here, not with this crowd watching. "Thank you, Jarrett," she whispered. "Thank you."

"Now I must go. I'll come back when I'm done. At five? Where will you be?"

"I'll be here," she said grimly.

She watched him go. Now she was all alone, witness to her repudiation. The fire had peaked, and now the frame of the building was groaning, preparing for its collapse. Just then she saw Hattie Winslow, hastily attired, coming toward her.

"Rebekah, my poor dear! What a terrible thing!" Hattie exclaimed. "It's a crime! Surely, it is! I've never seen the likes. Look at it—it's going up like a barn!"

Her lips parted, but she had nothing to say.

"Was that Jarrett Russell I just saw you with?" Hattie asked suddenly.

She could have laughed. "Yes, you know it was. Why do you ask?"

"I didn't realize you were in touch with him," Hattie continued.

Rebekah smiled a bit in spite of everything. "Yes," she said. "I am in touch with him."

"Do you think that's wise?" Hattie demanded to know.

"Why are you asking me?" Rebekah said, annoyed by the woman's inquisitiveness.

"I just want to know if you think it's wise for you to be seen with the son of a traitor," Hattie persisted.

"What do you care? What does anyone care?"

"Someone cares," Hattie cried. "Look at your store! Someone cares!"

"Is that what you came here to tell me?" Rebekah replied. "You're always coming around here with bad news. You're always eager to rub some salt in my wounds."

"That's utter nonsense. I came here because I heard what had happened and I wanted to help you if I could."

"I don't believe it!" Rebekah said. "I don't believe for a moment that you wanted to help me. I think you just wanted to see how badly I've been hurt. Well then, look, why don't you?" she cried, pointing to the burning building. "See? Are you pleased? Are you pleased that I've had my comeuppance?"

Hattie Winslow's face grew very stern. "You're intent on making all the mistakes you can?" she asked.

"Yes," Rebekah said defiantly. "Is that all right with you, Mrs. Winslow?"

The small, bonneted woman gave Rebekah a hateful look. "You're through in this town, do you understand?"

The woman's words suddenly made her find her fear. "What do you mean?"

"You've had your chance. You were smart. But you've broken too many rules. I warned you about that, and you didn't listen to me."

"I've only done what I've had to do."

"You had to see Jarrett Russell?"

"That's my business!" Rebekah cried. "Stay out of it, will you?"

"You don't do what you're doing if you want to stay in Mobile. You don't invite your betters to your home—especially if you're a shopkeeper and especially if you're a Jew. You don't get involved with a man like Jarrett Russell—especially if you're a Jew. You don't . . ."

"Don't tell me what I should and should not do!"

screamed Rebekah. "Who do you think you are? Damn you, you have no right to be talking to me the way you do!"

Hattie nodded briskly. "All right," she said calmly. "I've said all I've had to say. But just remember, Rebekah: you had your chance."

She watched the woman saunter off. Was she going mad? It seemed suddenly that the whole city, the whole world, was drawing a tight ring around her, suffocating her, destroying her. She found herself pacing back and forth. She was being destroyed, and she didn't know how she could save herself.

In another hour or so the sagging roof of the building did collapse with a great roar. There was nothing left. By tomorrow it would all be smoking ruins.

"You've lost, haven't you?" she heard a voice say.

She knew who it was before she turned to look.

"I thought you'd show up," she said.

"Of course. Everyone's talking about it," Simon said. "Everyone loves a fire, after all."

She hated him for coming here now. All of her enemies, come to see her downfall. "What do you want?" she said.

"My God, everything's ruined, isn't it?" he commented, ignoring her question.

"Just get out of here, Simon," she said. "Just get away."

"I will get away when you've answered a few questions for me."

"What questions?"

"Well, first of all, there's the obvious question: how do you plan to pay the rest of the money you owe me?"

She stared at him disbelievingly. "You came here now to ask me that?"

"What of it?"

"Why, you're just a leech, Simon. Have you no sense of decency? Have you no sense of what's right

and what's wrong? Do you think I'm about to talk
finances when I see my store burning to the ground?"

"This wouldn't have happened if you'd heeded the
warnings ..."

"Warnings? Those weren't warnings. Those were
threats."

"Whatever, I won't foot the bill for your recklessness."

"Listen to me, Simon. You won't get a penny more.
I'm coming out of this with nothing. You've got all
you're going to get. Now, why don't you just find
someone else to suck dry?"

Simon noticed that others nearby were listening.
"Lower your voice," he instructed. "You're carrying
on like a common fishwife."

"I don't care who hears it!" she cried even louder.
"You're nothing but a thief. That's right!" she told
the onlookers. "He's a thief!"

Reflexively he reached out and shook her roughly.
"Silence!" he said. "Do you hear me?"

"What are you doing?" she cried. "Don't you touch
me!"

As she cried out, he had an urge to hurt her further,
and he gripped her shoulders between his large blunt
hands.

"You're hurting me!" she cried, and it was what he
wanted to hear. She began to scream. "Police!" she
screamed. "Police!" Her cry woke him from his trance,
and he shook his head. "Don't," he muttered, but she
wouldn't stop. A circle formed around them, and he
broke through it, running down the street.

"You all right?" a woman asked her.

She too ran a distance down the street. No, she was
not all right. Everything had gone wrong. She tried
to think of Jarrett, the only thing in her life that was
good and whole, but it didn't seem strong enough
just now. All she could think of was the pain and the
punishment that she was experiencing. What had she

done to deserve it? Had she asked for too much? Had she done too well? Had she broken all the rules? Still now, even with the smell of smoke on her, she couldn't say what she had done for her to be punished this way.

She looked back at the fire. It was dying now; soon it would be over. Soon there would be ash where her fine store once stood. But it wasn't over; she couldn't believe in the finality of it. In her mind and spirit she knew that the core of confidence was still vivid and alive. With the Night Riders and Hattie Winslow and Simon all against her, she still felt that she would survive. As to whether she would prosper, she did not know. But she *would* survive if nothing else.

She turned and walked away from the fire, not looking back, no longer caring. Everything was done here; another end had been reached. She had Jarrett and she had her talent and she had her knack for survival. This portion of her life was closed. She had only to go on now, searching for new beginnings that poked out through the ash like fresh green shoots.

Part Three

CHAPTER SIXTEEN

In the aftermath of the destruction she seemed to be in a sort of dream. She woke often in the night, starting with a sense of peril, lighting the lamp and going halfway to the landing before she realized that it was too late. Nothing could be saved; the damage was done. And so she returned to bed, trying to seize some sleep before another such interruption.

Jarrett saw a great deal of her and tried to lift her spirits, but the task he set for himself was a difficult one. She had no taste for enjoyment now. All she wanted was to find a solution to her problems.

"You can't keep punishing yourself, Rebekah," he cautioned. "Come down to my office tomorrow, and when I'm through there, we will have ourselves a fine day."

She pressed herself close to him. They were together much of the time now. It would have been bliss if the black cloud hadn't shadowed other areas of her life. "I don't know, Jarrett. I should probably stay here and try to think."

"You think altogether too much." He put his long thin hand on her hip and stroked her tenderly. "Now I want you to join me tomorrow for a ride in the country. Will you do that?"

"All right," she said. "If you say so."

She went by his office at midday. It was located in the Negro section of town, a section she had only passed through once or twice before. There was something irredeemably dingy and threatening about the rows of shanties and the myriad black faces all staring at her as though she were a queen or an empress or some other form of interloper. She knew where the little shack that Jarrett used as an office was located, and quickly she made her way to it.

She entered quietly. She found him at his desk, reading from a great leather-bound volume. "Good morning," she said almost shyly, not immune to the awe she recalled from childhood that one showed the village doctor.

He looked up, and his haggard face was suddenly illuminated by a smile. "Is it noon already?" he asked.

"Yes," she said. "Are you finished for the day?"

"It appears so. Saturdays are not usually too busy. People like to do other things than come and see the doctor."

"Shall we go then?"

"Yes, of course."

They went outside and began walking to the wagon when they saw a young black girl, no more than fifteen at the most, rushing toward them with an infant in her arms. "Doctor!" she cried. "Doctor, wait!"

"What is it?" Jarrett said.

"My baby," the large, plodding girl cried. "He so terrible sick. Jes' you look at him, Doctor."

Jarrett could see right away that the child was suffering from measles. He went back inside with the girl, gave her some medicine and instructions, and told her that he would see her when he returned later in the day.

"Is it all right for us to go?" Rebekah asked.

"Yes, I would say so," Jarrett replied. "There's nothing more I can do for her now. The child will be all right until I return."

They got into the wagon and headed north. She sat close beside him, just barely touching him. She watched his fine strong hands on the reins.

"Where are we going?" she asked.

"Up toward Citronelle," he suggested. "Does that suit you?"

"I don't know. I've never been."

"You haven't allowed yourself much beyond the store, have you, Rebekah?"

"No. There was never time." She did allow herself a small ironic smile. "I suppose there is now, however."

"You should allow yourself time, Rebekah. The store is something very important to you, I know, but you can't make it everything."

She sighed. "What can I do, Jarrett? The business takes all of my energy and now I have to start over again and it's going to take even more out of me."

There was an extended silence, filled only by the sound of the horses' trotting, and then, with great tentativeness, he spoke. "Rebekah," he said, "will you give some thought to what I'm about to ask you?"

She stared at him, trying to get some notion of what it was he wished to introduce, and then she nodded.

"Rebekah," he said, "can we someday become husband and wife?"

She was genuinely shocked by his question. Almost imperceptibly she shrank from him. But he noticed even her tiniest withdrawal, and his face colored darkly. "I'm sorry," he murmured. "I shouldn't have spoken."

"No, Jarrett, it is I who am sorry. It's just such an impossible notion. In every way, Jarrett, can't you see? Why, I'm still a married woman and I . . ."

"He's left you!" Jarrett said heatedly. "It's only a matter of time."

"No, Jarrett," she said as calmly as she could, although she felt alarmed by his impetuosity. "It's more than a matter of time, you know that."

"All I know is that I love you. All I know is that my life was miserable before you came into it."

"And I'll stay with you, Jarrett," she assured him. "But marriage? How can you expect me to even begin to think about it?"

"Is it so far from your thoughts, Rebekah? And will it remain so?" he said, obviously hurt and troubled.

"Yes, I'm afraid so," she replied. "Right now the store must occupy my full attention. I haven't worked all these years to see the fruits of my labor turned into ash."

The tone in her voice was so thoroughly penetrated by bitterness that he was made somewhat uneasy. "The store may just be burned down to the ground in its next incarnation," he said. "Are you going to run your life according to the fortunes of the store?"

"The fortunes of the store *are* my fortunes," she said. The totality of the remark made them both fall silent for a moment. "I'm sorry, Jarrett, but that's the way it is."

"I'm sorry, too," he said. "I thought I was bound to this place, Rebekah. I thought Wild Oaks had cast a spell over me. But when I met you, and when I realized that I loved you, I began to think that I needn't stay here. I needn't keep myself in a place where my family name was reviled. I began to think that we could go off somewhere, to Chicago or St. Louis, and I could set up a practice and we would have enough to live well . . ."

"And what about me? Don't I have a right to my dreams? Is that something so difficult for you to understand?"

"Rebekah, it is you who can't seem to understand."

There was another long, tense silence. "No, Jarrett," she said definitively. "I'm afraid it is *you* who doesn't understand. And I thought you did." Again the silence. With a sidewise glance she could briefly discern the lush beauty of the route, with its cedar trees and tangled bowers of larkspur and golden glow. She didn't want the day ruined, but she couldn't deny the fact that the proposal had, strangely enough, angered her. "It's not just the store, Jarrett. It's more than the store. I'm a Jew and you're not. We can't ignore that fact."

"But we love each other, Rebekah. What does the rest of it matter?"

"It matters, Jarrett. You may think my faith unimportant, but I don't. It's what holds me—this new me—to everything that went before. You may think I have nothing to do with it, Jarrett, but you're wrong. Every Friday I light candles—even if I have to work on Saturdays. And when I light candles, I think of my mother and my father and my sister Sarah and my sister Hannah and my sister Clara and my cousin Miriam and all the people who have meant something to me."

He nodded, and then he spoke softly. "Do you think I would stand in the way of that?" he asked.

The sanity of his response only seemed to add to her urgency. "Jarrett, what else do we need? Isn't it enough that I'm a Jew from across the sea and you're the son of a coward? Do we want to mix those two things? Do you want us to be tarred and feathered and driven out of town?"

There was nothing to be said. They rode on in silence, and by midafternoon they were in the country-side around Citronelle, which was so named on account of the aromatic grass that grew profusely in the surrounding regions. The smell of the pine, which was used in the manufacturing of turpentine and rosin, and the citronella grass made Rebekah feel almost heady. This, combined with the agitation of their talk, threatened to cause her to faint.

"Please stop the wagon, Jarrett," she cried.

"Are you all right?"

"No. I'm not."

He helped her down, grabbed the bag she had prepared, and they walked to a clearing in the woods. It was, in spite of everything, a magnificent day, having that special quality of lucidity that makes all color and form so very crystalline and brilliant. He laid a blanket down on the pine-needle carpet, and there she sat, her face chalk white and suddenly drawn.

He reached inside the picnic hamper and drew out a bottle of red wine. "Here," he said. "This will put some color in your cheeks."

"No. I couldn't . . ."

"Don't be foolish. Now have a glass. Doctor's orders."

She sipped, and she did begin to feel more relaxed. "I'm a fool," she said. "I don't know what came over me."

He smiled. "It must be the way I proposed. I haven't had much practice, you know."

"Really? I would have thought you did."

"No. There was never anyone. There were many in contention, but never anyone worth getting down on my knees for."

She laughed. "And *I* had many proposals. Or at least my father entertained many proposals. There was the widowed baker and the cousin from Tulin and the miller's son and . . ."

"My, my. You were very sought after."

"Oh, yes," she said archly. "And they were all good matches. Prosperous matches. The only thing was that I didn't know or care for any of them." She was quiet for a moment. "But there was someone I loved and wanted to marry."

"Who?" he asked, genuinely interested and with no competitive edge to his voice.

"A boy named Jacob. My father hated him, refused to have him in the house. I often met him in places like this," she said, making a circular gesture that encompassed this clearing in the woods. "I did love him. And you remind me of him," she said, reaching out for his hand.

They kissed tenderly, trying to put behind the stress of this morning's conversation.

"I loved him, but I was only a girl then. I didn't know then that love was not the answer to everything."

He felt her pushing him away again. "It's the answer to many things, isn't that so, Rebekah?"

"Yes, Jarrett," she said. "And if I didn't have you in my life, then I don't know how I could bear it. I was so starved, Jarrett, until you came along. But there are problems that love cannot solve."

"I don't know if I believe that, Rebekah."

"Maybe you're right, maybe I'm right. All I know is that there are things I must do, and all the help that you give me will not alter the fact that I must do them for myself."

"But will you let me help you?" he said.

"Oh yes," she murmured, reaching out for him, drawing him close, and finding her comfort with him once again.

There was only one course of action open to her: she had to mortgage Saffron Hill. That was the only capital available to her. The thought of doing what she had to do filled her with dread. As soon as she had gained something, she had to give it back.

She also had to terminate the employment of the servants. She felt awful having to do so, for they had all been associated with Saffron Hill most of their lives. When told of their dismissal, Eulalie fell into the most calamitous weeping and Dover, normally of a sunny disposition, suddenly turned sullen. Only Sophronia remained in character, cool to the end and vaguely condescending.

"You know I've been trying to make ends meet since the fire," Rebekah told them. "But it simply won't work. I'll give you pay, of course, and references. That's the best I can do."

"You all goin' to try again in Mobile, Miz Rebekah?" Sophronia wondered.

"Yes. There seems to be no other way."

"And you think next time goin' to be different?"

"I think so, Sophronia."

Sophronia looked at her very hard. "You know what you doin', Miz Rebekah?"

"I think so," Rebekah said again. She waited a moment and then added: "And if I succeed, Sophronia, there will be a place for you and the others. Wherever it will be, even if it's in the store, there will be a place for you."

Sophronia scrutinized her employer to see if she were telling the truth, and then, satisfied, she nodded briskly, leaving Rebekah feeling foolishly, inappropriately sentimental.

One other matter she had to see to was an auction of her furnishings. This aspect of her reversals seemed to her almost heartbreaking. She recalled that when she moved into Saffron Hill, there was no money at first for furnishings; only after awhile was she able to afford the armoires and the side tables and the chifforobes and the carpets and all the things that had really made Saffron Hill her own. Now they were gone, and she would never again see the things she had come to love. But she netted a tidy sum from the sale, and this, along with the money from the house, might be enough to get her going again if she was lucky.

"What are you intending to do with the capital?" Jarrett asked her at the end of the auction.

"Triple it, if I'm lucky," she snapped.

"What do you mean?"

"What I mean is that I'm taking the money to a place where I can get more of it quickly if I play my cards right."

He stared at her. "You mean gamble it away?" he said disbelievingly.

"No. I mean gamble it into something bigger."

"I think you're being foolish, Rebekah. I think you're being foolish and headstrong."

"I don't agree, Jarrett. I'm willing to take chances. That's how I got where I am. And I know I can win— I feel it in my bones—I feel that I can get lucky again."

"And if you lose?"

"I don't know. Back on the road, I suppose."

"What about us?"

"Don't keep asking me that, Jarrett!" she cried. "I can't think of it now. Won't you just leave me be?"

It was their last conversation before she left Mobile for New Orleans. She could have tried her luck in Mobile itself—there were gambling establishments here as well, notably the shabby little houses on Shakespeare's Row—but she was intent on New Orleans for a number of reasons. First of all no one knew her in New Orleans, and so she wouldn't be adding more fuel to the efforts being made to sully her reputation. Furthermore she didn't trust anything or anyone in Mobile at this point. And, most important, she wanted to go where the stakes were high, and this kind of game she was sure to find in New Orleans. She regretted leaving Jarrett on this sour note, but she wasn't going to worry about it now. Now all she was going to think about was turning her money into something bigger, something capable of renewing her business.

She took the morning train to New Orleans, and she traveled first class, even though she could ill afford such luxuries. But it was not, by any means, a frivolous gesture. She went first class because to do so preserved her sense of worth and achievement. If she traveled as though she were worth something, then she could believe that she would be worth something once again.

When she arrived at the Terminal Station in New Orleans, she felt momentarily weak with tension. So much rested on this brief journey—the future of her happiness, to be exact. She went directly to the St. Louis Hotel, one of the two great hostelries in the city, the other being the St. Charles Hotel. When she arrived at the hotel, she felt herself being looked over with some degree of disapproval. She knew that it was unusual for women of her age and demeanor to be traveling alone, but the fact was that she had no other choice. She watched what was obviously a brief consultation between desk clerk and manager and then, with the inimitable hauteur of low-level employees, the desk clerk summoned the porter and had her luggage, one bag, brought to room 6.

It was a magnificent hotel, and she was given a beautiful room. The furniture was elegant, the view outstanding. But she couldn't stay here. If she stayed in this room all day, waiting to see what the night would bring, waiting to see if she would be lucky or if she would be ruined, then surely she would go mad. So then, twenty minutes after she arrived, she was out on the street again, looking for diversion, looking to get lost in the rush of the crowd.

She began to walk down Royal Street in the heart of the Vieux Carré, or the French Quarter. It was a brilliant, sultry day, and everyone on the street wore light, brightly colored clothing. She took a left and headed down St. Louis Street, looking at the large, fine houses that created contrast to the narrow streets. The homes were built flush with the street line, and, instead of affording a broad, flowered front-lawn vista from a wide veranda, such as one would find in the homes of Spring Hill, these dwellings hid their interior beauty from outside eyes. But here and there were glimpses of the patios filled with bougainvillea and cat's claw and oleander and crepe myrtle and mimosa and sweet olive. The fragrance of these blooms wafted over the garden walls and did combat with the odor from the stagnant pools of water that were not an irregular feature of these streets. Leading up from the garden walls were the intricately wrought iron balconies. Rebekah studied each lacy, weblike pattern and was able to discern such elements as tulips, bows and arrows, maize, morning glory, and rose vines.

She walked and walked and finally took refuge in a small park overlooking the Mississippi. She watched the passing parade of exotica with unbridled fascination.

"R-r-r-r-ramonay!" she heard.

She looked behind her and saw a tall coal-black man wearing shuffling shoes, a long frock coat that aspired to dignity, and, cocked over one eye, an enormous top hat with the crown bashed in. He was carrying a bundle containing rope, a sheaf of broom straw, and several bunches of palmetto.

"Ramonez la cheminée du haut en bas!" he cried up to the windows of the houses.

She could make out the word "chimney," and she realized that he was the chimney sweep. As soon as she had placed his trade, she was distracted by another noise. She turned and saw a "spasm band" coming down the street. The "spasm band" was a group of virtuosos on the soap box, tin cans, pan tops, nails, drumsticks. The fact that the virtuosos were little black boys only added to her enjoyment of it. A bumping rhythm accompanied one of the boys who was doing a wild shuffling dance. They spotted her watching them, and the whole group of them descended on her. She tossed them some coins, which only spurred them on further.

"Lagniappe!" one of the children cried.

She shook her head.

"Lagniappe!"

"I don't understand," she said.

"They want to give you a little gift, a *lagniappe*," a voice from behind her said.

She turned and saw a small, spritelike man in faded elegant clothes.

"Something for nothing," he said with a smile.

"I don't understand," she repeated.

"An old Creole custom. The tradesman presents his customer with a little gift for each purchase," the man said in his thick Irish brogue.

She nodded, although she was mystified by the idea. Instantly one of the boys walked down the street on his hands while another imp of a boy placed the crown of his skull on a tin can and whirled like a top.

"That's their *lagniappe* to you," the man said.

"Thank you for explaining."

"You got the look of a foreigner about you," the man said. "You never been to New Orleans before?"

"No," she admitted.

"Well then, it's quite a sight to see, it is."

"Yes," she said with a distant polite tone to her voice. "Thank you." She began to head up along the river, and she sensed that she was being followed.

"Are you following me?" she asked, turning to see the little man.

"Only with your permission," he said with a bow.

"Well, you haven't got it," she cried.

"But, miss, New Orleans is a friendly city, you know. I'm just in the spirit for some conversation. I promise you I ain't got no sinister designs."

She stared at him. He was so small and droll looking that she couldn't really be too wary of him. If need be, she could easily pick him up by his collar and dispose of him quickly.

"I see you're reconsidering, miss," the man said. "Allow me to introduce myself. William P. O'Donnell at your service."

She stared at him further and then nodded stiffly.

"You may be wondering how I might be at your service," the little man continued. "May I suggest that

I show you around the Quarter? I have years of experience here and know every nook and cranny."

"And what do you want in exchange for it?" Rebekah asked.

He laughed with mock embarrassment. "Perhaps a small gratuity, miss," he said, "but only if it please you."

She found him ridiculously amusing. "Very well," she said. "But when I say the tour is over, then it's over. Do you understand?"

"I ain't never worn out my welcome yet, miss, I assure you."

In the course of this guided peregrination Mr. O'Donnell gave her the histories and the legends of many of the fine buildings. He also managed to insinuate into his narrative enough of his personal history for Rebekah to know that he was born in County Cork fifty years ago, that he claimed to have come to the United States on a clipper ship, and that he had been living in or around the city of New Orleans for the past twenty years.

"What brought you here?" she asked.

He smiled ruefully. "Gambling," he said. "I must confess it. I've always had a weakness for it, and this city drew me to it like a magnet."

She looked away from him, suddenly feeling too warm.

"Is something the matter, miss?" he said.

She shook her head.

"You don't like gambling. Is that it? Many women share your dislike."

She faced him again. "No, that's not it, Mr. O'Donnell. The fact is that I, too, have come here to try my luck."

"You don't say!" he cried with a laugh. "Well, fancy that! You could feed me to the turtles! I never took you for the gambling kind, that's for sure."

"I'm not the gambling kind," she countered in a

voice rather too demure for the situation. "I need the money to launch a business venture, and the only way I can increase my capital is through games of chance."

"Well, I admire your pluck, miss. But the fact of the matter is that you're just as likely to lose what you got."

"I have no other choice!" she insisted.

He stared at her. "You know where you're going to try your luck?"

"I've heard talk of a place called Burgundy Street," she said hesitantly.

He snorted in contempt. "Penny-ante stuff!" he said. "And whatever you go away with, they'll take from you in the alley."

"Then where?" she said. "Where can I go?"

He looked at her shrewdly. "You didn't come very well prepared, did you, miss? You got your money in a safe place?"

She nodded.

"Where you got it?"

"Why should I tell you?"

"Because I'm an honest man," he said. "If I weren't an honest man, why would I be outfitted in togs like this? Now tell me, for your own good, where are you keeping your money?"

She felt herself trust this man, trust him instinctively. "In a money belt," she found herself answering.

"That's good. That's smart." He stared at her again. "Let me make you a little proposal, if I may, miss."

"All right."

"How's about I act in this enterprise as a sort of chaperon. A tutor, maybe you'd want to call it. And all I ask is a small cut of what you win."

The proposal interested her. "How small a cut?" she asked.

"Five percent?"

She didn't know what to do. She shook her head slightly, but it was not really a response.

"Come on, miss. Don't go it alone. It's so awful lonely that way. Anyway, maybe I'm your lucky charm. What do you say?"

She looked at him carefully. Maybe he was her lucky charm, she thought. "Very well," she said. "It's a deal."

He walked with her back to the hotel. "Now, what we're going to do tonight is to pay a visit to Colonel J. J. Bryant."

"Who's that?"

"He only happens to run the number-one gambling establishment in New Orleans. Oh yes, miss, you can win a lot and you can lose a lot at Colonel Bryant's."

"That sounds like what I had in mind," she said with steely resolve.

"But one don't go to Colonel Bryant's before midnight. So first I think we'll take dinner at Antoine's and then the show at the St. Charles."

"What do we want to do that for?" she said. "You've certainly got grand ideas of what to do with my money."

"Listen, miss. If you're going to lose it, then a good time ain't going to matter. And if you're going to win —it matters even less. This way we'll steady our nerves and be fresh as daisies when we get to the colonel's."

She thought about what he said and then agreed. The dinner they had that night at Antoine's was magnificent, even though a nervous stomach on her part limited her enjoyment. There was crayfish bisque, *pompano en papillote*, *poulet chanteclair*, and, for dessert, an *omelette souflée* followed by *café brulée*.

"I haven't eaten at Antoine's since my last run of luck, which was about three years ago," O'Donnell confessed, wiping his lips with his napkin. "I guess that's a good omen, ain't it?"

"I don't know, Mr. O'Donnell," she said. "Look at you now."

"Well, I ain't so bad, am I, miss? I mean, here I am in Antoine's again."

She would have smiled, but she was altogether too tense.

"Easy, miss," O'Donnell cautioned. "You got to get your nerves nice and steady if you're going to win tonight."

"Oh, that's easy for you to say. All you'll lose is five percent of something you hadn't counted on anyway. But I'll be ruined!"

"You ain't going to be ruined, miss. O'Donnell knows that much."

As planned, they followed dinner at Antoine's with the show at the St. Charles Theater. Tonight the performance was by the great stage personality Joseph Jefferson appearing in one of his most famous vehicles, *Rip Van Winkle.*

"You ever seen Joe Jefferson before?" Mr. O'Donnell whispered as the house lights were lowered.

She shook her head.

"Well, you're in for a treat, miss."

The spectacle was grand, and Mr. Jefferson handled both tragedy and comedy with marvelous deftness. But still, all she could really put her mind to was the forthcoming event, the part of the evening that would determine the course of her life, the game of chance that was much more than a game.

"Did you enjoy that, miss?" O'Donnell asked, beaming with delight.

"Not as much as I would have liked."

He clucked his tongue. "Well, first time out's hard for everyone, I suppose. Tell you what. What say we get ourselves a drink and then we'll . . ."

"Are you a drinking man, Mr. O'Donnell?"

"Well, now and again, miss, to be sure, but only . . ."

"This is not the time to indulge yourself, Mr. O'Donnell. This is the time to keep your wits about you."

They made their way down St. Charles Avenue to

Colonel J. J. Bryant's. They stood across the street
from it; she felt her heart pounding. She watched the
finely dressed men and women pass through the un-
imposing portal. "Will they let us in?" she said.

"Don't worry. I know people here."

And it turned out that he really did. They were
admitted into a large and impressive room that led
into a much larger chamber. The walls were all red
plush; there were Turkish rugs on the floor; there
were great red damask draperies on the windows; there
were crystal chandeliers illuminating the room;
there was the smell of cigars and whiskey and sweat.

"Welcome, welcome," said an august, white-haired
presence who turned out to be the colonel himself.
"We are so pleased you could join us tonight."

"Thank you," Rebekah murmured, suddenly, ridiculously shy.

"May we get you some sherry?" he asked.

She looked at Mr. O'Donnell who, of course, was
nodding eagerly.

"I said we shouldn't drink," she hissed when they
were alone.

"Just do what I do," O'Donnell hushed her.

They got her chips and went to the gaming tables.
They took their place and began to play the game of
lansquenet. The banker, a dark, snaky-looking man
who made Rebekah particularly uncomfortable, set
the stakes, and everyone matched him, even though
he had started high. He then turned up two cards, one
for himself and one for the others. His was a five of
diamonds; if anyone else was to get a five, they would
lose. When it got to be her turn, O'Donnell spoke for
her: "*Je tiens,*" he said, meaning "I'll hold." She won
that first round, and then she was forced to leave the
table because her heart was pounding so furiously.

"We did well there," O'Donnell said, after they
collected her chips. "Don't tell me you're going to
crack."

"I don't know. So much is riding on this."

"I know, miss," he said. "I know what it's like to have everything riding on your last hand. But you've come all the way here, so you may as well take your chances."

They went back to the lansquenet table, and she won more than she lost. Being ahead, she continued on to a game of euchre where the stakes were considerably higher. O'Donnell quickly explained to her the rules of euchre, wherein seven was the lowest card and five cards were dealt, with one being turned over. The turned-over card was the trump; the knave was the best card; the knave of trump was known as the Right Bower and the other knave of the same color was the Left Bower. Three tricks out of five won the hand.

"Do you get it, miss?" O'Donnell asked.

She nodded.

"You're a quick study, all right."

Three hands later she had lost heavily. She felt the sweat pour off her body, and her mouth was ash dry.

"Don't give up now, miss," O'Donnell whispered into her ear.

She listened to him. She kept on playing, and then her luck turned. When she won back what she had lost, she left the euchre table.

"I'd better stop," she said, as she poured herself some water.

"Not now. You're just getting it back."

"I'll be ruined!" she screamed in a whisper. "Don't you understand?"

"No such thing," the little man assured her. "You've got the glow about you now. Don't stop—you'd be a fool to stop. Try the faro game. You'll see."

She had avoided the faro table so far. That was where the heaviest activity was, faro being the most popular game of the day.

"All right," she said, feeling that if she lost, then

she lost and so it would be done and so she would
accommodate her life to this turn of events. "Come
with me."

They took their places at the faro table. This simple
game was a matter of betting against the dealer on
what order the cards would turn up. She looked
around the table at the other players. Old, young,
men, women—they all had the same expression, a
resignation that might lead at any moment to anguish
or ecstasy. She lost the first two hands, and then she
began to win. She felt her luck blooming; she felt it
take over the room like some great, large, yeasty force.
She felt Mr. O'Donnell's hand on her shoulder, and
she reached up to clasp it. A crowd gathered. The
euchre tables and the game of lansquenet were halted
as everyone in Colonel Bryant's establishment turned
their attentions to this phenomenon. She kept on
winning, feeling her head buzzing with excitement,
feeling Mr. O'Donnell's hand gripping her shoulder
tightly. When it was over, when she was told that she
had beat the bank, she sat there for a moment in a
state of wonder, feeling that she had been given a
wonderful gift more rare and precious than anything
she could ever have imagined.

"You did it!" O'Donnell cried, his normally red
face grown to crimson with delight. "I knew you
could! When I saw you the first time, something went
fluttering in me and I said to myself, 'Now there's a
piece of luck, Billy Boy!'"

She rose from the table. All eyes were on her. "I
want to leave," she whispered to Mr. O'Donnell.

"Well, let's cash in then."

Colonel Bryant stared at her suspiciously as he completed the transaction and gave her the cash. "What
is your name, madam?" he asked.

"Mrs. Weiss," she murmured.

"Have I ever met you before?"

She shook her head.

"Then you're not a professional game player?"

She blushed deeply. "No, sir. I am not."

"Just a very lucky woman," he said, his voice laced with an unfriendly, ironical tone.

"Yes," she replied. "There you have it."

Once out in the street they hailed a carriage and headed toward the hotel. She was carrying more cash on her than she would ever have dreamed she would.

"He certainly gave you the once-over," O'Donnell said.

She nodded. "I can't really blame him, I suppose."

"He would have liked to take you into another room and had you searched for *portées*," the little man chuckled.

She gave him an uncomprehending look.

"Prepared decks of cards," he explained. "Very dangerous stuff."

When they arrived at the hotel, she asked him to come to her room.

"I want to give you more than you asked for," she said.

"Oh, miss, that's not necessary. I was only along for the ride, you know. It was clear to everyone there that nothing could have stopped you tonight."

"Nevertheless I don't feel I could have done it without you." She gave him the sizable sum of money that she felt he deserved. "You were a comfort to me, Mr. O'Donnell, and I thank you for it with all my heart."

"Well, the pleasure was all mine," he said with a bow.

She stared at him. He was shabby and it was evident that he had led a life of some dissolution, but she liked him more than anyone she had met for some time now. She sensed something fundamentally honest about him, and that was a quality rare and valuable. "Let me ask you something, Mr. O'Donnell," she said.

"At your service, miss."

She smiled. "This may strike you as impulsive . . ."

"Well, miss, if I may be allowed to interrupt, I just want to say that I ain't got nothing against impulse."

She smiled, more broadly this time. "Yes, Mr. O'Donnell, I realize that. Well then, let me make you a proposition. How would you like to come work for me?"

The little man's jaw dropped. "Well now," he said, taking a deep breath and then exhaling slowly. "I wasn't banking on that."

"Then you're not interested?"

"Whoa, miss! I didn't say that, did I? Tell me, what kind of work is it?"

"Well, Mr. O'Donnell, with your help tonight I was able to recoup from a disastrous loss I suffered in a fire. My store—Weiss Dry Goods and Sundries in Mobile—was burned to the ground by the Ku Klux Klan."

O'Donnell's normally genial face turned angry. "Why, the dirty bastards, excuse my language. Doing that sort of thing to hardworking people like yourself. Why, they should be shot!"

She was pleased by his anger. "I'm going to start the store again. Except this time it's going to be different. This time it's going to be for a new clientele." As she spoke, she began to plan in her mind a whole new strategy. "I made the Weiss Store into a fine ladies' specialty store, and I did good business with it. But you have to play games to keep those kinds of customers, and I won't do it anymore. They have no loyalty to me, these ladies. All they want to do is tell *me* what to do, and I won't have it."

O'Donnell watched her with fascination. There was a fierceness to her that surprised him and that he rather stood in awe of.

"So this time out I'm going to aim my business at the freedmen. They're a force to be reckoned with,

Mr. O'Donnell. They may not have a lot of money, but they are large in number. The Weiss Store is going to be there to serve them and anyone else who cares to come and buy. And this time, Mr. O'Donnell, I'm going to have guards around the clock."

"Is that what you want me for, miss?"

"No, Mr. O'Donnell. I want you for something more important. But first tell me something—do you have any feelings against Jews or Negroes?"

He thought a moment before answering. "I admire your frankness, miss. And let me tell you right off that, as an Irishman, I know what it's like to have others looking down on you. 'Tain't a good thing at all, miss, and I ain't party to it. Never have, never will be."

"That's what I thought. I don't know why, Mr. O'Donnell—I may be gravely mistaken—but I trust you."

"You ain't mistaken, miss."

"I want you to come work for me, to assist me, to be a sort of right-hand man to me. When we were together tonight, I felt that your judgment was sound and that you knew what I wanted even before I did."

"Well, miss," he said. "I got a good feeling too."

"Will you come work for me then? I'll pay you well, and I'll treat you well. I promise you that, Mr. O'Donnell. As long as you treat me well, and that means no coming in drunk and no pilfering from the register. What do you say?"

He smiled. "I say you just hired yourself a man, miss."

She smiled back at him. "Then meet me tomorrow at the Terminal Station at noon, will you?"

"Sure enough." He turned to leave and then he turned back to her. "Just one question, miss. When we was in Colonel Bryant's, you said you was Mrs. Weiss. Do there be a Mr. Weiss then?"

She thought a moment. "No, Mr. O'Donnell. You are mistaken. I said no such thing. There is no Mr. Weiss."

"Very good then, miss. Until noon," he said, with his customary little bow.

Once Mr. O'Donnell left, she felt her utter exhaustion take over. It had been an extraordinary twenty-four hours. All she knew was that she had survived. No, more than that: she had won. Now she could go back to Mobile, and she could pick up where she left off. Now she had a clear idea of how to make things work. She was anxious for the morning to come; she was anxious to get back to Mobile; she was anxious to sink herself in her work, with her new aide at her side. And then there was Jarrett. Would he be there for her? She hadn't been caring of him; she knew that, and she felt so ashamed. Would he be there for her? She prayed that he would, for she loved him so, and she wanted him to be there to share the joy of this victory with her.

CHAPTER SEVENTEEN

As soon as she returned from Mobile, she sent Jarrett a note.

Dearest,

She wrote.

You know I had to do what I did. Can you accept

it? Can we see each other? I can't bear it if you say no.

She had it delivered directly to Wild Oaks. And then she waited, but she didn't have to wait long, because that same day he met with her at the Waverly Hotel where she was staying temporarily.

They sat in the small, lush garden at the rear of the hotel.

"I'm glad you came," she said when she saw him.

"Did you think I wouldn't come?"

"I didn't know. I haven't acted well, I know that." She fingered the stem of the delicate goblet that held the water and bitters. "But I did what I had to do."

"I hadn't wanted to stand in your way," he said sarcastically.

She was surprised by his tone. "You *are* angry," she said.

"Not at all. You made it clear that certain things come first in your life, and I can go along with that. Things have changed, but not necessarily for the worse."

"What's changed?" she said, her voice charged with urgency.

He gave her a smile that was supposed to appear tolerant but that was really meant to nettle her. "You've shown that I can't look to you for real love, or whatever love is. I thought we had that—that special understanding—but it's clear that we don't. We're just two people drawn to each other, which is fine. It's foolish to ask for more because more isn't available."

She felt chilled by his tone. "I don't understand, Jarrett. You sound like you're punishing me."

He smiled again, the same infuriating smile. "That's a rather petulant remark, isn't it? After all, you must expect that there will be consequences to your actions."

"You haven't even asked me what happened in New Orleans," she said, now, indeed, sounding petulant.

"I assume everything went your way, as it is wont to do."

She stared at him. She felt herself grow angry. "Yes, it went my way. It went my way splendidly. And if I'd listened to you, I would have been nowhere now."

"Well then, keep that as a rule of thumb. Never listen to me, and good things will happen for you."

She was so disturbed to hear this new tone that she could have burst into angry, betrayed tears right then and there. "You're being horrible. You know you are."

"Stop it, Rebekah. You make an unconvincing victim."

"All right, Jarrett. The fact is that I made a killing. The fact is that I broke the bank at Colonel Bryant's."

"Impressive," he said, nodding.

"Yes, it was. And I can start the store again."

"Yes, the store."

"*Yes.*"

The tension in the air was electric. She had the impulse to get up and leave, but she couldn't, being held there, as it were, by force.

"Have you thought of putting the store behind you altogether and becoming a riverboat gambler?" he said with another turn of the screw.

"I don't think that's at all funny. You seem to have misunderstood my purpose entirely. Just what is it, Jarrett? Have I offended your sense of propriety? Did you suddenly realize that a fine gentleman such as yourself doesn't take up with a Jewess who travels alone to New Orleans to play at the faro table?"

"There it is again, your Jew thing," he cried.

"Yes, my Jew thing," she said, flinging the words back into his face.

"That has nothing to do with anything," he said emphatically. "I asked you to marry me, didn't I?"

"Oh yes, on your terms."

"Were they so unreasonable? All I suggested was that we could start a new life together."

"I don't want to start a new life," she cried. "I did that when I was eighteen years old. I'm not a cat. I don't want nine lives. I want one! The one I choose."

"Well then, what do you want me to say?"

"Say that you'll be here with me."

"There? Where? Where do you want me to be? Comfortably, securely in the background?"

She closed her eyes and held her knuckles to her temples. "Oh, I'm so tired of fighting everyone," she moaned. "Why can't I just do what I want to do?"

"Do it. I don't care."

"Why don't you care? I *do* love you, I do. And I know you love me. But that doesn't mean we have to give up everything else, does it?"

"That's precisely what I said, Rebekah. You haven't been listening. You go your way and I'll go mine and when our paths cross, then we shall enjoy each other."

"I never heard anything so cold."

He shook his head. He reached out for her hand. "I don't feel coldly toward you," he said in a low, pressing voice.

"That's not what I mean," she said.

"It's what I mean," he replied, putting her hand to his lips.

"You can't do that, Jarrett. I'm not some sort of easy . . ."

"Whoever said you were easy?" he replied.

She looked at him. Where was her kind, gentle Jarrett? She wanted him to hold her and tell her that it was all forgiven.

"Let's go up to your room," he murmured.

"No. It's not right. Not when you say there isn't love. Not when you . . ."

"Come on," he said, rising, taking her by the hand.

They went to her room, the small, neatly appointed room that she was occupying in between residences.

She sat on the fine brass bed with the white candle-wick spread embossed with a large "W" for the Waverly Hotel.

"Here we are," she said nervously.

He sat down beside her. Boldly he placed his hand on her breast.

"Jarrett . . ."

"I want you," he said. He kissed her neck as he unbuttoned her dress.

She let him do what he wanted. At first she just stared at the ceiling, feeling hollow and abandoned. Then, when she saw his pleasure in her, she held him closely and tried to catch it from him.

"Here," he said, "touch me here."

She did what he said. She tried to please him; she felt she owed him something; she felt that if she pleased him, maybe they could go back to the way it was.

Afterward, when it was done, he fell into a sudden deep sleep, and she gazed at him. His face, in repose, brought back to mind all the goodness she had seen in him from that very first time at Locust Point. What had she done? she thought. She had altered him in some way, letting him suffer before the exercise of her will. She could hear Simon's words: *You're no woman, you don't know how to be a woman.* Desperate to get the words out of her head, she nudged Jarrett awake.

"What is it?" he asked, startled from sleep.

"Hold me," she cried, thrusting herself against him.

"What is it? Tell me."

"I'm sorry," she sobbed. "Forgive me, Jarrett, forgive me."

He took her face in his hands and looked into her eyes. "You want everything your way," he said, "but it isn't as easy as all that."

"I just want you to love me again," she pleaded.

He stared at her for a very long moment, and then he spoke. "Give it time," he whispered. "Give it time."

* * *

Time did pass and much happened. She opened the
store again, this time in a long, narrow, unobtrusive
building at the intersection of St. Anthony and Claiborne streets, the junction at the threshold of the
Negro district. From here Davis Avenue stretched for
three miles, the main thoroughfare of the city's black
section. It was here that Rebekah set about establishing a store that would draw upon the new economic force of the freedman.

Assisting her, in addition to O'Donnell, was the
maid Sophronia and Dover, the former groom. She
had promised them positions and, not yet wanting to
return to Saffron Hill or some other grand residence,
she kept her word by having them work in the store.
It also occurred to her that the employment of Negroes
in the Weiss Store would not hurt business any.

"How are we going to know what to stock, miss?"
O'Donnell wondered at the beginning. "Have you
experience with the tastes of these folks?"

"I have experience knowing what sells, Mr. O'Donnell," she said confidently. "The first thing we know
about the freedman is that, for the first time in his
life, he has money that he can call his own. It's not a
lot of money, of course, but it seems like a great deal
to him, and he's going to want to feel that he's getting
a lot for what he buys."

O'Donnell nodded, admiring her sage appraisal.

"Of course, when there isn't much money, there
isn't much of a market for luxuries. We'll aim at
women because that's where your real strength is, and
we'll stock fifty-cent corsets and twenty-five-cent stock-
ings. That will get a lot of people into the store, and
then we'll give them something. A *lagniappe*," she
said with a grin.

He laughed his joyous, beery laugh. "You are a
quick study, miss. I said it from the beginning."

"Indeed you did, Mr. O'Donnell. The point is," she

continued, "that we will offer, let's say, a free handkerchief with the purchase of two corsets. That will cost us next to nothing, but I have a feeling it will excite our customers."

"Something for nothing, ay?"

"Precisely. And there's nothing more exciting than that. Now are you prepared to get to work?"

"Yes, miss. I am pleased to begin."

As she and O'Donnell and Sophronia and Dover set to work, cleaning and polishing and building shelves and scraping floors, she tried not to think that this was the second time around. If she thought of all the work that had gone into setting up the store on Caroline Street, she might very well succumb to fatigue. Just now she felt the pain and bitterness that the merest brush with her recollections were sure to induce. She and Simon could have had so much if only he were willing. But it was foolish of her to entertain such thoughts, she realized. There was something profoundly, unalterably wrong with Simon. She was best relieved of him altogether, and she had heard through Sophronia that Simon and Lucy had gone to New Orleans. Well, she wished them well, she told herself, even though, in some deeper, less controlled part of her, she longed to see them punished.

She scheduled a grand opening on the day before Thanksgiving. She instructed Sophronia and Dover to spread the word in the Negro district that she was offering a free chicken with any purchase of five dollars or more.

"But isn't that a bit extravagant, miss?" O'Donnell said.

"Not really, Mr. O'Donnell. Chicken is cheap, and think of all the people we'll get in the store, not to mention the fact that many of them will come back because we'll be noted for our *lagniappe*."

"Well, we'll certainly see, won't we, miss?"

The day of the opening was a good deal different

than that day two years ago when she and Simon sat
in silence in the store on Caroline Street waiting for
the customers who refused to show up until she
dragged herself over to White Meadows to beg Hattie
Winslow for her patronage. Now Hattie Winslow
could rot in hell, Rebekah thought as she watched the
droves of people waiting outside the new, small, narrow Weiss Store—a store that would soon be obsolete
when business got too big for it.

"Miss," O'Donnell cried as he ran into her office
around midday, "there's some of them what's coming
in with baskets of eggs. What are we to do, miss? They
wants to pay us with baskets of eggs!"

"Then take the eggs, Mr. O'Donnell," she said
calmly. "Take the eggs and that's what we'll be eating
until they come in with money."

It was in this way that Rebekah and the Weiss
Store established themselves in the new community.
And every instinct she had was right. She established
credit freely, and she found that she earned more
than she lost with this policy. She allowed for returns
with few questions asked. She made sure that no one
had lower prices than she did. And she continued her
policy of *lagniappe*, so inscrutable to her when she
first heard of it, but now seeming so right. She gave
little gifts at holidays—fabric flowers and ribbons that
cost a penny a piece—and she had constant special
sales. "Two for the price of one" became an often-
heard refrain, and she instituted a schedule of linen
sales, lingerie sales, and remnant sales at various times
of the year.

"You're doing very well, aren't you?" Jarrett asked
her one night when he came to take her to dinner.

"Yes, I am," she admitted.

"And I was wrong, and you were right."

"I didn't say that, Jarrett, did I?"

"But you thought it."

"Don't tell me what I think, please."

The tension surfaced again, much to her regret. They had been seeing each other all along, in the months since she had returned from her gambling trip to New Orleans, but it had been less than good. Ever since Jarrett had discounted the need for love, there had been a hollowness to their relationship. She didn't know what to do about it. She would rather have died than give up altogether. There was no use, however, in saying that she was sorry, because he would know that she was lying. She would not abandon her pride; it was what drove her on to success. But as long as she had her pride, it would be hard for them to reclaim the gentle, good feelings.

"You certainly have a way of making money," he said in a tone that was meant to sound idle but that she knew was far from it.

"Yes," she said. "I do."

"Remarkable. Absolutely remarkable."

"Yes," she replied, her voice taking on an edge. "We Jews have a way with money. Is that what you're thinking, Jarrett?"

"Yes, Rebekah. That's exactly what I'm thinking."

"Well then, why don't you just leave? I don't need that kind of filth being spread around here. I don't need . . ."

He took her roughly by the shoulders and shook her until she was silent. "You impossible woman! What makes you turn my thoughts into insults? What gives you the right to do that? The fact was that I was admiring you, and yet you turn everything around."

The intensity of his feeling shocked her, and she stared at him, at a loss for words.

"Is that what you did to Simon?" he added cruelly.

She pulled free of him. "Don't you say that, Jarrett! I won't hear it. You can just get out of here if that's the way it's going to be."

"Do you want me to go?"

She retreated a bit. "I didn't say that, did I?"

"Did you drive him away, Rebekah? Is that what you did?"

She covered her ears. "Stop it, Jarrett!" she cried, not knowing why he was doing this to her.

He took her wrists in his hands. "I want to know, Rebekah."

"Simon and I had nothing. We were partners—that's all. We came to this country so that we could make a future for ourselves—that's all. There was never any love. There was never any affection. All there was was a sense of union, and that's what kept us together until he let his end of the bargain slip altogether."

"Partners? Is that what you want? Do you want a partner?"

"I don't know why you're doing this to me, Jarrett," she murmured.

"Ever since I asked you to marry me that day in Citronelle, there's been little between us. I know now that it was all my mistake, Rebekah. So I've put all those thoughts behind me, but I can't get you out of my life."

"Why, Jarrett? Why would you want to do that?"

"Because you're dangerous to me. Because you're keeping me here when I've felt that I was ready to leave again."

"It's because I want you, Jarrett. I want you with me always." She reached up for him and kissed him. "You know how much I want you."

He let his hands roam around her body, and she closed her eyes, making herself available to him, utterly available.

"I said I can't be without you," Jarrett whispered. "So what then? Shall we be partners? I'm willing, Rebekah. I'm willing to throw our lots together and ask for no guarantees. I'm willing to take on this city and whatever happens, happens."

His words excited her. She felt within her a stirring

for revenge. She felt that she wanted to show Simon
and Hattie Winslow and all of her enemies that she
didn't need them, that she was a free woman, that she
had gotten what she wanted. She had come here a girl
in search of her freedom, and now she had it. Now
she could show anyone who was interested that she
made up her own rules and that she survived all odds.
Let others call her brash or headstrong; the word she
chose for herself was none other than victorious.

"Is that what you want, Jarrett?" she said, testing
him.

"Yes, that's what I want."

"What about your practice? Aren't you worried
about what could happen?"

"What about your store?" he countered.

"I'm not worried about my store. I'm putting guards
on it at all times, and I have some other plans to
protect it."

"Well then, there's no problem. I don't care what
happens to my practice. It isn't much of a practice
anyway, is it?"

She shrugged. "That's for you to say."

He stared at her. "I've said what I have to say."

She felt infected by this new tone of recklessness. An
interior voice—eminently sensible—told her to retreat.
Don't match him, it said. Don't catch his fever. But
she couldn't help it. All the anger and aching for release that she had stored all these years had come to
the surface.

"Very well then, Jarrett," she said at last. "No more
hiding. No more discretion. We'll do what we want to
do, and whatever happens, happens."

He nodded briskly. "Then let's go to dinner, Rebekah. And let's spend some of that money of yours,
if it's all right with you."

She laughed, suddenly, incredibly gay. "Of course,
Jarrett. Let's paint the town red."

* * *

The fact that she and Jarrett had dedicated their relationship to high spirits and a wild, angry zest did not mean that her business was to suffer one little bit. As the new Weiss Store became thoroughly entrenched in the city's commercial life, she sought a way beyond the use of guards to protect her success against outside aggressors.

She and O'Donnell went over the books one night, and she started to think aloud.

"Tell me, Mr. O'Donnell," she said, "would you say that we were doing well?"

He laughed at the question. "What do you mean, miss? Here it is in black and white. Could anyone hope to do more splendidly?"

"Yes," she said coolly. "That's what I thought."

"Why, we got to turn customers away. This here little store just ain't big enough for the kind of business we could be having."

"So then it probably would be wise of us to put our profits back into the business rather than in the bank. Is that what you're saying, Mr. O'Donnell?"

He frowned and held his chin. "Did I say that, miss?"

She smiled. "Well, perhaps not in so many words, Mr. O'Donnell, but I think that's the gist of what you said."

"Now that's a big step, miss," he cautioned. "I don't know that we're ready for that one yet."

She folded her hands and spoke very calmly. "I don't think it's premature, Mr. O'Donnell. After all, as you said, we are turning customers away, and that's not very good business, is it?"

"No, I suppose not, miss." He leaned forward in his chair and asked, in a confidential voice: "What then are you planning, miss? A bigger store?"

"That's a possibility, Mr. O'Donnell," she replied. "I haven't put that one out of mind, although, of course, that would mean losing time here. Wouldn't it be better, Mr. O'Donnell, if we simply established another location?"

"You mean a second store, miss?"

"Yes. That's precisely what I mean."

"Well now, that's a novel idea, all right. But I ain't sure I get it. You mean two stores with the same kind of inventory?"

"Yes, Mr. O'Donnell. I mean two Weiss Stores."

"Sounds like the beginning of an empire, miss."

She laughed. "Perhaps, Mr. O'Donnell, but let's keep those lofty dreams to ourselves."

The very next day she put on her fine, pearl-gray dress and her veiled hat with the egret plumes, and she went to do business. The site that she had set her mind to was that of Mr. Chester Stiles, the man whom she held responsible for the destruction of the store on Caroline Street. She had been witnessing the downward curve of Stiles's business—he had never been able to recoup from the losses of the war years—and now, when it seemed that foreclosure was in the offing, she was prepared to make him an offer.

She walked into the dingy, bare store and found two men sitting in the dim light at the rear. One of the men was Stiles; the other obviously an employee. They were playing checkers.

"Good morning," she called.

Stiles squinted. "Who's there?"

She walked closer, into that dim arc of light. "Rebekah Weiss," she said. "Do you recall me?"

A sudden, palpable tension invaded the air. "What you want here?"

"May we talk?" she asked calmly. "I have something to say that might interest you."

He stared at her for a long, scrutinizing moment, and then he turned to his employee. "Get lost, George," he said, and George did what he was told. Then they were alone, ready to talk.

"Now, what's on your mind?" Stiles asked in his characteristically surly voice.

"I've come to talk business."

He gave her a contemptuous look. "Your kind can always sniff out a foreclosure."

That's right, Mr. Stiles, we're trained like dogs, she thought to say, but she kept her composure. "I don't know what you mean, Mr. Stiles," she said coolly, trying to cover up for his stupidity. "I've come to make you an offer. I would like to buy your business."

The man's eyes nearly popped from his head. "Buy the business, you said?"

"Yes, Mr. Stiles. You know I've just recently established a store on St. Anthony and Claiborne, and I'm thinking of acquiring another location."

"What's the matter? You gettin' tired of the niggers?"

She smiled a bit. "Then you've been following my progress, Mr. Stiles?"

"Yeah. That's right. I been keeping an eye on you."

"To the expense of your store, I might add. You don't appear to be doing a very vigorous business, Mr. Stiles."

"I got my customers," he said, muttering a feeble defense.

"Really?" she said, looking around. "Where do you keep them?"

He didn't laugh, but she had made her point. "I'm looking for a store with a good location, Mr. Stiles, and you have just such a thing. You get a lot of traffic here, even if you don't take advantage of it. I'm prepared to buy your store, lock, stock, and barrel, for what it's worth." She took from her purse a slip of paper on which she had written a figure. She handed it to him and watched him study it. She had deliberately set the figure much higher than what he could have expected on the open market and, accordingly, his face registered a hot rush of blood.

"Is that what you had in mind, Mr. Stiles?"

"Well now, ma'am, I wasn't really expecting to sell the store, and I think it's worth somethin' more 'n you offered."

"Of course, Mr. Stiles. You know what your store is worth. Anyway my price is firm. You know where you can reach me." She offered him her gloved hand. "Good day, Mr. Stiles."

She walked toward the front door and impulsively he called out to her. "Wait a minute, Miz Weiss," he said. "What about that day when your store was burnt down? What about what you said to me?"

"Did I say something to you, Mr. Stiles?"

"You said plenty."

"Well now, Mr. Stiles, I was quite beside myself that day. You wouldn't hold that against me, would you?"

She gave him an enchanting smile, and then quickly she left.

As expected, the sale was completed on her terms. She knew that Stiles's only alternative was foreclosure, and she had made him a handsome offer. The transaction was done in the most civilized fashion, and she knew that neither Stiles nor his cronies would cause her any more problems. She would be paying him out of the receipts of her business, and so he had nothing to gain by damaging her. Her mistake in the past had to do with playing the game by her own set of rules. Now she had given Stiles a piece of the pie, and everything would be that much smoother.

She presided over the opening of the second store. She put O'Donnell in charge, and he seemed to be thriving with this new responsibility. As the store opened in March, she called an inauguration spring sale with everything in the store reduced. The first day of the new store brought them the greatest receipts of any single day in their history. She and O'Donnell

stood in the emptied store after closing time, each of
them absorbed in their private thoughts.

"Well, miss, we seem to have done it," O'Donnell
said at last.

"I knew we would," Rebekah replied, not holding
back at all.

He looked at her. There was an extraordinary expression on her face. "You really are going to build
an empire, miss, aren't you?"

"If there's one to be built, then I'll build it, Mr.
O'Donnell," she said, feeling her heart pound like a
mighty engine.

CHAPTER EIGHTEEN

With the two stores launched, Rebekah felt herself
grow giddy with excitement. She had won, she kept
telling herself. She had tossed the rules back into their
faces. She had played the game the way she had
wanted, and she had broken the bank to top it off.

Don't, an interior voice warned. Don't, because it's
fragile and because there are dangers and because
you'll be hurt. She heard the voice repeat these words
in her head like a chant, but she shook it off. She
didn't want to hear warnings now. All she wanted to
do was savor her freedom.

Some of her giddiness was tied in to the mood of the
city itself. After all, it was Mardi Gras time and, for
five days culminating on Shrove Tuesday, the city
would surrender itself to a wild festivity. For weeks
before she had more than she could handle keeping in

stock the ribbons and brilliants and bugle beads that were being snatched up to decorate the mummers' costumes.

Jarrett came by the store a few days before the beginning of the carnival and caught her in the middle of the preholiday madness.

"You look like the headmistress of an insane asylum," Jarrett joked.

She didn't answer him, being busy ringing up a sale on the register.

"Are you giving away merchandise?" he laughed as a buxom black woman jostled in front of him.

"Jarrett, please," she cried. "Can't you see what's happening here?"

He laughed even further, enjoying her unique predicament of being run ragged by making so much money. He admired her ingenuity and drive immensely, even though it made him feel inferior to her. He knew he didn't have her strength; he had never met anyone who could rival her strength. She was an absolute dynamo, conquering everything that stood in her way. And if he tried to stand in her way—if he presented to her such conventional alternatives as love and marriage—she discarded them as mere trifles. Sometimes he felt so angry with her that he could thrash her, and it was then that he felt a kinship with her errant husband Simon. She could be maddening and arrogant, and many times he had contemplated walking away from her altogether. But then he would feel so ashamed. Could he not endure her strength? Was he so small a man that he could not acknowledge and permit the incredible indomitability of her spirit? He told himself at such times that he should get down on his hands and knees and thank God that he had met such a woman because she was someone who was full of life, and by being with her, he, too, might grow strong again.

He walked outside and lighted a cigarette. He

leaned against the doorway and watched the constant
flow of people in and out of the store. There were
more black faces than white, he noted. She was smart.
When he had first met her, she was as green as the
grass, a little immigrant girl screaming in terror at the
touch of the doctors. She didn't know any English
then. She called him "Herr Doktor." He smiled at the
memory now and marveled at her achievement. Everything about her was unusual: the way she had learned
English, so quickly, with such a gift for the idiom.
Her honesty and her acumen in the field she had been
thrust into was a remarkable thing too. Still, in the
end, the most remarkable thing was that he loved her.
She was so different from everything he had been
taught to love. He had been trained to direct his interests toward gentle, well-bred Southern belles who
knew how to please and serve a man. He smiled
ironically at the thought. All of that was over now,
at least for him. All his ties with the past were severed.
It was a new world now, and Rebekah was in the
vanguard of it. He admired her for it, but, even so,
he could not help but be proprietary about the past
and the lost glory that was the Russell family.

He went back inside and watched her further.
Everything about her was efficient; there was no waste,
no frivolity. At least not in the store. On their evenings
together she had become increasingly high-spirited.
They gambled—he always lost and she always won—
and they danced, and once they even went to a cock-
fight. She seemed to want to go faster and faster and
never stop to think. He knew she was running from
something, as he was. What was it? Each other? Their
love or the absence of love? The need for decisions?
The need to put the sorrows of the past behind them
and out of sight? She, as he, only wanted to laugh and
have fun and not think about all the difficulties that
their lives had seen already and that they doubtlessly
would go on to encounter.

"Five minutes," she cried, holding up five fingers to him.

He waited five minutes more and then Sophronia came back from whatever errand she had been performing. He smiled to see the young black woman; she had always been proud, but now her carriage was as regal as a queen's.

When she was free, they went upstairs to the little sun-filled room where she took her lunch. She turned to him on the landing, and they kissed passionately. Everything about the atmosphere was heightened, not least of all her color, which made her look blushed and warm to the touch.

They closed the door to her little private room and kissed once more.

"I've missed you," she whispered.

"But I just saw you last night," he said, excited by her urgency.

"I don't care," she said, holding him close. "I missed you."

"You weren't thinking about me a few moments ago," he said. "You were thinking about your register and you were thinking about all the sales you were ringing up and you were thinking about all the money you were making and you were thinking about bringing all that money to the bank."

She pulled away from him. "You're making fun of me again, aren't you?"

"Oh, don't be so sensitive, Rebekah," he chided her.

She was confused by him. She felt that he wanted her, desired her, but that he didn't have any respect for her. "You've ruined the moment, Jarrett," she said bitterly.

"No," he murmured, holding her, kissing her again, and he managed to bring her back to where they had begun.

"Will you have lunch with me?" she said.

"No. I've eaten. But I'll watch you if I may."

She smiled shyly and began to cut up an orange.

"Won't you have some?" she said, offering him a section.

He shook his head.

"You just want to watch me," she said tensely. "As though I were some strange animal whose habits fascinated you. Is that it, Jarrett?"

"What's wrong, Rebekah? You're jumping at me for everything?"

He was right, she thought. "I'm sorry, Jarrett. I suppose it's the hectic nature of the business this time of year."

"And the feeling in the city itself. I've sensed it too with my patients."

"There really is something in the air . . ."

"Yes, something feverish. I haven't paid a bit of attention to Mardi Gras in years . . . either I've been away from the city or just holed up. But this year I have my eyes and ears tuned to it, and it's all so ripe, so ready to burst."

They were silent for a moment, and then she spoke. "I feel so apart from it," she said ruefully. "It reminds me of Christmas."

"How so?"

"Oh, when I was a child, my sisters and I would watch from the window as the little Gentile children went to Midnight Mass, and we were so enchanted by the carols and the trees and Santa Claus." She laughed but, at the same time, she felt so lonely for her sisters. "We had our holidays—Succoth and Passover and Purim and Chanukah." She looked up to see his face. "You don't know them, I can see that, but they *are* joyous, Jarrett, and so lovely."

"I believe that, Rebekah."

"But still I wanted Christmas and could never have it. And now," she whispered, "even though I know better, I want Mardi Gras. Is that too ridiculous?"

His expression suddenly turned grim. "That's not for us, Rebekah. Not now, probably never."

"Why? We're of this city, and this city, for the next five days, will have nothing on its mind but Mardi Gras. Why shouldn't we be part of it?"

"Let's not try our luck, all right?"

"We said we were going to take on Mobile," she cried. "Didn't we? Or was that just idle talk?"

"It was foolish talk."

"It wasn't. I won't live as though my life were a secret. I won't do it. I won't live in the shadows. I want my place in the sun, Jarrett. And this is the time to seize it."

Her argument was powerfully seductive, but he made efforts to resist it. "Is it so important?" he asked, knowing that his resolve was weak.

"Yes, it is. I want to dance and I want to get dressed up and I want to do what everyone else in Mobile is allowed to do."

"You're *not* like everyone else in Mobile," he said. "Can't you understand that? You're not and I'm not. Everyone in Mobile doesn't open a store for Negroes. And everyone in Mobile doesn't set up a practice for Negroes."

"Then you're as bad as everyone else," she cried. "If we don't show our faces at Mardi Gras, then we're saying we're not good enough. We're saying we *should* hide. Is that what you want to say?"

He fell silent, confused by her words.

"It isn't, is it, Jarrett?"

"Why do you want to destroy what we have, Rebekah?"

His question went through her like a lance, but she managed to shake her head. "It isn't true, Jarrett. I want to celebrate us. That's all I want."

He stared at her and then nodded resignedly. He was powerless against the exercise of her will. "All right, Rebekah," he said, "we'll have it your way.

We'll do whatever it is you want, as long as you know to expect the consequences."

"Don't be silly, Jarrett," she said impulsively, reaching up to seal the agreement with a kiss. "It will be a holiday for us. You'll see—it will be a perfect pleasure."

The city grew boisterous with anticipation. Crowds of people gathered in the streets to exchange gossip and tips on the forthcoming festivities. Sophronia and Dover were hardly of any use at all in the store.

"No, you can't have today off, Dover," Rebekah patiently explained. "The day before Mardi Gras is not a holiday. Do you understand that?"

"But, Miz Rebekah, dere's goin' be marchin' right down Davis Avenue," he fretted.

"I don't care, Dover. There will be plenty of time for you to celebrate."

She knew he'd disappear anyway. There was no keeping anyone here today; she might just as well shut down the store. She herself had the impulse to go play —that was the feeling in the city, pervading absolutely everything.

"What will you be doing for the holiday, Mr. O'Donnell?" she asked when she met with him at the end of the day.

"Oh, I suppose I'll just take in the atmosphere, miss."

She smiled. She knew he had a "lady friend." Someone from Madame Valerie's, she had been told by Sophronia who seemed to know everything about everyone.

"Well, until next week then, Mr. O'Donnell," she said, offering her hand.

He bowed and kissed her hand. "Have yourself a fine time, miss. It's supposed to be the good time before we enter a period of deprivation."

"Yes, Mr. O'Donnell. I'm aware of all that."

She returned to her hotel room to bathe and dress in something more flamboyant and amusing than the habitual black dress she wore at the store. Sometimes, in that black dress, she felt like a nun, dedicated to a life of servitude to some ideal apart from herself. She hung the dress in the closet, wanting it quickly out of sight. Now she found something yellow in her wardrobe—a canary silk dress, vivid and glorious. She put it on and felt like she was dressed in sunshine.

She went down to the lobby, which was overrun with people. The city was like one great big party. A man she had never before seen, tall and red-faced and wearing a wine-colored frock coat, came right up to her, bold as could be, and with a rakish smile, he spoke to her.

"You all alone, miss?" he asked.

She ignored him, looking through the crowd for Jarrett.

He followed her as she moved through the lobby. "You look so pretty there, miss, in that there yellow dress. Why, you look just like a spring daffodil."

She found him repulsive and felt like telling him so. "Leave me alone," she instructed.

In the crush of people, many of whom were trying to get rooms (for Mobile was attracting during this madness all sorts of cardsharps and gamblers and predatory lowlifes looking for activity), the man was able to press close against her.

"Stop it," she said.

"Come on, lady, it's Mardi Gras," he replied, and he placed his hand on her hip.

She wheeled around and pushed him away. "Animal!" she cried. She ran out into the mobbed street. There were small, impromptu marching bands, with members dressed up in outrageous and exotic outfits. There were women with ostrich plumes and silver fans, and there was the sweet, cloying smell of absinthe in the air.

"Ooooh, look at the canary!" a fat, heavily rouged woman said to her companion. Both of them laughed like monkeys or some other kind of jabbering creature given to swinging from vines. Rebekah walked down the street a bit, feeling like all eyes were turned to her. She began to feel a real dread. Maybe Jarrett was right; maybe they should have gotten out of the city altogether; maybe they were mad to be here, in the middle of all this, when it wasn't really for them at all. She looked behind her, feeling that she was being followed, and she saw the red-faced man weaving through the crowd, a wicked, terrifying leer on his face as he pursued her, pushing his way through the mass of chanting and shrieking and laughing mummers. She began to run, and the horror of it was that no one noticed her fear.

"Rebekah!" she heard.

She stopped. She looked around. "Jarrett!" she cried. "Jarrett!" She saw him coming toward her, his face drawn and troubled. She met him halfway and held him closely, not being able to speak over the pounding of her heart.

"What is it?" he asked, holding her away from him so that he could look into her face.

She turned around again, saw the man look at her, and then she watched him disappear into the crowd. She felt herself actually shudder.

"What is it?" he demanded to know.

"Oh, an awful man," she said. "Following me. In broad daylight. Can you imagine?"

"Where is he?" Jarrett said, looking over the sea of heads.

"He's gone," she said. "Never mind."

"I want to find him," Jarrett said, outraged and intent.

"*Never mind*," she cried. They stared at each other for a moment. "Please," she said, genuinely frightened. "I don't want there to be trouble."

They walked along, getting a bite to eat from one of the many vendors, and they made their way to a suitable vantage point where they could watch the opening parade of the Krewe of Columbus, one of the mystic societies of Mobile.

"Did you ever participate in this, Jarrett?" Rebekah asked, looking to be diverted from her fear by conversation.

"Of course," he said. "All fine young Mobile gentlemen take part in the Mardi Gras doings of their society."

She was fascinated by the idea of a mystic society. She envisioned oddly garbed men sitting around a fire performing pagan rituals. "Tell me more," she whispered.

He laughed at her childlike excitement. "The Russells belonged to the Strikers. We are, of course, one of the oldest families," he said in a facetious tone, "and so we belonged to the oldest society. No one knows—or is supposed to know—who the members are, but there's hardly a distinguished man in the city who doesn't belong. Every New Year's Eve the lobby of the old Battle House is filled with an excited crowd. At nine the crowd enters the ballroom. The best debutantes get to sit in the front row of seats, facing a curtain that hides the stage." He turned to her and smiled. "Are you following me?"

"Oh yes, Jarrett, go on."

"The curtain is drawn, and there, making a striking tableau, are the maskers, dressed up perhaps as the court of Louis XIV or in the regimentals of the Revolution or in buckskin and Indian beads." Just then his expression dimmed.

"What is it?" she asked.

"That's when the Captain of the Ball comes forward and leads to the center of the tableau the girl who has been chosen as the princess. She wears a white gown, and her arms are filled with red roses. Then the captain leads the girl out onto the floor and then—then they lead the dance."

There was a heavy silence. "Were you once the captain, Jarrett?"

He nodded. "And the girl was Hattie Winslow's daughter."

"I didn't know you'd been that close," she said.

He laughed a little. "We were meant for each other . . . in everyone's eyes but our own. That was a very long time ago, however."

"And yet here we are, Jarrett. In the middle of it all."

He looked out over the crowd. "Yes, right in the middle of it all, and I never thought I should be here again."

"Perhaps we shouldn't be, Jarrett," she whispered in a low, urgent voice. "Perhaps we should run. Run for our lives. Do you think so, Jarrett? Do you? Suddenly I'm so frightened. I feel like there are too many people and that I recognize no one and that they're all looking at me, wanting to do me harm. I feel so afraid, Jarrett. Hold me, please hold me."

He put his arms around her. The air was filled with smoke and the odor of ripe fruit and the sound of mad, metallic laughter.

"Oh, Jarrett," she whispered, holding him close, burying her face against him so she would not have to see the army of revelers dressed in glitter and cock feathers coming down the street toward her.

As the spirit of the city grew wilder, burning brightly into the nights, she surrendered herself to the intoxication of it all. She felt, for a moment, like the heroine of a story, pursued by wicked spirits who were intent on charming her, drugging her, possessing her. She resisted the spirits with all her might until she was too tired and too worn, and then she succumbed to it all, powerless to defend herself. She pulled Jarrett down with her, and for the last two nights they drank with strangers, and they kissed passionately on street corners, and they sang with groups of fellow revelers on the street. Throughout it all, or, rather, underneath it all, was a quality of desperation, but she wouldn't confront it. She was here, home for the holiday, and she would witness the Mardi Gras as though she were a true Mobile native.

This morning they watched the floral parade make its way down Ann Street to the throngs of people who waited on Government Street. The air was filled with the odors of tuberose and azalea and crepe myrtle and camellia to the point that one could choke on it. Again she had the feeling of being trapped, being held prisoner inside the warm, fuzzy cup of a flower, and she ran through the crowd like a frightened deer.

"What is it?" Jarrett cried, pursuing her.

When she turned, he looked to her, for a moment, like the wicked man from the hotel lobby, and she shrieked. He took her in his arms and led her into the doorway of a darkened store.

"You fool," he said, his voice suggestive of pleasure.

She laughed, almost hysterically, warmed by the morning milk with brandy.

He leaned down and kissed her; he felt her breast. "I'd like to have you right here, right now."

"Don't," she said, a small, pleased smile on her lips that he licked, so suddenly, so thrillingly.

They left the floral parade and returned to her hotel room. He locked the door behind them and she waited for him by the bed. Through the open window they could hear the collective roar of people at play, a sound that made them feel like they were not alone. But they went ahead anyway, unfazed, intent on satisfying themselves.

They stripped off their clothing with great speed. They admired, desired, needed, each other's bodies. He walked over to her, his wanting vivid and persuasive, and she caressed him as he had instructed her in the past. Then he put his hands under her and lifted her onto the bed. He buried his head at her most intimate place. He gave her such pleasure that she heard herself, shocking as it was, begin to cry out. But it was all right because the hotel was deserted of its clientele, and, beyond that, her cry was lost in the great roar of the city.

"Oh, Jarrett," she moaned.

He made love to her as never before, with such intensity and imagination that she could have fainted as she went from release to release, as though she were climbing up and down the same high step. Then he, too, began to moan as she moved about, clasping him with her legs, and then there was such great, ultimate pleasure and then it was over. They lay exhausted, falling into sleep, and when they awoke, the roar of the city—the buzz, the strange stinging sound as though the city had been transformed into one giant insect—filled the plush little room.

They kissed again, happy with each other, but still with the same sense of dread that this interlude had not managed to eradicate.

"I love you," he whispered.

She began to weep. She knew now that something was going to happen, something that would ruin all of this for them.

"I don't ever want to leave this room, Jarrett. Promise me we won't have to. Promise me we can just stay here and hold each other."

He stroked her hair. "That isn't you, Rebekah. That isn't what you want."

"It *is*," she cried desperately, wanting to convince him or perhaps herself.

He smiled and shook his head. "No, my dear, it isn't. We have nothing to hide. We have nothing to be ashamed of."

"But we'll get hurt. I know it. I saw it. I dreamed it."

"Hush, will you? Just be still."

"No, I dreamed it. I dreamed of a man on a horse coming after you, and you cried out to me . . ."

"Hush," he said, putting his finger over her lips.

They lay there for what seemed hours. Then, finally, he rose.

"What are you doing?" she asked, so afraid.

"Come. We'll get dressed, and we'll go out."

"No. No, we mustn't."

"Rebekah," he said sternly, "this is all wrong. We'll do as we planned. We'll let Mobile see us and if they don't like what they see, then to hell with them."

She didn't want to do any of this, but he forced her to. She dressed in a magnificent red silk dress that she had had made from a French fabric of breathtakingly gossamer delicacy. He wore a fine black suit, looking handsome and renewed, and they took dinner in the hotel dining room.

A fine meal of squab and crayfish and Kirschwasser with berries was served, but Rebekah had no appetite. Her stomach seemed to be throbbing, or perhaps that was the beating of her heart that she heard.

"You look so nervous," Jarrett said. "White as a sheet."

"I . . . I don't feel so well."

He ordered a brandy for her, which did, in fact, have a calming effect. Soon she was feeling warmer and more capable of enjoying herself.

There was singing in the streets as they took their postprandial walk. They made their way toward a good vantage point for the parade of the Order of Myth. This was the great culminating event of the festivities, and countless torches borne by proud Negroes were lighted to illuminate the procession of Felix, Emperor of Joy, who presided over this carnival.

A sound of trumpets announced the emperor's appearance. People pushed to get a glimpse, and Rebekah felt herself surrounded by hot, reeking bodies. Again she felt consumed by dread.

"I want to go, Jarrett," she cried, but he couldn't hear her.

When the emperor had passed, Jarrett directed her to the Battle House where the ball given by the Order of Myth was to be held. This exclusive order, founded in 1868, was created to dispel the gloom brought about by the War Between the States, and so there was a tradition here of music and high spirits. The annual ball, one of the primary events of the Mobile season, was about to begin, and Jarrett was leading Rebekah to it, determined to capture some of the gaiety that was being dispensed so openhandedly.

"We mustn't go," she said. "Really, Jarrett, we mustn't."

"Don't be foolish," he said with too much liquor in him. "I've a right to be here."

She was frightened by his tone more than by anything she had witnessed in the last few days. And, beyond that, she was frightened by the spectacle that prefaced the ball. The emblem of the Order of Myth was the figure of Folly belaboring Death with colored bladders, much in the manner of a Punch and Judy show. At the beginning of the ball Folly chased Death across the room, whacking at him, while everybody laughed. But Rebekah wasn't laughing. She didn't want to encounter Death, even if it was dressed up like a grotesque clown.

"Why is everybody laughing?" she cried, covering her ears.

Jarrett looked at her as though she were some foreign creature, some alien, who had somehow wandered into his world. "Sssh," he said. "Just be quiet and watch."

But she didn't want to be quiet. She wanted to

scream at him to beware. She wanted to grab hold of him and pull him away.

And then, when Folly had captured Death and dragged him off the floor, the music began and the dancing commenced.

"Come, Rebekah," Jarrett said, taking her hand.

"No," she protested. She felt so obvious in her red silk dress. She felt that she had been bold and reckless, and now she wanted to hide.

"Come," Jarrett instructed, leading her out onto the dance floor.

They spun around to the gay, vivid waltz. She didn't want to look out at all the other faces, and so she stared into Jarrett's eyes, which were darting anxiously about the room.

"Here they all are," he muttered. "All the people I grew up with. All the men and women who used to come out to Wild Oaks and drink my father's whiskey and eat my father's food and be joyous that they were honored guests at Wild Oaks. Well, damn them, damn them all to hell!"

She looked away from him and saw that they were in the center of a ring of onlookers. "They're watching us, Jarrett," she whispered, feeling her knees weaken to the point that she might collapse.

"Just be still," he murmured as they continued to dance.

They were surrounded by an audience who was glaring at them. Just then she saw Hattie Winslow, and her heart skipped a beat. There she was—there she was staring at her, staring at her and Jarrett with a murderous expression on her face. Oh no, she heard her interior voice scream, oh no, we're done for.

The music stopped. They stood there, in the vast silence, still clinging to each other. And then a man came toward them, a tall, imposing man with hair the color of iron and a noticeable stiff-legged gait. She could see Jarrett's eyes widen and then narrow in recognition.

The man came very close, stood right before Jarrett, and appeared white-faced with rage. "You are to leave, sir" were the words he finally spoke (the words that she was to hear in her terrible dreams for so long afterward).

Jarrett smiled contemptuously. "Rebekah," he said, turning to her. "Allow me to introduce General Winfred Schuyler."

She remembered who he was. He was the brother of Hattie Winslow; he was the man who had brought up Jarrett's father on charges.

General Schuyler ignored her completely. "You are to leave here, sir," he repeated. "You are to leave here promptly."

Rebekah looked at the ring of faces, at Hattie Winslow's face. Their eyes stared at each other for a moment, and then Rebekah looked away. She felt naked in her red silk dress. She felt like she was in a cage. She took Jarrett's arm, applied a slight pressure, urging him to go. But he shook her off.

"We're staying," Jarrett said, his mouth formed into a bitter line. "Start the music!" he instructed the bandmaster, but the bandmaster just stood there, immobilized.

"Jarrett," she whispered, "come."

"We're staying!" he said harshly. He turned to the imperious general. "My family has been in this city for one hundred years. Don't you presume to tell me that I'm to leave."

"You dare to speak of your family, sir?" the general replied.

"Haven't you done enough punishing, General?" Jarrett said.

"You are not wanted here, sir. A gentleman has enough grace to go when he isn't wanted."

"What do you know of being a gentleman?" Jarrett said.

The general moved closer to Jarrett so that their faces were almost touching. "Get out of here," he whispered so that no one but Rebekah and Jarrett could hear him. "Get out of here and take this woman with you. No son of a traitor is welcome here."

"Shut up!" Jarrett cried. "You old war-horse! You stinking, fraudulent old . . ."

There were two stinging slaps, back and forth across Jarrett's face. She watched Jarrett reel slightly, more from shock than pain, but there was a small tear at the corner of his mouth and a slight trickle of blood. She saw Jarrett's hands clench into fists. She shook her head. Her lips parted slightly. No, she whispered.

"Now will you leave, sir?" General Schuyler asked again.

Jarrett took out a handkerchief and held it to his lips. "Yes, I'll leave," he whispered so that only the general and Rebekah could hear. "If you consent to meet with me tomorrow morning to settle this matter."

"I shall meet you outside directly to arrange for it," the general said. Then he turned and walked away, leaving them to stand humiliated before the hundreds of onlookers.

Jarrett offered his arm, and they made their way beyond the bristling, whispering crowd. The band broke into a lively Virginia reel to relieve the tension, and then they were on the front steps of the building, in the balmy night air that seemed so at odds with the mood of things.

"What are you going to do, Jarrett?" she cried.

"Go wait in the carriage, Rebekah," he said.

What did he mean? Was he mad? "What are you going to do?" she demanded to know. "I won't let you do anything foolish. I won't let you get hurt!"

"Go wait in the carriage," he ordered.

He strode off to his meeting with the general, leaving her there, trembling, distraught. Suddenly she felt a presence behind her. She turned to see Hattie Winslow.

"Are you happy now?" the woman said straight off.

Rebekah shrank away from her. She was like some wicked harpy, come to torment her.

"You're a spoiler, aren't you?" Hattie Winslow said in a hate-filled voice. "You came here and you wanted to wreck everything, didn't you?"

"No," Rebekah protested. "I want to live my life! And people like you—all you want is to take things away from me."

"Now one of them will die," Hattie said, ignoring Rebekah's words.

"What do you mean?"

"Are you a fool?" Hattie cried in a strangled voice. "Don't you know what they're going to do?"

Rebekah stared at her, and then she shook her head. "No," she whispered, moving down the broad flight of stairs, anxious to get away from her. But Hattie pursued her and grabbed hold of her arm.

"They're going to kill each other," Hattie screamed, "and it's all because of you."

"No!" Rebekah cried. "Stop it!"

"You evil thing. You Jewish witch. You evil Jewish . . ."

She slapped Hattie soundly across the face, a mimicry of what had gone on between the two men just moments before. Then she ran, tearing her skirts on the ground. When she got to the carriage, she was breathless, and it seemed that she would never get a deep breath again.

She waited for Jarrett. She waited for what seemed an eternity. She kept hearing Hattie Winslow's vile words. *Witch. Evil Jewish witch.* What had she done? Was she responsible for this awful turn of events? Yes, by bringing Jarrett here, by exposing him to this. She began to whimper like a child, out of sheer terror and anguish.

"Don't cry," she heard.

She turned and saw Jarrett in the shadows, looking so remote.

"What happened?" she asked, and then, more significantly: "What's going to happen?"

He didn't answer her. He got into the carriage, and they rode off through the bright, moonlit night.

"Tell me!" she screamed.

He cleared his throat, which had been made dry by all that had gone on. "We're to meet at dawn," he said.

"To fight?"

"To duel," he acknowledged.

There was a silence.

"There was no other choice," he said.

"You fool!" she cried. She began to sob, and though he reached out to hold her, she would not receive his comfort.

"There was no other choice," he repeated.

"Take me home," she said, rigid and white-faced. "Take me home."

He stared at her. "Is that all you have to say?"

"Take me home!"

The ride back seemed an eternity. She didn't want to look at him. She was so furious and so heartsick. When they got to the hotel, she jumped from the carriage, and he had to chase her.

"Don't go just yet," he implored her.

She struggled with him, and he let her go. "You're going to die!" she spat. "And what good will it have accomplished?"

"I won't die," he said. "I won't allow it."

She laughed, verging into hysteria. "Oh, yes," she cried, "oh, yes. And to defend your father's honor. How proud he would have been of you. How proud of his gallant . . ."

"Shut up!" he demanded, shaking her.

"You're going to leave me!" she cried. "You're going to leave me, and I don't want you to. I don't want you to leave me!"

She burst into tears and now she let him hold her as she sobbed, her face pressed against his coat jacket, just as in the past.

"Be brave," he whispered.

"Oh, Jarrett. I don't understand. What happened? And why did we let it happen?"

"There was no choice, Rebekah," he replied. "This had to happen. Ever since I came back to Mobile, this was bound to happen."

"Stay with me tonight," she pleaded.

He shook his head. "No. Tonight I'll stay at Wild Oaks." He laughed a little, wondering at the sense of calm that had come with this destiny. "Tonight I'll sleep with my ghosts, if you don't mind."

They embraced once more, and then he pulled away.

"Be brave," he reminded her.

"You'll come back to me, Jarrett, won't you? Promise me that you will."

"I'll come back to you, Rebekah," he said. But as she watched him move back into the shadows, she didn't know if she could believe him.

CHAPTER NINETEEN

The night, what little there was left of it, was so very hard to get through. Jarrett sat in his room at Wild

Oaks, the room in which he had grown up, the room he had come back to reclaim, and he stared out into the dark night, waiting for the appearance of dawn.

He was to kill or be killed at that appointed hour. The choice of weapons had been made; they would use pistols, and they would do their best to lodge a bullet in the breast of their opponent. Jarrett remembered sitting at his grandfather's knee and hearing the tale of how his grandfather's brother—a redheaded hellion named Jedediah—fought a duel with a man called Lazarus Purdy over a young woman named Caroline Marshall. He remembered how fascinated he was to hear of the meeting at dawn, the pearl-handled pistols, the drop of the white handkerchief, the firing, and then the powder burn at the heart of Larazus Purdy. It had seemed to him, throughout his childhood, a tale of triumph; but now, in this different slant of light, he found the story appalling. Two young men fighting to the death over a woman who probably didn't mean all that much to them to begin with. It was a horror story, and here he was, reenacting it two generations later.

He sat in his room at Wild Oaks and tried to come to terms with what he had initiated. Dueling—a medieval practice that had hung on in a vestigial manner in the South—was not only abhorrent but illegal.

And not only did he face death or maiming, but, even if he was the victor, he faced a trial and a probable incarceration. But, more than that, he faced the damage that this duel would cause to his spirit and to his sense of himself. He was a doctor, he had taken the oath of healing, and here he was, bent on revenge, ready to kill or be killed.

He had never killed a man. He had seen killing and death all around him during the war, but he had never had to kill. It had been his job to staunch the wounds; but he wasn't very good at his job. No one

could be very good at his job. There wasn't much to
be done in the field for sucking lung wounds or fractured larynxes or torn, ravaged abdomens. Sometimes,
even now, in his dreams he heard the wailing of soldiers, and when he awoke, he was in a sweat, his fists
clenched as he tried to fight his way out of this frustration and despair.

And now he was going to kill a man. Or at least he
was going to try. He hated Schuyler; he hated him
with an all-consuming passion that sickened him. The
man was an opportunist and a fraud. Schuyler had
always been in competition with his father—in school,
in the army, in the social structure of Mobile—and
when his father had weakened, Schuyler went for the
jugular. Schuyler had indeed been brave; Schuyler had
the wounds to show for it; but Jarrett knew that there
was more to Schuyler's attacks on his father than sheer
moral outrage. He had wanted to use the incident as
a stepping-stone to higher things, but nothing had
ever panned out for him, primarily because Schuyler
went too far and used the Russell incident to the point
that nobody wanted to hear about it anymore. Even if
the elder Russell was not a liked man, that didn't
mean that the people of Mobile wanted to be reminded at every juncture of a leading citizen's cowardice and betrayal.

He was prepared to kill General Winfred Schuyler,
even though he had never killed a man and even
though it went against everything for which he was
trained. He had no other choice. The hour was set; he
could show or he could run, and he could not run as
his father had.

What would happen if he lost? Which was to say:
what if he were to die? Then what would his life have
meant? It would have been nothing but a life of failure and shame. And now, just when he had Rebekah,
just when he had found a woman he could love, he
opened himself up to violence and annihilation. But

wasn't Rebekah to be held accountable as well? He had wanted to leave Mobile; he had pleaded with her to do so. They could have made a good life for themselves elsewhere, but she had refused. And now, because they had been reckless together, he had reached this point, four o'clock in the morning, staring out the window, waiting for the first terrible signs of light.

He heard a knock on the door.

"Who's there?" he called.

"It's me, Master Jarrett. It's Micah."

"Come in," Jarrett said.

The old black man entered the room. "I sees your light, sir. I says to myself, Master Jarrett, how he goin' to get through this night?"

Jarrett sighed and shook his head. "So soon, Micah. So soon it will be dawn." He had arranged for Micah to be his second, an unorthodox idea to be sure, but then any code of etiquette that was meant to govern these proceedings was a sham anyway.

Micah stared at Jarrett for a very long moment. "You ain't goin' to let yourself get hurt now, are you, Master Jarrett?"

"Who can say, Micah?"

"Oh, Master Jarrett, I remember when you was a baby. I remember when your mother did birth you, God bless her soul. She was a fine woman; she was all goodness, she was. And how good it be that she ain't here to live through this. Why, she loved you more than she loved life, and that's the truth, Master Jarrett. You know it is."

"Yes, Micah," he said quietly.

"And your father . . ."

"It's all right, Micah," he said shortly.

Micah's face sagged a bit. "No, Master Jarrett, you'll let me talk, won't you?"

"I'm sorry, Micah. Please go on."

"Your father was a man like no one else ever I met. I was scared by him; everyone was. But he never treated me unfair. He always says to me, 'Micah, you done your work good?' And I says, 'Sure did, Master Russell.' "

Jarrett had another seigneurial impulse to quiet the older man, but he controlled it. Let the old fellow talk, he told himself, wanting the minutes to pass less slowly than they had been.

"And he loved you, Master Jarrett. Oh, surely he did love you. Why you could read it clear in his face. Everything you did was something his curiosity wouldn't miss. You was his son, Master Jarrett, and he wanted only the best for you. Why, I remember when the groom, Caleb, told me that the master says to him, 'Caleb, you makes sure that my boy got the best horse in the county.' And you got it, sir. Now can you beat that, Master Jarrett?"

"Yes, Micah. I'm sure that's all true."

"Well now, I don't tell no tales, Master Jarrett. That man *did* love you, no matter what you thinks."

"Well then, he should be pleased, Micah. Because, you see, today I'm going to fight for his honor. If I lose, I'm dead, and if I win, I lose. Because you see, Micah, I'm not a killing sort of man."

"But you ain't got no choice, Master Jarrett."

"That's right, Micah. When my father's honor is at stake . . ." He let the sentence trail off in wry, brittle laughter.

"You shouldn't be laughin' like that, Master Jarrett. Your father *was* an honorable man. I don't care what nobody says . . ."

That was more than he could patiently endure. "You don't know what you're talking about, Micah. My father was a coward and a traitor. It was because of my father that scores of soldiers were killed. My father's name has no honor and never again will have honor, no matter how many duels I fight."

The older man looked shocked, and his lower lip trembled noticeably. "It ain't right, what you're sayin',

Master Jarrett. Your father was your father, and you got to have respect for him."

"Respect," Jarrett laughed. He held his head in his hands. "Why, he's ruined my life. He ruined my mother's life and he's ruined my career and now he's going to take my life altogether. I loathe him, and I wish I could erase his memory entirely."

"Stop it, Master Jarrett!" Micah cried. "It's a sin to be sayin' what you're sayin' on a day like today. You got to have love in your heart if you goin' to die. Don't you know that?"

"Please, Micah, just leave me be."

"Say the psalm with me, Master Jarrett," Micah implored.

He shook his head. He was not a religious man, something Micah should have accepted by now. "There isn't time, Micah. Just let me rest here and I'll . . ."

"Do it for your mother, Master Jarrett," Micah said. "She'll hear you."

He looked into the old man's mournful face, and he couldn't refuse. "Very well, Micah," he whispered.

Micah nodded gravely and then began to recite the words:

> Make haste, O God, to deliver me; make haste to help me, O Lord.

Jarrett stirred in his chair, feeling the words reach out to him and grab hold of his attention.

> Let them be ashamed and confounded that seek after my soul: let them be turned backward, and put to confusion that desire my hurt.

Would he be hurt today? He and his adversary would stand on that grassy knoll, just a few hours from now, under the glowering sky that hid all their shared phantoms, and they would draw their weapons and they would feel their pulses throbbing with fear.

> Let them be turned back for a reward of their shame that say Aha, Aha.

Who would bury him? Rebekah? Maybe so, with Micah's help and O'Donnell's help. But who would guard his grave?

> Let all those that seek thee rejoice and be glad in thee: and let such as love thy salvation say continually, Let God be magnified.

Would they rob his grave as they had robbed his father's? And would they do something vile and vengeful to his corpse, as if death were not a sufficient punishment?

> But I am poor and needy: make haste unto me, O God: thou art my help and my deliverer; O Lord, make no tarrying.

He looked again to Micah. "That was the psalm that was said over my father's body, wasn't it, Micah?"

The old man nodded. "It's a call for help, Master Jarrett. I thinks we need it now, don't you?"

He reached out for the black man's hand and squeezed it tightly. "Stay with me till the light comes, Micah. Will you do that?"

The old man nodded and placed his other hand over Jarrett's.

The light did come, more quickly than he had expected. With his doctor's eye, he watched all the signs of fear possess him: the dry mouth, the queasy feeling in the stomach, the cold, clammy hands. He couldn't believe that this was happening to him.

They got into the carriage and made their way toward Walnut Hill, located not more than a half-hour's ride from here. The morning was gray, curiously streaked with a sulphurous yellow; it had an unhealthy, foreboding aspect to it that chilled him thoroughly.

"You're clear on procedure, Micah?" he said suddenly, forcing himself to focus on the logistics of this mad enterprise.

"Yes, sir. I understands everything you done told me."

He laughed to himself, looking for humor as another alternative, but before he could test it, the laugh evaporated, and he was left with a breathless, choking sensation. He was going to face a man—his father's nemesis, his own nemesis—in a matter of moments, and he was going to try to kill him. My God, it had been too long since he had fired a gun. He no longer hunted, the days of fraternal hunting parties for boar and pheasant seemed lifetimes ago. Now he was a solitary, odd figure in the city, engaged in activities that were the antithesis of sportsmanship. Still he had once known how to fire a gun and hit a target with the best of them. As a youth he had excelled at everything he had undertaken. Riding, shooting, and all the other things that young men of his ilk were trained for came to him with a great, elegant naturalness. He was gifted, and, to some, he seemed almost godlike in his perfection. Not only was he strong and handsome and quick, but he had a guilelessness to him that won everyone to his cause. Still his powers of personal attractiveness had proved incapable of overcoming the perfidy of his father's crime. So here he was, en route to this long overdue confrontation.

"I be praying for you, Master Jarrett," Micah mumbled. "You too young to die, and you too good. I always felt you is a good man."

They arrived at Walnut Hill exactly at the appointed hour. This was the site of many duels throughout the years, renowned as a dueling place just as was the shadowed grove outside Memphis or the sandbar along the Mississippi near Vicksburg. He and Micah disembarked from their carriage. They walked toward where General Schuyler, Walter Wallace, his second and his son-in-law, Michael Carter, the surgeon who was on hand to tend wounds, and a group of the general's supporters had all congregated.

"This is your second, sir?" asked Walter Wallace, referring to Micah.

"Yes, sir. This is my second," Jarrett replied. Wallace was a man his own age, a man he had known in school, and an unregenerate fool. In this case the usual duties of the seconds had been dispensed with. Traditionally their role was to negotiate, to determine whether the duel might be avoided, but in this case settlement was a remote fantasy. This duel was inevitable; a man does not have his face slapped before hundreds of onlookers and settle for anything less than the right to retribution.

As the challenged party it was General Schuyler's right to name the weapons and the distance. The weapons were the general's dueling pistols, which were presented accordingly, and the distance was ten paces, which translated to approximately thirty feet.

The distance was measured and pegged by the seconds who then examined and loaded the weapons and handed them to the principals.

"God be with you, Master Jarrett," Micah whispered. "Aim low and don't bend to the side."

Jarrett nodded stiffly. Oddly enough he was no longer shaking as he had been en route to Walnut Hill.

The principals took their places. Once there they could not move, for this was a violation that allowed a duelist to be shot down by the second of the opposing party.

Jarrett and Schuyler began back to back and walked the designated paces. Jarrett felt like it was a dream, a very terrible dream. He saw the pines and live oaks all around him, and the thought flashed through his mind that this might be his last glimpse of earth.

Then, when they were ten paces apart, they heard Mr. Wallace, who had won the toss and the right to give the signal, yell: "Fire!"

They whirled around; there was an explosion; there was the smoke; there was the flight of birds from the trees. Jarrett felt his body buckle, but, seconds later, he realized that the pain was only an excess of anticipation and that no harm had come to him. Looking beyond the smoke, he could see that the general, too, stood fast.

There had been a firing with no injury. Jarrett felt his pulse quicken still; there had been a reprieve; he had upheld his honor, and still he had not killed or been killed. It was a miracle, he thought, feeling the pistol dangle at his side.

The seconds came out to the field. "There has been no injury," Mr. Wallace announced.

Jarrett waited for Micah to come to him. "Thank God, Master Jarrett," Micah said with tears in his eyes.

As the challenger Jarrett had the right to declare himself satisfied. He said this much to Micah, who conveyed the message to the opposing party.

"General Schuyler is not satisfied," Mr. Wallace said with a sneer. "You can tell Doctor Russell that General Schuyler wishes to fire at five paces."

"But, sir," Micah said, shocked beyond belief. "Do there be a need for such a thing? God didn't want no death here, don't you see?"

"Hold your tongue," Mr. Wallace said. He was a whippetlike man, small and pinched. "Get back to your principal and tell him that we are not yet done."

Micah stared at the man and then at General

Schuyler, whose face seemed drained of any human
emotion. He returned to Jarrett, who looked at him
with an uneasy, curious expression.

"What is it, Micah?"

"They wants another round, Master Jarrett," Micah
said in an anguished voice.

"What do you mean?" Jarrett cried. "Are they
mad?"

"At five paces, sir. That's what they wants, and
there be no talking to them."

He stared across the dewy field at the general, whose
eyes could almost be seen glinting at this distance.
"Very well, Micah," he said, angry, weary, and overwhelmed. "Tell them it's agreed."

They started anew. Back to back they walked the
five paces. There was the brief silent instance in which
Jarrett had the time to think that he wanted the man
dead, that he wanted to kill him and see his body,
drained of life, lying on the ground, and then there
was the cry from Mr. Wallace:

"Fire!"

And then they whirled about and discharged their
pistols, and again the sharp crack in the gentle morning and the smell of smoke and Jarrett felt himself hit
the ground with a thud, knocked over by this enormous force, this enormous unleashing of power. There
was a throbbing at his side, a pain that stabbed into
him like a dirk, and he reached down and there was
blood.

"Master Jarrett!" Micah cried. "Speak to me!"

His head was reeling; it seemed that he was turning
round and round and round. "Micah," he heard himself moan.

"Oh, thank God, Master Jarrett!"

"Schuyler," he murmured. "Tell me."

"He be dead, Master Jarrett. He took the bullet
straight in his heart."

The news stunned Jarrett, and then the combina-

tion of pain and remorse made him moan. "Oh, my
God, forgive me," he wept. "Please forgive me."

The surgeon, Michael Carter, an older man who
had been one of his early childhood models, rushed
over. "Let me look at you," Dr. Carter said, tearing
away the pants leg. "You're lucky," he said, quickly
assaying the damage. "One inch over and it would
have hit the femoral artery. Now all you've got is a
laceration."

"And the general?" Jarrett said, feeling dazed and
unsure.

"You know he's dead, man," Dr. Carter said harshly.
"You shot him right in the heart. You always were a
good shot if I recall."

"I didn't want to go on. You know that," Jarrett
cried. "After the first round I wanted to stop it, but
they insisted . . ."

"Hold your breath, Russell," the surgeon snapped.
"You let yourself be a part of this. Don't try to play
the innocent. You've just killed a man, and you, a
doctor."

Jarrett lay his head back on the jacket that Micah
had folded for a pillow, and he closed his eyes. Immediately, in the mind's eye, he saw the puff of smoke
and heard the sharp crack. It was horrible, and everything that Dr. Carter said was true. He had let himself
become a part of this. He had gone with Rebekah
to the ball of the Order of Myth when he knew that
they would be unwanted. He and she had sought out
trouble in the most provocative manner, and Schuyler
had called him on it. Well, Father, he said to the
ghost that controlled his life. Are you avenged now?
Are you at peace? And what has it cost but my life?

"You don't have to worry," the surgeon said contemptuously. "You're merely scratched. So congratu-
late yourself, Russell, for winning the fight."

He was helped off the ground by Micah, who was
sweating profusely and who appeared to be quite worn

out by the proceedings. As they made their way to the
carriage, Schuyler's second, Mr. Wallace, left his
principal's body to confront him.

"You may have won this duel," the thin hatchet-
faced man stormed, "but you've won no honor for
yourself, Russell."

"Go away from me," Jarrett warned.

"You can duel every man from Mobile to Montgomery, but you'll win no battle because you were
born a Russell and you'll die a Russell and everyone
knows that a Russell, beneath it all, is nothing but a
coward and a dog."

"I said go away from me, or you'll wind up like the
general," Jarrett cried.

"You and your woman, why you're nothing
but . . ."

With that Jarrett, weak as he was, seized the man
and dashed his head against the side of the carriage.
"I will not hear this!" he shouted. "I will not hear
this!"

"Master Jarrett!" Micah pleaded. "Come, Master
Jarrett!"

The old man's urgency made him see what he was
doing, and he released Walter Wallace, who staggered
in his place. Micah helped Jarrett into the carriage,
and quickly they rode off, to the shouts of Schuyler's
supporters. When they got some distance away, Jarrett
touched his leg and felt the ooze of blood.

"Does it hurt bad, Master Jarrett?" Micah asked.

Jarrett shook his head. "It hardly hurts at all."

There was a silence as they rode on.

"You'll have to do something for me, Micah,"
Jarrett said.

"Anything, sir. You just tell me."

"I have to leave Mobile today. I'm going to put you
in charge of Wild Oaks."

"But, Master Jarrett!" the shocked old man cried.
"Where you goin' to go?"

"I don't know, Micah. All I know is that I have to get away from here. You see what happened with Walter Wallace. It's going to happen again and again. The city is against me, Micah. What happened this morning is against the law, and they'll get me for it if I stay. So take me to the train station, Micah. Quickly, do you hear?"

"But, Master Jarrett, you're hurt. And you'll have no one to see after you . . ."

"I'm a doctor, Micah. I can take care of myself." He felt a twinge of pain in his wounded leg. "We'll stop at Wild Oaks. I'll get some money and some clothes. And then we'll be on our way."

They reached Wild Oaks just a bit later.

"Micah, send someone over to the Waverly Hotel. I want a message delivered to Miss Rebekah that she is to meet me at the station within the hour."

"Will she be going with you, Master Jarrett?" Micah inquired.

Another bolt of pain took hold of him, radiating from his leg up through the rest of him. "No, Micah," Jarrett said. "Miss Rebekah will be staying."

He was to take the next train out, which left in thirty minutes, bound to New Orleans. From there, there was no telling where he would end up. He felt himself aching with the pain of his wound, with the shame of the morning's violence, with the realization that his vocation as a doctor was unlikely to ever be resumed, and with the staggering thought that Rebekah would no longer be with him.

"Do you see her yet, Micah?" he asked, feeling weak from his wound.

"No, Master Jarrett," the old man said. He held a cup of sugared tea from which he had Jarrett sip, and the sweet, warming drink did revive him a bit.

"She isn't coming," Jarrett said bitterly. "Could she not come, Micah? My God, could it be?"

"She'll come, Master Jarrett. She'll come."

He dozed off for a moment, so utterly drained from the events of the day. When he awoke, it was because someone was nudging him, and he opened his eyes and he saw her.

"You came," he murmured, his throat so dry that he feared it would crack.

"What did they do to you?" she said, her eyes red, a kerchief wrapped around her head.

He shook his head, too heartsick to talk.

"You're hurt," she cried. "You're wounded. There's blood," she said, pointing to his pants leg.

"It's all right," he said.

"I don't believe you," she said. "You're hurt. And what about the other? What about him?"

"Haven't you heard?"

"How would I have heard?"

"He's dead."

She gasped, reaching up to cover her mouth.

"I killed him. He's dead."

"No. Jarrett, no. It's too horrible."

He felt wounded further by her response and sought to justify himself. "There was no injury after the first round. It seemed a miracle. I told him I was satisfied, but he wouldn't have it. He set the distance shorter, and there was nothing I could do. I had to go along with it and then it was over, Rebekah, and he was dead, and I'm glad for it," he heard himself saying. "I'm glad I killed him, and I'll kill anyone else who asks for it."

"Jarrett!" she cried, shocked by his belligerence. "How can you talk like that?"

"Now I have to leave here, Rebekah," he said, his voice alternately wild and remote. "If I don't, there'll be more violence. They've chased me from the city after all, don't you see? I can't stay here. I've broken the law, don't you see? I have to run, don't you see?"

She stared at him. Her beautiful face contorted with

some combination of fear and rage and despair. "You're leaving me?" she said.

"Come with me, Rebekah," he replied impulsively, knowing even as he suggested it that she would never consider it.

"Go with you?" she said. "To run? Don't you think I've run enough, Jarrett? Do you really want me to have to run more?"

"But I have no other choice, Rebekah."

"Then go!" she cried furiously. "My God, why did you let it happen? You're leaving me and I'll be all alone and I don't understand! I don't understand why you let it come to this if you loved me and if you wanted to be with me!"

"You were party to this," he accused. "Don't act as if you weren't. You wanted to be part of Mardi Gras, didn't you? Well, this is part of Mardi Gras, my dearest. Duels and death are part of Mardi Gras."

"You never told me," she accused. "Why didn't you tell me? You deceived me."

The shriek of the train whistle pulled them farther apart.

"I've got to go," he said, rising, his face grimacing with pain.

"Then go," she said bitterly, for now he was just one of the men in her life who had treated her badly, who had tricked her, and who had caused her sorrow.

"Have you no parting words for me?" he whispered.

She shook her head. "Just go," she said.

Micah carried his bag, and the two men walked toward the train. Her eyes were filled with tears, and she felt a searing sensation in her throat. Let him go, she thought. Let him go because there's nothing for you there, nothing. She felt sickened by the stupidity of men. She felt sickened by the idea of duels and codes of honor and the notions of bravery and cowardice. What had Simon once said to her? *Why is it that any fear I have turns me into a coward?* Now

she understood what he meant. Now she understood
him when he reproached her for subscribing to a
man's code of valor. She hated it all now; she thought
it all the most scurrilous bunk. So let him go, she
repeated to herself, now that he's sold his life out to
his gentleman's code of honor.

She watched him board the train. She watched
Micah hand him his bag. She watched him disappear
in a cloud of steam. She heard the train's whistle. She
felt overcome. She loved him, she loved him, and why
must he leave her? Jarrett! she cried. She saw the
train move; she saw his face in the window. Jarrett!
She began to run after him; she ran twenty feet;
and then she stopped, and they looked at each other,
he through the window and she on the platform, tears
streaming down her face, and the train moved slowly
out of the station.

"He's gone, miss," Micah said sadly.

"But why?" she said, still so confused, still so un-
believing that all of this had happened so quickly.

"Because there's a curse on him," Micah said, and
she watched the train disappear along the tracks.

CHAPTER TWENTY

With Jarrett gone, she returned to the business that
offered her some sense of security in a world that had
become so disordered. She must try not to think of
Jarrett, for he was gone now, and she didn't know if
he would ever come back. She had tormented herself
for weeks after his departure with the burning ques-

tion of whether she should have gone with him or not. Now she was resolved to the answer she had chosen. It was not her place to go with him. She had made a life for herself in this city, even if it was a life marked by strife, and she could not just throw it away. She could not dedicate her life to Jarrett and his sense of honor. She loved him and she missed him desperately, but she would have to stay on the course she had set for herself.

Despite the scandal of their joint appearance at Mardi Gras and the ensuing tragedy of the duel, the business flourished. Her customers, of course, were not the sort to take her social standing into account. She offered cheap corsets and cheap calicoes, and so they came to her in a steady and powerful stream. Her revenues were enormous, and, when she had the time to fantasize, she could see the Weiss Store spreading to other cities—Montgomery and Tuscaloosa and Vicksburg and Natchez. She drove herself to the very limits of her endurance and beyond. While others might have thought she was losing some aspect of her femininity and, indeed, her humanity, she gave it no mind. It was her purpose in life to succeed. If she couldn't have love and a warm home and children, then she could have success of another sort.

One evening, very late, O'Donnell went by the Claiborne Street store and found the lights still burning. Suspicious that something might be wrong, he entered and saw his employer sitting at her desk, going over the books.

"Why, miss," he said, "what might you be doing here so late?"

"Can't you see, Mr. O'Donnell?" She gave him a significant look. "The question is what are you doing here?"

He was a bit taken aback. "I was just in the neighborhood, miss," he explained. He had, in fact, been

visiting a new lady friend who lived just around the
corner. "And then there was the light . . ."

"In the neighborhood, you say. How strange."

"Yes, miss," he said uneasily. "I was here on personal business."

She stared at him. She knew that her tone had been
suspicious and vaguely accusing, and she pulled back.
"Well, Mr. O'Donnell, I'm here on store business."

"I see, miss," he said. She had been so difficult lately;
he didn't know what was to be done. "But it *is* awfully
late . . ."

"I don't need you to tell me that!" she cried, slam-
ming shut the ledger. There was a painful silence in
which she thought to apologize, but then she didn't
want to and wouldn't. "I don't need a nursemaid," she
said, her voice full of strain. "I need a manager!"

"Are you saying you're displeased with me, miss?"

"No. It's not that I'm displeased . . ." She let her
words trail off, feeling like she might scream or cry if
she continued to speak.

"Then what is it, miss?"

"Don't badger me so!" she warned.

He stared at her again. "I think I'd best be bidding
you good night, miss," he said in a voice marked by
regret.

She watched him turn to leave. She had an impulse
to call out after him, to tell him she was sorry, to ask
for his forgiveness, but she swallowed it all and sat
there silently.

The next day and the day after that and the day
after that were no different. She was making life miserable for everyone around her. Sophronia and Dover
were growing more and more sullen under her abuse,
and Mr. O'Donnell just watched her with his sad, uncomprehending eyes.

"Stop looking at me like a cow!" she shouted at him
one day. He threw down the bolts of fabric he had
been carrying and stormed out of the store. The next

day, when he didn't return, she had to send Dover out
after him.

"I'm here, miss," he said stiffly when he reappeared.

"I'm glad, Mr. O'Donnell," she said briskly, offering
no apology, and then she went off to the bank on
other business.

She couldn't seem to stop her rage from building up,
and at night, when she returned to her hotel room,
she often wept out of sheer exhaustion and sorrow.
Months earlier she had tried to find some solace in
resuming a correspondence with her family. She had
sent a letter to her sister Sarah, with whom she had
been out of touch for too long, and it was long and
chatty. She had enclosed money as well, because she
suspected that their need was great. Now, when she
was feeling her own need so acutely, she went each day
to the hotel desk and prayed that the clerk would have
something for her.

"Excuse me," she said this morning to the clerk.
"There is a letter for me?"

"Yes, Mrs. Weiss, as a matter of fact there is."

Her heart pounded as she took the letter, the letter
that had traveled across the seas, the letter from her
family. She tore it open, hungry for news.

> My dear sister-in-law,

she read, savoring the Yiddish.

> Thank you for your gift. I wish my dear wife
> could thank you herself, but, alas, there has been
> much sickness. Our Sarah has been taken from
> us, a victim of the consumption. She never wanted
> you to know of her sickness, but now there can
> be no more secrets. She died in March, surrounded
> by her loved ones . . .

* * *

There was more, but she couldn't read it. She let the letter fall to the floor. She shook her head slightly, not wanting to believe it, wanting to express her disbelief. Sarah, she thought. She looked at the letter, worn from its overseas voyage, and she closed her eyes and shook her head again. Sarah, *mein Gott, mein Gott.* What was left? Was there anything left for her? Nothing, she thought bitterly, nothing.

That night she looked around her hotel suite, which was well appointed and spacious and elegant, and she loathed being there. She wanted a home again. Now, being so alone, she wanted a place that was hers. She didn't want Saffron Hill; there were too many bad memories at Saffron Hill. She knew that Wild Oaks was for sale. She knew that Jarrett had sacrificed it when he left Mobile. And all at once she knew she wanted it.

"But, Mrs. Weiss," said her lawyer, William Carl Benson, when she told him of her plans, "do you think it wise?"

She smiled. "Do you remember when I invited you and Mrs. Benson to dinner at Saffron Hill some time ago?" she asked.

The lawyer averted his eyes. "I'm sorry, Mrs. Weiss. I can't say I recall."

She had never brought up the subject before and had continued to use his services, but now she enjoyed seeing him squirm. "Well, I remember, Mr. Benson. I received, at the very last moment, a letter from your wife, saying you were called to the capital."

"Yes, I'm sure I must have been . . ."

She looked at him with contempt. "I'm sure," she said. "But the point is that you and your friends never would have come to Saffron Hill and so now you never will come to Wild Oaks. The only difference is that I don't care anymore."

He looked at her and then, embarrassed, he looked down at the desk.

She rose and went toward the door. "Draw up the papers, Mr. Benson," she instructed him coldly.

And so she moved into Wild Oaks, which set the tongues wagging anew but which filled her with a distinct pleasure and excitement. She kept on Micah, of course, and she rehired Eulalie and she had Eulalie's niece Velma as the parlormaid and Velma's cousin Hannie as the pantrymaid and Dover's brother Orin as the groom. The house, ever since she had first encountered it, was in a sorry state of disrepair. But now she had the money to make it over into something grand.

"Miz Rebekah," Micah said, "the painter, he's here. He wants to know what colors you wants him to paint the rooms."

It was an enormous house and an enormous job to refurbish it. But she found herself with enormous sums of money and she wanted Wild Oaks returned to its former state of elegance in the hope that one day Jarrett might return.

"I never thought I'd see Wild Oaks looking so fine again, Miz Rebekah," Micah admitted at a later point. "It been such a sad house for so long now."

"Yes, Micah," she said. "But we'll make it well, won't we?"

Micah looked up at the freshly painted ceiling, and she noted his silence.

"Is it wrong for me to be here, Micah?" she said suddenly.

He was startled by her question. "Miz Rebekah," he said, "it ain't for me to say what's right nor wrong."

"Please tell me, Micah," she cried.

He stared at her. "I thinks Master Jarrett would approve."

And so she made Wild Oaks her home.

Some weeks later she was working in her office at the store when she heard a knock on the door.

"What is it?" she called, her voice querulous, her nerves strained further by the pressures of her business and by the extent of her loneliness.

Sophronia entered and stood before Rebekah with a sort of ill-disguised smirk on her face. Rebekah could never figure her out. She had always had a sullen, mysterious quality about her that rather held Rebekah at bay, and yet her efficiency and diligence were points in her behalf.

"There's a man here to see you," Sophronia said.

"Who is it?"

Sophronia raised an eyebrow.

"Just send him in," Rebekah said curtly, not wanting to play games.

In a moment her husband Simon was standing in front of her. She stared at him for a long moment, taking in his new, deteriorated aspect, and then she lowered her spectacles and waited for him to speak.

"Do I look good, Rebekah?" he said with a crooked smile.

She shook her head. "You don't look at all well, Simon."

He laughed. "You always were honest with your thoughts, Rebekah. Soon as you saw me, back in Korneuberg, you took a dislike to me and you let me know it. You said right off, 'Simon Weiss, you're not the kind of a man . . .'"

"You didn't come here to reminisce," she said, cutting him short. "What do you want?"

"And what makes you so sure I didn't come here for that reason? You're my wife, after all. You're my family."

"I'm not your family. I have no family," she said, thinking of her father, thinking of Sarah, thinking of her great loss.

"Well, that's for you to decide." He looked her up and down with an expression that seemed to her lascivious. "You're looking better every year, Rebekah. You're a beautiful woman."

"All right, Simon . . ."

"No, you are. You must take good care of yourself. Me," he said deprecatingly, holding forth his dirty, worn frock coat, "I ain't nearly so elegant as you, milady."

"What do you want, Simon? Tell me what you want, and I'll tell you your chances of getting it."

"Oh, you're a tough one, milady."

"Stop calling me that!" she said furiously.

He sniggered in a way that indicated to her the degree of his disturbance. "Sorry, Rebekah," he said, "but you got so much, and me, I got so little. You got your stores—two stores!—and the fine new house I hear about, and me, I ain't got hardly a thing."

"You've got Lucy," she reminded him.

His face, which was in need of a good wash and a shave, almost winced at the mention of the girl. "Lucy ain't too well, you see. She ain't been at all healthy and I thought . . ."

"You thought, you thought," she spat. She found him a disgusting creature. Before, in his arrogance, he had been a repellent individual, but now he was sordid and pathetic and she was made to feel dirty and itchy in his presence. "Well, keep me out of your thoughts from here on in," she instructed. "There's nothing for us to say to each other."

"Come now, Rebekah. I didn't come all the way here from New Orleans to have you tell me to go home without a cent in my pocket."

She looked into his eyes and she saw something dangerous, something violent. She was frightened by him, frightened by his unbalanced view of the world, frightened by the consistency with which he kept turning up in her life. "I settled with you, Simon," she ventured. "I gave you more than you deserved. I gave you more than . . ."

In an instant he took his fist and slammed it down on her desk. She jumped in her seat and, involuntarily, she began to tremble.

"What do you want?" she whispered.

"What do you think?"

"You're blackmailing me. You've no right to anything. "You've had your share and now you've come back to frighten me into giving you more."

"You've got plenty of money, you bitch," he said in a low, guttural voice.

She wanted to scream. She wanted to scream and she wanted Dover to come rushing in here and she wanted to have this madman seized. But she was too afraid; so she sat, staring at him, waiting for him to harm her.

"I need money," he said desperately. "Why do you doubt me?"

"I don't doubt you. That's not the point."

"I told you Lucy isn't well. And look at me. I've been working like a coolie."

"What do you want of me, Simon? Do you think I was born into this world so that I could take care of you and protect you?"

"Just help me, Rebekah," he cried, his voice suddenly changed over from something violent into something cringing.

"All right, Simon," she said. "I'll make you a deal."

"What? Just tell me."

"You give me a *get*, and I'll give you what you need."

He stared at her. "What do you want a *get* for?"

Was he mad? And why was she asking herself that at this late date. Of course he was mad. He claimed not to know why she wanted a *get*—a Jewish divorce—and she had to stare at him in disbelief. "I want a *get*, Simon, because I want to be free of you. You're not my husband anymore. We don't live together. You've taken another woman."

"It doesn't mean I don't care for you, Rebekah."

"Oh, Simon, Simon, Simon," she said wearily, shaking her head. "What's to be done with you?"

He gave her a boyish smile, thinking that she still found him irresistible.

"Stop smiling," she said, sickened by it. "Just tell me one thing: do you want the deal or not?"

"The deal?"

"Don't play the fool. You know what I mean. Money for a *get*—that's the deal."

He thought a moment, twirling his derby on his lap. "Very well," he said calmly. "If it's what you want. But it'll cost you a thousand dollars more than we agreed."

"Are you serious?"

"Yes."

She laughed all of a sudden, for there was nothing else to do. "Anything, Simon," she said in a voice full of hate and outrage. "Anything you ask."

She went to see Rabbi Lipman. It had been a long time since she was here last, for that anguished meeting when she couldn't seem to make him hear her plight.

"Welcome, my dear," said the rabbi, greeting her in his study.

"Good day, Rabbi," she said. She had dressed in a prim black outfit, wanting to appear as conservative as possible.

He peered at her, trying to discern her identity.

"I'm Rebekah Weiss," she told him. "I came to see you a long time ago about getting a *get*."

His benevolent smile faded immediately.

"You told me to be patient, to try to work it out. Well, it hasn't worked out, Rabbi, and now my husband is agreeing to give me the *get*."

"This is a serious business indeed," the rabbi said.

"If you won't give it to me," she said fiercely, "I'll find another rabbi in another city who will."

"You've been in much distress, have you?" the rabbi said.

"Yes," she replied, and if you had listened to me that time you would know how much distress. "I haven't lived with my husband for quite some time now."

"And have you sought the comfort of other men?" he asked bluntly.

"Yes, Rabbi," she said after a pause. "I have."

"So then you have committed adultery?"

She nodded. "Yes, I have," she admitted.

"Then there are grounds for divorce," he concluded, for in the Jewish law adultery was a concept predicated on only the wife's wayward path.

She and Simon were scheduled to appear at the temple the next morning. She wished she had someone to go with her—a sister or perhaps even a friend like dear Fannie, who had worked beside her sewing pockets in Baltimore. It had been so long since she'd had a woman to confide in. She dressed in an outfit similar to yesterday's, everything prim and proper, and she showed up at the temple at eight o'clock, the appointed hour. She found a tribunal of elders, waiting to judge her, waiting to give their word as to whether she would have her freedom from this man or not.

She settled in a chair and, along with the elders, she waited for Simon. He was ten, then fifteen minutes late. Had he decided against the deal? But why? What difference could it make to him? He was getting what he wanted, a tidy sum of money, and he was losing very little. Except, she thought, the power to control her.

"It seems your husband does not wish these proceedings to occur," the rabbi said sonorously as the minutes ticked by.

"He'll be here, Rabbi," she cried. "I'm sure he will."

And then, moments later, he did appear. He entered as if he had been chased, looking wild-eyed and disoriented. But the rabbi, being used to human crises, settled him. Then the proceedings were put into motion.

"It is a grave task we are asked to perform here today," the rabbi began. "The prophet Malachi says, 'Because the Lord hath been witness between thee and the wife of thy youth, against whom thou hast dealt treacherously: yet is she thy companion, and the wife of thy covenant.' "

Simon and Rebekah glanced briefly at each other and then averted their eyes.

"And in the book *Sanhedrin* the rabbis say, 'For him who divorces his first wife, the very altar sheds tears.' " Rabbi Lipman looked at Simon and then spoke very quietly. "My son, are you intent on the dissolution of this marriage?"

Again Simon looked to Rebekah who gave him a nod that was perceptible only to his eyes. "Yes, Rabbi," he said.

The rabbi nodded gravely. "The basis of the *get* is found in Deuteronomy," the rabbi intoned. "Let me read these words to you. 'When a man hath taken a wife,' " he read, " 'and married her, and it come to pass that she find no favor in his eyes, because he found some uncleanness in her; then let him write her a bill of divorcement, and give it in her hand, and send her out of his house.' " The rabbi looked up and addressed the gathering. "There has been the sin of adultery on the part of both halves of this marriage."

Rebekah, shocked to hear the confidence spoken before this group of men, felt her face flush. Simon, hearing this news, clenched his fists under the table.

"And so we may conclude that a *get* should be granted for the purpose of dissolving this marriage."

Rebekah's head was buzzing. More formalities were

spoken—laws and maxims and such—and then a parchment was produced on which there were twelve lines drawn. Together she and Simon read the document.

On the fourth day of the week, the thirteenth day of the month Tamuz, in the year 5631 of the creation of the world according to the number we reckon here, in Mobile the city which is situated on the Bay of Mobile and contains wells of water, I, Sholem Weiss, son of Yisroel Weiss, do hereby consent, with my own will, without force, free and unrestrained, to grant a bill of divorce to thee, my wife Rebekah, daughter of Chaim Kraus, who hast been my wife from time past, and with this I free, release and divorce thee that thou mayest have control and power over thyself from now and hereafter, to be married to any man whom thou mayest choose and no man shall hinder thee from this day forevermore, and thus thou art free for every man. And this shall be unto thee from me a bill of divorce, a letter of freedom, and a document of dismissal, according to the laws of Moses and Israel.

"And you are ready to sign this, Sholem Weiss?" the rabbi asked.

Simon looked at Rebekah. "Yes," he said at last, and the document was signed and witnessed.

She felt her heart pounding as she produced the *kittubeh*, the marriage contract, and gave it to the rabbi who presented it to Simon.

"This is to be destroyed," the rabbi said.

Simon, his face ashen, took the *kittubeh*, ripped it savagely, and threw the pieces into Rebekah's face. She gasped, and the quorum of elders looked on in stunned silence.

"You've been no kind of a wife to me," he accused.
She began to tremble and half rose in her seat.

"You've been no kind of a wife to me!" he bellowed.
"You're not a woman! You're not any kind of a
woman!"

She ran from the chamber, away from all of this.
She raced outside, into the warm, flowering morning.
She ran until she was winded, and then she stopped
and tried to collect her breath. She turned and saw
him coming toward her, his face dark now and glowering.

"Business is done then," he muttered. "To your
satisfaction, I hope."

"Yes," she whispered. "Yes, it is, and I've left the
money for you at the bank. Go and get it and just
leave me be, will you, Simon?"

He nodded heavily. "Very well, Rebekah," he said.
"But only remember that it isn't over between us, nor
shall it ever be."

CHAPTER TWENTY-ONE

Six months after her marriage was formally termi-
nated, Rebekah heard from Jarrett. He finally sent her
a letter; the postmark read "Galveston." She carried
the letter around with her all day, not sure that she
wanted to read it, angry with him, furious with him,
for taking so long. She didn't need him in her life. Her
life was smooth now. She was working hard; she was
making money; she had drawn up plans for a store in

Hattiesburg. She didn't need Jarrett; she didn't need the trouble he could cause her.

And yet she was living in his house. Even though she owned it, Wild Oaks was the Russell house and would always be the Russell house. One couldn't eliminate the Russell history from these surroundings, and Rebekah didn't have the inclination to try. She didn't move to Wild Oaks because it was a beautiful home—although it was, with its stately white columns, its broad veranda, and its great expanse of lawn—but, rather, she lived in Wild Oaks because she wanted to be near Jarrett. And so when she arrived back at Wild Oaks late at night and retired to her bedroom, she held the letter in her lap for several long moments and then she opened it.

My dearest,

she read.

Before you reproach me, do you really think I don't know how long it has been? Do you think I haven't counted every minute? Because if that is what you think, there is no point in your reading further.

She lay the letter down in her lap. Was there any point? she asked herself. She had loved him, and she didn't or couldn't believe that he loved her the same. She missed him so intensely; she felt a terrible yearning, a hunger for him; and so she had to read on.

Has it been hell for you, Rebekah? Surely it has been for me. There are times when I feel like the Flying Dutchman, doomed to journey aimlessly, never allowed to set anchor. It was like that, too, when we first met in Baltimore. I was sick then, sick in spirit, and I tried to make myself well and

with your help, I almost did but then the world
came between us, Rebekah, or did we ask for too
much? We were reckless—you know it, I know
it—and we were punished. Not only are we punished by being kept apart, but I am punished by
knowing that I can never return to my home
again. There are dreams, Rebekah, when I meet
Schuyler on Walnut Hill and I walk the paces and
I hear the command to fire and I shoot the general through the heart, shoot him dead, and yet he
rises, and comes after me, and I have to run.

She felt her throat and her nose and her eyes begin
to burn with unshed tears. She wanted to reach out to
Jarrett, to touch him and to hold him close.

I did run, Rebekah. All these months you haven't
heard from me, I've been running. From New
Orleans to Baton Rouge to Alexandria to Shreve-
port to Beaumont and then finally to Galveston.
I've stayed in Galveston now for a while. Its place
on the sea helps to remind me of Mobile. I've set
up a practice here and it would be a good life for
some, but not for me. Why? Because it isn't my
life. I feel like a shadow without you, without my
home.
    Come to me, Rebekah. Please come to me. If
only for a day, just so I could see you, just so I
could touch you. Perhaps there is no reason why
you should, except that I love you very much.

                                   With devotion,
                                   Jarrett

She stared at the letter, at the signature, at the
address, and then she folded it very carefully and
placed it in her purse.
    She rose. She removed her clothing and put on her

nightgown. She poured the water into the washbasin, and she cleansed herself. Then she got into bed and turned out the lights. Everything was dark and silent, except for the incessant chirping of the cicadas. She closed her eyes; she tried to sleep; she tried to put Jarrett out of her mind because it was trouble, sheer trouble, and she just wanted to be left alone, to live and work in peace. But she could not sleep, and she could not put him out of mind. She kept hearing him whisper to her that he loved her very much, and it was with those words ringing in her ears that she passed this troubled night.

The next day she tried to convince herself that Jarrett was over for her and that she must ignore all of his entreaties. She worked as hard as ever even though she felt confused and unhappy. By the end of the day she knew it was inevitable that she would make the journey, and it was thus that Mr. O'Donnell found her when he reported to her with the receipts from the Claiborne Street store.

"Good evening, miss," O'Donnell said, his manner reserved as it had been over these many months, ever since he felt that her personality and attitude toward him had changed.

"Good evening, Mr. O'Donnell." She stared at him, at his small red nose, at his rosy cheeks. He was a dear man and he had turned out to be a felicitous choice, for there was none more resourceful or faithful than he. She despised herself for mistreating him, for venting her anger at him.

"Here's the receipts, miss," he said stiffly.

"Thank you, Mr. O'Donnell."

There was an awkward pause.

"Will you be needing anything else, miss?" he said.

"Mr. O'Donnell," she replied, gesturing toward a chair, "won't you sit down a moment?"

He gave her a quizzical look and then did as she suggested.

"Yes, miss?" he said, his voice tense and so suspicious that it hurt her.

"I'm going to be going away for a few days, perhaps a week," she announced.

"You're not ill, are you, miss?"

She shook her head. "No, Mr. O'Donnell. There's some personal business I have to attend to, and I want you to see after the stores."

"Very well, miss. If I can be trusted."

The remark was overtly confrontive, and she paused before replying. "Do you think I don't trust you, Mr. O'Donnell?"

"I don't think nothing, miss," he said, trying to sound calm.

"Well, I just want to tell you that I do trust you, Mr. O'Donnell. I trust you and I respect you and I like you and I value you and I need you." She looked up at him and she saw that his eyes were blinking with surprise. "Can you forgive me, Mr. O'Donnell?"

He paused significantly. "Yes, miss," he said finally, barely audible.

"I know I've been wretched to you, and I'm grateful that you didn't leave me long ago."

"Just so long as you're back the way you was, miss," he said gallantly.

She leaned across the table and placed her hand over his. "Thank you, Mr. O'Donnell. Thank you so much."

"Where are you going, miss?" he asked, renewing his concern for her.

"Galveston," she said in a remote voice. Then, with forced brightness, "It's supposed to be a very gay place, you know."

O'Donnell stared at her, thinking of whether or not he should ask this next question. "Are you going to see Doctor Russell, miss?"

She felt an immediate urgency to deny and conceal, and then she decided against it. "That's right, Mr. O'Donnell," she admitted. She smiled ironically. "I may be a fool, but at least I'm a consistent fool."

"You ain't a fool, miss. Listen to your heart. That's no foolish thing to do."

And so that was precisely what she did. The next day she left for Galveston. She didn't bother to wire ahead, for she wanted to surprise Jarrett. She imagined how he would receive her when she walked up to him and tapped him on the shoulder. As she rode the train, she smiled at the thought of it, and her fellow traveler, a severe-looking clergyman, studied her face for a clue.

She looked out the window. Sea and pines and groves of oleander. It was a lovely country. For the first time in God only knew how long she felt unencumbered by the pressures of business. She didn't want to think of business now; all she wanted to think of was her reunion with Jarrett.

When she arrived, so many dusty hours later, at the terminal in Galveston, she felt a sudden weakening of purpose. This strange city—more resort than a place where people actually lived and worked—seemed ill designed for seriousness, and she had come here with serious intentions. She was willing to think about the proposal of marriage that Jarrett had made to her so long ago. As the thought went through her mind, she herself was a little shocked by it. Just several days ago she was questioning the continued existence of Jarrett's place in her thoughts, and now she was willing to give herself over to him. Was she mad? Perhaps, yes, perhaps she was, but she didn't care. All she wanted was to see him once again. And if she established the store in Hattiesburg, then perhaps they could live there, and he would be safe.

She went to the address that he had enclosed: 240 Water Street. There she found the Royal Poinciana Hotel, a ramshackle, rundown establishment with a group of unsavory characters loitering in front of it. She checked the address, feeling that there must be some mistake, but there it was: 240 Water Street.

She went to the desk and spoke with the rat-faced young clerk.

"Excuse me," she said.

He looked her up and down and then sort of smiled, exposing a row of discolored teeth. "What all can I do for you, ma'am?"

"Can you tell me if Doctor Rusell is registered here?"

"Who wants to know?"

"An old friend of his."

"Well, matter of fact is that the doc been stayin' here for a while now. He knows you comin'?"

"What business is that of yours?" she said.

He sniggered a bit, a horrible covert sound. "Well, I don't know, mebbe none a 'tall, but you all some kind of fancy lady and your old friend here, he ain't been payin' his bills and I thought mebbe you might like to . . ."

"How dare you," she said in a voice that was meant to be as withering as possible. "How dare you speak to me like that." She turned and walked right out of the hotel and into the blazing hot street. Even though she was dressed appropriately to the weather, in a light yellow dress, she felt a momentary faint that she attributed to the heat. She went toward the water, which was everywhere, for Galveston was an island. She walked down to the piers, and there she saw the collection of boats that was called the mosquito fleet, so named because when they went out to sea, they appeared to be swarming. She stood there, on the pier, watching the vivid orange sunset, watching the flocks of screaming gulls fighting over shrimp heads. The noise—the quarreling, hungry noise—set her on edge. Was it a mistake for her to have come here? She felt so anxious and confused. What was Jarrett doing living in a place like that? It wasn't right. He wasn't meant to live in a place like that. He was a fine person, born into luxury, unsuited to deprivation. She could sustain herself in whatever wretched surroundings she was committed to; she had survived steerage, she had survived the crowded noisy tenements of Baltimore, she had survived living in a wagon on the road. She was strong and resilient; she had a sense of herself. But Jarrett—she didn't trust his instinct for survival. She felt protective toward him, and she didn't want to see him hurt.

After a couple of wasted hours she returned to the hotel and sat down in the seedy lobby. There were beaten, worn-down people scattered about, people who looked like they drank too much and gambled too much and led utterly rank and dissolute lives. One such person, an elderly woman with a shocking frizz of white hair, sat down next to her and stared at her like a lunatic.

"What *is* it?" Rebekah said when she was no longer able to ignore the woman.

"Have you got some money for me, dear?" the woman whispered.

Rebekah shook her head.

"Just a *sou*," the woman said with a cackle.

Rebekah looked at the woman. She was obviously someone who had once had some education and here she was now, in these squalid circumstances, begging for money.

"Come on now, dearie. Just a *sou*. You can spare it."

Rebekah reached into her purse and pulled out a few coins while the woman nodded eagerly. She handed the coins to the woman who pocketed them without a word of thanks and went toward the stairs. At the foot of the stairs she turned around, and in the most strident voice imaginable, she screamed: "Whore!"

All eyes turned to Rebekah, who stared straight

ahead, not willing just yet to run from the lobby. She
would leave when everyone stopped looking at her,
and she wouldn't come back. She would leave a note
for Jarrett telling him that she could be reached
through the First Mercantile Bank. She would get a
room in the best hotel in town, and then they could
start again.

Just then, while she thought up her strategy, Jarrett
entered the hotel. She looked up and there he was.
He hadn't yet seen her, and so she watched him walk
toward the desk, studying him secretly just as she had
done that day in Biloxi when they met on the riverboat. He looked worn, she thought, just as did everyone in the Royal Poinciana Hotel. His clothes were
shot, and he looked exhausted. He walked to the desk
with a strange stiff-legged gait. When he reached his
destination, the rat-faced clerk pointed toward her,
and Jarrett turned and tried to focus in on her.

She knew, when she saw him doing that, that he
must have been drinking, and she felt her spirits crash.
The memory of Simon flashed into her mind—the
memory of a man destroying himself—and, in a feeling
of panic, she wanted to bolt. But there he was coming
toward her, and she had to sit there and she had to
see him this way.

He stood before her, his face drawn, but still there
was something so beautiful about him to her.

"You've come," he whispered.

She closed her eyes and nodded heavily.

"And look at me," he said straightaway, his voice
and manner a study in desperation.

"Oh, Jarrett," she said with a small moan.

He put out his arms for her and she rose and they
held each other, not caring that they were being
watched. She began to sob, and he stroked her hair.
She hid her face against him until she was ready to
look at him again. She saw that there were tears in his
eyes too, and she kissed him passionately, smelling the

whiskey on his breath but for that moment not caring what she smelled, not caring who watched her, not caring about anything except that they were together again and she loved having him hold her and she loved the feel of his body and she always would, always.

At last it was time to break away, and this they did, although it was painful to do so.

"You should have written me you were coming," he said awkwardly.

She was going to explain that she wanted to surprise him, but then she thought better of it and merely nodded her agreement.

"You must be tired. I . . . do you want to come up to my room?" he stammered.

He wasn't terribly drunk, she thought, defending him to herself, only just a bit. She wanted to be with him, surely she did, but not up there, not in a sordid little room. "I haven't even checked into a hotel yet," she said with a little smile. "I should do that, shouldn't I?"

He smiled back, but his smile was edged with bitterness. "You wouldn't want to stay in the Royal Poinciana, would you?" he said.

She thought to make some silly excuse, but then she realized that honesty was the only course. "No," she admitted, "I wouldn't."

"Well then, there's the Beach Hotel. That's the finest in town, that's where you should stay."

"Very good," she said, introducing the brisk, businesslike voice that she habitually used as her defense. "And we can eat there—I'm famished. Why don't I wait for you to get dressed and . . ."

"I am dressed," he said bluntly.

She looked at him, at the worn and soiled suit, at the faded, frayed collar of his shirt. "I see," she murmured. "Well, no mind. We'll have ourselves a fine dinner anyway."

"Anyway?" he said testily. "Listen, if you'd rather not be seen with me . . ."

"Jarrett . . ."

"Just save me a few crusts of bread, that's all I'll need."

"Jarrett, please," she said in a low, urgent voice. "Please don't do this."

Her request seemed to surprise him and to chasten him. "I'm sorry," he said. "Of course I won't. You haven't come all this way to be subjected to my rantings."

They dined at the Beach Hotel on lobster and steak and English cream custard and brandied peaches and other fine delicacies. She watched Jarrett eat with a lugubrious intensity, needing this sort of food but not allowing himself to enjoy it. There was little conversation until halfway into the meal when she decided to speak frankly.

"Aren't you pleased I've come?" she asked.

"Of course I am."

"I should think you would be. I got your letter. It's what made me come."

"Well, I am glad," he said tersely.

"No, you're not," she accused, feeling suddenly devastated, feeling suddenly that the whole thing— the journey, their love for each other—was a mistake, a terrible mistake.

"You should have prepared me," he reproached her.

"Why? I wanted to surprise you. I wanted to see you smile."

"There's no place for surprises, Rebekah," he explained. "I want everything simple and ordered," he said fiercely. "I want a home and a practice and a wife and children and honor and respect and community and I've none of it and now I never will. No, my dear, surprises won't make me smile."

She stared at him. His face seemed just now like a ruin of some fine, noble edifice. "What has your life

become, Jarrett?" she said. "Tell me. Tell me everything."

He laughed weakly. "Everything? Oh no, not everything."

"Do you drink?"

He looked away from her, across the sumptuous
dining room filled with prosperous, well-fed people.
"Yes," he admitted. "I do take a nip here and there,"
he added wryly.

"Why, Jarrett? Why?"

He looked back at her; he stared with his eyes that
were still brilliantly blue and unfaded despite all the
hardship. "Sometimes I need a haze to come in and
cover me up," he murmured. "A deep, wet haze that
will let me forget everything, everything; and Christ,
Rebekah, there's so much to forget."

"But that hotel, Jarrett. You mustn't live there. Is
it the money? I can give you . . ."

"No!" he said harshly.

She pulled back. "Why?" she wanted to know. "Why
won't you let me help you? Are you so proud that you
won't take my money?"

"Don't try to protect me, Rebekah. This is my life.
This is what I've made for myself, and if it means
living in the Royal Poinciana, then so be it."

"But you're punishing yourself."

"I deserve to be punished," he said in a controlled
voice.

"No, you don't."

"Yes. Yes, I do. I killed a man and why? Because of
a matter of pride. What stupidity! My God, Rebekah,
you said it yourself, and you were right. That's why I
deserve to be punished, because I was a fool, and
fools learn hard."

"But how do you live? You told me that your life
here was good enough but . . ."

"It is good enough."

"No, it's not. Not for you. Not for someone like you."

"Stop saying that!" he cried angrily. "I'm just a person. I'm no different from anyone else in the Royal Poinciana Hotel. We've all got our stories and our excuses. I'm no different. I'm not from noble lineage or anything of the sort."

"But how do you live? You said you had patients. Were you telling the truth?"

He paused a moment and then nodded.

"Where is your office?"

He shook his head, irritated. "What difference does it make? Do you know this city?"

"Who comes to see you?"

"Stop asking so many questions!" he said furiously.

There was a painful silence which lasted while the waiter cleared away their places.

"I'm sorry," Jarrett said. He leaned over and took her hand in his. He brought it up to his lips. "I can't tell you what it means that you've come to me. I feel like I'm in prison and you're the only visitor I've had. I don't want to talk about myself. I just want to look at you, Rebekah, and hold you."

Shortly thereafter they went upstairs to her room. He had picked up a bottle of brandy, and now he poured two glasses.

"Do we need that?" she said disapprovingly.

"Don't be the reformer. Not tonight."

She could see that he was nervous, that he must have felt dirty and inferior to her, and that he needed something to bolster himself. She held out her arms to him and he came to her and they embraced.

"Oh, Jarrett," she whispered. "There won't ever be anyone else for me, never."

He kissed her, her eyes, her lips, her neck.

"I love you, Jarrett," she heard herself say, choking back the tears.

They undressed each other, slowly, with unending

fascination. They renewed each other's memories of their bodies, and they rejoiced in the feel and the closeness. She could look at him now, freed of those awful clothes, and he was her great love. She didn't care what he said, he was not just another person and he never would be. He was gifted and kind and special; she cherished him.

"Your breasts," he murmured, wondering at their beauty, their white lushness, the skein of blue veins that mapped their fullness.

She took his hand and directed it toward the center of her longing. He touched her there expertly, and she became lost in her pleasure, closing her eyes and imagining herself falling again and again through a ring of fire. She moaned and she knew that she could have wept at how long it had been and how much she had been deprived of. When she was able to catch her breath, she took hold of him and stroked him with a touch that was at once firm and tender.

He ran his rough, unshaven face along her smooth white thighs and then grazed her sex with his lips. Oh yes, she cried, seizing his shoulders and pressing herself against him. Jarrett, Jarrett, she cried, pulling him up to her, and then he entered her and then they were together as they hadn't been for so long, as they had needed to be for so long, and she heard the waves crashing onto the beach below her window. And when it was over, they were there, holding on to each other tightly, as if the surf might reach up to them, grab hold of them, and pull them out to sea.

They breakfasted that next morning in the sunny rose-colored dining room of the hotel. They didn't speak much; rather they smiled at each other, sharing the significance and the joy of their reunion.

Over the second cup of *café au lait* she decided to give him some news. "Something good has happened," she announced.

"Oh?" he replied, arching an eyebrow. "What might that be?"

"I'm free of Simon at last."

"How so?"

"I divorced him."

He stared at her. "That's good," he said finally with a nod. "Very, very good."

She smiled excitedly. "So there are no barriers anymore, Jarrett."

"What do you mean?"

She sensed an inexplicable reserve enter his tone. "I mean nothing. It's just that we're free for each other now."

He sipped from the coffee, remaining silent.

After breakfast they strolled along the boardwalk. She felt a certain unease that was at odds with the freshness of the day and the pleasure of last night. He was withdrawing from her, she told herself, and she didn't know why. Didn't he love her? How could he not when she loved him as she did?

"Jarrett," she said, "you seem so far away."

"I'm sorry, Rebekah," he said, the reserve becoming even that much more apparent.

"I don't even know what your life is about anymore," she said. "You've told me nothing. I see you living in that awful place, and you haven't told me why, you haven't told me . . ."

"I have no explanations," he said shortly.

"But I demand them!" she cried. "Tell me what your life has become, Jarrett. I must know."

"No," he whispered. "You mustn't."

"Why? Are you doing something wrong?"

"Don't ask questions, Rebekah," he warned.

He began to walk on ahead, yet she stayed where she was, holding onto the railing that separated the beach from the boardwalk. He turned to see her standing there rigid, her eyes full of fear.

"Come now," he said gently, holding out his hand to her.

She shook her head.

"Rebekah, don't be foolish."

"Something's wrong," she said. "And you don't trust me enough to tell me."

He laughed. "Can't you see, darling? Everything's wrong. Why should I bore you with the details?"

"Stop it!" she cried. "Who do you think you're talking to? Do you think you're talking to some empty-headed, silly little woman? You're talking to me—Rebekah Weiss—and if you've nothing to say to me, then I may as well leave."

His face sagged as he walked the few steps back to her. "All right," he said. "I'll tell you everything."

She felt her heart pounding, but she nodded, trying to appear controlled.

"When I came here, I didn't have any money at all . . ."

"Then why didn't you wire me?"

"Because I didn't want to!" he said fiercely. "I wanted to make it on my own. I'd made my own mistakes, and now I wanted to bail myself out. But it was hopeless. Somehow—inevitably I suppose—my reputation preceded me. I couldn't set up a practice."

"But there must have been people who didn't care . . ."

He nodded. "Yes, there were some, but they couldn't pay me anything. And it wasn't like it was in Mobile, where I had my home and my belongings. I couldn't afford to have patients who couldn't pay their bills."

She thought of all the money she had been making and all the money she had put into Wild Oaks. She realized that he didn't even know about Wild Oaks, and here he was, all these months, living like a pauper.

"I tried to get some other kind of work, but there was nothing for me. And then, one day in the Royal Poinciana . . ."

He let his thought die out, and she waited for him. "What, Jarrett? Tell me."

He sighed heavily and then continued. "Someone in the hotel, one of the resident lowlife, approached me and said he knew I was a doctor and he knew how I could make some fast money. I was desperate, Rebekah, do you understand?"

She was beginning to feel a sort of numbness, but she nodded.

"He said if I cut him in for some of it, he could arrange something for me. He said a friend of his—a lady of the evening—had gotten herself into trouble, and all she needed was for me to clean her up a bit."

Rebekah stared at him, not sure she wanted to hear any of this.

"I must have done my job well, because I've become the whorehouse doctor. It's all right, they're nice friendly girls, and the money's regular. Pretty soon, I'll have enough to get out of these rags. Then I'll move to the Beach Hotel and take my coffee in a sunny spot and play faro with my earnings . . ."

"Stop it!" she cried. "Stop it!"

"And that's the way it will be, Rebekah," he said, his voice choked with emotion. "And that's the way it was meant to be."

In a flash she was down the stairs of the boardwalk and onto the beach, running away from him, running away from the spectacle of his ruin, running toward the sea, the sand in her shoes, the gulls screaming at her overhead.

"Rebekah!" he called, running after her.

She stopped at the water's edge. She looked out over the sea and it was limitless and there was nowhere to go.

"Can't you understand?" he said breathlessly when he caught up with her.

"I've bought Wild Oaks," she cried. "I bought it so that you could come back one day and we could live there together, but now I see it won't happen. Now I see you're abandoning yourself, just as Simon did, just as Clara did. You never told me you'd be weak," she cried. "I thought you'd be strong. I thought you'd survive, but now I see that all you want to be is a whorehouse doctor. Well, I want none of it, do you hear?" she screamed.

He came up to her, standing very close. She could see that his face was lined and showed the signs of destruction. "Can't you understand?" he said. "Have you no understanding? You ask me what my life is about, but, my God, what is yours all about? You're like some kind of wild, heartless battle maiden, you are. All you care about is your pride and your destiny and your womanhood, and you don't give a damn about the frailties of other human beings. Well, let me tell you, Rebekah, I'm weak and I'm tired and my life isn't honorable. For two cents I'd walk into that ocean and that would be the end of it. Not only haven't I your strength, but your strength makes me weaker. So leave me, Rebekah," he said. "Leave me in peace, and that will be the end of it."

They stared at each other, blocking out the white blaze of beach, the glowing orange sun, and the brilliant blue water.

"Very well, Jarrett, if that's what you want," she said in a voice that strained for composure but that betrayed at every point the heartbreak she felt.

CHAPTER TWENTY-TWO

She sat on the train, looking out at the same vistas she had passed en route to Galveston when everything seemed bright and hopeful. Now she was tired of this scenery, of this tropical lushness, with its dense, spiky vegetation and its tendency toward rot. She thought of the hayfields of her youth, of the warm soft greens of the linden forests, of the rose arbors and the flowering chestnut trees. Here, on this train from Galveston, this train taking her away from Jarrett and back into her life of loneliness, she felt again the fatigue of the voyage, the voyage that was her life. It seemed she could never stop; it seemed that there was always a ship to meet or a train to catch or a wagon to pull her down the road. In this first-class compartment (and this had changed, hadn't it? she thought with no real satisfaction, remembering back to the days of steerage), with its fine plush appointments and its absence of fellow travelers, she could pull down the shades and she could let herself weep without restraint, for there was much cause for sorrow.

What would she do now? She felt pummeled by the urgent dizzying sensation of wanting to run back to Jarrett, wanting to get down on her hands and knees and plead with him to make her life easier. But, instead, she sat on this train, in this fine expensive compartment with its undeniable bouquet of stale smoke, and she let the hope drain out of her. She was nearing thirty; she was without a husband; she was without a child. There was, in her life, no visible proof that she was a woman capable of love and nurturing.

She wanted, more than ever, to have a child. She felt a need, almost biological in nature, to gear her body toward the birth of a child. The thought of never having a child filled her with sorrow and shame. She remembered her mother and how kind she had been, how gentle and loving, and she wondered how she herself would ever achieve that state of loving without a child. Just before, when she sat in the dining car and had seen a woman younger than she organizing at table a brood of young ones, she felt that emptiness in her life, and she felt old and even withered beside this stranger. She had left the cup of consommé untouched, and she withdrew to her private compartment, like a sort of freak, not wanting to inflict herself on others.

Well, she told herself with infinite bitterness pretending to be resolve, it wasn't meant to be. One didn't get to choose one's life; it simply happened, and you either accepted it or you were destroyed. Her life had not to do with love and marriage and children and friendship and warmth but, rather, with ambition and commerce and money and power. She opened the shades, tired of the dark and of the weeping and ready to look out at the world again. More than anything, her life, she supposed, had to do with resilience. *You're like some kind of wild, heartless battle maiden,* Jarrett had told her, and the words felt like they were carved into her. But she couldn't help it if she had a knack for survival, could she?

She would do business in New Orleans on the way back to Mobile, she had decided. She knew that there was something fundamentally cold about that decision, as if she had to justify this trip by doing some business on it. But the fact was that she had to pass through New Orleans on the way back to Mobile, and that there were importers and manufacturers there whom she should see, and that she did want to justify this trip or at least find some worthy aspect of it to counter the sourness and disappointment.

She would stay overnight and wire Mr. O'Donnell that she would return that next day. Again she would be a woman alone in that great, raffish city. Well, she told herself encouragingly, the first time she had gone there on her own, she had been lucky. She had found Mr. O'Donnell; she had gone to the faro table; she had broken the bank at Colonel Bryant's. This time she didn't need to double or triple her money. This time she had all the money she needed. This time she needed luck to lead her in another direction, toward some other province of happiness that had been hidden from her too long.

She arrived early the next day, after a sleepless night on the train, at the station on Annunciation Street. She would stay at the Royal Hotel, as she had in the past, and she would avail herself of only the best. That was what she wanted in her life now: the best. That was what she demanded: the best. And if the best was something that money could buy, then she would have it.

She got off the train, in that damp, chill morning, and stood momentarily on the platform, feeling rather lost, with that enormously lonely feeling of being a stranger in a strange city. She began heading out of the station, out of the crowd of people whom she already felt she knew just because she had seen their faces over the course of a two-day period. She walked along the network of rail lines that fanned out to make a bleak, gray tableau. Then she heard someone call her name, or at least she thought she did, and she looked around briefly but saw no one on the platform. She sensed that she was hearing her name being called precisely because she was alone and in need of recognition. She hurried on, convinced of her delusion, and then she heard her name called once again. This time she was sure that she heard it for real, and so she stopped, put down her valise, and looked over the heads of the people behind her.

"Here!" she heard a voice cry from somewhere below, from somewhere on that network of rail lines.

She shaded her eyes and saw a tall, broad man waving at her. She saw him ask something of another man, who appeared to be the foreman, and then, evidently, he was given liberty to leave his work, and he raced toward her.

"Rebekah!" he called again.

Now she recognized the voice, and now she recognized the man. She watched him come nearer to her—that tall, broad man with blond hair and blond moustache—and she felt that this meeting was providential, a nasty, small-minded joke that Fate thought to amuse herself with. She suddenly felt her heart pounding, her head pounding, her knees weak, and she had to sit down on the valise, as jarred and depleted as if she had just been struck down by a horse and carriage.

"Rebekah, my God!" the strange, familiar man said to her.

"What do you want?" she cried in a voice that sounded, even to her, twisted with a terrible bitterness.

"I was working there, on the tracks, and there I look up, and I see you, and it was like a dream, Rebekah. I says to myself, Simon Weiss, are you dreaming? I gave myself a pinch," he said, demonstrating on his strong forearm covered with blond coils. "Naw, I ain't dreaming," he laughed.

Reluctantly she looked up and searched his face. There was such a deterioration in his manner. The very way he spoke, once so precise and, if not cultured, at least striving to be, had become coarse and untutored; his hair, once thick and shiny as a brass helmet, had thinned and looked in need of a good washing; his face was lined and sagged a bit at the jowls.

"So here you are," he said, looking at her intently.

"Yes, here I am," she said sullenly.

"You're looking so fine. Making a lot of money, are you? Yeah, that's what you know how to do, all right."

"And you, Simon?"

"I'm a working man, Rebekah. A hardworking man."

"But, Simon, here? You're working here?"

"That's right, Rebekah. A common laborer. That's what it's come to. And how about you, Rebekah? Are you happy?"

"Don't ask me questions, Simon."

"Where are you coming from?"

"Don't ask me questions, Simon."

"Why?" he asked innocently.

"Because you've no right!" she cried. Then, disturbed by her lack of control, she stood up, reached down for the valise, and began to walk away, but he took her by the shoulder and held her there.

"What are you doing? Unhand me! You've no right to . . ."

"Don't, Rebekah," he said. "Just talk to me a bit more. I'll let you go. I'm not asking for anything."

She searched his face to see if he were lying and then decided he had to be. "Who do you think you're fooling?" she demanded to know. "Do you think I don't know all your deceptions? I know your bag of tricks the way a rabbi knows Talmud."

He laughed a little, pleased by her witticism.

"What are you laughing about?" she cried. And why was she standing here? Why didn't she just walk away or call a police officer if he prevented it? "Look at you," she said. "Look what you've done with your life."

Reflexively his hand went to his collar, as if to straighten a tie, and then slowly he let his hand fall to his side.

"So in America, Simon Weiss, everyone has a servant, ay?" she said vindictively. "And the streets are paved with gold, and golden acorns hang from the trees, ay?"

"Don't, Rebekah."

"Why shouldn't I? The hell you've put me through! The hell you've put yourself through! Why, you could have been something. You had a mind. You had a fine, strong back. And I was there to help you!" She could almost have cried from the words, but her rage was more central, and she wanted to be able to speak. "That's all I wanted, you fool, you! All I wanted was to be there to help you and to have a family, to have children, to light Sabbath candles, to be a different kind of a person than I am now. You made me what I am. You forced me to be this way! And now where am I going to get a child? Where? Tell me where, you beast! Tell me where!"

She was quite hysterical, and he reached out to hold her. She slapped at him, but he took her into his arms and held her there tightly, on the now deserted platform, and she struggled but she couldn't break away. He was still too strong for her, and so she collapsed against him, against his sweaty, smelly body, and she cried, not even ashamed to have him see her this way.

At last she collected herself, and he released her. "You see," she said in a small, broken voice. "You see what *I've* become."

"But you're a rich woman . . ."

"It doesn't matter," she said. "I want a child. My God, I feel so empty inside. You wouldn't understand. You never thought of anyone but yourself. You never cared about the things I cared about."

"That's not true, Rebekah," he protested.

"It surely is, Simon," she cried, feeling it odd to hear his name on her lips once again.

"It isn't true," he said, preparing to show his trump card. "I have a new side to me now."

She laughed. "Do you? And what does it have to do with?" she said, mocking him. "Working with your hands? Has that made you into an honest man at last?"

"No, Rebekah," he said quietly. "It has more to do with being a father."

She stared at him. "You have a child?"

He nodded. "A son. Benjamin."

"Benjamin," she whispered, half to herself.

"He's only three months old, but he's meant so much to me. He's meant . . ."

She shook her head. "I don't want to hear," she cried.

He tried not to smile, but there was a faint line of delight at his lips which he couldn't control. "I'd like for you to see him sometime," he said.

"Oh, yes," she laughed. "I'll be the child's god-mother, why not?"

"If you'd like," he said with a false naïveté, mocking her now.

"Shut up," she said. "You never gave me what I want. I begged you for a child, and it wasn't till you found that whore . . ."

"Rebekah!"

"Well, a whore's a whore and a pimp is a pimp!"

He laughed at the spectacle she was creating.

"Stop it!" she screeched.

"I'm sorry," he said, covering his mouth.

"I must be mad to be standing here," she said suddenly. She picked up the valise and began to walk away.

"Two thousand seven hundred and thirty Rampart Street," Simon called after her. "Meet me there at six, Rebekah. I want you to see my son."

"And I want to see you burn in hell!" she cried back.

She spent the next day and a half going about the business that she had hoped would distract her but that failed to do so. She spent hours in the offices of

importers, looking over silks and linens that she
planned to carry in a new line aimed at the more
affluent of her customers. As the economy prospered,
so did many of the freedmen, and she felt they were
desirous of merchandise beyond the cheap corsets and
calicoes that had been her mainstay.

As always she participated in the cheerful bantering
that was part of the game between her and the men
who tried to sell her things, but she felt nothing cheerful deep down within her. She felt, more than anything, that she had been cheated and tricked. In a way
she felt like old King Midas—everything she touched
turned to gold, and yet she got nothing from it in the
end. She was being controlled by the business rather
than the other way around.

Finally, after these many appointments, she found
herself with time on her hands. She walked the streets
of the city, admiring it, loving it, as she had from the
first. She tried to convince herself that this was a
pleasant afternoon, geared to touring. But she knew
that it was a sham. There was only one thing on her
mind, Simon's son, and the address he had shouted at
her—2730 Rampart Street—kept coming back to her.

What did she hope to gain by going there? It was
such a strange, foolish idea. Why couldn't she get rid
of it? She felt it beginning to take her over, becoming
a full-blown compulsion, and she sat down on a nearby bench and tried to get her breath.

She had to see the child. She wasn't sure why, she
had no idea why, but she had to see the child. In a
way she felt the child was hers, or, at least, that she
had a claim. She had put years and years into Simon,
into sorting out her life with him. Just because he had
left her didn't mean . . . but this was madness; she
recognized it as such. Her life with Simon was over,
done. There was the *get*, for one thing. That had
ended it officially. It didn't matter what he had done

with his life. If he had one child or ten, it had nothing to do with her.

She resumed her walk. She strolled through the French market, crowded, pungent, noisy. There were men and women haggling with each other over the price of cabbages and tomatoes. Old black women with brightly colored *tignons* on their heads and great straw baskets filled with vegetables and fruits and sassafras leaves passed back and forth among the stalls that lay beneath the arches of the marketplace.

The sight of all this food reminded her that she hadn't eaten, and her hunger was suddenly pressing upon her. She sat upon a stool, drinking hot black coffee and eating a little cake drenched with honey, hot from the oven. Satisfied, she continued on, past the bloody slabs of beef, past the disemboweled rabbits, past the baskets of squirming crabs and eels, past the thousands of iridescent red and blue fish hanging on hooks and piled high in more baskets. Then there was the flower market and then the birds in cages, the noisy parrots, the little white lovebirds.

She felt suddenly that she had to get out of here. She walked quickly, away from this swarming humanity. She was not distracted by all of this gaiety, but, rather, she was wounded. She wanted so much, and she was not getting it. She wanted a child. Weren't there men who could give her that? Jewish men? Perhaps, yes. In Mobile there were some Jews, she knew that, even though she had kept herself a loner (but what about Jarrett? she wanted him; she wanted a child with him). She felt so utterly confused—so confused that she gave up trying to restrain herself and just kept walking down Rampart Street, feeling it inevitable, feeling that she had to see this son of his, this Benjamin, this child who should rightfully have been hers.

In no time at all she was standing in front of 2730 Rampart Street. It was a squalid little edifice, all muddy brown and capped by an incongruously jaunty red-tile roof. It was, moreover, an unlikely neighborhood. In fact it was a Negro neighborhood. All the while she had been walking there, she was too absorbed in her thoughts to notice the fearsome atmosphere. But now that she was here, she noticed the rough-looking men in the street, and suddenly she felt afraid. She supposed that Simon had come here because it was all he could afford; there was no other explanation for it.

She walked up the two front steps, and she knocked on the door. She had to knock several more times before there was any response. Then, finally, a woman opened the door.

"Yes?" said the dark-skinned woman, looking Rebekah up and down.

"Good afternoon, I've come to . . ."

"What is it?" the woman said impatiently. She looked tired to the bone and in no mood for visitors.

"My name is Rebekah Weiss," she said quickly. "Is this the home of Simon Weiss?"

The woman, who was quite tall and narrow and whose bushy hair had evidently been subjected to some cheap red dye, stared at her and then nodded.

"Mr. Weiss invited me to call," Rebekah said, feeling foolish at this formal, misplaced etiquette but not knowing how else to proceed.

"Did he?" the woman said with a smirk. "Such a fine gentleman he is," the woman continued in a sarcastic voice, "inviting people to call and all that."

"Is Lucy at home?" Rebekah said, so close to meeting this shadowy figure at last.

"Lucy ain't in no state to receive visitors," the woman said, looking away.

"Is she ill?" Rebekah asked with concern.

The woman stared at Rebekah. "She ain't well," the woman said at last. "She ain't well at all."

"Who's there, 'Malia?" came a dreamy voice from inside.

"Is that she?" Rebekah asked.

"She off on her cloud now," the woman named Amalia said with a mixture of sadness and bitterness. "And I don't know how or when she goin' to come back."

"Please," Rebekah said. "Let me see her."

Amalia thought a moment and then nodded heavily. Rebekah was led into the small dark hovel. It must have been a step down from the little shack on the heap of oyster shells at Water Street, Rebekah thought. This dwelling was stale, smelling of everything mildewed and rotten. There were great clots of dust in every corner, and Rebekah sensed that the walls were running with vermin.

Amalia led her into the larger of the two rooms which had a greasy little stove, a table, and a large bed upon which sat the figure of Lucy. Or, at least, Rebekah assumed it was Lucy. This wraithlike creature, sitting on the rumpled, unmade bed, had dark hollows for cheeks and waxy pouches beneath her eyes. Her hair, once so curly, was now dirty, matted even. And the girl's body, although it was disguised by a loose-fitting smock, showed indications of grave emaciation.

"Lucy?" Rebekah said. "Is it you?"

The girl nodded dreamily.

"My God," Rebekah said, "what's been done to you?"

This was a view of hell, Rebekah thought, nothing less. She saw before her the degradation of a human being. The girl had probably been a silly and shallow creature, not worth very much, but she had been alive. Now she was like some sort of pathetic, mindless shadow. What had Simon done? Had he beaten her? Was that it? He was capable of such things if he had enough liquor in him. Had he taken a club one night and smashed the sense out of the poor girl?

"Lucy," Rebekah said, moving closer, "are you ill?"

"No, ma'am," she said in a child's tiny voice, and then she looked around helplessly.

"What is it?" Rebekah asked with much concern.

"I'm thirsty," Lucy replied, still a child.

Rebekah found the pitcher of cool water and poured a cup for Lucy. "Here, Lucy," Rebekah whispered, offering the cup. "Drink this."

Lucy drank, and then she lay back and closed her eyes.

"What's wrong with her?" Rebekah demanded to know.

The black woman shook her head at Rebekah's ignorance. "Don't you know nothin', a fine lady like yourself?"

There was something in the phrase that reminded Rebekah of something. There was something in the situation that reminded her of something, some place else. The vagueness of the memory was no indicator of its force, and she held her head, feeling the dawning recognition bearing down on her. What was it? My God, yes, it was Clara; she was hearing Clara's voice. *Don't you know anything?* That night of nightmares, in that deserted warehouse on the piers, when she had met with Clara to try to reclaim her, to try to bring her back to life, and Clara turned on her and said she couldn't come, said she was held here, and Rebekah kept asking *Why? Why?* and Clara said, *Don't you know anything?* It was opium that had held Clara in its grasp and suddenly, piercingly, she knew that it was opium, or one of its relatives, that had claimed Lucy.

"She's taking something, isn't she?" Rebekah asked the tall black woman.

The woman stared back impassively.

"Some drug, some potion," Rebekah cried. "She's half-alive. Look at her."

The woman moved close to Lucy and bent down beside her. "Open your eyes," she said. "You got company here."

"No, 'Malia," Lucy whimpered. "Leave me be."

"Where is the child?" Rebekah asked, wanting to get out of here but wanting first to see Simon's son.

"Behind there," Amalia said, pointing to a tattered green curtain that was hung across a corner of the room.

Rebekah rose, pulled the curtain aside, and saw the big straw basket that held the naked baby. The baby, a beautiful black-eyed boy with a headful of dark hair and long skinny legs, began to bawl as soon as he laid eyes on Rebekah. She picked him up and held him and touched her cheek to his face.

"Is he hungry?" Rebekah asked.

"He's always hungry," said Amalia.

"But isn't he fed?"

"I feeds him," Amalia replied. Her voice was angry and troubled and close to tears. "But I ain't here all the time. And Lucy . . . well, Lucy never should've had the baby. Look at her. Do she look like somebody what ought to have had a baby?"

"But what about Simon?" Rebekah demanded to know.

"What about him?" Amalia said scornfully.

The baby's crying increased in volume and intensity, and Amalia got the bottle. Rebekah held him in her lap and gave him the bottle and felt a storm of emotions as she watched the infant feed.

"How long has Lucy been like this?" Rebekah asked.

"A long time," Amalia said. "Seems like so long a time to me."

"You seen my baby?" Lucy said suddenly from the bed, emerging from her reverie.

"Yes," Rebekah said.

"You want him?" Lucy cried in her high-pitched voice.

"What are you saying?" Rebekah replied.

"You can have him," Lucy said with a wild, squealing laugh. "I don't want him!" she suddenly screamed. "I don't want him!"

"Lucy! He's your son."

"I don't want him. 'Malia, don't let me see him," she cried, covering her face with the blanket.

"He tore up her insides," Amalia said. "That's when she began to use the stuff heavy. She done used it before, but not so heavy. The baby, he hurt her bad."

"And Simon? What does he do?"

"He drinks," Amalia said with a bitter laugh.

Rebekah looked at the baby again. Poor, sweet-faced creature. What kind of a life was he going to have? What kind of animals had he been born to? And what kind of justice was there when she did not yet have a baby and Lucy did?

"The baby needs someone with him all the time," Rebekah said. "Look at him. He's not strong. He can't be left alone with Lucy."

"I know," Amalia said. "Don't you think I know?"

"I don't understand," Rebekah said, genuinely confused. "Don't you work here full time?"

Amalia stared angrily at this stranger. "I don't work here," Amalia said imperiously.

Rebekah stared at her. "I don't understand," she repeated.

"I am Amalia Rougier," the woman said proudly, "and this here is my sister Lucy."

Rebekah was dumbstruck. So that was it. Lucy was a Negro. She was as light-skinned as Rebekah herself, but still she was a Negro. "I see, Mademoiselle Rougier. I didn't know. You'll excuse me."

"Does it make sense to you now?" Amalia said with a crooked smile.

"Yes, it does."

"Help us," Amalia said suddenly, desperately. "Help the baby. You got money, don't you? Take the baby from here. It's the only way."

"But I couldn't," Rebekah said, shocked.

"Listen to me!" Amalia said, clutching Rebekah's arm.

"Don't," Rebekah said, pulling away.

Amalia stared at her and then stepped away. "If you ain't goin' to help, then get out of here," she said coldly. "You hear me? Just get out of here."

Rebekah stared at Lucy and Amalia and once more at the precious baby. She didn't understand any of it; she didn't understand such people as this. "All right," Rebekah said. "I'm going."

"You want him?" Lucy cried again, this time with a squeal of laughter. "Then take him! Take him! Take him!"

And Rebekah went quickly from this hellish place, not wanting to look back but knowing that she would not be able to put this scene from her mind.

On the way to the station she kept running through her mind the events of the day. It was staggering: the self-destruction of Lucy; the brutalization of the child; and the revelation of Lucy's great secret. Did Simon know from the beginning? He must have and what did he care? But this son—this son of whom he had spoken with such pride and joy—didn't he see that the child was being treated worse than a mongrel dog? She shook her head, disbelieving, as if she had stumbled into the midst of some strange, primitive tribe whose behavior astounded and appalled her.

When she got to the station, she headed toward the platform where she would meet the Mobile train, and then she had a thought. She wanted to see Simon once more; she wanted to tell him that she had seen his son. She headed back toward the broad expanse of railroad ties, and she saw, in the distance, the same group of laborers, toiling in the same place.

"Simon!" she called. "Simon!"

She saw him look up, and she waved to him. Again there was the brief consultation with the foreman, and then he was bounding toward her.

"I have to talk to you," she said sternly.

"What is it?" he asked.

"I've been to Rampart Street. I've been to see your son."

His face broke into a brief smile, which evaporated when he saw that she did not join in. "I didn't think you'd go," he said vaguely.

"I didn't think I would either."

"You saw Lucy?"

"Oh, Simon, what have you done to her?" she cried.

"What do you mean?" he said stiffly.

"What do you think I mean? She's ruined, Simon, ruined."

"No," he said, shaking his head, trying to deny the truth.

"I know what she's doing to herself, Simon. Her sister told me."

His eyes darted away from her.

"Yes," Rebekah continued, "her sister Amalia."

"Stop your prying," he shouted in a sudden fury.

"You wanted me to go there," she countered. "You gave me the address. You wanted me to be in your life, your wretched wreck of a life. You wanted me to bail you out, didn't you, Simon, didn't you?"

"Stop," he said feebly.

"Do you know what's happening to your son? Do you care?"

"Don't," he said.

"He's hungry," she said. "Hungry! You're letting your own son go hungry!"

"What can I do, Rebekah?" he cried. "What can I do?"

"Oh, you're pathetic," she said, having to walk away from him because to look at him made her sick. But then she turned around and continued her tirade. "You take no responsibility for anything, do you, Simon? Why, of course you were excited to see me the other day because then you could have someone to prey upon, to suck dry, and who better than me?"

"It's not true, Rebekah."

"Of course it's true! What happened to the money I gave you?"

"The money?"

"Yes, you fool, the money. The money! Did you spend it all on liquor and dope and gambling?"

Simon's lips worked painfully, but no words emerged. Then there was a sort of whimper, and he covered his face with his hands.

"So that's your answer," she said, finding some sense of vindication in the midst of all of this.

"She didn't want the baby," Simon moaned. "She tried to get rid of it but she couldn't and she won't do a thing for him and I had to get her sister to come in and take care of him and I had to . . ."

He went on, but she wasn't looking. What he said made her think of Jarrett, of what he was doing, of what he was forced to do. Was it so wrong? But what if that child she had seen had been destroyed? But wasn't he being destroyed just the same?

"What should I do, Rebekah?" he demanded.

"You should begin to act like a man," she said scornfully, "even though it seems unlikely that you're capable of it. Why, any animal would take better care of its young than you and Lucy do." She shook her head and laughed unpleasantly. "Your son," she said with all the contempt she could muster. "Anyone can have a son, it seems."

"But there's no money, Rebekah . . ."

"Of course there isn't. You squander it all on your filthy habits."

"I won't, Rebekah," he said desperately. "I've learned my lesson. Please, you have to help me out."

"No, Simon," she said firmly.

"But the baby . . ."

"No."

He stared at her, and then he nodded. "You're right, of course you are," he said solemnly. "I haven't any right to ask you nothing."

"And that won't work either, Simon," she said. "None of your tricks will work."

His lips pursed angrily. "It ain't wise for you to be doing what you're doing, Rebekah," he warned. "It ain't wise at all."

"Don't threaten me," she said. There was a tense silence while they stared at each other, waiting for the next move. She was trapped—he had managed to trap her—and there was no way out. "Very well, there will be money," she said finally, fatalistically. "Not for you, understand, but for the child."

"Oh, Rebekah, you're good, you're so good," Simon said, his face brightening.

"Shut up," she said furiously. "It has nothing to do with you. I can't sit and watch a child being abused this way. It's no different than if I gave alms for the poor. It's for a hungry child that I'd be giving the money, that's all."

"I understand, Rebekah," he said obsequiously. "I understand completely."

She took out a considerable sum of money and placed it in his dirty, trembling hand. "I'm going to come down here again one day soon, and if the child hasn't a proper suit of clothes on and isn't clean and doesn't seem to be well fed, then I'm going to bring the law against you, Simon. Do you understand?"

She saw him looking down at the money, trying to get a sense of how much was there.

"It's enough to feed and clothe a baby," she cried, "if that's what you're wondering."

"Rebekah, how can I ever thank you?"

"I told you not to thank me. I want the baby looked after, do you understand, Simon?"

"Yes, Rebekah."

"And do you understand that I'll bring in the law next time if I have to?"

"Yes, Rebekah."

She nodded in her brisk businesslike manner. "Very well then. It's time for my train."

She began to walk away, and then he called her. "Rebekah! Wait!" She turned and saw him coming after her. He seized her hands and brought them up to his lips.

"Stop it!" she cried.

"Rebekah, dearest Rebekah," he wept.

"Simon, stop it," she ordered, looking around.

"I never wanted it to be this way. Don't you see? I love you, Rebekah. I always have, I always will. I never wanted my life to be this way. I couldn't help it. I couldn't."

If she had something heavy and blunt, a club or a poker, she would have smashed it down on him, destroying him once and for all. "Don't, Simon," she said. "It's no use."

He wept piteously and unabashedly. "Why, Rebekah?" he moaned. "Why has it come to this? Look at me!" he cried, his voice skittish with panic. "My God, look what I've become! And I don't know what to do, Rebekah! Tell me what to do!"

She stared at this wretched man, this man who had been her husband and her partner in life, and she spoke very softly. "I'm sorry, Simon," she said gently. "Truly I am sorry for you and for Lucy. But you have your life, and I have mine."

"But I'll never stop loving you, Rebekah."

"Simon, Simon," she said wearily. "You've lied so much and so long that even you don't know what's true anymore." She heard the church bells ringing, indicating the hour. "It's time for me to go."

"I won't let you," he said, holding tightly to her hand.

"Yes, you will," she said. He stared at her and then, reluctantly, he released her. She grabbed her valise and raced away from him, running for the train, running for her life.

CHAPTER TWENTY-THREE

In the weeks that followed the Galveston trip and the interlude with Simon and Lucy in New Orleans, she found herself tiring more easily and feeling less well than she had ever felt in her life. She went about meeting the demands of both the business and Wild Oaks, but she seemed to have no strength or energy.

"Miss, you look positively peaked," Mr. O'Donnell said one day.

She looked up from her accounts. "Yes, Mr. O'Donnell," she admitted. "I haven't felt all that well."

"You've been to the doctor?"

"No," she said. "It isn't necessary."

"Don't be foolish," he said. "You know the fever that's all around? If you don't catch what you've got, you'll pay dearly for it."

She ignored his cautions and continued about her business, but back at Wild Oaks she had Eulalie looking after her like a nurse.

"No, Eulalie, I cannot even touch it," she said, looking down at a bowl of honeyed hominy and butter.

"You got to eat, Miz Rebekah," the cook admonished. "You ought look at yourself. Why, you gotten so pale. I don't likes it at all, not one bit."

"Eulalie, you worry too much."

"No, ma'am. You don't look at all well."

"Well, thank you very much," she said with a wry little laugh.

"It ain't funny, Miz Rebekah. You got to take care of yourself or else the fever goin' get you sure as can be."

And she heard the same thing from Micah. "Miz Rebekah," the solemn old man said, "you got to go off to the springs. There just ain't no question."

"Oh, but that's ridiculous, Micah. I'm terribly busy."

"Then at least go see the doctor, Miz Rebekah."

"Very well, Micah," she conceded at last. "I'll see the doctor."

She sat before Dr. Michael Carter, the leading physician in the city, and he looked at her very knowingly.

"You're staring at me, Doctor," she said at last. "Is that part of your examination?"

He was a man of late middle-age, quite handsome and dignified, and he smiled ever so slightly. "You'll have to excuse me, Mrs. Weiss."

"What is it, Doctor? Am I so beautiful or am I so notorious?"

The doctor leaned forward across his desk. "You know I was at Walnut Hill the morning of the duel, don't you?"

Her face flushed instantly. "No, I didn't know."

"Yes. I treated Jarrett Russell for his wounds."

"Can we get on with the examination, Doctor?" she demanded to know. "Or should I find someone more impartial than you?"

"Please go into the dressing room and put on this robe," he said.

When she emerged, he had her lie down on the examining table.

"Now tell me what it is that's bothering you," he said.

"Really not so very much, Doctor. It's just that everyone keeps telling me how pale I am," she said with a nervous little laugh.

"Is that the extent of it?" he asked.

"Well, I have had a great deal of stomach distress."

"Vomiting?"

She nodded.

"When you eat?"

She thought about it. "Mostly when I rise, in the morning."

"And is there discomfort elsewhere?"

"Actually, Doctor," she said, "in my bosom, there is a certain tenderness."

He proceeded to give her a number of tests, and several days later he had her return. "I have diagnosed your malady, Mrs. Weiss," he said with a flicker of amusement.

She stared at this autocratic figure, comfortably lodged in his green leather chair, and she feared what he would tell her.

"Don't look so tense, my dear. It needn't be a fatal illness."

"What is it?" she cried.

"You are with child," he said, his lips curled into a smirk.

She fainted right there, in his office, which, she later thought, was a good place to faint if one had to. When he revived her, he was holding her hand and she couldn't for a moment remember where she was. Then it came back to her, and she felt herself totally overwhelmed by a barrage of feelings.

"I didn't think you would have that reaction," Dr. Carter admitted.

She shook her head. "I haven't fainted since I came over to America in the hold of a ship, Doctor. I'm not the fainting sort, but I really hadn't been expecting this."

"No, I don't suppose you were."

There was an awkward silence during which she could think of nothing to say. But then, finally, with the need for a confidant, she spoke. "It's Jarrett Russell's child," she said.

He nodded. "You really are out to shock the populace, aren't you, Mrs. Weiss?"

"I don't give a damn about the populace, Doctor Carter," she said fiercely.

"What are you going to do?" he asked.

"I'll do everything I can to have this baby, Doctor."

"Will he marry you?"

"That's no concern of anyone else's," she said strictly. The note of disapproval in the doctor's manner had dissipated, she noticed; perhaps he was impressed by her presence of mind. "I'm having this baby and if you'll help me, I'll pay you handsomely."

"I haven't such a great need for money, Mrs. Weiss," the doctor said coolly.

"And I haven't anything else to offer."

"If you want that baby as much as you say you do, I'll help you have it. There's no earthly reason on my part why I should do anything else."

"Thank you, Doctor," she said, trusting him. She told him in detail her history, and he advised her to head straight for Shelby Springs, a spa famous for its recuperative powers and as the site for innumerable camp meetings.

"But what about my business?" she protested.

"If you want to have this baby," he said firmly, "then you'll have to put your business behind you for the while. At least for several months, until the fetus is fairly secure."

"Very well," she said quickly, for there was nothing to ponder. The baby would come first, no matter what.

She called everyone together at the store to make her announcement. "Mr. O'Donnell, Sophronia, Dover—I have been told by my doctor that I must take a long rest."

"You see, miss," Mr. O'Donnell cried. "I knew it."

"You are very ill, Miz Rebekah?" Sophronia asked with a tone in her voice that suggested idle curiosity.

"No, not very. It's just that I need a rest."

"What about the store, Miz Rebekah?" Dover said.

"The store will go on under Mr. O'Donnell's direction. Hopefully I won't be gone more than six weeks or so. Are there any questions?"

Later on, when she met privately with O'Donnell to go over the logistics in greater detail, he seemed terribly worried for her.

"Oh, miss," he said, "I wish it were me."

She almost smiled. She wished she could tell the news, the thrilling news, but it was too early. She didn't want to have to deal quite yet with the public role of unwed mother. "Don't worry yourself so, Mr. O'Donnell. Everything will be all right."

And so, by the end of that week, she had left Wild Oaks, en route to Shelby Springs, which was approximately twenty-five miles from the city of Birmingham. It was a long and dusty journey; she was accompanied by Velma, the parlormaid who was Eulalie's niece and who had a sweetness of disposition that Rebekah found reassuring.

"Isn't the air good, Velma?" Rebekah said as they headed into the piny woods.

"Oh, yes, Miz Rebekah," Velma cried excitedly. "I ain't never traveled this far before."

Rebekah looked at the pretty young girl and had an urge to spill her secret. *I'm going to be a mother,* she wanted to say. I'm going to have my very own baby, and I'm going to love the child so.

The jolting of the coach stirred Rebekah's nausea, and they had to bring the vehicle to a halt so she could relieve herself at the side of the road.

"Oh, Miz Rebekah," Velma fretted, "I hope it ain't nothin' you et."

Rebekah was helped back into the coach, and not long thereafter they meandered into an upland cradle of the mountains, long and shallow, dominated at one end by a bluff that was presided over by a large, domed structure, like a temple, from which came the medicine, welling up in a reservoir several feet deep. This was the spring water, the source, the elixir.

The resort was roughly in the form of a hollow square, with rows of cottages forming the perimeter, and a larger wood-frame building which housed the dining facilities and the more luxurious suites. It was in one such suite that Rebekah established residence for an undefined length of time.

"Why, Miz Rebekah," Velma cried, "it's like heaven here, ain't it?"

She didn't know if it was heaven, but the days passed pleasantly enough. She ate well—lots of milk and greens and meat—and she took the waters. The days became ritualized: there were three daily trips to the springhouse and three more trips to the dining room; an afternoon nap followed by a leisurely stroll, and perhaps in the evening cards, dancing, or musicales. She began to feel relaxed and rested.

As the weeks passed, she felt her body change, verifying the pregnancy, and she decided it was time to tell Jarrett. She had a telegram sent to him:

Jarrett, I was wrong. I never should have judged you. You could never be unjust or cruel. Forgive me. I love you. I have news that I cannot tell you here. Contact me quickly.

* * *

She waited eagerly for a reply, but shortly thereafter her hopes were crushed. She received word that Jarrett was no longer in Galveston. He had left some time ago, without supplying a forwarding address. He had, in other words, disappeared.

"Bad news, Miz Rebekah?" Velma asked with much concern.

Rebekah did not answer. She retired to her room and would not emerge for several days. She felt now entirely abandoned. What had happened to him? she thought with a mixture of concern and anger. How could he have just disappeared? Had he taken their last meeting as an ending, and, if that were the case, why was he so quick to do so?

Now she had to think about her options. She must try to track down Jarrett, that was the first thing. If she were able to find Jarrett, then surely he would marry her. She would have to go to Galveston again. The difficult thoughts served to obliterate the rest and contentment she had built up over the precious few weeks. Now she feared for herself and for the baby. She would have to undertake a journey or else she would have to be a mother without a husband and she would have to brave the public wrath. She supposed she could do that if she had to, but the thought made her so worried and tired. If she had someone to help her—family or friends—then it would be less hard. But a woman alone, raising an illegitimate child—she felt all of her joy ebbing away.

"Won't you take the waters today, Miz Rebekah?" Velma asked after a third straight day of seclusion. "Or at least you should sit outside."

Rebekah shook her head. "No, Velma. I can't."

"But Miz Rebekah, you here to get well, and you ain't goin' to get well sittin' in this here hot room."

"Sitting in the sun or taking the waters is not going to solve my problems," Rebekah replied.

"Shall I pray for you, Miz Rebekah?" Velma asked shyly. "I knows you ain't of the faith, but . . ."

Again Rebekah shook her head, maintaining a grim silence.

"Tell me what's wrong, Miz Rebekah," Velma implored.

Rebekah searched the girl's face which did, in fact, appear to be unusually open and pure in its expression. "I'm pregnant," Rebekah said suddenly, feeling there was little to lose.

The girl just stared at her, the pretty impish face stunned.

"Yes," Rebekah reaffirmed. "I'm pregnant."

"Oh, Miz Rebekah, is it what you wants?"

"I thought so," Rebekah replied, "but now I'm not sure."

Finally, at the end of that week, Rebekah had sufficiently recovered from the shock of Jarrett's disappearance to go out into public again. Whatever her feelings were, whatever her fears were, she was resolved to have the baby and to love the baby.

That morning she went down to the springhouse. This resort, unlike the famous White Sulphur Springs, was not elegant, but it was peopled with the society of Mobile and Montgomery and Birmingham and so the taking of the waters was a social event. She had met many pleasant, cultured people at the spa, and these newfound acquaintances inquired after her health, having noted her absence. There was a pleasantness to all of this, but there was also an underlying sense of illness and waste in the environment. Many in the springhouse suffered: there were signs of consumption, gout, jaundice.

"You're looking well today, Mrs. Weiss," said a woman named Miss Parkins, an aged dowager from Tuscaloosa.

"Thank you, Miss Parkins, and allow me to return the compliment."

They chatted this way for a while, sipping from
the vile, sulphurous water which had taken some effort
to get accustomed to. Suddenly, however, she felt a
presence behind her, and she turned.

"I thought it was you," a woman said, but the
woman stood against the sun which came streaming
through the portals, and Rebekah was blinded by the
light.

"Can't you see me?" the voice asked.

Rebekah shaded her eyes and so discovered whose
voice this was. She was looking at Hattie Winslow, a
face she had never hoped to see again.

"So you've come to take the waters," Hattie Winslow
said in that voice that sounded to Rebekah insane
with hatred.

"Please leave me alone," Rebekah said. "I've come
here for my health as I assume you have."

"Oh, yes," Hattie Winslow said. "My health hasn't
been the same since the night you changed my life."

Rebekah glanced around and saw that Miss Parkins
and a few others were looking on in an attitude of
blatant curiosity.

"I have nothing to say to you," Rebekah insisted.

Hattie turned to this stranger, this Miss Parkins,
and utilized her willing ear. "She's responsible for the
murder of my brother," Hattie said in a deep, guttural, outraged voice. "She's the one!"

"Stop it," Rebekah whispered. "Stop it this instant!"

"Coming here," Hattie muttered, "acting like some
kind of fine lady, when everyone knows that you're
nothing but a common thing, a Jezebel, a good-for-
nothing tramp!"

Rebekah felt dizzied by the attack. "Get away from
me," she said. "I've nothing to say to you. Just get
away!"

"And now they're letting Jews in here, are they?"
Hattie continued. "Why, I've been coming here every

summer of my life, but now I'll have to stop because they've opened the doors to the vermin, haven't they?"

Rebekah tried to think of some way to retaliate, but then she decided that the best course of action was to flee. She walked quickly, silently, away from the woman.

"Don't you come back here!" Hattie Winslow screamed. "Don't you come back here, or you'll be sorry!"

When she got up to her room, she had Velma draw her a bath, and then she went to lie in it, hoping it would stop the trembling. She had come here for rest and comfort, but it was as though she had been consigned here so that she might be punished for some crime she did not even know she had committed. First Jarrett's disappearance and now the insane, shocking attack of a woman who had once posed as a friend. It was becoming still another test of her endurance rather than the therapy that had been prescribed.

From that point on she made sure that Velma checked for Hattie Winslow before she would venture out. It was a bizarre circumstance, almost a haunting; it made Rebekah think back to the Mardi Gras ball and the violence that had ensued.

As the weeks went by, Rebekah felt more tired than she had, and her breasts felt sorer. Her body was changing; everything was changing. The world for her would never be the same: there would be another life to consider, and everything she had would be shared. Was she ready for it now that it appeared at last to be here? Yes, she thought with a genuine, stirring excitement. She was ready to go beyond the needs that her own sense of destiny and individualism had dictated. She was ready to go into a realm of love and devotion that she saw as a good and selfless thing.

One fine day, however, when the sun was fiery in the pinkish sky and she had her hands placed on her stomach, wondering at the life encapsulated within,

she received news that was to bring change and chaos
back into her life. The desk clerk presented her with a
telegram, and her first thought was that it was Jarrett.
Eagerly she opened it and found herself staring at
something that was shocking, confusing, and unbelievable.

You are advised to return to Mobile immediately,

she read.

Your manager, Wm. O'Donnell, has suffered a
stroke. The store is in upheaval. Your presence
is required.

The telegram was from the office of William Carl
Benson, the attorney who handled all her legal affairs.
She held the message, full of mystery and oblique
signs of danger, and then she went into action. She
had Velma pack all their things, and she booked the
next coach to Mobile.

"But Miz Rebekah," Velma cautioned, "you
shouldn't. You aren't well."

"I have no choice," Rebekah cried. She thought of
what Dr. Carter had said to her in his office that day,
that she would have to put the business behind her,
but what could she do? The store was in upheaval.
The telegram had stated that much in black and white.

They traveled through the night and went directly
to the hospital where she found Mr. O'Donnell looking
pale and puny and terribly frightened.

"Mr. O'Donnell," she whispered, taking his hand.

His head turned a bit, and he stared, one eye trained
on her, the other seeming blank, unfocused, enlarged.

"What happened to you, Mr. O'Donnell?" she murmured, feeling so heartsick to see him in this condition.

He opened his mouth and struggled to speak, but it
was too hard for him and the tears came into his eyes.

"Don't worry, Mr. O'Donnell," she assured him. "We'll take care of you. And you'll get well, you'll see."

He tried to smile, but even that seemed too hard a task.

She held his hand against her cheek for a moment, and then she placed it on his chest and left him to sleep.

The next morning she went to see Mr. Benson, the attorney.

"What's happened, Mr. Benson?" she demanded to know.

"I hated to call you back from your holiday, Mrs. Weiss," the attorney said in his dry, unflustered way. "But when I tell you the events, I'm sure you will appreciate the urgency of the situation."

"Yes," she said impatiently. "Do go on."

"In your absence, Mrs. Weiss," the attorney continued, "your store was subjected to the malfeasance of one of your employees."

She stared at him blankly. "That word," she said. "I don't understand."

"Malfeasance?"

"Yes, Mr. Benson. My English is good but not that good."

"Your woman Sophronia," he said. "You've trusted her, haven't you?"

"Sophronia," Rebekah murmured. "What has she done?"

"Some very vile doings," the attorney replied. "It seems she has embezzled quite a bit of money from you."

"No," Rebekah protested. "I can't believe it."

"It's true."

But why couldn't she believe it? There was always something suspicious about Sophronia. The woman was always sullen and unresponsive, and now Rebekah wanted to know why she had kept her on, why she had been controlled this way.

"It seems she was sending the money down to some relatives in New Orleans."

"Where is she now?" Rebekah said.

"In the county jail."

"I must see her."

"Why? There's no need. You'll see her in court."

"No, I must."

"I don't think it's wise. Look what happened to O'Donnell."

"What do you mean?"

The attorney stared at her. "I thought you knew."

"No, I know nothing. Everything I know is through you."

"O'Donnell caught her with her hand in the till one night. He confronted her directly, and she flew into him. She accused him of lying, of trying to sully her good name, and she said she'd put a curse on him. Well, in the excitement of it all, Mr. O'Donnell had his attack. And so we called you back, and so here you are."

"Yes," she said remotely. "Here I am."

"I'm sorry, Mrs. Weiss, that this had to happen when your health was at issue."

She rose and offered him her hand. "Good day, Mr. Benson," she said. "I'll be at Wild Oaks if you need me."

But before she returned to Wild Oaks, she decided to see Sophronia. She had to see her; she had to make sure that Sophronia was really guilty.

At the jail the guard took her to a small, solitary cell that lay at the end of a dark corridor. She saw Sophronia sitting there in a straight-back chair, an open Bible on her lap.

"Sophronia," Rebekah whispered, "I am here."

The woman looked up. The long yellow face, never pretty, now seemed ugly and vengeful. She placed her long sinewy arms, which ended in long hands with long spatulate fingers, across her breast, and she rocked a bit, scowling at Rebekah. "They say I done it, but it ain't true."

"Tell me," Rebekah urged.

"Thou shalt not steal, the Bible says, and I reads the Bible!" she cried. "Look!" she cried, holding the Holy Book aloft. "Would I do what they says I done? Would I defy the Commandments?"

"Be still, Sophronia," Rebekah cautioned. "Charges are being brought against you. Mr. O'Donnell will bear witness against you. The fact that you read the Bible is small defense."

Sophronia sat stunned and silent for a few minutes and then spoke again. "Don't let them hurt me, Miz Rebekah," she said in a small, wounded voice that Rebekah had never before heard.

"Just tell me if you did it or not, Sophronia," Rebekah said. "Tell me if you stole from me or not."

"You wants to trap me," Sophronia said, the scowl returned to her face.

"You're trapping yourself, Sophronia."

Sophronia stared at Rebekah and then suddenly, with catlike swiftness, she jumped to her feet and seized Rebekah by the shoulders. "Let me go," the woman demanded. "Let me go. Tell them to let me free. They'll listen to you. Tell them."

"Stop!" Rebekah cried, struggling. "You're hurting me!"

Sophronia shook Rebekah harder. "Tell them!" she screamed.

The guard came at last and seized Sophronia. Rebekah watched in horror as the guard brought his stick down on the woman's shoulder and Sophronia yelped in pain. Dazed and sickened, Rebekah hurried, almost staggering, from the cell. She raced outside, down the steps of the jail, into her waiting carriage.

"Where to, miss?" the driver asked.

"Wild Oaks," she cried. "Quickly."

She never made it to Wild Oaks that afternoon. As they drove there in the jolting carriage, she began to sense a strange and ominous happening in her body. All of a sudden, without warning of any kind, she felt a strong, painful contraction. She told herself that it was nothing more than the product of the disturbing and frightening interview with Sophronia, but then, perilously, she felt her body seized by another contraction. She felt a wetness, and there, on her dress, was blood.

"Take me quickly to Dr. Carter," she told the driver.

Her mind raced faster than the carriage. She knew what was happening—the same thing that had happened at Locust Point—the baby was in danger, she was in danger, just as she was at Locust Point. But the difference was that this time she was three months pregnant, much more than she had been that time at Locust Point.

The doctor placed her in the hospital where she continued to bleed. By the second day it was clear that the miscarriage could not be reversed. Her bleeding was profuse; her cramps more intense. The afternoon of the second day saw her expelling the fetus, but the placenta remained within, and the doctor had to perform surgery to clean the uterus.

She lay in bed for several days afterward. The life within her had ended, ceased; and it was much as though her own life had ended also. The loss was so great and complete that she didn't wish to and could not talk to anyone, and yet she didn't want to be alone. She wept so painfully and so without cessation that she couldn't believe she would ever stop. There were moments, however, when her sadness rested and her anger took over. She cursed all the fates, all the people who had done wrong by her, and herself as well.

She watched as her body's signs of pregnancy were ruthlessly snatched away. Her breasts, which had grown large and swollen, were now returned to their normal size. Her stomach, grown hard, was once again soft. There was, she kept hearing a voice tell her, no child. No child. Never again a child for you, the voice cawed. When she managed to drift into sleep, she was savagely awakened by awful dreams of loss and pain.

What had she done wrong? Everything, the voice told her. She should never have come back from the springs. She should never have gone to the jail. She should never have exposed herself to anything that could be dangerous to the baby. The baby—my God, it was gone. The baby gone—and Jarrett gone. Jarrett, she cried, wanting him, feeling his absence, needing him to hold her.

Several days later she returned to Wild Oaks where she stayed in her room and continued her retreat. But the feeling that began to emerge, overcoming her sadness, was that feeling of anger. Simon and Lucy had a child when all they cared about were themselves. The child was left hungry while Lucy smoked some evil weed and while Simon gambled away the milk money.

She wouldn't have it. As she regained her strength, she formulated a plan, which, she knew on some level, was reckless and unfounded in reason but which seized her in its persuasive grasp and wouldn't let her go.

She would have Benjamin. It was right. It made sense. She would take him and she would raise him and she would make him hers and she would give him everything and she would love him. She would have Benjamin, this boy, this son that should have been hers, and nothing would stop her.

She had Dover nail signs to the two stores that said

"Closed Until Further Notice." She didn't care anymore. She didn't care about her business; she didn't care about her commitments. She wanted the rest of her life; she wanted everything that was owed her. She took the night train to New Orleans, intent on getting what she wanted.

Part Four

CHAPTER TWENTY-FOUR

When she arrived in New Orleans, she headed directly for Rampart Street. She would present Simon with an opportunity for money, and she was confident that he would accept. She would raise the child Benjamin as her own, and she would give Simon and Lucy whatever sum of money they wanted in exchange for the boy. What could they care? Their kind of shiftless, cruelly selfish people had no love for children and no right to children. It was a thing of amazement to her that the child had survived this long. You would think that their little rat's nest of a home would have already burst into flames like a mass of oily rags or that the child would have died of hunger or some sort of untreated infection. She was sure that they would take her offer, and if they didn't, she would counter with a legal attempt to have them declared unfit parents.

Was she being wrongheaded and reckless? She asked herself this as she sat in the carriage that took her toward Rampart Street. What right did she have to do what she was doing? This wasn't her child; there was none of her blood within him. How did she presume to say that Lucy had no love for the boy? But hadn't she heard Lucy scream for her to take the child away? *Take him*, Lucy had cried, *take him from me*. And that's precisely what she intended to do. Just so that the child would be healthy, she kept saying, even though she knew the real reason went beyond a concern for the infant's health. The real reason had to do with her own emptiness, her own longing, her own intent to ward off loneliness.

Still she would be offering the child a decent life. She would be giving the child a good, clean home and plenty of food and an education and all the love she had been storing up. Was what she intended to do so wrong. She couldn't believe it; she couldn't accept it; she couldn't see her motives as wrong or misguided.

She had the carriage wait for her in front of the Rampart Street address. She looked up at the squalid little house with its improbably jaunty red-tile roof, and something seemed ominous. There was a darkness here, a sense of uninhabitedness. When she went to the front door, she saw a sign that declared the premises CONDEMNED.

She stood there in confusion and increasing alarm. Could they just have disappeared? Had everyone who was in some way a part of her life just disappeared? A neighbor woman—elderly, black, with a bright yellow *tignon* tied about her head—came out, stood on the stoop, and studied her.

"Who dere you be lookin' for?" the woman inquired in a rasping, smoke-filled voice.

"Simon Weiss," she replied without hesitation, even though she didn't know this woman and, to look at her, there was not much reason to trust any information that she might get from her.

"Dey been carried off two day ago," the woman grumbled.

"Carried off? What do you mean?"

"Dey got de 'gue," the woman sniffed.

"What?" Rebekah cried, hardly able to understand a word.

"The 'gue," the woman replied impatiently. "Fell sick like dogs," she continued, and then she cackled to herself. "Dey carries on like cats, but dey falls sick like dogs."

Now Rebekah thought she understood. The mysterious word was "ague"; it was an ague, or a fever, that had visited here and that had stolen away the occupants.

"Where have they gone to?" Rebekah demanded to know.

The woman stared Rebekah up and down, assessing her worth. "How bad you wants to know?" the woman asked.

Rebekah withdrew a bill from her purse. "Here," she said, and the woman hurried over and grabbed it from her.

"They was taken to Pelican Island," the woman confided, whispering in her hoarse voice.

"Pelican Island?" Rebekah repeated, never having heard of it before.

"That's where dey takes them what's sufferin' from the 'gue," the woman said, exasperated at Rebekah's ignorance. "Dey done their share of stealin' and thievin' and whorin', ain't it so, lady?" she said, shaking her head.

"I'm sure I don't know."

"Oh yes, dey was trash. White trash, sure 'nuff. When dey done come to takes them 'way, I says loud and clear, 'Good riddance to bad rubbish.' That's what I says and ask me again, I'll tell you the same."

She left the woman and got back into the carriage. "Take me to a place called Pelican Island," she instructed the driver.

The driver, a tall, coffee-colored young man with astonishingly, improbably blue eyes, turned to stare at her. "What you want there, ma'am?" he said, not budging a bit.

"That's my business," she said angrily.

"Pelican Island ain't no place to go to, ma'am."

"I have someone there I must see. Now will you take me or not?"

"No, ma'am," he said, shaking his fine head. "You go near there, and you gets Bronze John."

"What are you talking about?"

"Bronze John, ma'am. That's the deadliest fever what there is. You go near Pelican Island, and you getting yourself a dose of Bronze John."

"Listen, just take me to wherever I can get a ferry to Pelican Island. There's no danger in that, is there? And I'll make it worth your while. Here," she said, thrusting some bills his way. "That should cover it, shouldn't it?"

He stared at the bills in his hand.

"Hurry!" she cried, jumping out of her skin. "Will you hurry?"

In a moment's time they were making their way through the city, along the banks of the great river, down along the coast. The air was steaming and fetid; New Orleans was no place to be in the summer months. Without proper drainage in the streets there was a marshy feeling throughout, with huge puddles the size of ponds covered over with a green slime in which one could discern heapings of garbage. Out of this culture bred millions upon millions of mosquitoes, regarded by the city as a nuisance, regarded by the first-time visitor as a true horror. Without one's netting one didn't dare to go to sleep at night; lawyers and other men of business were known to conduct their affairs from behind a gauzy web; and washerwomen and other domestics went about their chores with nets of muslin tied over their arms and head.

The city took a laissez-faire attitude toward its sanitation despite the fact that in 1853 an epidemic swept the city, claiming some fifteen thousand lives. Now, twenty-five years later, the city was still vulnerable to the deadly diseases—cholera, smallpox, typhoid, and above all the dreaded yellow fever. She feared for

Simon and Lucy, and most of all she feared for the poor little child named Benjamin whose life so far had seemed filled with nothing but all kinds of trouble.

"How far are we?" she asked.

"We's far," the driver said, anxious and annoyed. "This here place is way out. What you want to go there for anyhow?"

What *did* she want to go there for? It was a good question, a very good question. She could very well be endangering her life, for it wasn't at all clear what she would find when she reached this island. But her life was endangered anyway, she thought to herself with amazing calmness. Yes, it was. It was shaken to its roots, and if she didn't get to take this child away with her, then she didn't know what the point would be in her staying alive at all. The thought made her shudder, but she would not avoid it. Her life had come to this, to this pit, to this despair. If she didn't have the child to love, then there was no one for her, and she didn't know how she could stay alive under such circumstances. She couldn't be alone any longer. Each day she felt herself drying up, becoming sere and withered. What kind of an old woman would she make if she lived that long? It sickened her to think about it. She had a dream one night in which she saw herself as an aged queen, sitting on a throne of rubies, and there were dwarfs and jesters and ladies-in-waiting and gallants all about. She sat there on that throne, and she was all alone. She woke up in a sweat, and now, recalling it, she feared for herself and for the future that she had envisioned.

Finally they arrived at a little fishing village called Cool Water, and the driver took her to a jetty where one could get the ferry to Pelican Island.

"You sure you wants to go there, ma'am?" the driver said.

"Yes," she replied, speaking with more determination than she actually felt.

The driver nodded and then pulled away. She stood there on the deserted pier, looking out over the brackish water, seeing in the distance a spot of land that she knew must be Pelican Island.

She waited on the pier for what seemed hours, and then she saw a small launch making its way toward her. The captain, a small, wiry man with a gray beard and a fierce, bright-eyed expression, hopped out onto the pier.

"Is this the ferry to Pelican Island?" she asked.

"Yeah," he grunted.

"When is the next trip out?"

"Tomorrow."

"Tomorrow!" she cried. "But that's absurd! I must get there today!"

The grizzled man turned to stare at her. "What do you want on Pelican Island anyway?" he asked.

"I have a relation there," she explained.

"Well, there ain't no trip today no more," he said gruffly, moving down along the pier.

"I'll pay you!" she cried out after him.

He turned to look at her again.

"I'll pay you," she said intensely.

They settled on a price—more exorbitant than she had expected—and as soon as he refueled, they began to head out toward the island.

"You never been to Pelican?" the man asked.

She shook her head.

"Never been anywhere else like it myself," he said. "Went there first when my wife died. My Louisa. She was only nineteen. She got the Asiatic fever," he said, pausing to spit a stream of tobacco juice, "and this here is where she died. I couldn't leave. I jes' stayed here. Became a pilot fish," he said with a chuckle. "Never gets sick meself though. Got a hard hide. They calls me Saint Christopher."

She was hardly listening to his incessant babble. She

kept her eyes trained on the remote point of land looming ahead.

"Guess I been blessed one way or another. Somebody got to be doin' what I'm doin'. Sees all kinds of poor folk comin' out here, sent out here. No lepers, but everythin' else. You better pray to Christ, Our Saviour, you hear me, lady?"

She nodded.

" 'Cause most what comes out here don't come back."

"Do you remember taking a man out here with a wife and a child?" she asked.

"Could be anyone," he said, dismissing the question.

"A tall blond man with a dark-haired woman . . ."

"I jes' brings 'em out here, lady. I don't look on the color of their hair."

Within the hour they had reached the island. It seemed to have a mist surrounding it, but that, she thought, was a product of the wetness of the day. Still there was an aura, a palpable cloud, that one saw as one approached the spot of land. From the boat she could see the huts up on the shore, little squat edifices painted gray, with sparse trees offering no lushness and no protection. For a moment she felt the most awful fear, right in her stomach, and she felt that she would be sick.

"You don't look too good," the navigator said. "You look like you just might be coming home," he said, punctuating his remark with some insidious noise that she took for a laugh.

With a sort of groan the boat pulled up to the dock.

"Why, Mr. Jennings," a voice cried. "Back so soon?"

She looked up and saw a nun standing on the shore. The nun, who was a very large figure with a very large cap and glinting spectacles, held out her hand. Rebekah took hold of it and stepped out of the boat.

"Now who might this be?" the nun asked, rather too jovial for her surroundings.

"Rebekah Weiss," she murmured, feeling dizzy,

feeling that she must have a moment to readjust herself and collect her bearings.

"And what ails you, my dear?"

"No," Rebekah whispered. "You don't understand."

"I am Sister Agnes," the nun went on. "You seem to have a fever, poor dear," she added in a solicitous tone. "Come, I'll take your things and get you settled."

"No," Rebekah cried. "You don't understand. I'm not here because I'm sick."

The nun's face suddenly grew very severe. "What have you brought us, Mr. Jennings?" she said coldly.

"Where is Simon Weiss?" Rebekah demanded to know. "I was told he was brought here."

"You're not supposed to be here," Sister Agnes said. "Only the ill and the infirm and the nuns. You're not supposed to be here."

"Well, here I am," Rebekah said firmly. "Now tell me where they are."

"You really shouldn't have brought her here, Mr. Jennings," Sister Agnes reprimanded. "Now she'll fall ill, and what good will it do any of us?"

"Where is Simon Weiss?" Rebekah cried, tired, frightened because she had not been able to shake off her dizziness.

"He's in there," Sister Agnes said, pointing to one of the little huts.

Rebekah grabbed her bag and headed toward the destination.

"I wouldn't go there if I were you," the nun called, but she wasn't she and Rebekah ignored her. She knocked on the door of the hut—a gesture far too civilized for this environment—and she waited. Then she knocked again and then she turned the knob and then she entered into the darkness.

There was a groaning coming from this black room and then a shrill cry.

"The light!" cried a voice that she recognized as Simon's.

"Simon," she whispered, allowing more light as she admitted herself.

Again there were groans, and she realized that the light assaulted eyes that had become accustomed to the darkness. "Simon," she said, "Simon, it's me."

She could make out Simon, bare chested, in tattered pants, standing next to a bed of straw upon which lay a prostrate figure who, undoubtedly, was Lucy. The scene was so full of horror and poverty and sickness and despair that she felt herself almost swoon, the dizziness gripping her again and shaking her.

"Simon, it's me," she said. "Rebekah."

There was a silence and then he lowered his hands that had sought to block out the light. She saw his yellow eyes, and she gasped.

"Rebekah?" he said in a voice that sounded spent from having called incessantly for water over a period of days.

"Yes, Simon, it's me, Rebekah."

He staggered toward her. In the light she could see the ravaging of his person and she felt his pain and she felt the tears suddenly forming in her eyes. He walked a few paces, and then he dropped to his knees. "Rebekah, my wife, my wife," he cried and then he began to sob as though he would never stop.

She went to him and held him, stroking his sweated head.

"No," he said, cringing away from her. "Don't touch me."

She wanted to touch him; she felt, coming in here, as though this were the worst that life had to offer and she were an angel coming to spread her kindness.

"You're so sick, Simon," she murmured. "I want to help you."

"You'll die," he croaked. "It kills you. Yes, it kills you."

She walked over to where Lucy lay and what she saw was more horrifying than anything in her experience. Lucy lay there, her mouth agape, her teeth showing like a grinning rictus, her tongue furred brown, her yellowed eyes twitching in their sockets, and her body drenched in a fetid sweat.

"Simon, she's dying," Rebekah whispered.

Simon renewed his sobbing, laying down on his side and drawing his knees up to his chest.

"Simon, where's the baby?" Rebekah asked, feeling suddenly alarmed. "Where is Benjamin?"

He sobbed and sobbed, lost in his sorrow like a drunkard lost in his liquor, and she shook him. "Benjamin," she cried, fearing the worst, fearing that the child was dead and that she had come here for nothing, that she had been sucked into this hell and that she too would die.

"The nuns," he whimpered. "They're keepin' him away from us."

"Is he sick?"

"I don't know, I don't know, I don't know," he moaned.

"I want to die!" Lucy suddenly screamed, rising in her bed. Rebekah retreated into a corner of the hut, not believing what she saw but unable to doubt it. Lucy was like a corpse—starved, yellowed, her eyes aglow with some hideous transport of fever. "Water!" she screamed shrilly. "Water!"

Rebekah saw the pitcher, empty on the table, and she ran outside to the pump to fill it. The mist over the island seemed even thicker, hot and damp. She felt the earth turning around, and she kneeled to let the water from the pump wash over her face. Then she went back inside with the pitcher and gave them each their water.

"Bless you, Rebekah, bless you," Simon said, sobbing still more.

"What happened?" Rebekah asked. "How did this happen?"

He held his head with both hands and lay silent

for so long that Rebekah thought to ask her question again, but then he spoke up. "First the strangest feeling here," he said, pointing to his brow. "Just a headache one day, but you know it's more, you know something is coming. Then chill, terrible chill, and then . . ."

His voice trailed off, and he lay there, lost in the world of his sickness.

"But, Simon, you'll get better. You will get better, won't you?"

"I don't know," he said. "I'm better today than yesterday. But they say that with Bronze John, there's no telling. They say that with Bronze John . . ."

"What is this Bronze John, Simon?"

He stared at her, then he laughed uproariously until his laughter dissipated into the shakes. "Yellow fever," he said. "Don't you know? Don't you see?"

She shook her head, backing off. "No," she whispered. "No, they said you had the ague. They never said yellow fever."

"But what did you think? Look at us," he cried. "Look at the color of our skins."

Just then Lucy stirred on the bed of straw.

"No, Madame Jewel," she moaned. "I been a good girl, ain't I? Never did no wrongs, did I? I the prettiest girl you know, ain't I? So why I can't go to the circus, Madame Jewel? Madame Jewel? Madame Jewel, it hurts me. It hurts me, Madame Jewel! Madame Jewel! Madame Jewel!"

Rebekah covered her ears. It was awful; it was Clara. When Clara was delirious, this was how she spoke. Now it was happening all over again, the demons were back at work, and she couldn't bear to hear this screaming.

"I be a good girl," Lucy wailed. "Don't let that man take me. No, he goin' to take me from your house and what goin' to happen to Lucy?"

Lucy's expression, dazed and worried, suddenly altered entirely, and she lurched forward, making a horrible gurgling sound. Simon grabbed a basin, but it was too late. Lucy had already spewed forth her vomit, the ghastly black vomit that was the most fatal sign of this disease. Instantly the malodorous emission took hold of the room, and Rebekah felt the wave of dizziness again. Lucy lay back on the straw, her limbs jerking, her mouth, her nose, both dripping with blood.

"She's almost there," Simon said in a voice so hopeless and fatigued that it almost sounded objective.

"But where are the doctors?" Rebekah cried.

He turned to stare at her. "There's nothing to be done for her," he said, seeming angered by her ignorance. "My Lucy, my poor Lucy," he whimpered, the tears coming to him so readily.

She stared at this tableau, feeling herself an outsider, knowing that it was absurd to think in those terms at a time such as this but not being able to prevent herself from doing so. He seemed to love her, or, at least, he seemed to have feelings for her, and this was something for a man such as he.

"Mama," Lucy sang, "you are my pretty Mama."

"Sssh," Simon said, wiping her wet locks of hair off her burning forehead.

"I went to the river, Hop Fly," she began singing in a weird, otherworldly voice.

Simon held onto her, trying to calm her, but Lucy flailed at him and groaned so terribly that he had to let her go. She looked around, confused for the moment, and then, in the voice of her childhood, she resumed her little Negro song.

I went to the river, Hop Fly,
Set down under a willow tree,
Willow leaves roll down on me,
Roll down on me, Hop fly, roll down on me.

* * *

With that, she moaned and fell back on the bed of straw.

"Lucy!" Simon cried out in anguish. "Lucy!"

Then there was a noise at the door, and a doctor entered, accompanied by the nun, Sister Agnes.

"That's the woman, Doctor," the nun said, pointing to Rebekah.

Rebekah looked at the tall redheaded man, whose lined face seemed to have seen everything that nature and humankind had to offer, and she waited for him to speak.

"What are you doing here, miss?" the doctor asked sternly.

"I've come to nurse them," she replied quickly. "They are my family."

"Well, good nursing is the best medicine there is against the yellow fever," he said. "But do you have any notion how contagious an illness this can be?"

"I don't care, Doctor. I just want to . . ."

"Don't you remember the great plague of fifty three? Why, it nearly wiped out the city. This yellow death—it's no milder than the black death. You're mad to have come in here."

"But I'm here, Doctor," she said, sounding considerably more stalwart than she felt.

She and Simon watched the doctor and the nun apply mustard poultices to Lucy's chest and back. Then Lucy was given a bath of water and vinegar and a mild purgative to evacuate the bowels.

"Has she passed urine today?" the doctor asked Simon, who shook his head. The doctor glanced at the nun; this was a very bad sign, and there were further signs that Lucy had suffered urethral hemorrhages. On the girl's arms and back there were large, painful carbuncles from which blood was discharged freely. And this was once a beautiful girl, Rebekah thought, awed by the monumental cruelty of life.

"Is that all?" Rebekah cried as the doctor prepared to leave.

He turned to face her. "What more should be done?" he asked calmly.

"Something!" she cried. "You must do something!"

"I've seen everything tried against the yellow fever," the doctor said wearily. "Quinine, lime, calomel, even opium."

On the last word Rebekah glanced at Simon who kept his eyes on Lucy.

"I've seen people put onions in their shoes," the doctor continued. "And I've witnessed bleeding with cups and leeches. I remember in the city when barrels of tar were burned, when lime was spread everywhere, and when people put their faith in oysters to lend them protection. But we don't know what the protection is, and we don't know the cure. All we know is that the patient is best kept warm, with lots to drink, and with a nurse who cares. If you say that's what you've come here for, then they must thank the gods above because they've been blessed, and maybe now they'll have a prayer, even though the girl will need a miracle to pull through."

"I'll help her, Doctor," Rebekah promised.

"Sister Agnes will show you what to do," he said as he turned to leave. "Good luck to you."

She stared at the nun, and the nun stared at her.

"You don't look like any relation of the likes of them," the sister sniffed, assessing Rebekah from her clothes and her jewelry.

Rebekah said nothing to answer that, but instead posed a question. "Their child, their Benjamin," she said. "May I see him?"

"Don't let her, Sister," Simon groaned from his place beside Lucy, for he suspected why she had really come.

She whirled about and looked down at Simon. She wanted to scream at him to be quiet, but she mustn't.

"He's in with some of the other healthy children," Sister Agnes said. "At least they're healthy for now," she added grimly. "You can see him if you wish."

The sister showed her how to make all the poultices and preparations and how to wash the patients and keep them warm. Then she left her. Rebekah sat down for a moment, dizzy again and exhausted from her journey and her hunger and her fear.

She watched Simon sleep, and then she, too, fell into sleep. When she awoke, she saw Simon lying there, staring at her, and she started in her seat, the pain of her stiff back lancing through her.

"Do you want something, Simon?" she asked. "Bread? Water?"

He nodded.

She gave him what she offered, and she watched him eat, chewing slowly, painfully.

"What did you come here for, Rebekah?" he asked when he had finished. "To see me die? Is that it?"

"Hush, Simon, don't upset yourself."

"To see my poor Lucy in agony? Is that it?"

"No," she said, shaking her head.

"My poor Lucy," he lamented. "Such suffering. The fever and nothing to get her through it, and she so used to something to take the edge off." He looked up at Rebekah again, his eyes narrowed with suspicion. "What do you want to see Benjamin for?" he said. "What do you have to do with him?"

Rebekah waited a moment before replying. "Look at Lucy," she whispered. "Once she was beautiful. Yes, very beautiful. You always liked beautiful women, Simon. People have always told me I was beautiful and I always believed them, but I was never as beautiful as Lucy once was." She paused and walked closer to the prostrate figure. "But now that Lucy you knew is gone, Simon. There's something in her place— a shadow—and we know it's not the same Lucy."

"She's not even cold yet," Simon cried. "Won't you shut up with your doomsaying?"

"She's dead," Rebekah murmured. "She was dead that last time I saw her, when she was lost in that cloud of evil smoke. And now . . . you know, Simon, you know I've no reason to lie or deceive you, you know there's no hope."

He looked at Lucy, the blood dried at her nostrils and the corner of her lips, and he burst into tears once more.

"She's gone, Simon, and I want her child."

He looked up, putting aside the fist which he had been using to cover his eyes. "What are you saying?"

"I'll take care of Benjamin," she replied. "I'm the only chance he has, and he's the only chance I have."

"Stop it," he warned.

"Let me take him off this island, Simon. If he stays here, there's every chance in the world that he'll catch the fever and die just like his mother is about to die."

"Oh, it hurts," Lucy screamed suddenly, going into another spasm. She took deep, rumbling breaths and thrashed about on the bed of straw. "Oh, it hurts, it hurts."

"Listen to her, Simon," she said, disregarding the cold-blooded nature of her words. "I'll pity her and I'll even mourn her if it's what you want, but let me take the child away from here. Don't you think that she'd want it that way? Don't you think she'd want her child to live?"

"So that's why you came here!" Simon cried. "To nurse us back to health, you tell the doctor, but it's a lie!" He screwed up his lips, and then he spit at her. "There!" he screamed. "I hope you catch what it is that we've got. I hope Bronze John pays you a call. Coming here to suck our blood. You vampire, you!"

"Get me the pretty pink dress from the closet, Virgie," Lucy said suddenly, lost in her delirium. " 'Cause tonight I got Mr. Jasper, and you knows how Mr.

Jasper loves me in pink, he do. Oh, Virgie, men are such funny things, ain't they? All they want is lovin' and women, we don't care a bit, do we?"

"Lucy," Simon cried. "Lucy!"

"Leave her alone," Rebekah said. "Maybe it stops the pain for her."

"Lucy!" Simon screamed. "Look at me!"

"You'll never change, Simon," Rebekah reproached. "You'll always be the same. You don't care for anything but yourself."

"Shut up!"

"I told you to leave her alone!"

"Lucy!" he cried again, ignoring Rebekah, and he shook the girl by the shoulders.

Lucy turned her devastated face upon him and tried to focus. "Virgie, run quick! It's that man again, Virgie! Run quick and tell Madame Jewel! Run quick and tell Madame Jewel to send up Crocodile 'cause there's a man here what's goin' to hurt me!"

With infinite sadness and weariness he let go of Lucy and stepped away. "She doesn't know me," he murmured, more to himself than to Rebekah.

"She doesn't know anyone anymore."

"Did I do this to her?" Simon wondered aloud. "Did I ruin her? Everything I touch, everything . . ."

"I'm going to look in on Benjamin," she announced, not wanting to watch him pity himself.

"Don't you go near him," Simon warned in a furious voice.

"Don't you want to see how he is?" she countered. "Don't you care whether he's dead or alive?"

He stared at her, at a loss for words, and then he nodded.

She found the hut where the babies were being kept. There were three of them now, three healthy infants on this island, and they looked nourished and cared after, even if their mothers and fathers were dying all around them. She recognized Benjamin right away, with his dark hair and dark eyes that made him look alert and full of life.

"My sweet Benjamin," she whispered. "Are you lonely here, my precious?"

She picked him up and held him to her breast, and he made a sort of purring sound.

"Yes, my darling one, you need to be held, don't you, my angel?"

The closeness of this contact, and the pleasure that she felt, convinced her of the rightness of her mission. What good would it do anyone to have this child lying alone in this awful hut on this awful island when she had so much she could give him? She wanted the child; she wanted the child to grow up with her. She didn't care about all the things he would have going against him—the Negro blood, the shadowed months of infancy, the lack of a father. But what if Simon demanded to be taken back? What if, when Lucy died, the only way he would let her have Benjamin would be to take him in the bargain? No, it couldn't be done. There was no sense in it; the idea was unimaginable. The only man she wanted, the only man she loved, was Jarrett. Jarrett, where are you? she thought. How could you just leave me, so alone like this? She rocked the child in her arms. This wasn't Simon's child; this wasn't Lucy's child; this was her child; this was the child that should have been born from her love for Jarrett; this was the child she had lost, and this was the child she had found.

CHAPTER TWENTY-FIVE

In the bar of the Royal Hotel Jarrett sat drinking absinthe. He had never much liked it in the past, but the past now seemed so very far away. No, more than that, the past—his past—seemed no longer to belong to him. Now, when he thought about his days as the scion of Wild Oaks and the dashing young gallant of the cotillions, his youth seemed more remote than anything from Dumas or Sir Walter Scott. He was a Russell, a voice kept telling him. But what did that mean? It had come to mean not nobility but disgrace—his father's disgrace, his own disgrace.

He had been in New Orleans for two days now. He was searching for Rebekah, the woman he loved, the woman he had lost. He had written to Mr. O'Donnell, who was sufficiently recovered from the stroke to write him back. He had learned that Rebekah had come to New Orleans in search of Simon Weiss. He couldn't imagine what she wanted of Simon Weiss—the man had always been portrayed as nothing less than an utter scoundrel—but she had closed the store to come down here in a manner that could only be described as precipitous.

He had to find her. He had stayed away from all thoughts of her for so long now, hoping that she would leave his memory and his consciousness, but she wouldn't. He loved her more than anything in the world; she was the thing that made him feel alive. After she had left Galveston, there seemed no point in remaining there. She had made him feel dirty about what he was doing, even though he knew that there would always be someone who had to do what he was doing. But, beyond that, he wanted to make a new life for himself. Yes, it was undeniable, but that was what he wanted: to be one with Rebekah and to marry her and to have a family with her.

The sins of his father would weigh against him until he himself was a father. He kept thinking this even though he knew, on some level, that it might be totally wrongheaded. But when he saw children in the street, he wanted to reach out to them and hold them and feel his love for them. He was thirty-eight years old. Men half his age had families, and yet he wandered and wandered. His father had never loved him or anyone else. But if he had a child, he would love that child and if he had a wife, he would love that wife, and if it were Rebekah, he would be the happiest man alive. If he allowed himself love, he thought, then maybe he had a chance of throwing off his father's ghost.

He held the glass of absinthe between his thumb and forefinger. This was the liquor talking, he told himself. He wouldn't find her. It was a big city; there were so many places to lose oneself. And what if he did find her? What assurance was there that she would be his? Maybe she found him repugnant after all of this. Maybe she thought him a pathetic failure of a man. Well, was she wrong to do so? He was a failure, it was clear to see.

After Galveston he roamed again, and then, finally, he decided he had to get away from this land altogether and at Corpus Christi he got on a steamer headed for Venezuela. He was the ship's doctor, a post usually reserved on such vessels for the chronically alcoholic or otherwise disgraced members of the profession. He thought himself a natural for the position, and yet, in many ways, he thrived during this experience. He made a decent salary for one thing, and he got to see foreign lands—Honduras, Guatemala, Panama, and then Venezuela.

It was in Venezuela that he had the most extraordinary experience. He was in a bar on the waterfront one night, drinking heavily as had become his custom, and when he left and began walking down the dark streets, he felt a hand on his shoulder. He started, ready to draw his gun, but then he heard a moan.

"Who is it?" he demanded to know.

It was a bedraggled figure with haunted eyes who faced him. The man had a bullet in his leg, obviously the end result of some criminality, and he implored Jarrett to help him.

"But you must go to a hospital," Jarrett said. "I've nothing to do with this. There's clearly been trouble . . ."

"No," the man whispered. "I cannot." He reached in his pocket and pulled out something green and brilliant—an emerald. "For you," he said, "if you take care of me."

Had he killed a man? His partner perhaps? Jarrett stared at the emerald, and he didn't care. They found a deserted warehouse where Jarrett performed the surgery, excising the bullet and staunching the wound. That night he became a man of property, and he guarded the precious stone with his life.

He had taken the steamer to the Indies and then finally back to the States. He sold the emerald, got himself a new suit of clothes, a shave, and a manicure, and wondered what next to do with his life. It was then that he decided he must contact Rebekah. His life was ready to begin again, and she must be a part of it.

Now, sitting in the bar of the Royal Hotel, he wondered how he might find her. Mr O'Donnell had sent him a list of importers and wholesalers, and he had checked with them all, but to no avail. It was as though she had intended to disappear from this earth altogether. There was no record of her registry in any hotel. There was no record of her with the police or the hospitals. Had she become a phantom? There were moments when he thought so. There were moments when he felt that she had ceased to exist in this real, temporal world; and it was at such moments that he wondered what he would do with the rest of his life.

He toyed with the idea of going back to sea, where there was adventure at least and all the anonymity he could want. But he found that he couldn't pull himself away from New Orleans, not as long as Rebekah was missing, not as long as there was any chance of his finding her. And so he sipped the last drop of absinthe, and he went on his way, looking for his love and wandering, wandering.

Rebekah sat on a straight-back chair in front of the hut where Lucy lay dying. They knew now that her death was a matter of time, moments really, and her low, tortured, cavernous moans had filled the hut all night and all day and had driven Rebekah out into the broiling August sun.

She had just been in to feed little Benjamin. These past few days she had assumed all responsibility for his care. She fed him and she changed him and she bathed him and she rocked him. It was Benjamin that kept her here. She asked herself every moment of the day why she was here, here in this hell, the infection all around her, waiting to jump on her and grab hold of her and destroy her. It was madness for her to be here, and yet she was here for the child. The child needed her and she needed the child and she would have the child, the child would be hers if she just waited a bit longer.

The door of the hut opened. She looked around and

saw Simon, whose yellowed eyes stared at her and made her feel sick.

"What is it?" she cried. "Is it . . . ?"

"Not yet," he said. He knelt down on his haunches and held his head in his hands. "I can't bear to listen to her anymore," he muttered. "Why doesn't she die already? She holds on and on, like a horse she is . . ."

"Stop it, Simon!" Rebekah ordered. "How can you possibly talk this way?"

"Don't tell me how to talk," he replied. "You didn't come here to tell me how to talk. You didn't come here because you wanted to be a sister to Lucy, did you?"

She thought to protest, but then she just sat there, in silence.

"She was such a beautiful girl," Simon said. "When I first saw her, I couldn't believe it."

"I don't want to hear this," Rebekah said.

"And Madame Jewel said to me, 'This is Lucy. She can be naughty, you know.'"

"I said I don't want to hear this," Rebekah cried.

He stared at her. "Go inside," he said. "She needs something. She needs a woman's hand."

Rebekah listened to the awful moaning, and then she rose and did as Simon requested. She took the compress from Lucy's brow, dipped it into the cool water, wrung it out, and replaced it. The girl gave a little moan in acknowledgment—there was very little language left—and Rebekah stroked her hair.

"There, there," Rebekah said. "You'll be all right."

The girl rocked back and forth in the bed, her legs going up and down as if she were running or dreaming of running or dreaming of escaping from this wretched bed.

"Ssssh," Rebekah murmured. "Be still, Lucy dear."

She sat by the bedside and, after a long while, the moaning eased down, and Lucy opened her eyes, which had become a bilious yellow, and tried to speak.

"Hep," she squeaked. "Hep me."

She was calling for help, but she couldn't even make the word. "Here," Rebekah said, offering a sip of water, and the girl tried her best, but most of it dribbled down to her neck and her chest. Then the girl began to whimper, and Rebekah stroked her hair some more and whispered endearments to comfort her.

"So young, so awfully young," Simon said, entering the room. "What kind of God would do such a thing? Our Jahweh? Our God without mercy?"

"Don't, Simon," Rebekah warned. "Where there is sin, there is punishment. Nothing less."

"Rebekah, I prayed to God that he take me instead of Lucy. I swear I did. When I felt the fever coming toward us, I said, 'Here, take me, but don't take Lucy.' And yet I survive, Rebekah. The fever won't kill me. I've beaten the fever, but Lucy . . ."

"Yes, you survive, Simon," Rebekah said. "And I survive. We could have had such strength together, but maybe that was our weakness."

"What? I don't understand."

"Maybe we knew that we could fight each other off, that we were both strong in our ways and that we could hurt each other. Maybe we knew that we were both cut from the same cloth, and that we both wanted things our way or not at all."

"Not me, Rebekah. You fought me and you won."

"I thought so, Simon," she said. "I thought so and you wanted me to think so, but then here I am, Simon. Here I am on Pelican Island. How do you explain that?"

"Hep me!" Lucy suddenly screamed with surprising strength. She half rose from the bed of straw and then, with force, she projected a stream of the hideous black vomit.

"Oh God, let me out of here," Simon wailed.

"Stop it!" Rebekah screamed.

"Help me," Lucy babbled, lost in her own effluvia.

"Shut up!" Simon screamed at Lucy. "Can't you see there's no help? Now just shut up, shut up, shut up!"

Lucy stared with her yellow eyes which then rolled back as she sank to the bed of straw.

"Lucy!" Simon screamed.

"She's gone," Rebekah whispered.

Simon ran to his wife and shook the prostrate form. "Lucy!" he cried. "Lucy!" He felt Rebekah's hand on his shoulder. "Lucy," he moaned, clutching her to his breast, "Lucy."

"She's gone, Simon," Rebekah said, having seen, clear as day, the life leave her ravaged face.

"What are we going to do, Rebekah?" he wept.

"We're going to see her beyond this, Simon," she said gravely. "We're going to see her to her proper rest."

There was a small graveyard on Pelican Island, but this was reserved for those who had no survivors. It was, in a sense, a potter's field, undistinguished by names, reserved for the forgotten. They could not bury Lucy here, that much was clear.

"I can take her off the island for you," Rebekah said.

"No, I can go with you."

"But you're ill."

He laughed with something that sounded like disgust. "You said I shall survive, didn't you?" he cried. "This fever, it ain't going to kill me off. But if I stay on this island any longer, I may have to go mad from it."

"But will they let you off?"

"I ain't a prisoner, am I?" he challenged. He went off to see the redheaded doctor. When he returned, awhile later, he had something that looked like a smile on his face.

"What is it?" she asked.

"I been given a discharge," he said. "The doctor

says I'm over the fever. He says I only had a mild case of it anyway."

"So you see," she said, unable to control the bitter tinge in her voice. "You are a survivor, Simon Weiss."

"So get your gear, and we'll be off on the next boat."

"I want first for the doctor to check the baby," Rebekah said.

"There ain't nothing wrong with the baby."

"It's what I want!" Rebekah insisted, intent on establishing the primacy of her judgment in all things concerning Benjamin.

"All right," he muttered. "Do what you will."

Benjamin was given an examination and so was she. Both had escaped the fever, which was not in as virulently contagious an incarnation as it had been in previous years. She washed and fed the baby, dressed him in a light shirt, and met Simon at the pier. He was waiting there, spent, and bleak looking, standing sentinel over the coffin that held Lucy's remains.

"The boat is due here in an hour," Simon said.

She nodded, already feeling both the fatigue of waiting and the fatigue of being with him wash over her.

"Where will she be buried?" Rebekah asked.

Simon paused a moment before answering. "In New Orleans."

"That's where her family was from?"

"Yes, what little she had of it."

The boat did come when expected, just over an hour later, and she saw the grizzled man who had ferried her over days earlier with his imprecations of doom.

"Just the two of you?" he said.

"That's right," Simon replied.

"And whoever's in the box," the old man added gratuitously.

"That's right," Simon said somberly.

He and the ferryman hoisted the coffin onto the launch, and then Rebekah stepped on with the baby in her arms. As they pulled away from shore, they stared at Pelican Island. They had their last look at the nuns wandering among the squat little huts. Then Simon turned away, his eyes brimming with tears.

"What a place to die," he murmured.

"I'm sorry, Simon," Rebekah whispered. "Truly I am."

"Ay, you say so, but then you've got her baby in your arms, don't you?"

"It wasn't right for her to be a mother," Rebekah said defensively. "The baby wasn't taken care of. It simply wasn't right."

"The fact is that you still came and took the child away, stole the child away, while she was on her death-bed. That's the fact, ain't it?"

She shook her head. She wouldn't speak, because if she spoke, she might explode.

"Just came and stole him out of her arms . . ."

"Stop it!" she cried. "Why, you should get down on your hands and knees and thank God that I've come to save your son. Who would you have raise him?"

"We'll raise him together," Simon said.

"Don't be ridiculous," she replied impulsively.

"What do you mean?"

"I mean that I will raise the child!" she cried.

"Are you mad?" he asked with a half laugh.

"I'll pay you whatever you want, Simon. I'll even let you see the child. We'll draw up a contract. I'll pay all the legal fees. We'll come to a fair arrangement, I promise you."

He stared at her. She could see that there was already a glimmer of interest at the mention of money. "No amount of money in the world could separate me from my son," he replied sententiously.

She looked away from him. She knew business well enough for her to be able to translate this remark into "only a great amount of money could get me to separate myself from my son." She held her tongue and resolved to wait until a later point to open the discussion again.

"You folks be goin' back to the island?" the ferryman asked.

"No," Simon said. "Never."

"Never say never," the ferryman laughed.

They got off the boat, and Simon went to hire a horse and wagon. He was gone for a long while, for the town of Cool Water was two miles up from the pier. She sat with Benjamin; she fed him slices of peach. "There, my sweet," she said. "You're hungry now, aren't you?" She held the baby closely; at her feet was the coffin that held Lucy's remains. She wondered at the inexplicable rotations of life. Lucy, really just a child herself, now dead. And she with Lucy's child. And she with Simon, her former husband. What had she done? What madness had she reinstated in her life? But when she held dear Benjamin this way, it seemed as though she didn't need a reason. It seemed the most pure and right action she had ever taken. Already she loved this child. Already she felt the bond of motherhood in effect. It was a miraculous occurrence, and she accepted it as a miracle, not looking for reasons, not looking for any kind of an explanation.

Simon returned with the wagon and, with great effort, he managed to load the coffin into it, thus transforming it into a hearse.

"You're breathing so hard, Simon," Rebekah said with alarm.

"It's nothing," he said brusquely.

"You're not well."

"We know I ain't well," he said angrily. "So why bring it up, ay?"

"But what are you going to do when we get Lucy buried? Where are you going to go?"

"I'm going with you, I said. What are you trying to pull anyway? You trying to kidnap my son or what?"

"We can't live together, Simon," she sought to explain. "We aren't husband and wife. Don't you remember how we ended it?"

"I remember what I want to remember. No scrap of paper's going to tell me what to do one way or the other."

The ominous words stayed with her throughout the journey. When they arrived in the city, Simon drove directly to the cemetery of St. Vincent de Paul and went to speak with the pastor. The pastor came outside and stood by the wagon. He was a tall, frail-looking black man, perhaps sixty years old, with long, pendulous cheeks and sad, watery eyes the color of fruitwood.

"The deceased, she be sharing the crypt with her mama?" the pastor said in his high, tremulous voice.

"Yes, sir. With her mother, Madeline Rougier."

"And what do the name of the deceased be?"

"Lucy Rougier Weiss."

The pastor looked confused and worked his mouth strenuously, as though he were eating a fruit full of pits. "What do your name be?" he asked.

"Simon Weiss."

"You was her husband?"

"Yes."

The old man's watery eyes stared at Simon for a long, undisguised moment and then he nodded. "What of did she die?" the pastor asked.

"Bronze John," Simon said.

"Dear Lord, she must surely have been a sinner," the pastor grumbled.

Rebekah glanced at Simon, and truly she felt sorry for him. To hear his wife described thus, it was unkind, it was untrue. Lucy might have lived recklessly and unwisely, but sinned? That was something else altogether, and Rebekah did not like hearing the word.

The gravediggers were called out and carried the coffin out to the cemetery. This was a cemetery with a strange history, having been established by a Spanish

native named Pepe Llulla, a duelist with so many
killings to his name that he founded the cemetery in
order to have a convenient place to deposit his victims.

Like virtually all New Orleans cemeteries St. Vincent de Paul had to deal with rain and water seepage
and so relied on tombs, usually consisting of two
vaults, with a crypt below in which the bones were
kept, carefully sealed to prevent the escape of gases
from the decaying bodies. They were sometimes built
in tiers, resembling great, thick walls, and were called
"ovens." After a period of time prescribed by law, the
tombs could be opened, the coffins broken and burned,
and the remains deposited in the crypts. By this
method a single tomb might serve the same family for
generations.

The pastor directed Simon and Rebekah to the tomb
of Madeline Rougier and now her daughter Lucy.

"Her mother was beautiful like Lucy," Simon said,
the tears already coursing down his cheeks. "She was
in love with a French count and when she died of
tuberculosis, he brought her here to this great tomb
and had flowers sent to it every day until he died. His
thoughts went to Clara and the funeral he never
attended. Then suddenly he turned to Rebekah. "You
remember my mother, Rebekah?"

"Yes, Simon."

"God only knows if she's still alive or my brother
Joseph." He took Rebekah's hand and held it tightly.
"What life was that, Rebekah? Mine? Yours? Can you
remember?"

She shook her head. "No, Simon," she said, not
wanting to encourage him on this course even though
she remembered it all so vividly. "It's far too long
ago."

The pastor said no special words about Lucy. He
mumbled a few chants that were foreign and inscrutable to Simon and Rebekah's ears and then they began
to lower the coffin into the tomb.

"Lucy!" Simon cried, and Rebekah stepped back into the shadows with Benjamin. She didn't want to share Simon's grief. She'd had too much of Simon's grief in her lifetime.

"Lucy!" Simon screamed, and he threw himself upon the coffin. Was it Lucy that he tortured himself over? He didn't know. Once he had loved her, but now he had trouble remembering her face. And yet he held tightly to the sharp-edged torso of the pine box. Lucy! My God, Lucy! Was it Lucy he cried for? Or was it himself?

He felt the hot fetid breath of the fever—the breath of death—cover him up, and he screamed out in agony. What kind of a life was this? Once he was a young man, once he was a strong man, once he was a bold man, once he was a lusty man, once he was a dreaming man—and now what was he? He was a yellow man, touched by death. Seeing this love of his lowered into the ground, he could think of nothing else but his own mortality and Clara's so many years ago now.

Clara, it had all started with Clara. If he had only chased her away . . . if he had only said, 'Go home, Clara,' then she would not have died and he would not have been responsible for her and she would not have haunted him. "My God!" he screamed like a wild man, not for Lucy, not for himself, but for the world, this dreadful world, this cruel world, this mocking and wounding and killing world.

When the pastor and the gravediggers pulled him away, and the interment of Lucy was completed, Rebekah led him from St. Vincent de Paul.

"I don't know what happened to me," he said, his face now more ashen than yellow.

"You saw your life open up like a book before you, didn't you, Simon?"

He stared at her; he nodded.

"I know you did," she murmured, "because so did I. It was like the day they buried Clara." She paused a moment; she realized that she was thinking of Jarrett and that his name was at her lips and that it wouldn't be good to say his name. It wouldn't be good at all.

"It's Clara," he said, seizing upon her reference. "I saw her standing there. I saw her laughing at me."

"Stop it, Simon," she said crossly. "You saw no such thing."

He stood where he was and grabbed his head with his two hands. "I don't know what to do," he moaned. "I don't know where to turn."

They sat down on a bench in the brightest part of the cemetery of St. Vincent de Paul, and she gave little Benjamin his milk. She looked at him. He didn't know his mother was dead and buried now. Or maybe he took her for his mother, she thought, allowing herself, in the midst of all of this, to feel something approximate to joy.

Jarrett had finally found a lead. He had begun focusing his attention on Simon Weiss. Knowing his reputation for gambling and other profligacies, he asked after him in the seamier sections of town. He spoke with a wicked league of prostitutes, pimps, croupiers, and assorted thugs. Eventually he met someone, a dark-skinned young lady of the evening who, when she was through propositioning him, gave him a tip. She referred to Simon Weiss as "the Jew," and she said she knew his wife Lucy, that they used to work together. She told him to go talk to Lucy's sister, a woman named Amalia, who also was working as a prostitute at an establishment on Conception Street.

He went there directly that night. He climbed the rickety flight of stairs and entered a shabby, musty anteroom that was presided over by the madam who sat in a large green leather armchair. She was an enormous woman, whose rotundity was unparalleled in his memory and whose small puff of a face was characterized chiefly by the black moustache that seemed to perpetually tickle her nose.

"Good evening, gentleman," she said. She spoke with what sounded like a Teutonic accent, and she leered at him with undisguised delight.

"Good evening," he replied.

"Can I help you? Can I offer you something nice?"

"I am looking for Amalia."

She gave a little shrug, which sent a tremor through her fat bodice. "She is *engagé* at the moment, gentleman, but there are others."

"No, I'll wait."

And he did wait, not terribly long, and when it was time, he paid what they were asking, not terribly much, and he was shown to a room down a dark hallway.

He entered the room and he saw a tall, dark-skinned woman whose bushy hair was dyed a cheap red. She was not beautiful, he thought, and she looked at him in a manner that was perfunctory and that offered no charm.

"You are Amalia?"

She nodded and began to unbutton her peignoir.

"No, wait."

She looked up. "You want . . . something else?"

He shook his head.

"Then what?"

"You know Simon Weiss?"

She stared at him.

"You do, don't you?"

"Who wants to know?"

"My name is Jarrett Russell." He thought to add "doctor," but he didn't feel entitled to just now. "I'm looking for Rebekah Weiss. Someone sent me here, said you'd know where Simon Weiss was, said you were sister to his wife."

She continued to stare.

"You have to help me," he said desperately.

"You've nothing to do with the law," she remarked.
"No, I swear it."

She eyed him suspiciously. There was something so guarded about the woman that he didn't know how to break through to her.

"I've got to find Rebekah Weiss," he cried.

"You love her," she said, drawing the conclusion from the urgency in his voice.

Now it was his turn to stare at her. "Yes," he said finally.

"Then you'll pay," she murmured.

He nodded. "Yes, I'll pay."

They settled on a sum, and then she spoke. "The last I heard of them was a week ago." She took out a long dark brown cigarette, lighted it, and languorously extinguished the match. "I don't know if I ever be seeing them again."

"What do you mean?"

"They got the fever."

"What do you mean?"

"Don't keep saying that," she replied sullenly.

"What happened to them?"

"Bronze John," she said impassively.

"Yellow fever?"

She nodded.

"Are they dead?"

She shrugged. "I don't know. They was taken to Pelican Island."

He had, of course, heard of Pelican Island but knew it only as a backward facility that he himself had never witnessed firsthand. "Thank you for your time," he said, having gotten everything he could from her.

He turned to leave and she stopped him. "If you see my sister, tell her . . ." But then she let it drop, and he pulled away from her and left.

He traveled directly to Pelican Island. It was a long trip. He could not find anyone to take him there. So he had to hire a carriage and make the drive on his own. He arrived at the ferry just as it was pulling away, but the ferryman returned for him and took him across the bay.

"You know what you're going to find there?" asked the grizzled old ferryman.

Jarrett shook his head.

"All kinds of death."

They pulled up to the pier.

"Them's what goes onto that island don't always come back," the ferryman said, the remark being a fixture in his repertoire.

Immediately Jarrett found one of the nuns who took him to the doctor.

"What can I do for you?" asked the tall redheaded doctor.

"I'm looking for Rebekah Weiss."

The doctor turned to the nun. "Do you know the name?"

"No, Doctor," the nun replied.

"Simon Weiss?" Jarrett ventured.

"Did he have a baby?" the nun asked.

"I don't know," Jarrett said.

"There was a man here with a wife and a baby," she said. "Yes, I'm sure now. Simon Weiss. Yes. He left a few days ago. His wife died."

Did she mean Lucy or Rebekah? "Can you describe his wife?"

"A pretty thing, dark haired . . ."

It could be Rebekah, he thought desperately. "And he left with a woman?"

"Yes," the nun said.

"Let me see the death certificate," he demanded.

The doctor went to his files and searched a bit. "Here," he said, showing Jarrett the document.

He looked down. LUCY WEISS, he saw, and then his pounding heart eased a bit. "Where did they go?" he asked.

"We don't know that," the doctor replied.

He looked out across the water. She was still out there somewhere. He had to find her, he had to. He raced back to the pier. "Take me back," he demanded of the ferryman. He had to find her, and this time, when he did, he would never let her go.

CHAPTER TWENTY-SIX

Rebekah was staying with the baby at the Royal Hotel. Tomorrow she and Simon would meet with her lawyer and, if it all went well, Simon would sign the papers and Rebekah would have Benjamin all to herself. She loved the child. This was a life meant to be saved and she was saving him and, in the process, she was saving herself. If something pure and good and innocent was to be rescued from all these years of sorrow, then weren't they all redeemed? She, Clara, Lucy . . . but what about Simon? Was Simon redeemed? Would he let himself be redeemed? In her heart of hearts she could see no way that Simon could be saved.

She'd given him money. She assumed that he had rented himself a room, even though he still had the look of death on him and there weren't many boardinghouses desperate enough to take such lodgers. Yesterday he had come to the hotel and waited for her in the lobby. She saw him as she stepped from the elevator and she raced back into that iron cage and had the operator return her to her floor. She wouldn't see him outside of her lawyer's office, for to do so meant that she would be sucked back into the vortex of his madness.

This morning she outfitted the baby in the fine new clothes she had bought for him, and she took him out to the park. His color was pale; he needed fresh air if he was going to be the healthy, active child he was meant to be.

She sat on a bench in the park and the sun was bright and there was the smell of jasmine in the air. Was she happy? She didn't know if she could answer that question. She wasn't sure what happiness was; all she knew was that she hadn't had it these many years. When the baby cried, she took him into her arms and she fed him and she sang to him a Yiddish song she remembered from her own childhood. She thought of her mother and she allowed herself to feel that she too was a mother. Yes, she was, even though the child she held wasn't her blood, even though the child she held was the blood of a hated husband and his black mistress. She didn't care. She was a woman who could give comfort to a child, and wasn't that what being a mother was all about?

Was she happy? Yes, she supposed she was. She loved Benjamin; she loved the way his black eyes focused on her and his face broke out into a smile. But was she happy? She couldn't help but think of Jarrett. She would never be happy without Jarrett in her life. She prayed that he would contact her. She prayed that he would reappear and that she could tell him she loved him, for she did love him. He was good; he was kind; he was her lover; he was her friend. She knew that if they could find a way to live together, then he would love Benjamin too, for Jarrett had much capacity to love.

She was so lost in her thoughts that she didn't notice the figure approaching her until it was a shadow. She looked up, and she saw that it was Simon.

"What are you doing here?" she said, feeling herself begin to tremble.

"That's some question for you to ask. What do you

think?" he snarled. "Don't you think a man's got a right to see his son?"

"Your son?" she said. "Just because you planted a seed, does that make you think you have the right to call yourself a father?"

"You saw me yesterday in the hotel. Why did you run?" he demanded to know. "Am I a monster? Is that it? Is that what you're saying?"

Yes, you're a monster, yes you are, yes, yes, yes! She wanted to scream it, right here, right now, in this park; she wanted everyone to know what a monster he was. But she held her tongue. What wisdom was there in provoking him further?

"Answer me," he said.

"Just leave me alone, Simon. Please."

"That's my son," Simon whispered. "That's my Benjamin."

Something in Simon's tone—the violence lurking right below the surface—alarmed the baby who began to cry.

"Now look what you've done," Rebekah said.

"Me? So I'm the villain of this piece, am I?"

"Just go away, will you?"

"Why not? And then tomorrow we'll meet and I'll sign the papers and I'll sign my blood over to you. Why, you're a witch, that's what you are! Lilith!" he hissed, invoking the name of the female demon who dwells in deserted places and attacks children.

He was dangerous, Rebekah thought, and he was frightening her. She began making preparations to leave, collecting the baby's things and all.

"Do you think you can buy me off? I know you. You've put the curse on me. Do you think I'm going to lie down and take it? Is that what you think? You're wrong! You're wrong, I say!"

He was ranting now; his mind had snapped. She began to wheel the carriage away from him.

"Come back!" he bellowed, and she walked faster. Spectators began to gather.

"What's the problem, miss?" an elderly gentleman asked.

"She's taking my son!" Simon screamed, but it came out an inchoate roar that went misunderstood.

"Leave the lady alone!" said a burly fellow, his large hands forming reflexively into fists.

She walked faster. Simon ran after her and wheeled her around. "Don't run out on me!" he said, and the burly fellow was upon him and pinned Simon's arms behind his back. When Simon struggled, Rebekah could see the burly fellow aim two blows to his back and kidneys. Simon crumpled into a heap.

"Oh no," she whispered, staring at the pathetic spectacle at her feet.

"Should we call the police, miss?" the elderly man asked.

"No," she said, "leave him be." Then she hurried from the park, back to the confinement of her hotel room.

In the three days that followed his trip to Pelican Island, Jarrett almost gave up hope entirely. He would find a lead and then the track would simply evaporate. Still he combed the city for her, giving descriptions, following clues, and then, at his hotel suite, he received a message that was brief and intriguing.

Meet me soon. You know where.

The message was signed Amalia Rougier.

He went directly to the bordello. She received him in her room, her impassive face giving no indication of anything.

"I received your note," he said right off.

She nodded.

"What is it?" he demanded, irritated by the inscrutable aspect she presented.

"I got more information for you if you wants it," she said.

"Of course I want it."

"It'll cost you."

She stared as he withdrew a billfold. She nodded after he pulled out six of the bills; then she spoke.

"Simon Weiss is back in New Orleans," she sighed.

"How do you know?"

"There be lots of people that's looking for him," she said with a little laugh. "He owe money to everyone. One thing about a man like Simon Weiss," she said, shaking her head, "is that he gambles without luck, but he don't know when to stop."

"Where is he?"

"I hear he's on Chartres Street."

"Is he . . . alone?"

She smiled unpleasantly. "That's for you to find out, Dr. Jarrett Russell."

He went to the address he had paid her to disclose. It was a small, depressed lodging house in the Vieux Carré. He went to the third-floor room and knocked on the door.

"Who's there?" a voice cried out.

"A friend," he answered.

Simon was in need of a friend, and so the door was opened. Jarrett found himself face to face with a tall, broad blond-bearded man whose eyes, yellowed as if by jaundice, stared at him in the most unfriendly manner possible.

"You are Simon Weiss?" he said, barely able to identify this man who he had once grappled with in Rebekah's store.

"Who wants to know?" Simon responded, staring at a face that he thought was familiar, but succumbing in a moment's time to his alcoholic haze.

"I am Jarrett Russell."

"Do I know you?" Simon said, staring at him.

"We met once, many years ago."

"Well, what is it you want?" Simon demanded.

"I want to know where Rebekah is?"

Again Simon studied the strangely familiar face. "What do you want of her?"

"That's not important. Just tell me where she is."

Simon began to nod up and down. "Oh, yes. I can see it now. It's a conspiracy, that's what it is. Sure enough, you're all plotting against me."

The man was severely paranoid, Jarrett noted. He felt that everyone was persecuting him, and Jarrett had the sense that he could be dangerous in defending himself. "I'm a doctor," Jarrett said. "I must see her. She isn't well."

Simon shook his head. He was drunk and deranged, and he didn't know where to turn. "She wants me at the lawyer's tomorrow," he mumbled. "She wants me to sign over the baby, and she says she's going to give me some money. How much money do you think she'll give me?" he asked.

"I don't know," Jarrett said quietly.

"Not enough. It'll never be enough," he said fiercely. "What's Simon to do if he gives over the baby? I'll be lost then." He began to whimper and wring his hands. "I'll kill her. Yes, that's what I'll do. I'll go right over to the hotel and I'll rip her apart."

The hotel? But he had checked all the hotels just two days ago. "How long have you been in New Orleans?" he asked.

"What's all these questions?" Simon roared. With a sudden, pantherlike movement, he grabbed Jarrett by the shirtfront and held him fast. "You're her pimp, ain't you? The whore, she went and died on me." He screwed his face up into a mask of hate and anguish. "Whores! All of them! Why do they hurt poor Simon!"

Jarrett shoved Simon against the wall, freeing himself in the process. Simon fell and knocked his head and made a small, pathetic moan. "You hurt me," Simon said. "Why you gone and hurt me? Everybody hurts me, everybody."

Jarrett, red-faced and shaking, shook a warning finger at the drunken oaf. "Don't try anything, do you hear? You hurt Rebekah or the baby and you're dead, do you hear?"

He turned and went to the door. Just as he was about to leave, he saw over his shoulder the terrifying spectacle of Simon rushing at him with a knife that he withdrew from the sheath he had hidden on his pants leg. Jarrett swerved, avoiding the attack, and Simon wheeled about, following him around the room.

"You doing devil's work?" Simon cried. "I'll show you, I will!"

But Simon, for all his brute strength and insane fury, was still too drunk to do the job well, and Jarrett seized a wooden chair and sent it smashing down upon the head of his adversary. Simon fell to the ground, slashing his hand on the knife.

"Blood," Simon moaned, staring at the wound like some dumb beast.

Jarrett had the thought of giving him aid, but he wasn't a doctor now. Now he was a man in pursuit of the woman he loved, and he wasted no time renewing his search for her.

He found her registered in the Royal Hotel. He had been here just two days ago, checking for her as he had done routinely since coming to the city. Now he saw her signature in the registry, and his heart pounded.

He went up to her room and knocked on the door.

"Who is it?" she asked, for she was living in fear of Simon and had to be most careful.

"It's me," Jarrett said.

There was a pause—a thrilling moment—and then, tentatively, she opened the door. When she saw him standing there, she burst into tears. He held her, and then they kissed each other.

"Sometimes I thought I'd never see you again," Jarrett said, his voice choked with emotion.

"I wrote you," she said. "I wrote to you in Galveston to tell you how sorry I was and to tell you something else."

She fell silent, and he touched her under the chin, lifting up her face so he could look into her eyes again.

"I was to tell you we were going to have a baby," she said in a voice that was inconsolable.

"There, there," he soothed. "Don't cry, Rebekah."

"I lost it, Jarrett. I lost our baby, and I'll never be able to have my own."

"I don't believe that."

"It's true. It's true and that's why I'm here. That's why I've started in with Simon again, and I won't give up. Benjamin will be mine." She took his hand. "Come see him," she whispered.

She showed Jarrett the beautiful child, sleeping soundly in the bassinet. The baby's nightgown, the sheets, the blankets—everything was clean and fresh and sweet, and he looked at the radiant expression that appeared on Rebekah's face as she watched the baby sleeping so comfortably.

"How did this all happen?" Jarrett asked, the sequence of events too confusing and startling.

"After I lost the baby, I came down here to buy Benjamin from Simon and Lucy."

"Buy?" he asked incredulously.

"Why not? They needed the money to support their dissolute habits. And I wanted a child and he, Simon, had kept me all these years in misery."

"Go on," Jarrett said.

"It turned out that they had gotten the fever, and then Lucy died a horrible death. Simon said he'd sign papers giving me the child if I gave him more money, and I'll do it. I'll be glad to do it, but now he's gone crazy, totally crazy. He's mad, Jarrett, and I'm afraid of what he'll do."

"I know," Jarrett said. "I've seen him."

"You've seen him?"

"Yes. A woman named Amalia sent me to him."

"What did he say to you?"

"He thinks it's all a plot against him. He said he'll kill you."

"Oh, Jarrett," she said, clutching him. "I'm afraid. I'm so afraid."

"We have to get out of here. I'll put you on a train to Mobile."

"But what about the papers? The lawyers?"

"Forget that now. Your life is in danger."

"But what about you, Jarrett? Will you come to Mobile with me?"

"How can I, Rebekah?" he cried.

"Then what are you saying, Jarrett?"

"You'll just have to get away for now, Rebekah. Till Simon is under control or dead or out of this city. You're in danger, and it's madness for you to stay here."

"But you can protect me, Jarrett," she whispered, pressing her lips up against his. "Please don't send me away. It's been so long, so horribly long."

They kissed passionately, but there wasn't time. "There's a mad, violent man who holds you responsible for everything that's happened," Jarrett explained. "I want you out of New Orleans tonight, do you understand? Go home, Rebekah, and we'll see each other again as soon as possible."

He went to the station to get her tickets and to arrange things for her return to Mobile. She packed her things and the baby's things, hardly able to think for all of the confusion. A short while later the bellboy knocked on her door and presented her with a note.

I am in the lobby,

the note read.

I am prepared to accept your deal. There's nothing else for me to do. I will go with you to the lawyer. At least my son will be cared for.

She read the note again and again. It sounded sane to her. He was agreeing to the bargain, and he was willing to make Benjamin hers. It was what she wanted, and yet she didn't know how to proceed. She would go down to the lobby, where it seemed safe to conduct a discussion. She dressed the still sleepy Benjamin, and she headed for the elevator.

She saw Simon sitting in the lobby, his disheveled outfit making him stand out against this elegant backdrop.

"Simon?" she said.

He looked up from his bandaged hand. He stared at this woman, this bride of his with the baby in her arms, and he shook his head. "All right then," he said in a hoarse voice. "It's the end of the road for us."

"You'll sign the papers?" she said.

"And you'll give me the money?"

"You know I will," she replied. "I keep my end of the bargain, don't I?"

"Very well, Rebekah," he said. "Let's go."

"No," she said. "I want to wait for Jarrett."

"Jarrett? Your good friend? What is it? You want him to protect you from me?"

"I want to wait for Jarrett," she insisted.

"I won't have another man watching this," he said. "I won't have it. It'll be between you, me, and the lawyer, or it'll be not at all."

But I'm afraid of you, she wanted to say. You've hurt me so many times.

"Well? Are you coming or not?"

"No."

"Then give me my son," he said. "You've no right to him."

"Neither do you."

"Do you want me to call the police?"

"All right, Simon, all right," she said, wanting the whole thing to be done with. "I'll go with you."

They headed toward the lawyer's office. It was a brilliant, sunny day, and the streets were crowded with people, all of whom seemed to be chattering gaily like so many parrots. Only she and Simon were silent, walking beside each other, the baby in her arms.

As they passed the park, he grabbed his chest and staggered slightly.

"What is it?" she cried.

"I don't know," he said, rubbing his chest. "Let me sit for a moment."

They went to a bench in the shade. His face was flushed, and he was breathing with difficulty.

"Are you in pain?" she asked.

He laughed bitterly. "What do you think?"

"Shall I call someone?"

"You'd like to have me shot like an old horse, wouldn't you, Rebekah?"

"Don't say that, Simon. I don't want to hear anything else like that from you."

"Isn't it enough you have the baby? Do you want to see me dead as well?"

His madness was emerging again. She shook her head angrily. "Just be still until you feel better to go on."

"Let me hold the baby," he said.

"No," she cried.

"He's my son. One last time. Please, Rebekah," he said piteously. "Then we'll go on."

She wavered and he reached out and took the child from her. He held the baby tenderly, cooing at it, tickling it gently. The baby began to cry, complaining about something.

"You're disturbing him," Rebekah fretted.

"No, no. He's just thirsty, it being such a hot day and all. There's the fountain over there. Why don't you fill up his bottle?"

"He's probably hungry," Rebekah said.

"No, no. Just a little water."

She took the bottle and filled it up at the fountain. When she turned to come back, she didn't see them. She felt disoriented; she looked around thinking that she had left them somewhere else. But no, they had been right there. "Simon!" she cried, thinking he had gotten up for a moment. "Simon! Simon!" She raced back to the bench and then she raced down the little hill that was behind the bench. "Simon!" she screamed. "Simon! Benjamin!" She screamed their names as she raced through the park, but they were nowhere to be found. He had taken the baby and he had disappeared, like one of the phantoms he himself feared so much.

She ran and she ran. She didn't stop until she got to the Royal Hotel. Jarrett, Jarrett, Jarrett. He was there in the lobby, waiting for her.

"Where have you been to?" he cried.

"Oh, Jarrett. Oh, Jarrett, I've been a fool," she said, weeping bitterly.

"What is it?" Jarrett said, gripping her shoulders. "Tell me, Rebekah."

"He has the baby," she moaned.

"What do you mean? How did it happen?"

"I was a fool," she cried. "Oh, I hate it! I'll kill myself!" she screamed, her hysteria mounting. He shook her until she was quiet again. "He told me he'd sign the papers," she said abjectly, "and I believed him. And now he has the baby and what am I to do?"

"We'll find him, Rebekah . . ."

"He's mad. He's mad and he's dangerous and he has Benjamin," she cried, seeing something she loved being taken away from her. "How will we find him?"

"We'll find him, Rebekah."

"Jarrett, if we don't find him, I don't know how I'll be able to go on. I'll never forgive myself. I love Benjamin. My life was different when he was mine. Now I'm going to be alone again, Jarrett, and it's more than I can bear."

"I promise you we'll find him, Rebekah," Jarrett said, "and remember that you'll never be alone as long as I'm here."

She tried to believe him, but all she could think of was that this joy was gone, stolen away, and she had only had it so short a time.

CHAPTER TWENTY-SEVEN

Jarrett had Rebekah at his side, but still he was searching. This time, again, he was searching for Simon Weiss and for the baby that Rebekah had made the focus of her life.

"How shall we ever find him?" Rebekah demanded to know.

"I found you, didn't I?"

"But Simon's determined to disappear," Rebekah said. "After all, I wasn't hiding from you. There's no telling where Simon has gone to or what he's done with the child."

"We can do our best to find him, Rebekah. All we can do is our best."

"Oh, it's hopeless," she cried. "What's the use? We'll never find him."

"Be strong, Rebekah. You can be. You always have been."

She didn't feel strong now. She was tired; she was spent. And yet she couldn't just stop. She had to find Benjamin; his life was in danger. Simon was mad, totally mad, and the child's very life hung in the balance.

After some preliminary inquiries at his lodging, Jarrett suggested that they contact Amalia Rougier, who had been helpful to him before. They went directly to the house on Conception Street where the obscenely fat Teutonic madam eyed them with unbridled curiosity.

"Amalia *encore?*" the madam said with a lewd little smirk.

"Yes," Jarrett replied.

"*Pour deux?*" she said with a raised eyebrow.

They were admitted to Amalia's room. Amalia knew why they were there, yet she eyed them with a lynxlike hauteur.

"Will you help us?" Jarrett said, first thing.

"I don't know what you mean," she said. She turned to Rebekah. "So you're back in town, ay?" she said with a little bit of a laugh.

"Tell us, please. Have you any knowledge of Simon Weiss's whereabouts? We'd appreciate it if you told us whatever you know."

The woman remained still for a moment and then, stiffly, artificially, she shook her head no.

"Are you absolutely sure?" Jarrett asked.

"Yes," she said coldly. "I am absolutely sure." But she kept her eyes averted from them.

They stood there for a moment, hoping that she would give them a lead, but there was nothing forthcoming.

"Let's go, Rebekah," Jarrett said. "We have nothing to be gained from standing around here."

Outside in the hall they held a hurried conference.

"She's lying," Rebekah said. "Can't you see from her face that she knew something?"

"I don't know," Jarrett replied. "That woman is like a sphinx, by God."

"I'm going back in there," Rebekah cried.

Amalia looked up from the cards she was laying out on the table when Rebekah entered the room again. When Rebekah got closer, she could see that it was tarot cards Amalia was using.

"Intent on telling the future?" Rebekah asked, her voice laden with sarcasm.

"Ain't you taken up enough of my good time?" Amalia drawled.

"Tell me something about the future," Rebekah challenged. "Tell me what happens to little Benjamin."

"Get on out of here," Amalia said. She looked up at Jarrett; there was fear in her eyes. "Tell her to get on out of here."

"No, you're the lady with the cards," Rebekah cried. "Tell me what happens to Benjamin? Does he get carried away by wolves? Does he get lost in the forest? Or does his daddy just forget to feed him until he shrivels up and dies?"

"Shut up!" Amalia ordered. "Shut yourself up, or I'll call someone to shut you up!"

"I was with your sister when she died," Rebekah said. "I held her hand when she was spitting her guts out."

"Don't," Amalia said while Rebekah and Jarrett watched the first human emotion—sadness—pass over her face.

"Help us," Jarrett said.

"Don't let Benjamin die," Rebekah pleaded. "You're his aunt. Don't you care anything for him?"

Amalia looked up from the cards. "My sister," she said. "She had a decent burial?"

"What did Simon tell you?" Rebekah parried.

Amalia shook her long, stony face. "Don't you go try to trick me now," she said. "Just answer me my question."

"We took her to your mother's crypt," Rebekah said, her voice gentler now. "We had all the right things said over her."

Amalia touched her hand to her cheek. "Lucy always did love to go to that there place. Always she loved to go sit under the magnolia tree and say her thoughts to Mama."

"Help us, Amalia," Jarrett said.

She stared at Rebekah. "You love the baby," she whispered.

"I do," Rebekah said, her eyes suddenly burning with unexpected tears.

"And you'll take care of him?" she said somberly.

"I swear it. He'll be like my own."

Amalia took out one of her long brown cigarettes and lighted it.

"We'll pay you," Jarrett said in the intervening silence.

"Of course you will," she replied. "But that ain't why I'd tell you anything." She looked back to Rebekah. "You'll raise the boy to be something?" she said.

"Yes," Rebekah promised.

"And you won't just treat him like a nigger whore's son?"

"I'll treat him like my own," Rebekah said.

Amalia nodded gravely. "Lucy shouldn't have died," she said bitterly. "Lucy shouldn't have taken up with Simon Weiss. You take one look at Simon Weiss, and you know he's trouble. He a heartless sort of a man. But then you know that, don't you, miss?"

"Yes," Rebekah said. "I know that."

"Simon Weiss been here," she said, exhaling, letting her control ease up. "He wanted me to take the baby. He wanted me to take the baby and then he was goin' to send you notes, saying to send him money and he'd give you the child. But he weren't goin' to give you the child, miss. He jes' wanted your money." She paused and puffed on her cigarette. "It made me sick, it did. Playin' with a child's life that way." She looked at Rebekah. "I know what you thinkin'. You thinkin' how is it that I let the baby go hungry that time you came by the place on Rampart Street. Well, you think it was what I wanted? I had a feelin' for the child. It was my own blood, weren't it? And it was a sweet child, but what could I do? I didn't have no one to give me money for takin' care of the baby. That wasn't no way for me to make my livin.' " She sighed and drew from the cigarette. "Lucy should've known better. She was the babe's mama, but she didn't know nothin' of how to live. Me, well, I don't live so fine, but I lives, don't I?"

There was a long pause during which the woman puffed on the cigarette and seemed to blink back bitter, angry tears.

"It's good of you to tell me all this," Rebekah said. "But do you know where Simon Weiss is?"

"He's a crazy one. Mad as can be. I didn't know what to do. He said he'd kill me and the baby and hisself if'n I didn't help him. I thought of my Tante Josephine. I didn't want to lose track of the baby, so I tells him to go and stay with Tante Josephine out in Barataria Bay. I says, she'll put you up, she'll give you food, and then when I'm free, I'll come and I'll take the baby. You see, miss, I didn't want him to run off 'cause I didn't think the babe would ever make it through if he just runs off like that."

"Where's Barataria?" Rebekah asked.

"On Bayou Teche," she said.

Rebekah turned to Jarrett. "Do you know it?" she said.

He shook his head.

"But then how can we ever find him?" Rebekah cried.

"He be on Barataria Bay," Amalia said. "That's where he be."

"Can you come with us?" Jarrett asked.

She laughed. "I never heard such foolishness in all my born days. I swear I haven't."

"Please," Rebekah implored. "You know that country, and we'll never find him without you."

"What you want? You wants me to give up my whole life right here and now so that you can get what ain't even rightfully yours?"

"I'll pay you anything you ask," Rebekah cried. "Please, the child's life is at stake. You must care—you have to care. He's the only thing that's left of Lucy."

Amalia stared at them, taking puffs off her cheroot. "I wish you hadn't of come here," she said. "You gettin' me into all sorts of trouble, you know that?"

"Please, Amalia," Rebekah continued. "As one woman to another, I'm pleading with you to help me."

Again a pause and again the woman exhaled, making that simple action into a significant gesture. "All right," she grumbled. "I'll come with you, but I'll tell you one thing: it'll cost you."

"Whatever it costs," Rebekah said. "It doesn't matter. What matters is that we find Benjamin before it's too late."

They hired a wagon and two horses, and they started on the trip to Barataria Bay. The day was stifling; the sun was like a punishment, and waves of heat shimmered before them.

"He doesn't know anything about children," Rebek-

ah said. "I don't think he'd know to take Benjamin
out of the sun."

"There ain't goin' to be a whole lot of sun where
we goin'," Amalia remarked.

"What do you mean?" Rebekah asked.

"You never been to bayou, ay?" said Amalia.
"Bayou's a different place, a different world. Bayou's
like no place you ever seen before."

And, when they had been riding several hours, the
landscape began to change. It grew wilder, wetter;
the oaks were twisted into tortuous positions, and
there were thickets of oleander and fields of sedge
and palmetto. It grew darker; towering over them
were the oaks and the tupelo.

"We gettin' near," Amalia said.

"Where are we going to?" Rebekah asked.

"A place called Lost River. My mama, she was born
there."

"I hope Simon listened to you," Rebekah said. "I
hope he followed your instructions."

Amalia gave a sort of laugh. "Simon Weiss? He's
the kind of man who listens to other people, ain't
he? He's the kind of man what don't know his own
mind, ain't he?"

They rode on. The air was getting more and more
humid. Jarrett wet a bandanna and tied it around
his head. At one point a rattlesnake lay in the road,
and Jarrett had to shoot it so that the horses would
pass. Rebekah thought back to that first time she went
selling by herself, outside Pensacola, in country that
looked as wild as this. She remembered that bravery,
and she admired the girl who undertook it. Everything
was new to her then; her energy was unbridled. But
by now she'd seen the dark side of things; the sense
of evil and despair was etched into her brain. Clara's
death, Lucy's death, the burning of the store, the
loss of the babies, Hattie Winslow, the duel, the death
of General Schuyler. *I'm so tired of life*, Simon had

said, and she felt his words. Even with Jarrett here beside her she felt his words. Was it too late for love? She looked at Jarrett. She couldn't think of love now. All she could think was that things were coming full circle and that there would be resolution of one sort or another very, very soon.

"I tol' my sister Lucy to stay away from him," Amalia said suddenly, without provocation. "She come down from Mobile, and she says to me, ' 'Malia, what am I to do?' She tells me that Madame Jewel been good to her, treats her well. And I says, 'I know, Lucy, Madame Jewel, she run the best house in Mobile. You don't leave Madame Jewel 'less you got some place better to go.' And she says, ' 'Malia, there's a man who say he loves me. His name is Simon Weiss . . .' "

Rebekah felt, even now, a twinge of regret as she heard the history of the infidelity.

" 'Do you believe what he says, Lucy?' I ask. And she says, 'Nobody ever said they loved me before.' And I says, 'And do you love him, Lucy?' And she says, 'He such a strange man, 'Malia. Sometimes he be sweet and kind, other times he scare me 'cause he seem so far away.' And I says, 'Lucy, there ain't no trusting men no how, so if you wants him, you might as well take him.' "

She got more than she bargained for, Rebekah thought. She thought of Lucy, in her haze of opium, on her fever bed, and she felt with her, even now, the peculiar kinship of women who have been wronged.

"Then they moves down to New Orleans. Simon Weiss, he gambles every cent away. And he has Lucy out doin' business. Then she gets the baby, and she says to me, ' 'Malia, I don't want to tell him that I'm with the baby 'cause he make me get rid of it and I don't want to get rid of it. If I keep the baby, then I don't got to be out on the street no more.' "

The filthy pimp, Rebekah thought. She felt like covering her ears; she felt ashamed for Jarrett to hear these tales of the man she had once been married to.

"So that's what she did," Amalia continued. "She didn't tell Simon Weiss nothin' until it was too late, and when she told him, I thought he'd beat the baby out of her. She came to me, all beat up, and then Simon Weiss came after her, cryin', weepin', beggin' that she forgive him. That's when he started her on the dope."

"You told me that she started when she had Benjamin," Rebekah said. "You told me that he tore up her insides."

"I said that's when it got heavy," Amalia replied. "But it was Simon Weiss who got her on it. After he done beat her up, he got her on it. It was the thing he gave her to make up to her."

They rode on, the route becoming a narrow path that snaked through the marshy fields of salt cane and oyster grass and Spanish dagger.

"Now we got to watch close," Amalia said, " 'cause the road grows different ways from season to season."

A short time thereafter they arrived at a fork in the road and went left. They came to a large clearing in the woods, at the far end of which sat a small, squat house with a mud chimney and a cypress shake roof.

"This is the place," Amalia said.

A woman, tall and stringy like Amalia, emerged from the house and stood on the porch, her eyes shaded, staring at them, trying to figure out how strangers came to be here. Amalia jumped off the wagon and called out, "It's me, Tante Josephine. It's Amalia." The woman stood there, not moving a muscle, making Amalia's past impassiveness now seem positively animated in retrospect.

"Why for you come here?" the woman said. She, like others in this bayou, was a strange mix of Negro and Spanish and French and Acadian. "You think nothing I want but for you to come here?" she added, haranguing rhythmically.

"You got to help us," Amalia said. "Has there been a man here?"

"You send him, no?"

"Where is he?"

"With the baby, you send him here. Why for?"

"Just tell us where he is," Rebekah cried from the wagon.

"In a heap of trouble he is, that so?" Tante Josephine said. "He come here, he look like a wild man. He got a baby, the baby crying like there ain't no tomorrow. He says, 'Feed the baby,' and I says, 'Why should I?' He says, ''Malia sent me. I'm Lucy's husband. Here's Lucy's child.' And sure thing, I had to sit myself down and gather my breath."

"Is he here somewhere?" Jarrett interrupted. "It's very important that we find him."

"He came here last night," Tante Josephine said. "This morning he went off into the bayou. He says they'll be lookin' for him."

"Oh, my God," Rebekah cried. "You mean he went with the baby?"

Tante Josephine nodded. "He took the baby into the bayou," she said. "Into that blackness, he took the babe. Black black," the old woman said, pointing ahead of her. "He done took the babe where it's darker than night."

Tante Josephine had a pirogue, one of the narrow, flat-bottomed boats used for passage through the bayou. Amalia knew how to navigate one. As a girl she had spent a good deal of time here with her mother's aunt, and she proposed that they set out in search of Simon.

"But how can we find him?" Rebekah said. "It's hopeless."

"He couldn't have gotten far," Jarrett said. "He doesn't know where he's going, and he's got the child to boot."

"It's an easy place to get lost," Amalia said. "You can go back and forth in the bayou and never find your way out and never have nobody to find you neither."

"Well, what choice do we have?" Jarrett said impatiently. "He's taken the baby and there's no way that the child will survive unless we find him. His father is mad. Simon Weiss is mad."

Simon Weiss is mad. Rebekah repeated these words to herself. Yes, somebody else saw, she thought, somebody else knew. And he had Benjamin. He had the child that was supposed to be hers.

"Let's go," Rebekah cried. "We're wasting time."

"Will we be able to track him?" Jarrett asked.

"Did he go on foot?" said Rebekah.

"He surely did," Tante Josephine replied. "He wants to take my boat, but I wouldn't let him. I held the gun on him and says, 'Don't you touch that there boat.'"

"But you let him get away," Rebekah reproached.

"I can't stop the man from that," Tante Josephine grumbled.

They set out in the pirogue along one of the many channels that radiated from this clearing. The boat floated on shallow water, at spots no wider than two people standing side by side.

"There's tracks," Amalia said, pointing to indentations in the earth alongside the channel.

"Let's go faster," Jarrett said. "There's no telling how much time we have."

They moved along the channel, following its sinuous path through the thickets of sedge and alligator grass. The channel broadened after awhile and showed varying shades of purple and brown and black under the filtered sun. Along the banks were blooms of indigo iris and the extraordinarily beautiful water

hyacinth in whose tangled tentacles they were momentarily trapped. Stirrings in the water turned out to be
crawfish or terrapin, and once they saw an alligator
peering at them, its long lizardy snout poised at the
surface of the water.

There was a feeling of otherworldliness as they
made their way through the bayou. Rebekah felt as
if this was her entry into hell, and that all that had
gone before this had been merely pointing the way.
At one point Jarrett took her hand, trying to give her
comfort, but she pulled away. She could take no comfort now; things were happening too quickly and too
dangerously.

The channel narrowed again so that the leaves of
the water hickory on the banks grazed their faces.

"Let's stop here," Jarrett said. "I want to check for
tracks."

They moored the pirogue, and Jarrett hopped onto
shore. Just then Rebekah heard a strange noise. Was
it a bird? Perhaps yes, perhaps it could be, but no, no
it wasn't, no, it was no bird, no, that was a baby
crying.

"Do you hear that?" Rebekah demanded.

Jarrett stopped, and Amalia leaned forward, still in
her seat in the pirogue.

They followed the noise through the thick, insect-
infested woods. Jarrett kept touching his holster, reassuring himself that the pistol was there. Rebekah felt
her heart pounding so hard that the whole wood, the
whole world, seemed to be throbbing along with her.

"Don't come any nearer!" a voice cried out.

"Simon!" Rebekah screamed.

Simon—wild-eyed, his hair matted, his counte-
nance still yellow, his clothes in tatters, a gun in his
hand—jumped out in front of them, and Rebekah
felt that her pounding heart would surely stop in its
place.

"Where's the baby?" Amalia cried.

Rebekah ran ahead, going past Simon, who shoved her back as roughly as if it had been a man.

"Pig, you are!" Amalia screamed.

Jarrett stood there watching. He was waiting for a chance to use his gun, and he would not squander his attention for the sake of rage.

"Where's the baby?" Rebekah wailed, hurting from Simon's assault, fearing that none of them would ever get out of here alive.

Simon pointed to a heap of leaves behind him upon which he had placed the child who was bawling in the most piteous fashion imaginable. His cries were expressive of any number of woes: hunger, the chill of exposure, the ravaging by insects.

"The baby needs help," Rebekah said. "Can't you understand, Simon? The baby needs help."

"No!" Simon said angrily, shaking his head. "You're trying to trick me."

"Listen, man, can't you?" Jarrett shouted. "Let me see the baby. I'm a doctor. Let me look at him."

"Get back, all of you!" Simon roared, waving the weapon. "There ain't nothing wrong. Leave us alone!"

"You need help, Simon," Rebekah persisted. "Benjamin needs help."

He ignored her and turned to face Amalia. "You brought them here, did you?" he said, the corners of his mouth white with spittle.

Amalia stared at him, her normally impassive face now registering fear.

"Whore," he said, his mouth twisted with contempt. "You sent me here, to this godforsaken place, and then you came to hunt me."

"You got death on you," Amalia said, unable to hold her tongue.

"Shut up!" Simon shrieked alarmingly.

"Give me Lucy's baby," Amalia said, her fear turning back to anger.

Simon raised the gun, pointed it at the sister of

Lucy, cocked it, and saw fit to carry out the execution. "Simon!" Rebekah cried. Then Jarrett withdrew his pistol, and Simon, seeing this from the corner of his eye, whirled about and fired, catching Jarrett in the shoulder. With a muffled sound, a groan very short and pained, Jarrett fell to the ground. Rebekah and Amalia raced to him, and Rebekah cradled Jarrett's head in her lap.

"Oh my God," Rebekah kept saying, unable to stop, unable to do anything but look for some kind of help from a greater force. "Please, God, please."

"I'm all right," Jarrett managed to say, although the pain was intense.

"You murderer," Rebekah screamed at this madman.

"He killed Lucy," Amalia said, "and now he kill the rest of us."

Simon's yellowed face was made even more grotesque by his astonishment. What have I done? he asked himself. "Will he die?" Simon whispered, terrified, seeing his life come to such a horrible turnabout and yet unable to do anything except run the course that Fate had provided.

"Oh, Jarrett," Rebekah whispered, pressing her lips to his brow.

"I'll be all right," Jarrett whispered for her ears only, but he was bleeding heavily, and there was no telling how long it would be before he received medical attention.

"But you're bleeding . . ."

"Rip from your skirt a long thick strip," he instructed. When she had done so, he had her rig up a tourniquet. He was growing very weak, and the pain was enormous.

"You shouldn't have come," Simon said, trying to make some sort of explanation. "If you hadn't have come, this wouldn't have happened."

"You've shot a man," Rebekah said, "and if he dies, then I'll see to it that you die. I swear it, Simon."

"Just let me get away," Simon said, panicky. "You can keep the baby. Just let me get away." He looked around wildly. "I'll take the boat," he said. "Yes, and I'll have help sent back for you . . ."

"So you'll leave us all to die, Simon?" Rebekah accused. "Is that your idea?"

He saw the pool of blood that had collected beneath Jarrett's arm. My God, he thought, he had done that. And the baby, what if it were true, what they said. What if he had harmed the baby and what if the baby could not be brought back to health? Then there was murder on his head. He wanted to run deep into the woods, fast as a roebuck.

"Give me the baby," Rebekah ordered, unable to endure the sound of the baby's shrieks any longer.

"Come then," Simon said. "Take him."

Rebekah picked up the child and held him in her arms. The child's spasmodic weeping filled her with pain. "Don't cry," Rebekah soothed. "There, there, Benjamin. Don't cry." But the child could not stop; he was too tired and too frightened.

"What have you done to him?" Rebekah said.

"Nothing," Simon swore.

"I don't believe you. You've abused him. He's terrified."

"I said I've done nothing!" Simon shouted. "Why do you torment me?"

She handed the child to Amalia, and she kneeled down to where Jarrett lay, touching her hand to his brow. "I'm sorry, Jarrett," she whispered, breaking into tears anew. "I'm sorry you ever had to meet me."

"Don't," Jarrett said, wincing from the pain.

"Get away from him!" Simon ordered. He looked around wildly, searching for some avenue of escape. "Let's go," he said, pointing the gun at her. "Take the baby, and we'll get out of here."

"What are you talking about?" Rebekah said.

"We'll leave them," Simon explained. "Amalia can take care of the doctor. Now take the baby, I said."

"I won't leave him!"

"If you don't come with me, I'll go without you."

"You'll never find your way out of here," Jarrett said. "Only Amalia knows the way."

"Let him go," Amalia said contemptuously. "Let him go and let him get lost in the bayou and, good enough, he'll become the ghost of the waters."

"Shut up!" Simon screamed. His fear of ghosts—beginning with Clara's death—was total, and the prospect of his ending as one was unendurable.

"There's no way for you to get out of here by yourself or just with me," Rebekah pressed. "You need Amalia."

Simon stared at her. "You're trying to trick me."

"No."

"Yes, you are. Oh, Rebekah, what am I going to do?" he began to moan. "Oh, my life, what's happened to my life?" He held the gun rigidly. "I've got five more bullets," he screamed. "I'll kill us all. Yes, me and you and your doctor friend and the whore and Benjamin too. I'll kill us all and then Lucy will be happy and Clara will be happy and finally it will be over."

"It's not too late for you, Simon," Rebekah said. "You're just afraid. All of this can be behind you. Just don't fight anymore. We'll go back to Tante Josephine's, and then you'll rest. You want that, don't you, Simon? You must want very much to rest."

"Yes," he whispered, "to rest."

"Come then," Rebekah said.

They went back through the woods to the pirogue. Amalia and Rebekah helped Jarrett into the boat, and then Rebekah held the child, whose cries had become whimpers. Simon sat in the prow of the boat, keeping the gun trained on them.

"Let's go," Simon said, and they pushed off into the channel.

It was becoming dark; the bayou was being overtaken by night.

"How shall we find our way now?" Rebekah demanded.

Amalia lighted the lantern, and by this dim light they made their way along the channel. Everywhere were the sounds of life—the whoosh of wings and the sudden splash in the water and the sound of hooves on shore. It was a chilling place. There was the smell of rot in the air and the feeling that at any moment something unseen, something unknowable, would swoop down upon you and suck the life from you.

"I don't like it here," Simon said, his fear lodged in his throat, his heart pounding, his hands sweaty. "Get us out of here!" he ordered Amalia.

"That's what I'm doin'," she replied. "Can't you see?"

"Jarrett," Rebekah whispered, "how is it?"

"It's pretty bad," he admitted. "I think we'd better get some help for me quick as we can."

She felt herself begin to cry again; it seemed that was all she was capable of doing. "I don't want you to die," she wept. "Please, Jarrett, please don't die."

"Shut up!" Simon cried. "Stop saying that!"

"Be still everyone," Amalia said. "The ghosts will find us."

"What are you saying?" Simon demanded.

"The ghosts, all the ghosts, they will come and find us."

"You're a witch, aren't you?" Simon accused.

"All the headless horsemen," she murmured in a hypnotic voice. "All the crab-faced men and all the whistling shadows."

"Make her stop!" Simon ordered. "Make her stop!"

"I know Lucy goin' to come back," Amalia said with a little chuckle. "You know how I know? 'Cause

Mama done teach us how to come back from the dead."

"Shut up, you witch!" Simon said, paralyzed with fear.

Rebekah and Jarrett sat there, silent, knowing that Amalia was up to something, but something that seemed very dangerous indeed.

"You done sealed her up in the crypt, didn't you, Simon Weiss? You done put her in the crypt and, sure enough, you done give the pastor silver coins to keep her spirit bound tight, didn't you, Simon Weiss?"

"Shut up, I said! Shut up or I'll shoot! I swear I will!"

"Then you just got one more ghost, Simon Weiss," Amalia whispered. "And then what you goin' to do? You know Lucy goin' to come back. You know she got a score to settle with you. Why you beat her and you doped her, didn't you? So she got to come back, you see. Yes, sir, she goin' to come out at night, in the white dress you buried her in, and she goin' to pluck out your eyes and she goin' to eat your heart 'cause you done wrong by her, Simon Weiss, you done wrong."

"Oh God no!" he screamed in pain. "Rebekah, help me!"

There was a sound in the brush. "Over there!" Amalia screamed like a succubus, and Simon whirled about and fired the gun at the unseen phantom. Just then Amalia rose, the oar in hand, and she struck him three times fast, and over the side he went.

"Simon!" Rebekah screamed.

For a moment there was utter silence in the black night. Then, a slight ways off, there was a splashing in the water and then a harsh, tortured scream. "Help me!" Simon screamed. "Help me!"

"My God, he's drowning!" Rebekah cried.

"Leave him be," Amalia said. "Leave him be."

They heard Simon's deep, frenzied intakes of breath. "Help me!" he screamed gutturally once again.

They couldn't see him, and Rebekah seized the lantern, swinging it in their radius, illuminating the area in search of Simon. Then she saw him, thrashing in the black water, his face contorted by his fear and his efforts.

"Hold on," Rebekah cried. "We're coming!"

But then there was another splash in the water, and they saw something swimming toward Simon. It was a long, dark shape, and it moved very quickly and very surely.

"Don't look," Amalia said, gripping Rebekah in her arms and holding her head tightly pressed against her bosom.

"What is it?" Rebekah whispered in a child's voice.

"Don't look," Amalia said sternly.

And then there was the sound of a struggle, and then there was another awful, harrowing scream. "Help me! Oh God, help me! It hurts! Rebekah! Rebekah!"

She pulled away from Amalia and held the lantern high. There, in the dim arc of the lantern's light, was a sight that would haunt her forever. It was Simon, Simon being pulled under by a horrible beast, Simon being devoured by a beast of the swamps, and she heard herself screaming just as loudly as he, just screaming, just screaming so loudly and so wildly and so despairingly that she doubted she would ever stop and couldn't remember when she finally did.

She lay sleeping, her head on Amalia's lap. They were back at Tante Josephine's; the baby was fed; Jarrett was resting comfortably. With a combination of his own fortitude and presence of mind and Tante Josephine's knowledge of folk medicine, the two of them had collaborated to save him. And, indeed, he had been saved.

"What time is it?" Rebekah murmured, her mouth so dry she could hardly talk.

"Morning," said Amalia.

All at once she remembered. "Jarrett?" she said.

"He'll be well," Amalia said. "He ain't goin' to die."

"And the baby?"

Amalia smiled and, for the first time, Rebekah saw real warmth on the woman's face. "The baby is good as can be."

"And Simon . . ." she began, but she remembered what had happened to Simon. She felt a deep shudder pass through her. She would never forget the sight of him in the jaws of the alligator, the great lizard pulling him under that black water. It seemed like the ending to a medieval tale of sin and retribution, and she buried her face against Amalia who held her tightly.

"He's dead," Amalia said in a voice of calm and inevitability. "He's dead, and that's the way it had to be."

"But such a horrible death."

"God punished him," Amalia said somberly. "And he had his punishment comin', sure enough he did."

She lay there silent. She couldn't believe he was dead. She couldn't believe that he was gone from her life. She felt a sense of loss, so acute and piercing, much like the sense of loss she had experienced when she boarded the boat at Bremen and saw the continent of her birth fading away. Part of her history had been erased; part of her history had been swept beneath that black, oozy water. At the end, or well before the end, Simon was mad, and she pitied him for it. His life was a definition of waste. Had she conspired to let it happen? No, she told herself. She had tried to help him; she tried to bring him into the realm of decency and judgment and hard work and loyalty. He had accused her of never having loved him, of never having been kind to him, of never having given him affection—well, maybe it was so, but when had he allowed such things? She realized now that she could never have saved him, just as she could never have saved Clara, just as no one could ever have saved Lucy. They could only have saved themselves; they could only have redeemed themselves.

She thought of Jarrett. She knew that he would ask her to run with him, but that wasn't the way it was going to be. It was up to Jarrett to save himself, to make himself strong and whole again. She wanted him to be that way, she prayed that he would be that way, she prayed that they could come together—but she couldn't save him. The question of his survival was up to him.

"You want to see the baby?" Amalia asked.

They went into the back room where the baby slept so soundly. Poor thing, Rebekah thought. He was so tired and worn out. But the fact was that he looked none the worse for all of it. He was a beautiful boy; she would give him a good life and, when he was older, she would try to explain to him what his mother and father were about.

"He's my blood," Amalia said.

Rebekah glanced at her. The remark frightened her; did Amalia have designs on the child?

"No," Amalia said, knowing what she was thinking. "I wouldn't try to take the child from you. What could I give him?"

Then what did she want? Rebekah thought. What *would* she take from her?

"I don't got much of a life," Amalia said in a voice so low it was barely audible. "I never did have much of a life. I weren't never pretty like Lucy. People never liked me like they did Lucy. And being in the life—it ain't so good, you know?"

The woman's tone was so plaintive that Rebekah reached out and took her hand. Startled, Amalia looked up.

"Can I take care of the child?" Amalia pleaded. "I don't want much, and I know I ain't done good by him before. I know I was lazy with him, but that ain't the way I feel about him now. Why, if you take him away, then I'm all alone in the world and I don't want that, missus, please."

All of Amalia's innate pride and dignity was crumbling in the face of this desperation. "You've helped me," Rebekah said, still holding the woman's hand. "Without you, I wouldn't have anything. Of course you can come with us and you can stay with us as long as you wish."

Tears formed in Amalia's eyes, and she blinked them back. "I'll like that," she said, regaining her control. "I'll like that so much."

She left Amalia with the baby and went into the next room where Jarrett lay, still in his deep, recuperative sleep. She sat by the bed and watched him. She was troubled by what she would tell him when he awoke. The one thing that was sure was that she would have to return to Mobile. She knew now that she wouldn't give up her life for anyone, but that didn't mean she was unwilling to share it.

He stirred, his face screwed up in pain, and she leaned over and touched his brow with her lips. Sleep well, Jarrett, she whispered, and become strong again. She left him alone, convincing herself for the moment that he was out of danger.

CHAPTER TWENTY-EIGHT

They sat beneath the chinaberry tree at Tante Josephine's. Rebekah peeled an orange for Jarrett; he sat with his face to the sun. He felt himself growing stronger each day, but no surer of what the next step would be. He wanted to be with Rebekah, he had to be with Rebekah. Just looking at her now, as she sat across from him, her face intent as she peeled the fruit, he had the feeling that they must spend the rest of their lives together, for it was right to do so. And Benjamin—in the past few weeks he had held Benjamin as a father would, and he had rejoiced in Benjamin. This was a life saved, and he wanted very much to have something to do with the development of that life.

But where was his own life going to go? He felt that he was ready to begin again, that he wanted his life to become whole again, and that meant practicing medicine and living with the woman he loved and not having to run anymore. But things weren't yet solved. He was still an exile; he still could not return to the place where he had his roots. When would he be able to return? Perhaps never, he thought grimly.

"Here, Jarrett," Rebekah said, offering him the orange.

He took it and peeled off a slice. "It's good here, isn't it?" he said, feeling safe, feeling protected, wanting her to join him in this opinion.

But she couldn't agree. Each night she awoke in

a sweat, reliving Simon's end, seeing him pulled under that black water. She didn't think it was "good" here. She wanted to be home, in Mobile, in the city that she had claimed as her own.

"You seem far away," he said.

She shook her head.

"Well, not so very far away, I suppose," he added in a voice that was light but in which she could detect a dose of bitterness. "Only so far as Mobile, isn't that so, Rebekah?"

"I don't know, Jarrett. If you're asking me whether I think of my home, the answer is yes."

"And your business?"

"Yes, my business too."

His face became very dark and troubled.

"What is it?" she said, having to ask the question even though she didn't want to.

"I thought you loved me."

"I do!" she cried.

"Then how can you leave me? How can you even think of leaving me?"

"Jarrett, how can I explain it to you? I love you more than I've ever loved anyone. Ever since the first time I met you, I loved you or, at least, I thought about loving you. You make me feel good; you make me feel happy. But you can't be everything to me, Jarrett, nor can I be everything to you." She stood up and walked to where he was sitting. "When we were in the boat with Simon, I suddenly understood that there was no way I could save him. I suddenly understood that there was never any way I could have saved Clara. They had to make their own peace, Jarrett, and they weren't able to and they died for it. That doesn't mean I didn't feel for them. It doesn't mean I didn't weep for them. But I couldn't right their wrongs for them, Jarrett. I couldn't make their peace for them."

"And you can't make my peace for me. Is that what you're saying?"

"Yes, Jarrett. That's what I'm saying."

He maintained a troubled silence, which she shared with him for several long moments. Then she spoke again. "Can you walk a bit today?" she asked in a low, intimate, urgent voice.

He stared at her, and then he nodded.

"There's a meadow not far from here," she said. "We can go there, can't we?"

They walked along the channel and then up a hill that was dotted with oleander. At the crest they saw a field some yards away that was not large but was bright and yellow. She helped him through the thickets for he was still weak from his wound.

They sat down in the warm yellow grass. The sky was azure, and there were flocks of cottony clouds floating overhead. It was a perfect place; he wished never to leave here; he wished never to have this moment pass.

"What will you do in Mobile when they find out where Benjamin comes from?" he said, pulling himself deliberately out of this moment that had to end.

"I don't know," she said. She turned to him and smiled. "I love Benjamin. Do you know, I think he knows me already."

"Of course he knows you."

Suddenly, without warning, tears came to her eyes.

"What is it?" he said, taking her hand.

"You don't know what that means to me," she managed to say. "No man can know what that means to a woman."

"I'm happy for you," he said, taking her into his arms.

She held him closely; they kissed. They hadn't been together . . . since Galveston. She felt shy with him, and perhaps, she thought, he felt the same. But he kissed her with greater passion, and then they lay down on the soft dry grass.

"I want you," he murmured, and she pressed herself against him.

There was a series of movements—unbucklings, unlacings—and they didn't want to stop touching each other for to touch each other was a wonder of the world, and each of them had been starved for wonder and joy and delight. Oh yes, she said when he sucked on her breasts. He wanted her so badly; so badly he wanted her and then they were moving together and there were the cries of blue herons flying through the trees and she said his name, Jarrett, Jarrett, and he felt that he existed, he felt that he was alive, he felt that this must never stop, he felt that he couldn't get enough of her, and she held him tightly, and they were together, so close together, and it was joy.

"I love you, Rebekah," he said, moments later.

"Jarrett, I love you so."

They held each other, and the cool breeze fanned over them.

"I didn't know that it would work between us again," he said, "but now I know that what we have won't ever end."

"We mustn't let it, Jarrett."

There was a silence, filled only by the herons and, now and again, by the distant cry of a loon.

"You're going back to Mobile," he said finally, expressing what he had regarded all along as the unthinkable.

What could she say to temper it? There was only the truth, she thought. "Yes, I must. You know I must."

"But I don't understand," he said. "Isn't this what life is about? Isn't it love that makes life worth living?"

"Of course it is, my darling. But it isn't the one and only answer," she said soberly. "It can't be the answer."

"Then what is?" he demanded to know.

"Something within ourselves," she whispered. She

pressed into the crook of his arm; she brushed the hair away from her eyes. "When I was a girl in Korneuberg, I thought the answer would be a boy named Jacob. I was content to be his wife—that's all I wanted. And when that wasn't allowed, I thought the answer would be in my going to America. I was willing to commit myself to Simon Weiss; I was willing to share his dream. And all these years I worked to achieve something, and I did, Jarrett. I built up the Weiss Store, and it grows and grows. But it isn't the answer either. Benjamin? Yes, I needed to be a mother and I was willing to risk my life and yours and Amalia's to become one. And you, Jarrett—I need your love too. But all of that doesn't make up the final answer, the real answer."

"And you have found the real answer?" he said, unable to prevent the tone of sarcasm from entering his voice.

"I don't know that I have," she said. "All I know is that I have to do what is right. I have to find my own answers. I can't have my father or Jacob or Simon or you or even, someday, little Benjamin telling me what I must do."

"I'm not telling you what to do, Rebekah. I'm just saying that I love you."

"And I love you, Jarrett." There was a pause during which she stared at him, terrified by the prospect of losing him. "Come to Mobile with me," she said.

"How can I go there?" he cried.

"You can," she insisted. "It's your place. You can come back."

"So they can throw me into jail?"

"They won't," she said. "You've done your penance. You've exiled yourself. You've wandered without a home. Now it's time for you to come back."

"You just don't want to leave your store," he accused. "That's it. Why don't you admit it? Don't you think I know what's behind all of this?"

"You can think that if you want to," she said. "But you're wrong. You see, Jarrett, I know that as long as you're running, as long as you're away from Mobile, as long as you're denied your home, you can't give me or yourself as much as you have to give."

"Don't you think I want to go home, Rebekah?" he said in a voice so muted and saddened that it tore her to hear it. "But how can I? Just tell me how I can?"

"You know how I can, Jarrett," she said. "I don't think you're afraid of punishment. I don't think you're afraid of the courts or afraid of the jails. I think, like Simon, you're afraid of your ghosts."

He lay there in silence, his jaw tight as a bowstring, his head filled with a thousand old fears.

"I'll make a home for you, Jarrett, and I'll love you and I'll cherish you," she said. "It's all I can do, Jarrett. It's the very best I can do."

She left for Mobile the very next day. Tante Josephine's nephew, a reedy giant named Jacques, drove them into New Orleans. The ride was very bleak and silent; Jarrett and Rebekah had nothing further to say to each other. All the cards were on the table, and they were left to the interior world of their own thoughts.

They parted at the station on Annunciation Street.

"You have everything?" Rebekah whispered to Jarrett.

"Yes."

"You're sure?"

"If it's money you're talking about," he said angrily, "I'm sure."

Sadly she turned to leave. She walked a few steps, and then he called out to her. She rushed back to him, and they embraced. "I'm sorry," he said. "I don't want to hurt you. Believe me, I don't."

"I know, my darling, I know."

"We'll see each other again," he promised. "I know we will."

On the train she locked herself in the water closet and wept until there were no tears left. The thought kept crossing her mind that she must go back to him, that she must rescue him, that she must consecrate her life to him, but she wouldn't. No, she just couldn't. It wasn't right; it wasn't an answer. She didn't know what the answer was, but she knew that wasn't it.

When she returned to her compartment, Amalia gave her a scrutinizing look. "You all right?" she asked.

"Yes. Yes, I'm all right."

Amalia smiled. "Benjamin know where he goin', don't you, baby? Look at him smile. He ain't never been so happy."

Rebekah took him in her arms and held him up to the window. "Choo-choo," she said. "Choo-choo."

The child, bright and thoroughly alert, shocked them both by imitating the sound.

"Oh, sweet thing," Rebekah cried, hugging him. *"Mein kind,"* she whispered.

"Lucy can rest knowing where the baby be," Amalia said.

When they arrived back at Wild Oaks, the reception was muted. Micah and Eulalie were there to greet them, but when they saw the baby and Amalia, their expressions changed.

"This is Benjamin," Rebekah said. "He's come to live at Wild Oaks, and this is Amalia who will help us care for him."

Now the expressions of these two servants warred between the acceptance that they felt it their duty to give and the dismay that they were experiencing as a result of the presence of these interlopers.

"Micah," Rebekah continued, "will you see to it that the rooms are set up for their comfort?"

She left Amalia to feed and change Benjamin, and she went upstairs to see Mr. O'Donnell, who had been moved into Wild Oaks on release from the hospital. She knocked on the door, and then she heard him, his voice stronger than she had expected, telling whoever it was to enter.

"Jesus Lord!" Mr. O'Donnell cried. He was sitting up in bed, his face ruddy, a bright yellow robe keeping him warm, piles of books and newspapers scattered about. "If it ain't my dear miss!"

She went to him, and they embraced.

"You look so much better than I had hoped," she said. Seeing him now—her friend, this good man who was loyal to her—she felt quite overwhelmed and moved to tears.

"Oh, miss," he said, patting her hand, "it sure is good to see you."

"Are you well, Mr. O'Donnell?"

"Why, of course I am, can't you see? The doctor says another week, maybe two, in bed, and then it's up and about." He laughed a bit, his laugh wheezy and totally idiosyncratic. "The doctor says this was just a warning. You see, miss, it turns out that I'm kind of an old gent, and I can't be working so hard as I was."

"Well then," she said, adopting his joking posture, "we're going to make you the honorary chairman of the board and all you'll have to do is accept testimonials and cut ribbons and be very august in everything you do."

They laughed together now, and she felt better than she had in so very long. She felt that she was home again.

"Now," he said, growing serious, "tell me about yourself."

She shook her head. How was she to begin, where was she to begin? The events of these past weeks were so outrageous, so twisted in their course—how could she arrange them and how could she hope to explain them?

"Your eyes look like they seen trouble, miss. Is it so?"

She nodded. "All kinds of trouble, Mr. O'Donnell."

"Tell me," he urged.

"Simon is dead."

He nodded gravely.

"And so is his wife Lucy." She got up from the bed and walked around the room. "They had a child. Benjamin. He's mine now, Mr. O'Donnell. He's mine and I love him and he's here in this house and I'm going to raise him as my son."

"I'm happy for you, miss."

"Thank you, Mr. O'Donnell. Wait till you see him. He's such a beautiful boy. He's smart and he's strong. God knows, he had to be strong to live through what he's had to live through."

"A survivor, miss?"

She stared at him. He made his point. "Yes, Mr. O'Donnell. A survivor."

"And what will Mobile say?"

"I don't think Mobile will have any more to say about Rebekah Weiss. I think Mobile's said everything it's going to say."

"And tell me about Dr. Russell, miss. He found you, I trust?"

"Yes, he found me."

"And did you find each other?"

She walked to the window. She didn't want to answer the question. She looked out at the sweeping grounds of Wild Oaks. This was her home, but it was Jarrett's home too.

"You're not answering my question, miss."

She turned to face him. "I wanted him to come back to Wild Oaks," she said. "I asked him to come back with me. But he says he can't, even though I know he can. He says he can never come back here."

"What will you do?"

"What can I do, Mr. O'Donnell? I know that if I run with him, we'll never stop until we grow apart. I

can't run, Mr. O'Donnell. This is my home. Everything
that I have is here."

"Except Dr. Russell."

"He'll come," she said in a voice that was more sure
than her emotions.

"Do you really think so?" Mr. O'Donnell asked.

"You disapprove, don't you?" she said harshly. "You
think I should have stayed with him, don't you? Well,
do me a favor, will you, Mr. O'Donnell? Don't tell me
what to do."

His ruddy face was utterly surprised by her remark.

"I'm sorry," she said. She went and sat on the bed
again and took his hand in hers. "It's just that everything has changed. Yes, my whole life has changed,
and I feel so lost."

"I'm here for you, miss."

"I know you are." She looked around her. "I didn't
think I'd be lost here," she said. "I thought I'd be at
home in Wild Oaks. But a part of me is missing, Mr.
O'Donnell, and I don't know how to get it back."

The Weiss Store—the one on Claiborne Street, the
one that had seen the rebirth of her business—was
dusty and smelled of stale air. She threw open the
windows and let the fresh air in. She put on her smock
and, with the help of Dover and the maid Velma whom
she had brought over from Wild Oaks, she set to putting things back into shape.

She felt consumed by this activity. As she worked—
sweeping, dusting, polishing the display cases—she
couldn't help but think of that first store, the one on
Caroline Street. She couldn't help but think of herself
and Simon, standing outside, looking up at the fine
sign that they had had painted for them, the sign that
said WEISS DRY GOODS & SUNDRIES, and that was a
moment of pride, unalloyed and shared between them
and doomed from the moment of its inception. Poor,
lost Simon. He was a monster, and she pitied him. She

thought of them together in the gazebo at Korneuberg; she thought of the young girl named Rebekah Kraus and the young man who had come to claim her. How tall and straight he was then. There were so many girls who would have given anything to have him. He was blond; his hair shone in the sun. And yet there was something so wrong with him. She remembered telling her cousin Miriam, as they sat in the garden by the primrose hedge, that she was afraid of him and Miriam said, "Of course you are, cousin. What young girl would not be afraid of a man so big and bold as Simon Weiss?" She hadn't understood at all—and where was Miriam now? Gone, yes, and Sarah gone. Everyone gone. That life of hers gone, gone, faded away, lost forever.

She resumed her work, polishing the brass fixings on the display cases. The store was scheduled to reopen the next morning. She had had the neighborhood plastered with signs that declared: EVERYTHING ON SALE— THE GREATEST SALE IN THE HISTORY OF THE WEISS STORE. She wanted everything out; she wanted everything new. And she would have success, she felt it in her bones. She knew that there was no stopping the Weiss Store from becoming bigger and better and spreading out to other cities.

That night, the night before the reopening of the store, she felt so curiously alone. She felt like a new life was beginning and she was already longing for aspects of her past. It was September now; very soon it would be the Jewish New Year; very soon it would be High Holy Days. She would go to synagogue and she would say *Yiskor* for Simon and she would say *Yiskor* for her father and she would say *Yiskor* for Sarah. There was a whole part of her life that she saw fit to mourn; as the survivor she owed it to those who were lost. And, moreover, she wanted Judaism back in her life. She wanted to be part of a faith; she wanted not to be alone. There was much that she had to atone for—

greed, willfulness, cruelties intentional or otherwise—
and she would go to synagogue on Yom Kippur and
she would let nothing pass between her lips. She felt
the need to purify herself after all the horror that she
had been party to.

"Everything ready for the sale tomorrow?" Mr.
O'Donnell asked that night.

"Yes, quite," she said. "I predict receipts such as
we've never seen before."

"You're certainly confident, miss."

"If there's one thing in my life that I'm confident
about, it's that the Weiss Store will thrive again."

But then there *was* one other thing she was confident
about. When she went into the nursery that evening,
she was confident that Benjamin was the best thing
that had happened to her. Amalia was bathing the
boy—sharp contrast to the disregard she had displayed
on Rampart Street—and singing a gentle lullaby of
some arcane origin.

Honey bee,

she sang.

Come sit on my shoulder,
My shoulder's a flower,
You'll surely like it.

"Hello," Rebekah murmured, and Amalia turned
around.

"Why, look who's here, Benjamin," Amalia said.

Who indeed? she thought. She hadn't given herself
a name yet. She had given Benjamin a name—her
child, her baby—but she hadn't called herself anything.

"It's Mama," she said tentatively.

Amalia looked up, startled.

"Do you think it's wrong?" Rebekah whispered.

Amalia thought a moment and then spoke. "If you're goin' to be a mother to the child, then I guess there ain't no wrong in it. Least of all, I can't see that Lucy would mind. After all, she'd want Benjamin to have a mother, wouldn't she?"

"Mama," she said, more strongly this time. "Mama's here."

"There's only one thing," Amalia said.

"What's that?"

"Do you think it'd be all right if he knows me as his aunt?" she said very quickly.

A host of questions immediately descended. What would Amalia's role then be in the household? How would things be explained? But Rebekah put them aside. The situation was unorthodox; Rebekah knew that much from the moment she had entered into this affair. "If I can be Benjamin's mama," she said, "then is there any reason why you couldn't be Benjamin's aunt?"

"I love him," Amalia said. "He's full of life, ain't he? You'd never know what kind of end his mama and papa came to."

"Let's hope he'll stay that way," Rebekah said, "and that he'll grow straight and proud and that the world will be good to him."

She left the nursery and retired to her room. She passed a restless night, filled with thoughts of her new, sudden motherhood and of the store's reopening tomorrow, but mostly with thoughts of Jarrett. Already she missed him so. He was a rare person. Sometimes she wondered what greatness he could have achieved if his life hadn't taken its particular turns of fate. Other times, though, she felt angry with him, for wasn't that what life was all about? Wasn't it about taking what was sent your way and making the best of it? Why didn't he understand that? And why wasn't he here with her?"

She awoke very early in the morning, moments after

dawn, and her whole body was racing with anticipation. Today was the day that the store would come alive again, and she washed and dressed and went down to the kitchen.

"Up so early, Miz Rebekah?" Eulalie said. She was standing over a heavy black iron skillet, making the morning's cornbread.

"It's a special day, Eulalie," Rebekah said. "And how is my angel today?" she said to little Benjamin, who was sitting at the table being fed wedges of cornbread by his aunt Amalia.

"He was so excited this morning," Amalia said in a voice that had grown positively lilting since she had assumed responsibility for the child's care. "He must've known that his mama's store was opening up again."

"Maybe one day he'll run the store," she said, running her fingers over his silken black curls.

Amalia stared at her. "You think the world goin' to be ready for that?" she asked.

"We'll make the world ready for it, Amalia. It's up to us, isn't it?"

She rode off to the store. In two hours the doors would be opened and the enterprise would be officially renewed. Dover and Velma dusted again and swept again and made sure that all the merchandise was neatly arranged and in its proper place. She checked the cash in the box, seeing that the bills were in neat piles of tens and fives and singles and that there was enough silver to make change.

"It's going to be a big day," she announced to her assistants. "Are you ready?"

They nodded, caught by her enthusiasm.

She went to the front door. There was a crowd of people—old ladies in flowery cotton dresses, prosperous-looking young matrons with children in tow, husbands and wives in from the outlying rural areas—and they were straining to gain entrance. She counted two minutes and then she rolled up the shades, unlocked the doors, and let the crowd in.

The rest of the day was organized havoc. People came in droves and left with baskets of merchandise under their arms. She was selling merchandise practically at cost, but she was making a profit, God knows, and she was pulling the customers back into the Weiss Store. They hadn't forgotten—or even if they had, they were glad to be reminded so long as there were bargains to be had. And it cheered her to see them, because it reminded her that there was something she did well, there was something that she did better than anyone else in Mobile.

When they closed the doors at eight o'clock that night, the store was fairly well stripped of its merchandise. She was satisfied. She had expected as much and she already had her orders of new goods: combs and brushes and bolts of calico and worsted and denim and linen and hand mirrors and bath salts and slippers and rugs and pots and pans and tea kettles and writing papers and fancy grosgrain ribbons and so many other things that all served to make the Weiss Store the place to shop.

"I never seen so many people, Miz Rebekah," little Velma exclaimed. "I declare, I don't never think my feet'll stop hurting."

"Well, we'll all take a good soak when we return to Wild Oaks," Rebekah laughed.

"We sure did good, didn't we, Miz Rebekah?" Dover asked.

She stared at the young man. He had become a real aid to her. He had proved himself to be smart and trustworthy and even creative at solving problems, and she would give him more responsibility very soon. "We did better than good, Dover. We did splendid."

She took the books in hand; she would show them to Mr. O'Donnell tonight when she returned to Wild Oaks. Then she closed the lights and locked the door behind her. The day was a success, as she knew it would be, and tomorrow would be more of the same.

Mr. O'Donnell went over the books like a proud father. "You're some businesswoman, miss, let me tell you."

And she accepted the praise like a daughter, fairly blushing.

He looked up at her, and then he took her hand. "I'm so proud of you, miss," he said, and then his expression changed. "I'm sorry I failed you."

"You didn't fail me, Mr. O'Donnell . . ."

"Oh yes I did. You went off to the springs and, fast as could be, I get this crazy attack."

"It was provoked, Mr. O'Donnell, don't forget."

"How is your health, miss?" he said forthrightly.

"It's fine," she replied after a pause.

"It was a baby, wasn't it?"

She stared at him. "How did you know?"

"Word gets around, miss. There ain't never no secrets, remember that."

"The doctor?"

"The doctor, the nurses. There ain't never no secrets."

"So then everyone knows."

He nodded. "Everyone knows."

She couldn't help but laugh.

"What is it, miss?"

"Oh, it's nothing," she said, her laughter dying out. "It's just that I have so many strikes against me."

"Indeed you do, miss," he said with a frank nod.

"The doctor said I wasn't ever going to have a baby. He said my womb wouldn't hold a baby. And I didn't want to live without a baby. It was an idea I couldn't bear."

"Well, now you got the baby and you got the store back to the way it was. You got everything you need, ain't it so, miss?"

"Don't tease me, Mr. O'Donnell."

"I ain't teasing you, miss."

"Yes, you are. But what do you want me to say? That I miss Jarrett? Well of course I miss him. There isn't a moment in the day when I don't think of him. I love him, Mr. O'Donnell, and I miss him, but I can't have him, so what's the use of talking?"

"You can have him . . ."

"I won't go to him!" she cried. "I won't run! I won't, I tell you!"

There was a difficult silence between them and then O'Donnell spoke. "I don't want to upset you, miss. You know what you're doing. You have my blessing."

But did she know what she was doing? When she returned to her room, ready for sleep, the sleep wouldn't come. All she could do was ask herself the same questions over and over again. She wanted Jarrett—her life wasn't full without him. The store wasn't enough, even Benjamin wasn't enough. Why is it, she wondered, that when one gets some of what one wants, it only makes you want more. She wanted Jarrett. Lying here in bed, so acutely aware of her aloneness, she wanted to be held by him and she wanted to hold him. She wanted to be stroked by him, and she wanted to touch him. She wanted to feel him close to her. Her body ached with dissatisfaction and longing, her body ached toward that something, that someone, who would complete her.

But what was she to do? She couldn't run. She couldn't exile herself. She wouldn't be the immigrant all over again. She wouldn't do that for anyone—no, never again. She had made a place in the world for herself; this was her greatest achievement, and she couldn't throw it aside in order to help Jarrett find his place.

Then what was the answer? To live her life with dignity, yes. To do the best for the people she cared for—Mr. O'Donnell, Eulalie, Dover, Velma, and now

Benjamin and Amalia. To have faith in herself, yes, for this was what had kept her going through all the hardship and sorrow. To remember that she was a Jew and that her people had overcome. To hold on to the hope that she and Jarrett would be reunited and could live together without shame and with love and happiness. The answers were clear; she knew them; she lived them. But knowing the answers did little to alleviate the pain, and when she closed her eyes that night, she knew that she was surrendering herself to a sleep that was raw and troubled and full of phantoms.

CHAPTER TWENTY-NINE

Jarrett sat on the train to Mobile. In damp weather such as this his shoulder hurt but not intolerably. In many ways the pain had been good, giving him something real and tangible to hold onto, giving him an anchor for his feelings and his thoughts. Everything that had gone on since he had found Rebekah and since it seemed that he had once again lost her threatened to overwhelm him entirely. It took him weeks after her departure to be able to gather his thoughts and pull himself from the miasma of pain and confusion.

He had finally come to acknowledge that what she had said at the end was true in every way. *You're afraid of your ghosts*, she had said. Yes, of course, that was the story of its entirety. He had even fought the duel so that there would once again be some legitimate reason for him to flee Mobile. Ever since the war he had found reasons to stay away from his home. The issues of honor and filial duty lured him back, but again and again he broke away. Now he was willing and anxious to return for good. Rebekah, the woman he loved, was waiting for him. At last he was able to see that the enemy was himself, and he was ready to conquer his fears.

He knew now that there was no honor beyond the honor with which one leads one's own life. Everything else—codes of chivalry and proud histories of noble families—meant nothing. His father was a product of centuries of so-called "honor." The Russells could trace their tree back to a brave and valorous knight, but all of that meant nothing. His father was afraid, afraid of death. His father didn't want to die, the vast unknown was too much for him, and so his father surrendered himself to infamy. It was a thing so terribly sad. He thought of his father's last moments, sitting alone in an army tent, backed up against the wall, forced to commit against himself that of which he was most afraid. He thought of his father putting the gun to his head. Oh Father, he cried, feeling the waves of sadness that were such a new sensation for him after so many years of shame and resentment.

Suddenly he realized that he'd been weeping. He was alone in the compartment; the train was moving quickly, and he was moving quicker still back to his sources. He felt pity and forgiveness for his father; he felt his bonds breaking. He was through with shame and resentment; he wanted love and, miracle of miracles, love was waiting for him. Dearest Rebekah, he thought. They would be husband and wife and they would support each other and they would love each other and it was good, it was so very good, and it wasn't too late. He had the rest of his life ahead of him; it wasn't too late.

He didn't know quite what was ahead of him. He imagined there would be punishment of one sort or

another. But it wasn't forever. There might be public
censure; there might be hardship and prejudice. But
it wasn't forever. The rest of his life was waiting for
him. Once again he would be a doctor. And this time
he wouldn't take the living from the wombs of wayward women and destroy the life. No, this time he
would treat the sick and the infirm. He loved what he
did; he felt proud to know what he knew. He had
helped many return from the brink of death, and he
knew the thrill of breathing life into blue babies. He
had gone too long without using his gift, but now he
was ready. He had healed himself; with the help of a
fine woman he had made himself strong again. It
didn't mean that he was invincible. He anticipated
the familiar wave of pain when he walked through the
gates of Wild Oaks. But at last he was ready to come
home; at last he was ready to live his life again.

It was time for some sort of celebration, Rebekah
had convinced herself. It was still six months away
from Benjamin's second birthday, but did one really
need a reason to host a party for a child? She wanted
a table set up on the lawn and she wanted balloons
and noisemakers and party dress and coconut cake
and orange jelly and chocolate cheese pie.

"Here 'tis, Miz Rebekah," Eulalie said, showing off
the beautiful white cake trimmed with coconut that
she had baked for the occasion. "Ain't it pretty?"

"Why, it's a picture, Eulalie."

Velma was making the lemonade punch while Dover
was carrying a table and chairs outside. It was a
glorious fall day. The air was crisp, and the sky was a
gentle shade of blue. She was happy—at least when she
didn't think of Jarrett. There was the store and there
was Benjamin and there was Wild Oaks. If she didn't
think of Jarrett, then her life seemed very good indeed.
But how could she not think of Jarrett? She had heard
nothing from him since leaving New Orleans. She had

to conclude that it was over between them. Very well, she thought; it was meant to be. She would live without that kind of love, because if she didn't have Jarrett, then she didn't want anyone. She would have the store and she would have Benjamin—that was enough, or, at least, it would have to be enough.

The party commenced at noon. She and Benjamin and Amalia and Mr. O'Donnell and Eulalie and Micah and Dover and Velma. It was a good group, she thought. The cake was superb, and Benjamin smiled rapturously as he opened his presents—a hobby horse and building blocks and a wagon and a cornhusk doll that Eulalie had made.

"Can you say thank you, Benjamin?" Rebekah said.

Benjamin laughed as though she had told the funniest joke, and everyone laughed with him.

Dover took out his mandolin and sang a few songs, and then he and Velma did a jig. It was a fine day, she kept telling herself, although there was a strain of sadness and a certain feeling of unease. Why couldn't she put these feelings behind her? She had to go on with her life.

"Miz Rebekah," Micah said suddenly, "look who be comin' 'cross the lawn."

She looked up. A woman dressed in black. A tall yellow-skinned woman. Sophronia. Sophronia was coming toward them.

"We'll throw her out," Mr. O'Donnell said. "We'll call the authorities."

"No," she said, shaking her head. She rose and left the table; she crossed the lawn to meet with the treacherous woman.

"What are you doing here?" was the first thing Rebekah said.

"They let me out, missus," Sophronia replied, her voice cool and quite collected. "I served my time."

"That doesn't answer my question," she said. "What are you doing here?"

"I comes to visit."

"You're far too bold, Sophronia. I would have thought your time in prison would have taught you a lesson."

"It taught me a lot of lessons, Miz Rebekah," Sophronia replied, her voice etched with bitterness.

"I'll ask you one more time: what are you doing here?"

"This is where I'm from," she said. "Wild Oaks was my mama's home and my grandma's home. Don't I got a right to pay a call."

"Not after what you did," Rebekah said. Her pulse was racing as she confronted this woman. "You betrayed me. You stole from me, and you did me great harm."

Sophronia stared at her and then, wordlessly, she picked up her skirts and showed her legs that were crisscrossed by scars.

"Don't," Rebekah gasped.

"Why not?" Sophronia challenged. "That's what they done to me in prison. That's how they taught me my lessons."

"I'm sorry," Rebekah said. "It's wrong and they're brutes and I'm sorry for you. But it has nothing to do with me."

"You sent me . . ."

"No! The law sent you. You stole from me. I gave you responsibility, I gave you the opportunity to become an important part of the store, and you used that opportunity to betray me. You're the cause of Mr. O'Donnell's illness and . . ."

"And what?" Sophronia said brazenly.

She wouldn't say anything about the lost baby. She didn't want to use that against her. "I want you to leave now," she said coldly.

"You got yourself a baby, did you?" Sophronia said, ignoring Rebekah's command.

"That has nothing to do with you."

"Pretty little thing. Got coloring just like you."

"Get out of here."

"Not so quick. I'm lookin' at that baby of yours." She gave an awful little laugh. "Bet I know how you got him."

Rebekah stared at her, paralyzed.

"Sure I know," she said, making her voice ominous. "I got friends, all sorts of friends. I got friends what knew Simon Weiss and Lucy down in New Orleans."

"You're making a mistake . . ."

"No mistake, Miz Rebekah. That there's Lucy's baby. That there's a nigger baby."

"Shut up!" Rebekah cried.

"I won't neither," she said tauntingly. "How'd you like it for the world to know what color that baby be? You goin' to raise him as your own, but he ain't your own and I mean to tell everyone 'less you pay me to keep quiet."

"You're filthy," Rebekah said. "You're filthy and you're loathsome and you're very, very wrong."

"Wrong?" Sophronia said. "We'll see who's wrong."

"I don't care what you do," Rebekah said. "Do you think I could give a damn what you say? I've had a lot worthier enemies than you, Sophronia. Why, you're nothing but a petty thief."

"I'll make life miserable for you," Sophronia said angrily. "I'll make it so you'll wish Lucy took the child to the grave with her."

"You don't scare me," Rebekah said, standing her ground. "I love that child, and nothing you do or anyone else does will make me sorry that I've taken him for my own. There's nothing you can do to hurt me, do you understand?"

"You don't know what I can do to hurt you," Sophronia threatened. "The rest of my life is goin' to be lived to hurt you."

The woman's hate was chilling. "Why?" Rebekah said, having to ask the question.

" 'Cause you got everything," Sophronia said.

What could she say? How could she explain to Sophronia that it wasn't true, that, in fact, nothing could be further from the truth. "Go now," Rebekah said in a low voice. "Go now and don't come back."

"You'll be hearin' from me," Sophronia warned, turning to leave.

She returned to the table where all the revelers sat silent. She couldn't stop trembling, and the glass of lemonade shook as she tried to drink from it.

"What did you say, miss?" Mr. O'Donnell asked.

"Oh, she wants to make more trouble," Rebekah replied in an offhand manner. "But we won't let her, will we?"

"She should be flogged," Mr. O'Donnell said furiously.

"Don't excite yourself," she warned. "It isn't worth it."

The silence lay over the party, smothering it. "Dover, please, another song," she called, and he got up and began to play.

> I caught a big green frog,

he sang.

> I put it in a wooden box,
> I fed it turnips and watermelon seeds,
> And the frog began to sing.

Was this a harbinger of things to come? Rebekah thought, losing herself in a faraway world of imagined fears. Blackmailings, arson, threats on her life or Benjamin's—was this what was in store? She hadn't expected it. Sophronia's visit had taken the wind out of her. She felt dizzy under the suddenly hot sun.

> The frog began to sing,
> He sings a lullaby,

And I began to fall asleep,
And the frog ran away with the fly.

The innocent nonsense of the song seemed so at odds with this turn of events. Sophronia had entered like a shadow; she had done her best to frighten her, and she had succeeded. She looked at Benjamin, with ice cream on his face, and she felt her love pour out for him. Don't let him be hurt, she prayed. Whatever happens, don't let him be hurt.

It was twilight. Benjamin had been taken inside by Amalia; Dover and Velma and Micah and Eulalie were cleaning up, removing all signs of the festivities. Rebekah and Mr. O'Donnell sat on lawn chairs, watching the fading of the light.

"You're brave, miss," he said. "You're very brave to have come back here."

"Was I wrong?" she said, consumed by doubt.

"Trust your instincts, miss. They seem to work—they've gotten you through a lot of hard times."

"I don't want the day to end, Mr. O'Donnell," she murmured. "I've gotten so afraid of the dark. I've gotten so afraid of being alone."

He took her hand and held it tenderly, but it wasn't enough. Only one thing would have been enough. They sat like that for several moments, and then Mr. O'Donnell began to grow cold and they headed back toward the great white house.

"You're staying out here, miss?" Mr. O'Donnell said to her on the veranda.

"Just for a while, Mr. O'Donnell. I want to be alone."

She stood there, holding onto the railing, looking out over the broad sweep of lawn. How had she come to be here? She felt so confused. Her life was so charged, so full of change, so much in flux. There was

nothing constant, nothing except the need for love
and the need for a place in the world that was hers.

The daylight faded, leaving the large and brilliant
moon. She stood there and she was cold, but she
couldn't move. She was immobilized, gripped by a
combination of fear, longing, and a realization of
destiny. *You got everything*, Sophronia had accused,
but Sophronia was so very wrong. No one had everything, no one escaped the trials of life, no one escaped
grief and despair and loss. She was a mourner; she had
many to say *Yiskor* for. Her father, Sarah, Clara,
Simon, even Lucy. So much had happened, and yet
she understood so little. She didn't understand life;
she didn't understand death. All she knew was that
she had to believe, she had to have faith, she couldn't
give up hope, she couldn't surrender. She wouldn't
surrender—no, never—she wouldn't let the evil forces
drag her down. *And they blessed Rebekah, and said
unto her, Thou art our sister, be thou the mother of
thousands of millions and let thy seed possess the gate
of those which hate them.* Like Rebekah, Isaac's wife,
she was barren, and like Rebekah, Isaac's wife, she
had seen a miracle. Isaac's wife gave birth to twins, and
she, Rebekah, had been given the child Benjamin.
There was much ahead; there was much to do; there
was no time for bitterness; and she wanted so very
much to believe in miracles.

"Miz Rebekah," Dover said. "There's someone
comin' up the path."

Sophronia, she thought. No, not again. Stay away,
please stay away. She peered out across the lawn. But
it wasn't Sophronia. No, it was a larger figure—a man
—a man whose stride she recognized.

"Miz Rebekah," Dover said in a voice full of wonder,
"Miz Rebekah, is it him?"

And then the figure lifted his arm to salute her. Oh,
my God. My God. She walked down the broad flight of
steps. She walked out onto the lawn, damp now with

moisture. She wanted to run, but she couldn't. She could only move so very slowly, as if in some sort of a dream.

"Rebekah!" he called to her. "Rebekah!"

And the dream became reality. She raced toward him and he to her. They caught each other; they held each other, and before she could speak, she was sobbing and he was holding her tighter still.

"You're here," she cried.

"Yes, my dearest, yes."

"Will you stay now?" she wondered, not yet knowing if it was safe to believe.

"Of course, my darling. I'm home now. I'm home."

"But will you never leave me?" she persisted, wanting him to promise, wanting him to give her his word.

He held her close; she pressed herself against him. "I'll never leave you," he whispered. "I'm here to stay, Rebekah. We're home together at last." He looked up at Wild Oaks. There were candles burning in the windows, and he sensed the warmth she had made there. "It's for us now," he whispered, and they led each other back along the path.

Dell Bestsellers

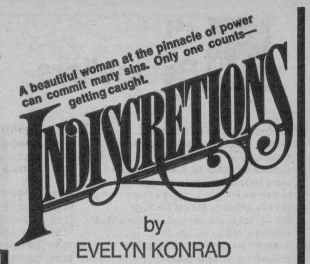

THE PASSING BELLS

by

PHILLIP ROCK

A story you'll wish would go on forever.

Here is the vivid story of the Grevilles, a titled British family, and their servants—men and women who knew their place, upstairs and down, until England went to war and the whole fabric of British society began to unravel and change.

"Well-written, exciting. Echoes of Hemingway, Graves and *Upstairs, Downstairs.*"—*Library Journal*

"Every twenty-five years or so, we are blessed with a war novel, outstanding in that it depicts not only the history of a time but also its soul."—*West Coast Review of Books.*

"Vivid and enthralling."—*The Philadelphia Inquirer*

A Dell Book $2.75   (16837-6)

Sometimes you have to lose
everything before you can begin

To Love Again

Danielle Steel

Author of *The Promise* and
Summer's End

Isabella and Amadeo lived in an elegant
and beautiful world where they shared their
brightest treasure—their boundless, en-
during love. Suddenly, their enchantment
ended and Amadeo vanished forever. With
all her proud courage could she release the
past to embrace her future? Would she ever
dare TO LOVE AGAIN?

A Dell Book $2.50 (18631-5)